Books by

STAR FOI

Su
Extinction
Rebellion
Conquest
Battle Station
Empire
Annihilation
Storm Assault
The Dead Sun
Outcast
Exile
Gauntlet
Demon Star

REBEL FLEET SERIES
Rebel Fleet
Orion Fleet
Alpha Fleet
Earth Fleet

Visit BVLarson.com for more information.

City World

(Undying Mercenaries Series #17)

by

B. V. Larson

Undying Mercenaries Series:

Illustration © Tom Edwards
TomEdwardsDesign.com

Copyright © 2022 by Iron Tower Press.

ISBN-13: 979-8429261751
BISAC: Fiction / Science Fiction / Military

"The army in the field is useless without wisdom at home."
—Cicero, 63 BC

-1-

After coming home from Ice World, the warm swamps of southern Georgia Sector felt good. Instead of being chilled to the bone all the time, I was sweating in the late spring heat. Being native to the area, I didn't mind a bit.

By the time the spring wore on into summer, however, warm turned to downright hot. I was still good with this, mind you, but I was considering upgrading my army of powered fans into a real cooling unit. They had better air conditioners these days than ever before, systems that used alien technology and some odd tricks of physics.

Captivated by an advertisement on my tapper, I considered a small, expensive box that just plain sucked up heat from around it without noise or fans or anything. After a particularly sweaty night, I woke up early and tapped in my authorization code. The unit was on the way, being drone-shipped straight to my sagging porch that very afternoon.

When the drone arrived, the sight attracted my dad to make a rare visit to my shack. I went up to the main house all the time, mind you, but my parents made a point of avoiding my more modest domicile. After all, they never knew who or what they might encounter if they dropped in unexpectedly.

1

My dad tapped on the door diffidently, peering into the dark interior of my place through the screen. He looked this way and that, clearly uncertain as to what his eyes might witness.

I was in a good mood, so I threw the door wide and invited him in. I took him straight to the new cooling unit, which I'd set up on the coffee table. It was a bluish metallic color, but I wasn't sure if that was just a paint job or what.

"See this, Dad? This thingamajig hardly uses any power, but it feels like a block of ice if you put your hand on top of it."

"Careful, I've heard those things can burn you like dry ice if you touch them."

"Only if you turn it way up. This one is set to winter mode, not arctic or glacier."

Cautiously, my dad put his leathery fingers near the unit. He waggled them there, making satisfied noises.

"It's nice," he said, "but it won't chill a whole room like that, will it?"

"You're supposed to put a fan next to it if you want more cold. If you crank it and blow air over it, it's supposed refrigerate an entire apartment."

"Well, let's set it up, then. I never did understand how you could stand living out here without air conditioning all these years."

We did some fixing, and we soon had two fans blowing over the cube, which was about as big as a six-pack of beer. One of its functions was to cool down your drink if you put it on top.

I set the box to "arctic" and things quickly got a lot nicer. With two fans going, one aimed at each of us, we were completely comfortable.

It didn't take long for my dad to get an idea. He went to the house and came back with a six-pack. He placed this on the flat top of the cooler, and after a minute or two we dug into a couple of icy brews.

The next half-hour passed by in a very pleasant fashion, but then someone else rattled at my door.

My mom poked her head into the living room and wrinkled her nose. She'd never yet learned to knock—at least not in the daytime.

"There you are, Frank. What are you two doing out here...? Oh, I get it. Is that one of those iceboxes? I've heard a lot about them. We should get one for the house."

"What for?" Dad objected immediately. "We've got traditional air conditioning. It works fine, and we just had the repair bot out to juice it up again."

"It's old fashioned and boring. James, you tell him."

"Huh?" I asked in surprise. I'd only been half-listening. There was a game on, and I was quietly watching it on my tapper with the sound turned down.

Seeing as she wasn't getting any help from me, Momma came to the table and messed with the cube for a bit. She found after a while she didn't like it.

"It gets too damned cold. It's dangerous. A kid or a pet might burn themselves," she said, reaching a final verdict.

"That's right," Dad said excitedly. He sensed he was slipping out of a major purchase with very little effort. "It's dangerous. What if Etta has a baby someday? It'd take the kid's arm off."

My dad often invented imaginary grandchildren to justify just about anything he wanted. The tactic always seemed to work on my mom.

"Well... if you two are done drinking and goofing off, I'd like to see you work on knocking down that old barn in the woods before it gets dark."

We both looked up in alarm. It was Saturday, but around most farmsteads that wasn't a day of leisure. Both my parents were notorious for coming up with something vital for me to do on weekends.

"Today?" my dad asked. "The day's half-gone."

"That's because you've both been sitting in here for hours. You promised, Frank."

"All right," he said, standing up and walking toward the door. "Come on, James."

"Huh?" I shot my dad a look of genuine betrayal. I should've known there was a job lurking under those beers.

3

"Aren't you listening, boy? We're going to go knock down that old barn."

I blinked at both of them in confusion and a growing sense of alarm. "We are?"

"Yes. Right now. Today."

"But why?"

My mother sighed and put her fists on her hips. "Because, as I've told you about a hundred times, we're going to sell that land. They've got a new road in with some proper sewer pipes. People are going to want to buy and develop it."

"They are?" I asked, honestly baffled. I wasn't sure if I'd not listened to my parents—not an uncommon thing—or I'd simply forgotten. Either way, I wasn't happy.

Standing up, I felt a fresh worry creep into my mind. That barn... I'd done things out there.

The land was swampy in our backwoods. All the land surrounding ours was a bog for the most part. I'd figured no one would ever go out there. Accordingly, I'd hidden things there... dead bodies and such-like.

"Uh..." I said.

"Come on, come on," Dad said, heading out the door and waving for me to follow. "Don't even try to come up with an excuse. There's no point. We've been listening to your excuses for around sixty years now, and we've heard them all by now."

"Uh..."

In the end, I followed my dad to the toolshed. We got out an automated walker and a power-axe. I could tell right away my dad meant business.

"I think this is a really bad idea," I said. "That land isn't safe, pop. Besides, if people move in back here... well, it just won't be the same."

My dad wasn't listening. I knew him well, and I knew he wanted mom to ditch the idea of buying an alien icebox so badly he was willing to do actual work. What's more, he probably thought he was going to get rich off some otherwise worthless land. That was my dad for you. If you wanted to know which way he'd lean on any topic, you just had to follow the money trail, whether it was real or imagined.

Even though I knew all this, I kept on complaining during the walk through the bog. Finally, he pulled up short and looked at me crossly. "I'll do it myself if I have to, James, but I'd rather have the help. Which is it going to be?"

The thought of my dad going out there alone and finding something evil concerned me greatly. I sighed and agreed to help.

"Come on then, boy. The sun will fade in another four or five hours. I want to get this done tonight."

We made our way through the bogs and the bugs until we came near the barn. It was really old, hailing back two centuries, maybe more. It was a sagging ruin with the roof partially caved in and the stone foundation overgrown.

"We don't have to take out the stones," Dad said. "Just the timber."

"Why don't we just let the new buyers do it themselves?"

"It's a matter of marketing, son. There are all kinds of regulations that govern a structure like this. For one thing, it's considered an historic landmark."

I looked at him, then the barn, astonished. "What the hell...? Are you serious?"

"Yep. The rules say anything that predates Hegemony is protected—but only from development. If we destroy it now and claim it was done for safety reasons, we'll get away with it. The inspectors will come and see it as a done deal. No one will ask any questions."

"What if we sell it as-is?"

"Then the new owners will have to bring it up to code."

My jaw sagged. That would cost a million credits, easy, and no one would even want a barn out here anyway. I could see how it could screw up a land deal right-quick.

Thinking fast, I decided to try another dodge. I pride myself on always having more than one lie in my hip-pocket for emergencies. I caught my dad by the arm.

"Hey," I said, "I'll make a deal with you. I'll work on this today, alone, and you can go back to my shack and test the hell out of my new icebox. There's another game starting, you know."

I showed him my tapper, which was playing highlights from last week already.

My dad frowned. "Are you saying I'm too old and good-for-nothing? Is that it, boy? You really don't want my help, do you? Fine."

Tossing down his power-shovel, he turned and began to walk dejectedly toward home.

Torn for a moment, I bared my teeth. I came up with one last move.

"Hold on, hold on. I welcome your help—I can't really do it all alone in one afternoon. I just wanted to do the front yard area myself. You know, where that old well used to be. You can do the rest."

My dad stopped walking. He stood there, facing away from me. I wasn't sure what he was thinking, so I waited.

Finally, he turned around. Instead of a grin, he had a suspicious expression on his face. His head was canted to one side, and his eyes were as narrowed down as a hissing cat.

"James… is there something about this old place you aren't telling me?"

Now, as anyone who knows me can attest, I'm a gifted liar. I consider the practice an art form, in fact. No one I'd ever met could do better. No one.

The trouble was this was my father. He knew me better than anyone, and he knew bullshit when it came on the wind from any direction. Accordingly, I didn't tell any tall tales. I didn't dare.

"Uh… no," I said.

His voice became stern. "There better not be some kind of drug-stash or alien spaceship out here on my land, boy."

"No, no! Nothing like that!" I laughed at the idea, but Dad didn't laugh with me.

We stared at one another for a bit. Finally, my dad walked around to the back of the barn. He fired up the power-axe and began working on the rear walls, which were relatively intact.

Taking this chance to work fast and dirty, I took the power-shovel and the automated-walker around to the front. I began cracking the stones on the well as fast I could and casting them down into the black round hole in the middle. I figured that

6

anything buried under a few tons of rock would stay buried forever.

Not eight minutes went by before someone tapped my sweating shoulders. I whirled to see my dad, standing almost as tall as me with his arms crossed.

"What's in that well, boy?"

"Nothing."

"Come on. Are you really going to make me dig it up to find out?"

Several lies came to mind. I used them all, one after the other—but it was no dice. My dad smelled a two-meter-tall rat, and he wasn't going to let him slip away. Not this time.

I was caught red-handed. There was nothing else to say. Heaving a sigh, I considered my options.

Normally, I would have just killed whoever had caught me. That had been my tried-and-true approach for decades. Unfortunately, that wasn't an option with my dad... so I confessed instead.

"It's aliens," I said. "There are aliens down there."

Frowning, my dad leaned over the black circular hole. He sniffed experimentally. "Doesn't smell like anything weird."

"I mean there are *dead* aliens down there."

He looked at me, eyebrows riding high. "You killed aliens and tossed them down my frigging well?"

"Yeah... A long time ago. You remember those guys who came out here to the farm in air cars and threatened the family?"

"Yes, of course. The Tau died in a fiery air car crash—along with you, as I recall. Why would you toss burned bones down my well?"

I stepped up and lowered my voice to a conspiratorial whisper. "Not all of them went down in that crash, see. Some of them came back later..."

His jaw sagged low. I could see he didn't know what to think. This made me happy, because there weren't any aliens in the well. The dead down there were all quite human.

"But you said it was a long time ago," Dad protested. "Those Tau fellas were here just months back."

I shrugged. "A long time is a relative thing, I guess."

7

The next thing I knew, he was grabbing me by the shirt and shaking me—or trying to. "You idiot! How can I sell this land with dead aliens in the frigging well? Environmental inspectors have gizmos that will sniff out a fish-fart!"

"Relax dad, this is a swamp. Everything smells like decay. Don't worry, I'll take care of it. Just give me a couple of days."

I promised to work on the problem and get it done fast—but he didn't believe me. I could tell.

Dejected and defeated, my dad decided to knock off work for the day. He took a few of his tools back home, but I got him to leave the digging machines with me.

After he left, I got to work. The day wore on and darkness began to fall. I cranked up the lights on the walker and shined them into some bad places. Sometimes, in twilight, a bright light worked better than sunshine to show the worst things on Earth.

I ended up working until midnight and then some, but the job still wasn't done. Along about one a.m., a voice spoke to me. It was a familiar voice, and it startled me, because I thought it must be a ghost I'd disturbed.

"What are you looking for out here, McGill?"

Whirling around and casting a bright light in the direction of the speaker. I saw a familiar round face.

It was Carlos.

-2-

"What are you doing on my land, Carlos?" I demanded.

"Relax, cowboy. Your dad said you were out here farting around in the swamp. He said I should know all about why. When I told him I didn't know what he was talking about, he scoffed at me."

Carlos and I blinked at each other for a minute. My mind was tired and swirling, but I soon caught on.

My dad had bought my bullshit about more buried aliens, apparently. He'd bought the story hook, line, and sinker. Accordingly, he figured Carlos was in on the secret. After all, Carlos had been in one of the two air cars we'd brought down.

The truth was that Carlos didn't know anything about this private mortuary of mine. No one but me really knew what had happened out here in these dripping woods.

Now I had a whole new problem to solve, and it was frowning up at me, wanting answers.

Automatically, my mind conjured up my usual solution: murder. It was my knee-jerk reflex when I needed to exit any difficult situation—one might even say that killing people had become a crutch for me to lean on.

But after a moment, and for the same reasons as before, I passed on the option again. One lie had already caromed into a second one, and murders had a way of doing the same thing.

Deciding it was best to stick to a single cover story, I went with the tried-and-true.

9

"It's aliens," I said, with the same gusto I delivered this lie to my dad.

"What?"

I gave him the same cock-and-bull story, and just like my pop, he seemed to buy it. His jaw was hanging lower than mine before I was done explaining.

"This is unbelievable... how do you get yourself into shit like this, McGill?"

I shrugged. "It's a gift, I suppose. You want to help with the shoveling?"

"What? I don't want any part of your skullduggery. I came out here to tell you to turn on your damned tapper. You have to talk to Central."

I glanced down at my arm. It was still quietly playing sports.

Carlos followed my gaze. "You don't even have it wrapped in aluminum foil? I'm stunned. Why can't anyone reach you?"

"Because... maybe... well, I might have done a little bit of jail-breaking."

"Don't even tell me that. I don't want to be an accessory to any more of your crimes. Not tonight."

"Fine, fine. But you're not going anywhere."

He had just turned to leave, but he looked back over his shoulder in annoyance. "Why not?"

"Because you're going to help me hide these aliens. You know the truth, and that makes you a co-conspirator. You're just as guilty as I am."

Carlos frowned. "What if I squeal?" he lifted his tapper into the glare of the floodlights coming from the walker. "What if I call Turov, or Graves, or—?"

I reached out a hand and covered his screen with big fingers. "You don't want to joke about that. You're not squealing. Not tonight—not unless you want to squeal on the way down to the bottom of this here hole in the ground."

Carlos looked from me to that round black hole and back again.

"Are you going to help me or not?" I demanded.

He shrugged. "All right, all right. You don't have to twist my arm. I'll help."

10

We worked together, and while we did so I questioned him about the reasons Central had seen fit to send a man of his low reputation all the way out here into the darkest swamp in Georgia.

"Because there's a Mogwa battlecruiser parked in orbit," he said, pointing a thick finger up into the black sky. "Apparently, your name came up in their conversations with Central."

I covered my mouth with one big dirty palm. I groaned aloud. A few days ago, I'd been looking forward to a lazy summer and an even lazier fall. I was in the full swing of vacation mode, and I'd been enjoying each day thoroughly.

But today, everything seemed to be shifting under my size-thirteen boots. As every hour passed, I'd begun to doubt my immediate future would be peaceful.

"All right," I said. "Help me finish this—and pick up the pace. We've got to work fast. We've got to knock down all these stones and throw them into the well, along with enough muck from the swamp to fill it in."

"Is that what that puddle of slime over there is for?"

"Yep."

Carlos wrinkled his nose. "It stinks. It really stinks. There are sticks in here, too…"

He began poking around in my sludge pile, and before I could stop him, he held up a long dripping bone that was slick with black mud. "Hey, this looks like—"

I snatched it out of his hand and tossed it into the well. It clattered on the way down.

Carlos faced off with me. "That wasn't a Tau bone."

"It sure as hell was. What do you know about it?"

"I'm a bio, remember? I took anatomy and all that."

"Oh yeah…"

We stared at each other for a second, then I sucked in a deep breath. "Look, do you really want a full report? I'll turn on my tapper, here, to record it all. You can hear about every dark deed that's gone on out here in this swamp, all the way back to the Unification Wars. Is that what you want? Really?"

Carlos blinked. He looked around the place. He was really thinking now, I could tell. "The Unification Wars…? Shit, no—I don't want to hear another word."

11

"That's what I thought."

I went back to shoveling, but Carlos was looking around with growing alarm. "I don't think I ever want anyone to know I was out here."

"They won't hear it from me—but you *are* here. Anyone who wants to check will know the truth. Your tapper knows it."

Breathing hard, he lifted up his arm and stared at it. "Wrap it up for me. Or hack it. Or maybe stab it with your knife—I don't care."

I grinned. Carlos had had a change of heart. He was realizing that he wasn't just antagonizing me, he was endangering himself. His life, limb, and Healthy Citizen scores were all on the line.

These days it didn't matter if you innocently stumbled upon a heinous crime against Hegemony. You were indelibly stained by such moments, becoming permanently associated with whatever you'd found. Innocence bought you jack-squat. Only powerful associates, like Galina's father, could save you.

Carlos didn't know many powerful people—and whenever he did meet one, they soon started hating him.

"Come on, hurry up," he said as I trussed up his tapper. "Let's just bury everything. You're right, McGill. It's the only way. Oh, and thanks by the way for involving me in more of your subversive evil."

I shrugged. "No charge. But you should remember I didn't ask you to come out here when you stole those illegal coins, either."

Carlos' breathing slowed when he saw his tapper was sealed up tight. No telltale signals were escaping his arm now. Not anymore.

An hour or two later, he straightened his sore back and groaned. "What else can I do? The well stones are about gone."

I had him move the sludge into the hole. It was the worst, dirtiest job I could think of. Skulls showed up now and then while he worked. Mostly, they were human skulls. Any fool could see that.

But Carlos didn't say anything. Oh, he grimaced, and he spat grit, and he cursed a lot—but he didn't *say* anything. He saved his breath for working.

About an hour before dawn broke, we finished our work and stumbled back to my place. We washed off with the hose and drank beers on the porch.

"Hey!" Carlos said. He got up and walked out into my weed-pit of a yard. He pointed up into the sky. "Look out there, up to the northeast."

I walked out into the open and looked up with him. I squinted, and then I saw it.

A diamond-shaped object hung in the sky. The sunlight was hitting it, as it was far above the curvature of the Earth. The edges were a silvery gray, and they were unnaturally straight.

"That's an alien battlecruiser," Carlos said. "The spooks figure the Galactics probably sent it."

"What's that doing here?"

He grinned tiredly. "Drusus at Central wants to know the answer to that question even more than you do. That's why your tapper is filling with urgent messages."

Sure enough, when I looked down at my arm, I saw it crawl with red text. Now that I was near the house, they could find me despite my hacks.

"Shit…" I said.

"Come on," he said, slapping me on the back. "You can sleep in my air car while I drive you up to Central. As soon as we get there, though, you've got to promise me my name will never come up again. Okay?"

"You got it—as long as you forget what you saw out there in my swamp."

Carlos glanced out into the bog, and he squinted in disgust. "I can't remember a damned thing. It must be the beer. Did you put something in this can?"

He lifted the beer I'd given him accusingly. We both smiled tiredly and headed for his air car.

There wasn't time for a shower, or breakfast, or much of anything. That ship was waiting up there—and it didn't look like something that liked to wait around on grubby humans.

-3-

On the way to Central, I finally looked at my tapper. It filled every minute or so with fresh, frantic texts. I turned off all my illegal mods, knowing that would only make things worse.

"Look at all this crap," Carlos said. His arm was getting bombed as well. "Most of these love-notes are accusing me of goofing off. What a bunch of dick-riding haters."

"We are wanted men, Carlos. At least they haven't called us directly yet. They're probably all in a meeting."

Still, frowning at his arm, he finally sighed and lowered it without reading any more of the messages. "It's a relief I'm getting all this now, really."

"Why's that?"

"Well, since I didn't see this spam while we were… uh… out *hiking*… that means we must have been off the grid."

I nodded, unsurprised. Most of the Earth's surface was within range of a grid pickup these days, but not everywhere. Spooky backwaters like my family's private swamp still qualified as offline, apparently.

Bored after a short nap, I tapped at my tapper with a grungy finger. Most of the texts were from officers such as Graves, Winslade—even Galina Turov. Finally I saw an interesting name on the list.

"Drusus himself?" Carlos asked. Even though he was driving, he was still snooping.

14

"Piss off," I told him, turning away from him and shielding my forearm from his prying eyes. Then I tapped on the message in question.

McGill, the message read, *contact me before you speak to any of the others.*

"I'll be damned..." I said, and I tapped on the message, initiating a direct call. I shushed Carlos when the call went through.

Primus Bob appeared on my screen immediately. He looked as bald and sour as ever.

"Hey, Primus!" I said in a cheery tone. "I got the boss' message loud and clear. You can tell him I'll be in Central in an hour flat. You can take that to the bank."

"Not good enough, McGill. Your appointment began at 0700 hours. It is now 0714 hours. Accordingly, I've been authorized to take drastic action for the purposes of personnel retrieval."

"Uh... what?"

Primus Bob smiled. It wasn't a nice smile. "I see that you're in an air car. Please land and await extraction."

After that cryptic suggestion, the screen went blank.

"What the hell is he talking about?" Carlos asked. Despite my best efforts, he'd been listening in.

"I don't know. But you'd better land."

"That's crazy," he said. "We'll make better time if we thin the airfoils and hit the gas hard."

My tapper was quiet, but I frowned at it, thinking about what old Primus Bob had said. "I think you'd better land. They're planning something."

Carlos frowned and gazed all around him at the skies. "I don't see any fighters or anything."

"Just land the frigging car, Carlos."

"All right, all right."

We spiraled down, putting our skids into a green field. We were in the Carolinas somewhere, south of Virginia sector.

Craning our necks, we gazed at the skies suspiciously—but we were barking up the wrong tree.

A bluish glow flashed into existence just above the car's hood. Two big boots thumped onto the front panel, making some big dents.

"Goddammit!" Carlos shouted, climbing out of the driver's side hatch in a hurry.

I scrambled out of the passenger's seat with equal urgency.

The teleport jumper was a hog soldier in stone-gray coveralls. He wore a teleport harness, and he handed me a matching unit.

"You dented my hood, you asshole!" Carlos told the man.

The hog ignored him—which I didn't think was a good move on his part, but it was his funeral.

I took the harness and put it on. There was only one big button on the harness. Even a dummy like me couldn't get it wrong.

"Let me guess, I press this thing here, right? Where will this take me?"

The hog veteran didn't answer. He reached out a glove and rudely pressed the button for me.

I began to blur out, and I would have given the man a piece of my mind, but you can't really talk when you're in an energy field and about to jump.

The single thing that gave me joy was the fact that I saw Carlos coming up behind the thoughtless hog. He had a tire iron in his hand, and I knew he meant business.

Smiling and giving the jump-jockey a wave, I winked out of existence.

A moment later, I appeared inside Central. I was standing on a circular landing pad on an indoor Gray Deck—probably the highest floor in the building that had such a facility. Unsmiling hogs were there waiting for me.

They didn't grab me—and that was a good thing for them. Maybe they'd been briefed or something.

"Centurion McGill? This way, sir."

As I hadn't been shown any undue disrespect, I followed the security people without injuring them. It was moments of forbearance like this that allowed me to assure others I was no threat to polite authority figures, despite past misunderstandings.

16

Marching briskly, we headed for the lifts and shot upward at a dizzying pace. In the meantime, I whistled a forbidden tune and looked out the windows at the clouds and the city that sprawled out below them.

"Um..." one of the hogs said. "I can't help but notice that you've got a powerful odor coming off you, sir. Is that mud on your hands... or maybe manure?"

"A little of both, I suspect. I was called in from my farm without much notice."

"I see... Do you maybe want to stop by a restroom and wash up?"

I considered his thoughtful offer. I really did. But I shook my head. "Nope. Duty calls, and they're telling me I'm already late. A smear of grit and filth is nothing the brass hasn't seen before. We're all soldiers here at Central."

"Okay..."

The two hogs looked at each other doubtfully and shrugged. I ignored them.

When I marched into Primus Bob's domain a few minutes later, he gave me a tight grin of greeting. I could tell he thought he'd pulled a fast one on me, what with the teleportation kidnapping and all.

As we got closer to one another, however, his grin faltered. "What are you wearing, McGill...? Is that a filthy flannel shirt? And what is that god-awful smell?"

"That would be the fine soil of southern Georgia Sector, Mr. Primus, sir. I didn't have time to wash-up, see, what with your sudden abduction and all."

"Good God! This will never do. Come with me."

Primus Bob rushed past me with a finger crooked over his shoulder, indicating I should follow him toward the lavatory. I did so with reluctance.

Before we'd taken six steps, however, the doors to the main conference chamber flew wide. A stormy-faced Drusus appeared. "Bob? You texted me that McGill had arrived. What's the hold-up? Ah, there you are, McGill! Get in here immediately."

"But sir—" Bob began, but Drusus ignored him.

Drusus gestured furiously for me to follow him.

As Drusus outranked his bald butt-monkey by a factor of around a thousand, I switched directions and followed him instead. On the way past old Bob, I patted him on the shoulder. "Thanks for looking out for me," I said. "Too bad the brass is in such an all-fired hurry."

Primus Bob didn't answer me. His mouth hung open a centimeter or two instead. Then he frowned and sniffed at his collar in disgust.

I didn't get to see all of his reaction, unfortunately, as the big doors swung shut behind me at that moment.

Turning to look around, I was immediately impressed. The meeting wasn't large—but the attendees were big-wigs, one and all.

There was Praetor Drusus himself, Praetor Wurtenberger, plus a few flunky tribunes and imperators. My eyes widened when I spied the one person present who wasn't wearing a military uniform—other than myself, that is. Dressed in the ceremonial black robes of a Public Servant, Alexander Turov sat at the head of the conference table.

Alexander was an old dude with a wrinkled face, a hoary beard, and quick eyes. He had a funny East-euro way of talking. One glance told me he was in charge of this assembly.

"I see McGill has finally arrived," he said. "Good. We will proceed with the briefing."

"Great to see you, Servant Turov!" I said with gusto. I approached him and offered him a grimy hand to shake.

Old Alexander wasn't fooled. He glanced at my offending hand like it was a dog-turd—which it just about was.

"Remove your filthy paw from my vicinity, Centurion. Drusus? McGill is your beast. He will sit next to you."

Still smiling, I walked to the other end of the table and squeezed into a spot between the two praetors. Drusus and Wurtenberger looked horrified. I grinned and nodded to them both.

Old Alexander then reached a hand out toward the conference table. He made a few practiced gestures.

The battlecruiser that hung above the planet appeared. It was majestic and impressive. The sun shined over the hull, giving it a silvery outline.

"An envoy has arrived from the mid-galaxy provinces," Turov began. "We are all accustomed to our barbaric local warlords such as the Rigellians. We also frequently suffer the attention of our rightful masters from the Core Systems—but this ship is from the Mid-Zone."

My dirty hand was already up and waggling. A few dribbling bits of grit flaked off as I performed this gesture, but it couldn't be helped.

Alexander glanced at me in surprise. "There is an inquiry? Already? All right, I will suffer your existence one more time, McGill. What is it?"

"Sir, what the hell is a Mid-Zone alien? I mean, are these people from a planet like Earth, or are they something special like the Galactics of Trantor?"

Alexander pondered the question for a moment before answering. "It's a mix of the two. As we all know, the Empire spans outward from the core, covering two thirds of the star systems in our galaxy. In the hot, blazing center, there are countless ancient suns circled by worlds that are billions of years older than our beloved Earth. There, the Galactics hold sway."

I nodded. I knew all this stuff already, of course. I'd been to grammar school and studied Astrological Civics just like everyone else in the room.

"Minor civilizations such as ours are much less significant. We reside on the fringe of the Empire. Frontier provinces such as our beloved 921 are almost entirely devoid of value. However, many middle-tier provinces also exist. These span the region between the Core Systems and the frontier."

To illustrate his point, Alexander flicked at the table before him. He stood, using both hands like a wizard conjuring a demon.

What appeared was indeed an image that impressed me. I could tell by sweeping my eyes around the table that the others were intrigued as well.

A star map showing the entire galaxy spun between us. It was fantastically detailed, so much so that each sparkling star was like a glittering mote of diamond dust. The lights lowered as Alexander continued casting his spell.

Then, as I was about to slam my crusty hands together in applause—things got wild.

The gently spinning galaxy rose up, lifting itself from the depths of the conference table and taking life as a three-dimensional hologram. It spun slowly between us all, and I saw officers gasp and recoil physically when the gauzy spiral arms ran themselves over their faces. It was like being touched by a gigantic alien ghost.

"Wooo-hoo!" I hooted, standing and clapping. "That's the coolest damned thing I've ever seen!"

"Sit down and shut up, McGill," Praetor Wurtenberger ordered. He tugged at my pant leg, but then quickly regretted it. He withdrew his hand and rubbed his fingers together in horror.

Reluctantly, I obeyed. A quick look at old Alexander told me I wasn't in any real trouble, fortunately. He had a wintry smile on his face, and although he wasn't looking my direction, I could tell he'd enjoyed my outburst. He was proud of his massive hologram. In my book, he deserved some hooting and hollering.

The image itself was more than gaudy, it was instructive. Our galaxy was shaped like Saturn's planetary system, with a large mass in the center and relatively thin rings circling it. Instead of a planet in the center and dust spinning around, however, our galaxy consisted of billions of stars.

In the center, there was a tight ball of suns. These bright stars were bigger and more densely packed together than the rest of the total collection, which spread out thinner and thinner to the wispy fringes at the edges of the great disk.

Alexander worked some more magic. He began to paint various regions of his beautiful map. He touched the center basketball of stars, and it turned golden. An inscription appeared at his whim, labeling the region the *Core Systems*.

His fine-boned hand then moved to the fringe. There he touched the far edge, lighting up a wide band of stars that entirely encircled the galaxy. He turned this band a rust-red.

The red region lit up with the label: *Unknown*.

Next, he lit up a similar band of stars, one step inward from the Unknown region. He turned this band blue and labeled it *Frontier*.

Extending one thin finger, he touched a tiny point in the Frontier near the Unknown, causing a star to brighten. The spot was right on the border. The dot lit up and turned green. The label said: *Earth*.

"You can see our position is precarious," Alexander said. "We are located at the very border between the known and the unknown. We ride a local spur of stars, a region that sits like a lighthouse on the edge of a stormy sea. Past our location, mildly civilized life forms give way to the utterly barbaric."

My hand was up and waggling now. Reluctantly, Alexander called on me again. "Yes? What is it now, McGill? Do you need to relieve yourself?"

"What? Well... no... maybe... it doesn't matter. I'm bothering you because you haven't yet finished your map, Mr. Servant, sir. What's with the big band of stars between the golden basketball in the center and the blue Frontier?"

Alexander gave me another cold smile. "That is the Mid-Zone." He reached out and touched the zone, lighting it up with a sickly green glow. "These peoples are more important than lowly creatures such as humans. We are grunting frontier savages. These people are considered important, but not as important as the Galactics themselves. Many of these civilizations are made up of colony worlds. Outcasts from the Core Systems, but still somewhat respectable."

My hand was up again, and I shouted out my next question the moment he pointed at me.

"But sir, are they slaves like us, or are they full-fledged citizens?"

Alexander nodded to me. "Another good question. They are in-between. In our ancient history, we once had a system known as feudalism. In that social construct, the nobility were at the top," here he indicated the Core Systems, "with serfs and peasants at the bottom." He tapped at the blue frontier.

"But also, there existed a middle-tier. Such people were tradesmen, skilled artisans and bureaucrats."

Praetor Wurtenberger lifted a hand then. Alexander called upon him immediately.

"You mentioned bureaucrats, sir?" he asked. "Are we to assume from this that our own local officials might hail from this region? I'm talking about, of course, the Nairbs?"

"Yes, Praetor. You're exactly right. We haven't yet isolated their homeworld, but it is definitely within this region."

My jaw dropped. I'd long wondered where the hell the Nairbs came from. After all, they weren't Galactics, but they were definitely more important than humans. Now, looking at the green band of the Middle-zone, I knew the truth.

Suddenly, a new idea struck me.

"Wait a second! Are you telling us that battlecruiser up there is driven by Nairbs? That they're here, hat in hand, asking for our help?"

Alarmed, everyone turned toward Drusus to hear his answer.

He looked thoughtful. "That would be an interesting situation. In fact, I wish that it was so... it would be good for the Nairb race to owe us a favor, would it not? But alas no, this ship isn't manned by Nairbs. The very idea is amusing."

I thought about that, and I realized he was right. The Nairbs were capable of many things, but they didn't build fantastical warships. At least, I'd never seen one, and it didn't seem to be within their natural character to construct such a thing.

Who then? Who was flying that big ship from the Mid-Zone? Who had come all the way out to Earth to visit us and cut my vacation woefully short?

Old Alexander had us in the palm of his hand at this point. Every eye was locked upon his wrinkled hands as he reached up again to paint more detailed illustrations.

With a sweep of his arm, he obliterated the galaxy map he'd drawn. The looming shape of the battlecruiser that hung above Earth reappeared. It seemed oddly-designed and mysterious now. It *looked* like an Imperial warship—but the details weren't quite right. I knew one battlewagon from the next, and this one didn't match the profile of a ship from the Core Systems—not exactly.

"And so, we have gathered to discuss the nature of these visitors we have in our skies today," Alexander said. "No, they aren't Nairbs. They aren't from any planet we recognize. Nor have they yet deigned to identify themselves to us."

"Our fleet stands ready, Servant Turov," Praetor Wurtenburger said. "We aren't crowding this guest, but should they make any hostile move, we're ready to pounce."

"That's... somewhat encouraging," Alexander said. "But I doubt our reaction would come fast enough to save the souls meeting in this chamber."

Right then, I felt mildly impressed. Sure, Old Alexander had probably made sure he had a backup of his files in Russia somewhere—but the fact remained that he'd dared to stand with us today, under the guns of a big warship that possibly had evil intentions.

Looking around the table again, I noted many of the big brass types I might have expected to be present were nowhere to be seen. Imperator Turov, for example, or Tribune Winslade. One would have thought... but no, they were probably tucked away somewhere playing it safe.

Alexander was talking again, so I forced myself to listen-up. Staff meetings usually bored the living shit out of me, but today's case was an exception to that long-standing rule.

"...we have, naturally, made every attempt to communicate. They have yet to respond, except for a single pulse of data. After deciphering the code, which was a dialect of Imperial standard, we determined there was only a single word of meaning buried within."

Here, Alexander turned and looked at me for the first time. His eyes were piercing. He was as old as the hills and maybe what was buried under those hills, too—but his mind was still sharp.

"Uh..." I said, wondering if I'd missed something. Often, during meetings that lasted more than, say, twenty minutes, I zoned out. If I was expected to speak at that point, I'd almost certainly miss my cue. I suspected this might be another of those times.

Reflexively, I looked as clueless as possible, hoping someone would give me a hint—but no one did. They all just stared at me.

Finally, Alexander began speaking again. "Can you guess, Centurion, what that single word might be?"

"Oh… No, sir. Not a clue."

I felt a wave of relief. I'd misread the situation. Alexander was just being unfairly accusatory, due to my often-misunderstood involvement in alien visitations. As I had no idea who these Mid-Zone visitors might be, I felt like I was in the clear.

But Old Alexander continued to stare at me thoughtfully. He was a hard man to read. He had the expressions of a lizard—an unhappy lizard—most of the time.

Falling back on ignorance as my standard defense, I tried to resemble a man who was as dumb as a bag of hammers. It came naturally to me.

Finally, Alexander spoke again, breaking the uncomfortable silence. "The single word they transmitted to Central was this."

He touched a virtual button in the air, and a projected audio player coalesced into being. It had a red jangling line showing a waveform of sound. He played it, and a haunting alien voice spoke a single, damning word.

"…*McGill*…"

-4-

Every eye in the place turned toward me then, and those eyes were wide. Many were bloodshot. Some were angry. Almost all of them were slitted in suspicion and prejudice.

"Holy Hell!" I boomed. "Did you guys hear that? It almost sounded like it said my name... almost."

My ploy failed miserably. No one even responded. They all just sucked in a breath with tight lungs and muttered dark things to one another. Words like *traitor* and *perming* were mumbled right next to me.

"Hey, hey now!" I said, faking a laugh. "Come on, guys. You don't think I have anything to do with that big ship up there, do you? I'm just a hick from the sticks. I'm a six-pack guzzling moron, just ask anybody."

Alexander rustled his robes, sliding them back to reveal his tapper. It had a lot of wiry gray hairs growing out of it, and it was kind of nasty to look at, I don't mind telling you.

"I've taken it upon myself to retrace your recent locations, McGill. You often drop off radar—and last night was no exception. This vessel appeared late in the evening, and not only did you ignore all summons to Central—you were also unreachable."

"Uh... yeah. I do go off-grid sometimes. Everyone does that now and again."

The assembled officers shook their heads.

"No," Alexander said. "No one here goes off grid while on Earth. The only possible exception is myself, when I enter a counseling session with other high level Public Servants."

"Oh… that's a crying shame, sir. I could show you how to tape aluminum foil over your tapper and vanish if you want to. You really should try it, you'll enjoy yourself more."

He gave me that humorless smile. "A kind offer, I'm sure, but I'll pass, McGill. Let us return to where you were last night. Were you on Earth?"

I blinked several times. "Of course I was, sir."

"Do you know that both drones and a tracing grid-spider could not find you?"

"Huh? Really? Well… I live way out near Waycross. We don't get the best service there, see."

Praetor Drusus lost his cool then. He stood up and slammed a fist on the table. The image of the battlecruiser jumped a little. "McGill, I'm in your direct chain of command. In fact, I'm at the top of that chain. I hereby order you to stop bullshitting and come clean about this visitation."

"But sir, I'm trying to help in any way I can. Old McGill is as honest as the day is long—everyone knows that."

"Just tell us what's going on," he implored me. "Are they here to find and arrest you? Are they cutting some kind of deal you privately arranged? Or might this be a prelude to another invasion?"

"Uh… I don't rightly know, Praetor, sir. Seriously—I spent the night out in my swamp with a lady-friend. That's all. There's an old rotting cabin out there, see, and… well… sometimes it's good to be away from prying eyes for a while."

They all stared at me distrustfully.

Drusus wasn't done yet. "You're telling me you were out screwing some woman in the woods, and you had no idea that new and threatening aliens were knocking on our door with your name on their minds?"

"That's exactly right, sir. As God is my witness, I have no clue what they want or who they are. That's not a Nairb ship. It's not a Mogwa ship… It looks kind of Mogwa-like, but the design is different."

"We know all that. Thanks for being utterly unhelpful."

Drusus sat down in a huff. I tried not to look at him. In my experience, when someone was mad at you, it was best not to kiss-up or glare. You just ignored them and went onward. That usually settled them down the quickest.

Old Alexander had watched this exchange carefully, and he hadn't missed a trick. He and I had had dealings recently—not all of them of an entirely cordial nature. For one thing, he knew I'd been mounting his daughter for years, and—

Oh, shit.

A spike of instant regret stabbed into my fool brain. I'd screwed up. When pressed, I'd reflexively turned to my girlfriend defense. That normally worked well, as I was one of the more infamous horn-dogs in my legion.

But I'd forgotten during Drusus' tirade that Galina Turov, Old Alexander's daughter, was supposed to be my main squeeze. I didn't see any way in which confessing to infidelity would improve my standing in his cold, ancient eyes.

"Uh…" I said. "What I meant to say was… I was indisposed in the swamp. That's the truth, sirs. You've got to believe me."

"This is getting us nowhere," Praetor Wurtenberger said. "I suggest we forget about McGill helping in any substantial way. What are we going to do about that ship up there? As a representative of Earth's Fleet, I can say without reservation that we can destroy her almost without effort."

"No." Old Alexander had spoken, and his single word was uttered with finality.

Wurtenberger threw his flabby hands high. "What then? Do we wait for them to transmit a second word? Or perhaps to launch a spread of hell-burners onto our green Earth?"

Alexander shook his head. "Not that, either. We have only one option. We shall have McGill transmit a message to them. If that doesn't work, we'll send him up there in an unarmed shuttle to tap politely on their hull until they either destroy him or allow him entry."

I blinked and frowned at these ideas. Was it my imagination, or was old man Turov sour on me all of a sudden? Could it be over his daughter? I thought that it might be, and I thought that was mighty unfair. After all, it wasn't like we were engaged or anything.

"Uh…" I said. "What should I say to them, sirs?"

Drusus threw up his hands with the palms out flat. He looked very alarmed. "Sir, I can't condone this action. McGill isn't a diplomat. He isn't even a proper officer most of the time."

"Yes. I gathered that. But they've ignored us for too long. They asked for McGill, we brought him here, and they will get their wish. Proceed."

Drusus sat down in defeat. He massaged his neck with one hand while I was given a microphone and some staffers conjured up an open channel to transmit over.

After clearing my throat, I began to talk. "Hello, alien brothers. I'm Centurion James McGill, from Legion Varus. I'm sorry about the wait, but I'm here now and listening. If you have some message of peace, joy and enlightenment, I'm all ears down here at Central."

Nothing came back in response to my message. I repeated the transmission in several different ways, but no one so much as launched a peep or a ping back at me. After about three solid minutes, I gave up and threw my hands wide.

"I don't get it," I said. "Maybe it's all a big misunderstanding. Maybe they were saying something like McGillicuddy, you know, but it got cut off, or something. That kind of thing happens all the time in my neck of the woods."

They didn't even look at me. They seemed more depressed and worried than ever. On the other hand, I was beginning to sense an opportunity for an exit.

I faked a yawn and touched my gut suggestively. "You know, if you guys don't mind, I think maybe I should take my leave. I'm sorry I couldn't help you guys out, but I'm feeling a mite hungry, see—"

"Shut up," Drusus said suddenly. "Look!"

My eyes followed his pointing finger. An object was falling from space. It was small, dark, and slightly reflective.

"A bomb?" Wurtenberger demanded, standing up suddenly.

Drusus shook his head. "No, it's got jets, see? It came right out of the ship's belly. Project the trajectory!"

A red arc appeared, connecting the object to the roof of Central. The missile, or bomb, or whatever it was would soon be landing on our heads.

"Evacuate the building," Drusus ordered.

"Impossible," Wurtenberger said. "There's no time. We must shoot it down."

"No."

We all stared toward the head of the table. Old Alexander had spoken again, and as before, everyone listened to him.

He extended one hand toward me, and one toward Drusus. He unrolled a single finger from each hand, and pointed them at each of us.

"You two will accompany me to the roof. The rest of you can evacuate if you want—but no one is to take offensive action until our visitors' intentions are clear."

"If they drop an A-bomb on the city, will that be sufficient provocation to take action?" Wurtenburger asked. His tone seemed almost mocking, but Alexander didn't take offense.

"I should think so. In such a situation, you'll be in charge of the response. The rest of us will be obliterated."

Alexander marched out, with Drusus and me trailing in his wake like ducklings.

"So, Mr. Servant, sir. You think they're sending down a ship? A delegation?"

"It's possible. It is the best case scenario, one that I'm willing to entertain even at this dark hour. Pray that I'm correct."

"I'm praying, sir. I truly am."

We rode the elevators upward. We stepped out onto the landing pad on the windswept roof of Central. Fortunately, the wait was a short one.

"Whatever it is, it's firing landing jets. That's a good sign," I said.

A few hogs rushed to stand between us and the landing ship. They tried to order us back inside, but when they saw the ranks on Drusus and Servant Alexander, they melted away in a big hurry.

The ship—because it really was a ship, that much was clear now—came in for a fiery landing. Once it was down, sitting on

29

six skids with vapor pouring off the fins, we approached and stood at a respectful distance.

Less than a minute later the hatch opened—and we were all in for quite a shock.

-5-

Two marines stepped out—they were Mogwa marines in power armor. I'd seen their kind before. Our Galactic overlords often used such troops for security on their ships.

But these alien marines weren't identical to those I'd seen in the past. They were rougher-looking, somehow. They had the same funky, multi-limbed walking machines—but their armor was differently shaped.

Whatever the case, they were essentially one-alien tanks that could crush your toes if they wanted to. The machines reminded me of the dragons that we used on Earth sometimes.

The two marines split apart and stepped to either side. From the dark interior another Mogwa emerged. This one was in a naval uniform, but not wearing power-armor.

At first, I didn't recognize him. He was young and proud, walking with the odd six-legged gait of all his kind. There was a hint of a swagger buried in the movement.

I squinted at him, and he squinted at me.

Finally, his translator lit up. "Ah, I believe I recognize a favored slaveling of the past. Are you the McGill-creature?"

My jaw dropped low. I couldn't believe it. "Grand Admiral Sateekas? As I live and breathe, it *is* you! You look all young and healthy, sir!"

"You speak truth. I've been rejuvenated to my prior state."

Sateekas was the only Mogwa in existence that I could call a friend—sort of. The Mogwa weren't exactly easy to get close

31

to. They were arrogant, self-centered and downright mean most of the time.

But Sateekas and I had shared a lot of battles, and a lot of difficult moments. We'd come to an understanding of sorts.

He'd never been the luckiest of admirals. He'd lost fleets out here in Province 921 more than once. Because of these costly defeats, he'd been forcibly retired out of the military.

"I don't think I've met up with you since we fought three Skay together at Clone World…" I said. "Can that be right?"

Sateekas winced at the mention of that campaign. "Do not mention the Skay, McGill. They were my downfall."

"But we won that battle in the end!"

Sateekas made a shrugging motion with his two front appendages. "Perhaps so, but we won at too great a loss for the Mogwa Admiralty to accept. Never a day goes by that I'm not somehow reminded that this entire province isn't worth the value of the ships I lost while defending this worthless dribble of stars."

I wondered if that could be true—and I suspected it was.

Drusus cleared his throat, and we all looked at him. Old Servant Alexander stayed quiet, however.

"McGill, perhaps you can introduce us."

"Sure thing. Admiral Sateekas, this is Praetor Drusus and Public Servant Alexander Turov. He's a big cheese in our local government."

"How exciting," Sateekas said, but I could tell he was anything but excited.

I glanced over at Drusus and Alexander, but neither of them moved to speak. Drusus finally gave me a tight-lipped nod. He wasn't going to try to take over. He knew from long experience that I had a certain rapport and perspective with the Mogwa elite—as upsetting as that was for everyone.

"Uh…" I said. "Well your lordship, can you tell me what we can do for you? You're honored guests, of course… but you must have come out here for a good reason."

"A grim reason," Sateekas admitted. "Be it known that I swore off Province 921 many years ago. I've long considered it a benighted backwater. A stew of villainy and misfortune."

"You've got the right of that, sir."

"Yes… but now, due to unforeseen circumstances, I've been forced to end my retirement and stand upon the bridge of a warship once again."

"How's that, your lordship?"

The Mogwa made a dismissive wave with one of his hand-things. "All will be explained in due course. First, I must establish my authority."

At this odd turn of phrase, we three humans frowned at one another. Sateekas turned toward the dark hatchway of his shuttle craft. He made a motion suggesting someone else should come forward.

Establish authority? My dim mind puzzled over those words. Drusus, Alexander and I were all contemplating what they might mean, and why such a thing might need to be done.

Finally, another figure appeared in the hatchway. I recognized her immediately.

"Governess Nox?"

The female Mogwa ignored me. She eyed the overcast skies with disdain. "This ghastly planet is always cold," she complained. She clutched at her pouch reflexively. It squirmed at her touch. "There's a cutting wind up, I can feel it from here."

The squirming thing in her pouch… that stunned me. I knew Nox had had a kid with Sateekas in the past. But that kid would have to be pretty well grown-up by now. Could it be they'd spawned a second child? I was gob-smacked by the idea.

But as I was now seeing Sateekas in his rejuvenated form, I could better understand the situation. I'd been thinking of him as the nasty, wattled old sad-sack he'd been years ago. Now he was a rejuvenated alien in his prime, and he might seem quite dashing to Nox.

"Come, come, milady," Sateekas said, urging her forward. "Tell these slaves they must listen to me."

Nox shuffled forward and peered at the cloudy skies. The truth was the weather was quite pleasant by human standards. It was the end of summer, and although we were pretty high up on a windswept landing platform, it wasn't all that chilly. She was probably just feeling protective about her new offspring.

"Earthlings, you are the enforcing species for the Empire in Province 921," Nox said. "Do you acknowledge this fact?"

"Yes," Drusus said. "In fact, I'm the chief officer in charge of—"

"Yes, yes, whatever," she interrupted, cutting him off. "Do you also acknowledge that I am Governess Nox, the rightful civilian authority here in this pathetic hinterland?"

We three humans couldn't help but exchange concerned glances yet again. We all had the feeling we were being buttered up for something heinous.

"Yes," Servant Alexander stated at last.

Nox peered at him, hugging her squirming pouch with two hairy, leathery hands. "Who and what are you, being? I know Drusus and that over-sized speaking-ape named McGill—but you're new to my eyes."

"I represent the civil authority here on Earth. I represent Hegemony at large, just as Drusus represents our military."

She squinted at him for another moment or two. "I see… I suppose your presence is tolerable. Listen to me now, slaves. I am about to make an official decree, and I don't wish to repeat myself."

We stared with worry in our hearts. None of us said anything.

"Your armed forces are hereby commandeered. They will be placed at the disposal of Admiral Sateekas. Your armies, your fleets—they must all serve him until this emergency has passed."

Drusus sputtered. Alexander stood as still as a stone.

"Uh… sirs?" I dared to speak up. "Can I inquire as to the nature of this emergency?"

Nox made a flicking motion with her hind leg as she retreated back into her ship. She gave a little shiver as she did so.

Sateekas watched her go, and then he turned back to us expectantly. "Well? Where is the required response?"

"Um…" Drusus said. "We will of course comply with the wishes of the Empire."

Sateekas screwed up his face in disgust. "Hmph. Your rejoinder lacks in both decorum and enthusiasm. Although I found it woefully lacking, I accept your acquiescence. Now, you will arrange our welcoming feast, which will commence within the hour."

"Oh... yes, sir. Of course," Drusus said, caught by surprise.

Sateekas turned as if to go, but then he paused. "Ah, and don't forget I have a personal preference for those large flying insects of yours, roasted to perfection. Xlur shared them with me long ago, and I want to enjoy the flavor again."

"Large flying insects?" Drusus asked, baffled.

"Squab, sir," I interjected. "I think he's talking about squab. Xlur ate a bunch of them one time, and the Mogwa seem to love them."

"Er... um... yes, of course. We'll do everything we can, Admiral—"

But his words were again cut off when the hatch slammed closed in our faces.

There was a scowling, whispering conference that began as we left the shuttle and hurried toward the terminal. When we reached the rooftop elevators and began the downward plunge into the guts of Central, both Alexander and Drusus seemed to be in a foul mood.

"Never in two score decades of life have I been dealt with so abruptly," Alexander complained.

"A feast of squab?" Drusus complained. "A banquet planned and presented in less than one hour? How are we going to arrange that?"

They both seemed to be missing the big picture. "Sirs... what about his business of commandeering our armed forces?"

Drusus shrugged. "Unfortunately, they have the authority to do that. It is well within their rights to demand our ships and troops."

I frowned so hard my face hurt. I didn't like the sound of all this. Sateekas, after all, was best known as an officer who excelled at losing armies and navies. If we were being dragged off to some conflict in the Core Systems, that sounded very dangerous.

While Drusus wrangled with his tapper, making various calls to banquet halls and concierge-types, I thought hard about the situation we now found ourselves in.

Old Alexander was watching me. When the elevator stopped and Drusus trotted away, the old buzzard tapped my shoulder. He pulled me aside in the corridor. "McGill? What are you thinking about?"

I faked a smile. "Squab, sir. I love it. Duck is better, mind you, but—"

The old man shook his head. "No, you're not thinking about birds. Never take me for a fool. It will only embarrass us both."

"Uh…"

"What are you thinking about?" he repeated, gazing up at me with intense eyes.

It took a moment for me to answer that. Sure, I could have come up with another lie. I thought about telling him I was thinking about how lovely his daughter was at sunset, or some other such nonsense.

But I knew somehow he already understood my line of reasoning. That was bad. The old bastard was scary-smart.

"Well, Mr. Servant, to tell you the truth I'm thinking about getting the Mogwa to change their plans before they get started."

Alexander nodded. "Coincidentally, I'm thinking along similar lines. Can it be done?"

I shrugged. "Sure it can. I've done it before. I've talked aliens out of all kinds of dumb ideas."

He smiled. "Usually, you are a man of action. Tell me what you are really contemplating."

"Uh… well… that's not—"

"How many Mogwa have you assassinated, McGill?"

That question took me by surprise. It wasn't something that I dared even to think about. There had been, after all, quite a number of Mogwa who'd died at my hands. Some of them had even been permed.

"Never mind," Alexander said when I didn't answer. "You and I have worked together before, for the good of our shared planet. If you get a chance to fix this situation, I want you to take it. End this threat to our fleet, to your legion—to all our legions. Do you understand me, Centurion?"

"I think so."

36

"Good."

Then he swept away and followed Drusus. Together, they planned a feast and a grand celebration. They were also calling all our armed forces back to duty.

The Mustering Halls would soon fill with troops. Then the skies overhead would fill with ships.

Earth was going to war again—unless I could find a way to stop it.

-6-

The banquet took an hour and ten minutes to pull together. By that time, I'd washed up and put on a fresh uniform.

The two Mogwa showed up before the tables were properly set, and they complained about everything.

"Such shameful disorganization," Nox said as Sateekas seated her at the head of the main table. "If I wasn't famished and in a hurry, I'd demand executions."

"I urge you to go with your instincts, my dear," Sateekas said. "A public display of justice might bring about a welcome surge in your digestive enzymes."

Nox considered it, but she passed on the idea. "No. We shall hold back upon judgment until we taste their offerings."

The two Mogwa then turned toward me and Drusus. Alexander stood back, a quiet shadow behind us.

"Sit down, McGill," Sateekas ordered. "I wish to be entertained."

I did so, and I grinned and talked lavishly about his accomplishments in battle. I'd witnessed him in action commanding ships on several occasions, and although the engagements often turned into disasters, they were always glorious and dramatic as well.

Drusus sat with us. He appeared glum. Across the room, Alexander Turov sat at a nearby table and stared.

He wasn't the only one watching us. Mogwa marines guarded the exits and observed everyone at the buffet. They tasted every plate heading toward our table. It seemed to me that they weren't in a trusting mood.

Nox was the first one to fall out of my spell of words. Sateekas was eating it up, enjoying my enthusiastic retelling of the fleet battle at Rogue World. In my version, he was the undisputed hero.

Suddenly, Nox pointed an appendage toward Alexander. "That one. He stares. He doesn't eat. Who is he again?"

"Uh… that's Public Servant Turov, sirs. He's the highest civilian authority in this room—other than yourself, of course."

"Of course… I don't like him. He doesn't seem trustworthy. I want him removed."

"What?"

Before I could say anything else, Nox motioned to her marines. They crowded near us, their armored suits bumping the table.

"Hey, hey," I complained, trying to keep the plates from sliding, and the wine glasses from spilling.

Nox pointed toward Turov. "Remove that withered crone from this assembly."

Immediately, the marine squad leader sighted an energy weapon on old Alexander.

"Whoa!" I said, but it was too late for objections. Mogwa marines were trained to act upon their orders, not overthink them.

A gout of blue-white energy blinded us all as it fired from the tip of the marine's projector—it missed, however, as I had knocked the muzzle upward. A burning stripe of fire scorched the ceiling.

The marine and the rest of the Mogwa turned on me, glowering with rage.

"I'm sorry, sirs! I didn't mean to bump your man. Didn't realize the slightest touch could spoil a marine's aim so easily. Hold on a second, I'll pin the old buzzard by the shoulders for you. You can burn his face off if you want to—uh…"

I made a show of looking for the Servant, but he'd taken the hint and run out of the place.

"He's pretty spry for such an oldster," I commented.

"This is entirely unacceptable!" Nox complained.

"Don't I know it, Governess. I apologize profusely. How about if you have your boy here shoot me, instead? Would that make you feel any better?"

Nox glared at me. "You have thwarted my direct order. Your life will be forfeit!"

Sateekas cleared his throat. "Hmm, let's not be too hasty, my dear. McGill is the only element of this gathering that isn't stupefyingly dull at the moment. If we kill him, we'll have to listen to these others prattling on all night."

Nox calmed herself with difficulty. "All right... I don't want to spend another minute listening to the idle chatter of this simpering creature." She pointed at Drusus when she said this, but we all pretended not to notice.

Fortunately, the food arrived about then. It came in the form of a large platter heaped with roasted squab. A few feathers still clung to the meat here and there, and it was slightly raw in places—but the Mogwa dug in anyways. They didn't seem to mind or even notice that the birds weren't cooked to perfection.

I joined them, tearing into the food. Drusus, however, only poked at his dish. When the aliens weren't looking, he shoveled his half-raw bird onto my plate.

I didn't mind. I ate with gusto that almost matched the Mogwa themselves.

Once everyone had been fed, the mood at the table improved dramatically. Only Drusus seemed tense, wearing a pasted-on smile that belied his wrinkle-furrowed brow.

The good news was that after being told how dull he was, he let me do most of the talking. That state of affairs was just fine with me.

"Let's get down to business, shall we?" I asked.

The Mogwa eyed me with immediate suspicion. That was their way, when they met up with anything unexpected.

"Business?" Sateekas said. "Is this a code word for payment? If so, there shall be none. Possibly, fueling stations might be arranged for your fleet during transport, but only if we find it convenient to supply such niceties."

"Uh..." I said, blinking, "that's not exactly what I meant, sirs. I was just wondering if you might share where our target star might be? Where are we going to war to spread the glorious will of the Empire?"

Nox and Sateekas exchanged wary glances. Nox signaled in the negative. Sateekas turned toward me thoughtfully.

"You ask too much, McGill."

I glanced at Drusus, who looked kind of gray. He wasn't any help. He probably hadn't eaten enough.

"Hmmm…" I said. "Okay then. We'll load up a transport and our best legion. We'll follow your battlecruiser wherever you need us to go."

Sateekas scoffed. "You'll do no such thing. All your ships will gather. When a great host has assembled, my vessel will serve as the fleet's flagship. It will be something of an embarrassment to lead a horde of militia vessels to war, but it can't be helped in this case. We have to face realities out here on the frontier."

"Um… okay…"

Drusus finally couldn't contain himself any longer. After all, he was the man who would have to command this fleet on Earth's behalf. He couldn't very well plan a monstrous voyage of this type without more information. I could tell he was hungry to hear the details.

"Sirs, please. We must know at least the distance in lightyears we'll be required to travel. We can't plan without that information."

"Obstinance!" Nox declared. "Impudence! Who is this being who dares to demand things of an Imperial Governess?"

"I—I didn't—"

Fortunately, Sateekas intervened on our behalf. He was an old navy man, after all. He knew the truth behind Drusus' words.

"It is true, you can't load a ship with fuel if you don't know how far you will be traveling. I understand your need for logistical details, Drusus. I will give you a modest goal: plan for a voyage of five thousand lightyears, six thousand to be on the safe side."

"Six thousand…?" Drusus was gob-smacked. Our entire province was only a thousand lightyears across, more or less, and five hundred deep. To the best of my knowledge, Earth had never gone so far across the cosmos in any direction, by any means.

"Is this a problem?" Sateekas demanded.

Drusus gathered himself and made an effort to seem professional. "Yes, it is. First of all, I have to know if you are talking about the full distance, there and back, or only about the distance to the target one-way."

"My figure would be for the round trip—assuming any of your ships survive the battle and manage to return."

"Of course… well sir, the good news is some of our vessels can make a journey of that range. Not many, but some."

Sateekas made a blatting noise. "Range… of course. I had not considered it… Earth would naturally build only local defense vessels, not real ships-of-the-line. I'm disappointed."

"They're probably lying, Sateekas," Nox said. "I suspect they're holding back on us as would a tax cheat. Let's bring in Nairbs to tally their real fleet and measure their capacities."

"No, no, I won't have that kind of talk. These beasts are feral, stupid, and primitive in the extreme, yes. But they are creatures of honor. I've watched them fight and die with cunning and bravado. That's why we're here to gather them to our banner, my dear."

Nox appeared to lose interest. "The military side of this is yours to run as you see fit, as we agreed. Just don't be too trusting."

"Never."

Sateekas turned back to confront us. "How many of your ships could travel a distance of three thousand lightyears, Drusus?"

He shrugged. "Maybe twenty or thirty percent of them. The largest vessels of the newest classes. But you were talking about six thousand, not—"

"Indulge me. Give me a precise number by morning. Name and describe every ship, and transmit the roster to my vessel. Now, we shall take our leave."

The two Mogwa got up, and I felt a certain urgency overcome me. They were leaving too soon. I'd hoped to get them drunk or something. Their Marines were already crowding forward, their clanking machines crushing feet and ramming aside diners who took more than a half-second to get out of the way.

"Uh…" I said, wondering if this was the moment.

I have a good sense for these things. Opportunities are rare and fleeting when it comes to assassination. Right now, I had the element of surprise and proximity in my favor. The two Mogwa could be killed in a dozen ways. I could grab onto a Marine's energy projector, for example, perhaps inducing him to fire through me and burn his masters in the same moment.

But then I saw something. Nox… she had her nasty hands on her pouch again. The pouch was squirming on its own.

I frowned. She'd brought her baby down here to the banquet? That seemed weird—but maybe it wasn't for a Mogwa mother. Their babies never seemed to squall and carry on like a human child would have. If they didn't represent a disruption to a social event, why not bring them along?

In the end I stood, and I smiled, and I saluted and bowed. The Mogwa were ceremoniously led by their color guard out of the hall and upstairs to their shuttle.

I tried to come up with a reason why I should accompany them aloft—but my mind was a blank. Nothing I could say would have worked on these two. I knew them both, and they'd sooner have taken a bag of dog turds up into space with them.

The night didn't end with the Mogwa exit. Instead, it had only just begun for one bored, yawning James McGill.

"It's unbelievable," Drusus said, pacing around in an elaborate pattern in his office. "The arrogance of these creatures—the sheer gall!"

"Yes..." Old Alexander agreed. "They are even worse in person than I had imagined they could be. You once described Galactics to me, Centurion McGill, and I thought your judgment was too harsh. I now stand corrected. You were being kind."

"Six thousand lightyears?" Drusus demanded, throwing his hands high. "That's insane. Our ships are built to go two thousand, round trip—twenty-five hundred if we push it. That's enough to cross any of our borders into a neighboring province and conduct a lengthy campaign. We never planned to go on a voyage farther out than that."

"Hmm..." Alexander said. "Let's project the range as described."

He brought up his shimmering map of the galaxy again, and we all stared at it, mesmerized.

"Such a vast distance..." he said. "That would be approximately this far..."

A sphere appeared. It was orange in color, and it stained space around the tiny green gem that was Earth. All of Province 921, 928, and 926 were encompassed in this sphere. It reached well beyond these familiar regions, however. It reached all the way into the Mid-Zone.

Alexander turned to us. "Now, let us use deductive reasoning. Where do our friends hail from?"

Drusus took over. He stepped up and drew an intersecting line that reached into the Mid-Zone stars. Not that many targets lit up. There were only a few hundred that were within reach.

"What do we know of these stars?" Alexander asked.

Drusus waved dismissively. "Almost nothing. We've never even dared to send probes out that far. Our knowledge ends just beyond the borders of Province 921. The Mid-Zone?" He scoffed. "You might as well ask a tropical shark what it knows about the Arctic Ocean."

Alexander ignored his bad attitude, and he made some cryptic notes. "I must take my leave of now. I will convene with my peers in Geneva. It's morning over there, and they will want to stay apprised of these developments."

"Of course, Servant Turov. We thank you for your support and advice. Earth's military won't disappoint you."

It didn't sound like Drusus meant it, but his words were well-chosen.

Alexander, however, didn't even look at him. He was staring at me.

"Support..." he said. "Advice... and disappointment. These are powerful words. Opportunities have already been ignored. I hope—no, I pray—that we didn't miss our best chance to guide events in our favor tonight."

I put on a dumb-ass expression, but he didn't look like he was buying it. We both knew what old Alex was telling me—that I'd blown it. I'd let the Mogwa slip from our grasp.

Both Alex and I were wondering if we'd ever get a second shot.

When the old bastard had left us, I turned to see Drusus was looking at me funny.

"What was that about, McGill?" he asked.

"Huh? What was what about, Praetor?"

"The Servant was looking at you, and he seemed disappointed."

I brightened. "Oh, that. Well sir... you might happen to know that Galina Turov is the Servant's daughter, right?"

"Yes, I knew that."

"Well sir, can you imagine being a daddy and learning that your little girl is spending *way* too much time with the likes of one James McGill?"

Drusus blinked. My lie had been a good one—one of the best, because there was a grain of truth in it.

"Oh... he mentioned disappointment... wasn't that the word he used?"

"I believe so."

That was good enough for Drusus. He soon forgot all about the weird moment between Old Alexander and me.

Moving on, he began to plan in earnest. He worked numbers and charts, trying to figure out how to get Earth's battlewagons to fly farther and longer than they'd ever been designed to do.

Along about midnight, I snuck out of the place and made good on my escape. Yawning and thinking about finding a bunk somewhere, I received an urgent call on my tapper.

I almost ignored it. My finger was hovering over the decline button—but I hesitated. The call was from Imperator Galina Turov.

Grumbling, I answered the call. If I didn't, I knew she'd hound me all damned night long. It was one thing to hide while I was living down in Waycross and furloughed—it was quite another to dodge the brass while working at Central in the lion's den.

"James? Where are you?"

"Uh... Central, I think."

"I know that, you idiot. I mean why aren't you here at my office?"

Blinking in confusion, I noticed a slew of messages on my tapper. I'd been ignoring them as I'd been in an important meeting. That was a great excuse to dodge work, and I always played such cards to the fullest.

But despite my best efforts, some vicious techno-deviltry had informed Galina that my meeting was over, and my time was up for grabs again. She'd pounced on the moment immediately.

"I'm headed for a bunk, sir," I told her. "I worked all last night, and—"

"Sleep is for the dead, McGill," she said, quoting a legion proverb. "Get to my office and drink some coffee. We've got a campaign to plan out."

Groaning aloud, I did a one-eighty in the corridor and headed to Galina's office. She wasn't running Legion Varus this year, she'd been promoted out of that role and now enjoyed a desk job. Unfortunately for her, she was still considered an eligible field commander due to her experience among the stars. A big mission like this would need a big staff to run it. Apparently, someone had decided to make her role official.

Pouring a midnight coffee was a sad thing for a man like me. I liked midnight beers much better, but no one was interested in old McGill's preferences tonight.

The room wasn't full-up, but there were several other officers present. Tribune Winslade was there, having been wrongfully awarded the command of my beloved Legion Varus after the Ice World campaign. Graves should have gotten the job, but justice was too lofty of a goal for the folks running Hegemony.

Graves was there too, sitting at Winslade's side. That wasn't a surprise. He'd end up doing all the work and probably handling Winslade's laundry, too.

Turning my head in the other direction, I did a double-take.

"Hey!" I boomed, pointing a big finger at a face I knew well. "What's Primus Bob doing here? Isn't he a hog who works for Drusus?"

Turov had been fooling with her display settings, but she looked up to answer me.

"That is a rude and pejorative statement, McGill. Primus Sweeney is now Sub-Tribune Sweeney. He's been promoted by Drusus no less than hour ago."

"Uh... why?"

She glared at me. The question was legit, but I could tell she didn't want to answer it. "Everyone needs field experience

47

at some point. This mission—ill-defined and grandiose as it seems to be—will serve as the perfect training ground for an officer such as Bob, here."

I stared at him, marveling. He looked too shell-shocked to be angry. I wondered if being reassigned to running a zoo legion on a dangerous mission into the unknown had left old Bob without much to say.

"Sub-Tribune Robert Sweeney…" I said, marveling and staring at him. "Have you bought yourself some nose-plugs yet, Bob? You might find them useful when you mount up and ride in the belly of *Dominus*."

"That's enough, McGill. Sweeney, I apologize for the crude manners of your legionnaire brothers. They have a unique way of welcoming newcomers."

"That's all right, Imperator," Bob said. "I'm sure we'll all come to respect each other in time."

Galina began the briefing then, going on about using tight storage supplies economically, transmitting supplies via gateway posts, waste management and everything else from food to water tanks. I was bored immediately, and I tuned out all the nerd-stuff.

All the while she talked, something was bothering me. I wasn't sure what it was until…

Slam! My open hand crashed down on the table, making everything and everyone jump.

"Wait a minute!" I shouted. I pointed at Bob accusingly. "Wait just a damned minute. I thought Hegemony had gotten rid of the whole sub-primus and sub-tribune bullshit. Hasn't Bob here rightfully earned the rank of a full tribune?"

Galina folded up her face and her arms. She glared at me. "No, McGill. That's all changed again. After the shocking events of last year—some of which you participated in personally, I might add—Hegemony reinstated the Sub-ranks for the time being. That was announced months ago. You really should do more reading, James."

"Yeah… I guess so. Was this change due to the evil of that traitor-squid, Tribune Foam?"

Galina showed me her small white teeth in a line. "The events of the past year did affect their decision. Tribunes Fike and Foam were both posthumously stripped of their ranks, by the way."

"Uh… really? That's only right, I suppose."

"If you're done with making loud outbursts, can I proceed with the briefing now?"

"Sure thing, sir. I'm sorry, sir."

Galina went on then, and I tuned her out promptly. The whole meeting seemed to be about planning to fly Earth's fleet out farther and faster than our ships had been designed to do. That was reasonable, and planning was certainly needed for any new campaign, but I still considered it nerd-work. Give me a tactical battle map, and you're much more likely to hold my attention.

Along about one in the morning, I managed to sneak off to the bathroom. I promptly fell asleep sitting on the toilet. I wasn't bare-assed or anything, just bone-tired and bored shitless by all-day meetings.

The door rattled eventually, and I snorted awake. A small fist pounded on the door a moment later.

I snatched it open, spreading my eyes as wide as I could. I smiled down at Galina, who was looking cross for some reason.

"Uh… sorry sir, but I might have spoiled your bathroom. You'd best leave the door shut and run the fan on for a while… just saying."

I stepped out and pulled the door shut behind me.

Looking around, I noticed her office and conference room were empty. "Uh… where'd everyone go?"

"I dismissed them, James. How long were you in there?"

"I'm not rightly sure. I must have lost track of time, what with it being after midnight and all."

She studied me while I made a show of washing my hands and toweling them off. I finally noticed that she wasn't talking, but she was staring.

"What seems to be the trouble, sir?" I asked finally.

"Why did you fail us tonight? How could you underperform so spectacularly the one time Earth truly needed your crude talents?"

49

"Uh…" I said, uncertain as to what the hell she was talking about. "Are we still talking about me being rude to our new zoo-keeper? I'm sorry about that. Primus Bob will command his Blood Worlders with vigor and style, I'm certain of it."

Galina stepped one pace closer. She looked intense and kind of worked up about something. When she spoke, it was in a low tone. I got the feeling she didn't want to chance anyone else overhearing her words—even though no one else was in her offices but us. Hell, I suspected the entire floor had emptied out by now.

"No, James… No, that's not it at all. I'm asking why you didn't take action and end all this when you had the opportunity. I assured my father you would do so if asked properly—but you failed to perform. You not only embarrassed me, you let down all of Earth."

"Huh? Are we still talking about Bob, here?"

"No! We're not talking about Bob! We're talking about you having the perfect opportunity to assassinate Sateekas and Nox at dinner."

"Oh… I was supposed to do that? So soon? How could I have pulled it off? They had the place crawling with their marines in those weird suits of walking armor."

"So what? Mogwa are weak and almost helpless. You didn't even need a weapon. All you had to do was knock their heads together or something."

What she was saying was undoubtedly true. The Mogwa were from a relatively low-gravity world. Their bones were thin and light. One good crack and they'd have flopped dead.

I looked down, and I frowned at her carpet. "I didn't do it, because I didn't want to," I admitted.

She looked more alarmed than ever. "What? Are you kidding me? Since when did you begin taking bribes from aliens? Are you in their employ right now? Are you wearing some kind of recording device?"

Galina looked scared, but I laughed and lifted two big hands, palm-out, to calm her. "Nah. I'm loyal to Earth. But I know Sateekas. I even know Nox, a little. They seem happy together as a couple, and—"

50

Her demeanor transformed again. She'd gone from curious, to scared and suspicious, to downright hissing-angry. All that had happened in the span of two minutes. Galina was a woman who often blew hot and cold, like a spring day in the mountains.

"Are you shitting me?" she demanded, getting into my face. "This isn't time for you to go soft, McGill. All of Earth's military could be destroyed. Do you trust the Mogwa not to squander our ships and troops?"

"Uh... trust? Not really. Sateekas is brave and honorable, but he's not the sharpest commander I've ever met."

"No. No, he isn't. He's a loser. That's why Mogwa High Command ditched him. Now, you just let him go. They've already flown up to their battlecruiser, where we can't reach them. We're going to have to either destroy their ship, or follow them six thousand lightyears out into the unknown. The brass is freaking out, James. Can't you understand that?"

I nodded and hung my head low. "I get it. I was there, the man on the spot. But I couldn't do it."

Looking up, I saw she was stewing and fretting still. She looked tired and worried.

"Hey," I said, snapping my fingers under her nose. "I've got an idea."

"What idea?"

"A way to get up there—onto their ship with them."

Galina looked hopeful. She cocked her head. "Really? Seriously? How?"

"You just leave everything to me."

She narrowed her eyes in instant suspicion. "What are you hiding?"

I shrugged. "If I reveal my plans, someone might hear them. You might even accidentally let the cat out of the bag. Wouldn't you rather be ignorant anyways? What if there's an inquiry later on? What if the Nairbs come and interview everyone?"

She blinked and nodded slowly. "You're right. I don't want to know. I just want you to do it."

I grinned a big fake one. I had no ideas in my head—at least not concerning the Mogwa. But I knew she'd feel better if

51

she thought everything was going to be all right. It was only natural.

Experimentally, I put a big hand on her small shoulder. "Don't worry about a thing. They're as good as dead and gone. But... hmm..."

"What?"

"Do you have anything to drink around here? It's been a long day."

Galina sighed. "It certainly has. You know where it is."

I found a bottle that wasn't too fruity, and I poured us both a dose. She took hers reluctantly. Soon, we were both in better spirits.

The night wore on, and I ended up spending it in her quarters. We'd been a couple off and on over the years, and although we didn't always see eye-to-eye, we'd never lost our mutual attraction. When we were stressed, and needing a break, Galina and I often took comfort in one another's arms.

Half-drunk and entirely exhausted, I slept the sleep of the dead.

-8-

In the morning, we got up and started scrambling. Meetings and appointments filled Galina's day. I tried to get the hell out of her office as fast as I could, worried I'd be caught up in the bullshit if I dawdled.

At promptly 0600 hours, I stumbled out of her private apartments. The suite she commanded as an imperator was arranged so that her quarters were directly attached to her main office. That was a design flaw in my mind. How could the brass get in any goofing-off time with such an arrangement? It was one more reason I didn't want to join their vaunted ranks.

Today wasn't my lucky day in any case. In my hurry to leave her bed, I didn't even put my shoes on. Worse, Gary beat me to the door.

There he was, walking into the office at the same moment I was walking out of Galina's quarters. He slid his sleeve down over his tapper, having just convinced the door lock AI he was legit. Then he glanced up. He spotted me and my sheepish grin and responded with mild shock.

It must have been quite a sight. Instead of a coffee auto-pot signaling it was hot and ready, the first thing his bleary early morning eyes spotted was me. A hulking James McGill who was sneaking out of his boss' bedroom with a pair of boots in his hands.

"Hey there, Gary. Long-time-no-see. I was just checking in on the imperator. She wasn't feeling well last night, see..."

"Sure, McGill," he replied in a flat tone. I could tell right off my lies were going to have zero impact on him.

"Say," I said, deciding to shift gears, "does the imperator have her calendar clear for lunch today? I'm just wondering…"

The look he gave me wasn't a happy one. Either his lips were twisted up in disgust, or he'd just detected a bad odor. I wasn't entirely sure which it was. I waited while he checked his calendar, occupying myself with pulling my boots on.

"She's all booked up," he said after a moment. "There's some big military planning going on, as I understand it. All hush-hush, I'm afraid. I can't give you any details."

"Uh-huh…"

I realized Gary was under the wrongful impression that I didn't know what was going on at Central what with the Mogwa visit and all. The sad truth was he was probably more in the dark than I was.

"You got a duffle packed, Gary?" I asked him.

"What?"

"Well… if the imperator is deployed soon, she might need her best aide."

He looked alarmed at the idea. "Um… she usually doesn't take me into the field. I usually prefer to manage her office at home. I'm not combat-arms… not really."

My face lit up with a sudden idea. I snapped my fingers at him. I wondered why I'd never thought of this before.

"Seriously? They've kept you cooped up and flying a desk all this time? Damn, boy. I think I see some tufts of gray at your temples. That's a crying shame. I think I might be able to fix this injustice."

"What? I… what are you talking about, Centurion?"

I grinned at him. I grinned real big. Some would say I had a predatory gaze, but I would say I had the look of inspiration and enthusiasm. I leaned on his desk with both hands and lowered my head and voice. "How'd you like to see the dirt of a new planet on your boots, Gary? For reals?"

He swallowed. His face had moved quite quickly from an expression of bored disgust to fright. Those eyes were wide, and I saw the whites all the way around.

"I don't know, McGill. I don't—"

Slam! I brought both my hands up and down again, crashing them onto his desktop.

"Say no more, Gary! Your fondest wish is about to be granted." He gaped at me like a fish, but I waved away his objections and headed for the door. "Don't thank me now, you can do that later, after you've had the time of your life. I'll see you in space!"

I skedaddled after that, leaving him in a raw panic. If there was one thing a dedicated hog feared more than losing his pension, it was the idea of going out into space and serving in a real ground-based military operation.

They all talked big about it, mind you. They liked to swagger around non-military types with what-if stories. But the truth was, if they weren't chickens in the first place they would have signed up for combat arms on day one.

Feeling I'd done my good deed for the day—and it was only six in the morning—I headed for the officers' mess. There I devoured a sumptuous breakfast. Real eggs, real ham, country-style red potatoes and more. I was probably the lowest-ranked man in the hall, which earned me a few glances, but I ignored all the haughty tribunes wandering around. The key was not to make eye-contact with anyone who was looking for trouble. They shrugged and let me eat in peace.

Soon I was well-fed and feeling great, so I made my way down a few hundred floors to where my legion headquarters was posted. There, I found Winslade was already at work. He was scrambling, and his staff was hopping.

"There you are, McGill. Fancy seeing you after you've arranged a hell-tour for all of us."

"Huh?" I asked. "What do you mean by 'arranged', sir?"

He glared at me, rattling a wad of computer scrolls with moving text and pictures on every paper-thin screen. "Imagine that a sudden requirement for a mobile legion comes up. Imagine that it requires one of our newest, longer-range transports to reach this distant objective. Who do you think would be selected for this hazardous duty?"

"Uh... is there a reason I'm imagining all this, sir?"

"Yes, you imbecile. You're the one who sat at that banquet last night and grinned in support of every insane thing the

Mogwa said. Now, they want Legion Varus on the mission roster. Never mind that Victrix is orbiting as well, snobs who are just as mobile and ready. I've just received word that we're to deploy to space immediately."

I nodded, rubbing at my chin. It was a little stubbly, as I hadn't had a chance to shave yet. I would probably need to get out some nanite paste and smear it on to do a quickie job later.

"Uh…" I said. "Don't worry, sir. I don't think this is going to be a one-legion show. Victrix is likely to come along and keep us company."

Winslade eyed me then. His expression grew thoughtful. "Were you in that late-night planning meeting with Drusus?"

"Yessir, I surely was."

He showed me most of his small, white teeth. "Insane. Utterly insane. Here I am, the newly appointed tribune in command of the first legion they commit to the operation, and I wasn't even given notice of these deployment orders going on until this morning!"

His hands were fluttering around. I could tell he was upset, and I could even understand his problem, to a point.

"Sir, if it helps ease your mind, I would have gladly switched places with you last night. I hate long planning meetings."

"That doesn't help at all, McGill. What can you tell me about the plans?"

I thought that over. I hadn't been specifically sworn to secrecy—not even concerning the part about Alexander wanting me to kill the Mogwa. Fortunately, I knew enough to keep that part under my hat.

I made a show of doing some hard thinking. Winslade watched impatiently, making remarks about my poor mental health all the while.

"Well, sir… I think I can give you a quick briefing—in private, of course."

Winslade considered. Finally, he nodded and waved me into his personal office. It was a lot less roomy than Turov's new one was upstairs, but it was neat and functional.

"Talk," he demanded when the door was closed.

I rattled at his liquor cabinet, but it wouldn't open. I looked up in surprise.

"I locked it," he said. "Good God, man. It's not even eight in the morning yet."

"Yeah… okay. Have you got something fizzy to drink? My mouth is parched."

He tossed me a soda, which I consumed without gusto. I'd kind of been hoping for a beer. Making the best of it, I briefed him concerning what we knew of the Mogwa operation.

Winslade was aghast. "Six thousand lightyears round-trip? All the way out to the Mid-Zone? Are you joking?"

"I wish I was, sir. What's more, *all* of Earth's ships and legions were officially commandeered last night. The only reason most of them aren't doomed to fly out to the Mid-Zone is that most of them can't make it, even with refueling and what-not along the way."

Winslade wasn't really listening to me. He was bent over his battle computer, working the table-like surface. He soon had drawn up range limits similar to those that Drusus and Alexander had worked out the night before.

His tapper buzzed, and he checked the message. He looked up at me in shock.

"You're right. Victrix has just been officially summoned to join us on this children's crusade across the cosmos."

"Is that good or bad, sir?"

He shook his head. "I'm uncertain. Whatever it is, I'm unsettled about it. Overall, the entire situation is unbelievable." He stared at his handiwork, checking his numbers and nudging at the map lines. The scenario stayed pretty much the same. "This will be the greatest reach of naval power in Earth's history."

"I would say you're right about that, sir."

-9-

I tried to hide. I tried to take naps, find a bar to squat in, and I made up reasons why I couldn't be located—but it was a losing battle.

As a centurion with orders to scramble to my transport on an emergency basis, there were a thousand things to do. Sure, I managed to delegate as much of the busy-work as I could. People like Adjunct Barton thrived on checking everything twice. Leeson was good at logistics, so he worked on packing our heavy gear. Harris... well, Harris was good at yelling at people. I put him in charge of locating and harassing everyone who hadn't reported in for duty yet. He excelled at that, and our ranks swelled by the hour.

Modern transportation was such that even people taking vacations in the Australian Outback, on the Moon, or at those getaway resorts on the bottom of the ocean—they could all get back home within twenty-four hours. We had gateway posts set up between major locations all over Earth these days. Tickets weren't cheap, but if you could stand up and walk straight, you could be transported to Central in an instant.

Of course, with thousands of people trying to do this all at once, the lines were long. But the troops kept trickling in steadily hour by hour. Soon, we were ready to head up to *Dominus*.

Reporting with all our gear and seventy percent of our personnel to the spaceport, my unit was one of the first in 3rd

58

Cohort to lift off. I got a little bit of shut-eye on the ride into space, but it didn't last long enough. By the time I was dreaming, the ship was docking up and big blasting noises filled the lifter's main chamber.

After some jostling around, the cabin pressure equalized, and we were hustled off the ship and onto the deck of our fine transport.

Dominus was downright luxurious compared to older ships. It had the biggest Green Deck I'd ever seen. On top of that, if you were able to sneak in, Lavender Deck had real high-quality restaurants.

After getting my unit tamped down into our assigned module, I asked Kivi out on a date. I promised her a Lavender Deck restaurant, and she squinted at me for a few seconds.

"Am I just the first girl your eyes landed on?" she asked.

That was the bitter truth, of course, but I shook my head vigorously. I even managed to look hurt. "Are you kidding me? You're the *only* girl my eyes can even see!"

Kivi glanced around, thinking things over. Her usual boyfriend of late was Sargon—an excellent fellow, by the way—but he wasn't on board yet. He was one of those who'd yet to straggle in. Carlos, another distant love of hers, was likewise absent.

"All right," she said. "But you have to get me into a good place. I'm not going down to Lavender Deck to wash dishes."

"I hear you. Don't worry about a thing."

A few minutes later, we boarded an elevator that whisked us away to the lower decks. Kivi was a little nervous as the doors opened, expecting a pack of frowning hog-like crewmen to try to shoo us away.

Regular grunts like us weren't normally allowed to set foot on Lavender Deck. Only ship's crewmen, high ranking officers and civilian guests were supposed to linger down here. Seeing as I was only a centurion, I normally wouldn't have made the cut.

Kivi's situation was much worse. As a mere specialist, she would be seen as a walking insult to any member of the brass who'd come down here for a good meal in good company.

Naturally, I had a bullshit story all ready to go. My mouth split into a grin, and I launched into my attempt to con my way past the wannabe hogs—but the words died away. My jaw dropped all the way down and stayed there.

"Where did everyone go?" Kivi asked me. She was kind of half hiding behind me, but now that she saw no guards—no one at all—she stepped around me and put her hands on her ample hips.

"I don't know…" I said. I put my big hands to my mouth and bellowed, "Hello?"

Kivi elbowed me. I shut up and made a woofing noise.

"If the guards aren't here, you idiot, we've already managed to sneak in. Come on!"

I followed her, frowning and rubbing at my gut. "I don't think anyone's home, Kivi."

Excited, she ignored me and led me to her favorite shop—some kind of money-trap that sold goopy creams for your face. The place was closed and dark.

Disappointed, we walked onward. Everything was closed. Every shop, every restaurant—frigging everything.

"Uh…" I said. "I guess the Lavender Deck people haven't opened up for business yet."

Kivi whirled on me angrily. "I get it now. You brought me down here for a quickie, didn't you? The trick isn't on them, it's on *me* this time."

I looked surprised, because I hadn't even thought about that move. At least, not yet… "Well… how about it?" I asked. "Seeing as there's nothing else—"

She rabbit-punched me in the belly, which was now beginning to ache a bit.

"Hey, that's not—"

"I should never have let you talk me into this, James. You haven't changed at all."

She stomped away and went back to the elevators. Soon, she'd been whisked away to the upper decks, leaving me alone.

Still rubbing my guts a little, I poked around. The place was nearly deserted. Finally, a power-broom operator happened by. His rig was sweeping and sucking at every millimeter of the passageway.

"Hey buddy," I said to him. "Do you know if there's a place down here a man can get some grub—or better yet, a drink and a date?"

He stopped his machine and frowned at me. "Centurion? I don't think you're supposed to be down here."

"I sure as hell am. Imperator Turov sent me."

He blinked a few times. "Well, she's a few months too early then. This deck is shut down for now. They don't tell me much, but they say it might not open again until we get back to Earth."

"Why the hell not?"

He shrugged. "They don't want to waste the power and supplies, I guess. We're going to be flying for a long time, don't you know."

I heaved a sigh. "Yeah... I guess I do know. All right, thanks."

Once I left him in peace, he switched his whirring, howling equipment back on. I walked back to elevator lobby, planning to return to the upper decks in defeat.

The situation was bleak. I was seriously disappointed. Taking girls down to Lavender Deck for some R&R had long been one of my signature moves. With that vital source of entertainment closed off to me, this trip was going to feel twice as long and dull.

Touching the elevator call-pads repeatedly, I frowned. It wasn't opening. Someone was using the lifts—all of them.

A full minute later, the doors still refused to open. "Aw, shit..." I said aloud.

I was struck by a new worry. What if the elevator was programmed to let people come down without authorization—but not to return to the upper decks without approval? But then... how had Kivi left? Had some robot clock decided to shut down the lifts?

Worried I was trapped on Lavender Deck until I got that janitor to let me out, I began banging a big fist on the doors and hollering. This did precisely jack-squat to fix the situation.

Finally, however, after I spent a full minute howling at the doors like a wolf in heat—they suddenly swept open.

61

Inside was a delegation. A crowd of crewmen gaped at me. They were wearing their finest whites, which meant they were dressed up like waiters at a royal wedding.

What was even more surprising was the large amount of quality food they had with them. There were cartloads of meats and fine gravies on silver trays. Sparkling cut-crystal goblets were already filled with wine and lined up on yet more carts.

"What the hell?" I asked.

A portly, older man with a familiar face stepped forward. It was Captain Merton, the Fleet puke who commanded *Dominus*. "McGill? What are you doing down here?"

"Uh..." I said, dumbfounded.

"Never mind. Step aside, we're in a hurry. Why don't the Mogwa ever give us enough advanced warning to set things up properly?"

I got out of the way, and the crewmen hurried down the passages. "The Mogwa?" I asked aloud, talking to nobody.

Turning back to the elevators, I saw by the indicators they were all in motion. More doors were about to open—any second now.

My mind is slow, but it was right about then that I figured out what was wrong with the elevators. They were all full of VIPs and service people. They were all coming down here at once for a banquet of some kind.

Licking my lips and sniffing the finest of foods like a dog under a dining table, I was struck by an idea.

I quickly stepped after Merton and his crew. I didn't want to lose them in the dark, lifeless passages.

-10-

My reasoning, such as it was, went something like this: if I took the elevators back up topside, I'd be missing out on a banquet. Sure, I hadn't been invited to said banquet, but a man like me rarely lets such details get in the way.

If, on the other hand, I stood around like a dummy with my thumb in my butt and waited to ask permission from the load of brass that was doubtlessly coming down in those elevators right now, I might, just maybe, get an invite. The trouble with that safer approach was obvious: they might say no.

So, to the mind of James McGill, there was only one reasonable solution in this situation. I'd follow Merton and his pack of Fleet waiters and pretend I belonged. It might not work—but it was worth a shot.

As I snuck along the dark passages in the wake of humming power-carts, I considered contacting Kivi and inviting her to join me. That might work out—but then again, it might make a mess of a sweet deal. It was one thing to claim I should be at a banquet honoring Mogwa, but inviting a noncom date was definitely pushing it. Hell, Galina and her father might be among the guests. No, no, Kivi was just going to have to hear in the morning about how she'd missed out big-time.

The crew with the food carts stopped at one of the best restaurants on Lavender Deck. It was called "the Blind Fish" and the place had an underwater grotto theme. The walls glimmered with blue diffused light when they powered up the dining room, and it looked pretty cool. There were gurgling tanks all around the tables, tanks filled with swimming drones that mimicked sea creatures.

When the crew was busy setting up, I waited until I heard footsteps behind me. The guests were coming in. Walking calmly into the place, I stood at the "wait to be seated" sign and looked bored.

Behind me, a gaggle of brass showed up. They looked at me funny, but the waiters were fooled. They noticed the crowd and ushered us in, suggesting we sit where we wanted, there was plenty of room.

Choosing a small table very near the growing buffet, my mouth watered. My eyes were glowing almost as much as the fish tanks. Damn, I might have missed out on Kivi's talents, but I sure wasn't going to go hungry.

"McGill?"

Glancing up and turning my head, I did my best not to look startled or alarmed. I smiled and waved at Galina, who was frowning in my direction. She came walking toward me, her eyes as narrow as a pissed cat's.

"What are you doing here?" she demanded with her hands on her hips.

My mouth opened, and I was about to give her some hornswoggle lie about being invited by Sateekas—but then I was struck by a flash of sheer genius.

Lowering my voice and leaning toward her a bit, I spoke fateful words. "You should ask your father about that."

That sentence changed her mood instantly. She blinked, and she looked concerned. She glanced over her shoulder—her own staffers were hanging around. Gary was among them. He looked like a lost kid at the zoo. Once she looked his way, he began walking over to her.

"Oh hell…" Galina said.

For my part, I was all grins. I'd told Gary he might be coming along on this trip just to scare him—and then I'd forgotten all about it. The chances he'd be dragged into deep space with us legion types were low, to my way of thinking. Galina didn't always take her ground staffers, but this time she'd given the order.

I had to wonder if it was all chance, or Gary himself had acted on my idea. How had that happened? Had he brought the idea up to Galina, and then she'd agreed? Had he possibly decided I was right, that he did need field experience to rise in rank, and Galina had gone for it?

The wherefores and the why-fors hardly mattered at this point. However it had happened, Gary had been brought along for this special ride to the stars. I found the situation funny.

"Hey, Gary!" I boomed, standing up and offering him a hand to shake. "Glad you could get off your duff and make it out into space at last. This is a proud moment for you and yours, boy."

Galina looked furtive. Gary looked shell-shocked. I, however, was as happy as a clam.

"So," I said, "you must be playing secretary for the brass on this trip, huh? Have you had a chance to sit in on a high-level meeting yet? Take any good notes?"

Galina cleared her throat. "Gary, I've reconsidered my plans for tonight. It looks like this is to be a social occasion, with little need for support personnel."

"What...? Oh... okay, sir. I'm sorry. I'll head back to Gold Deck, then... if you won't be needing me?"

Galina nodded. "Thank you for understanding, and I'm sorry about the sudden change of plans."

He slunk away, and I almost felt sorry for him. Almost.

Something had finally impinged on my dull mind—I got the feeling Gary was doing more than taking notes for Galina on this trip. That thought wasn't a happy one, but there it was.

"Uh..." I said. "You wanted to talk in private, Galina?"

She set her jaw. She seemed ruffled. "James, you mentioned my father."

"Yep."

"Have you been talking to him?"

I held up two fingers wrapped around each other. "We're like this."

She nodded and stared at the table. She looked kind of freaked out. "So you're the agent in play tonight... I should have known."

"Uh... what?"

65

She looked at me. "You don't have to pretend around me—but you're right, it's probably best that you do. I'm going to move away from this table before we eat. I want you to forget we spoke tonight—during the aftermath, I mean."

"Uh…" I was dumbfounded, and it wasn't even an act. Then I suddenly caught on and snapped my fingers. "Oh, you're talking about if I kill the Mogwa, right?"

"Shut up!" she hissed. "Your tapper might be recording you."

"Not mine. I hack it regularly."

"Maybe so… but under torment, you're more likely to confess words you spoke aloud than thoughts you had. They stick better in a delirious mind."

I blinked a few times. "Torture?"

Galina shrugged. "Whatever happens. I don't want to think about it, or even hear about it afterwards. I'm sure you've got your contract with my father aligned and peer-reviewed by legal experts. Most do."

I was gaping again. I hadn't done any such thing. I wasn't getting paid or anything. I'd just thought that his assassination idea was a good one, in order to save Earth's military, and so I'd agreed to do my part.

But Galina was giving me some second thoughts.

She kept on talking about something, but I wasn't listening any longer. Looking around the room, I didn't spot old Alexander. Most of the crowd was made up of suits from Hegemony and Fleet pukes. I only recognized a few of them.

It just so happened that as my head was swiveling around, Galina was chattering and my good mood was deflating, another crowd showed up at the entrance.

The honored guests had arrived. Governess Nox, Sateekas and Drusus all stepped into the dining room. Every conversation died at once.

"The Galactics Nox and Sateekas have graced us with their presence," Drusus said loudly. "All rise."

We stood up as one. Drusus led us in singing a song called *Submission of the Glorious Collective*. We'd all learned the tune as kids in school. It was catchy, but I'd never liked it much.

The Mogwa looked around with disdain. Then Sateekas spotted me. He pointed me out to his wife, and they began wobbling in our direction.

"Oh hell," Galina said through clenched teeth. "I waited too long to get away from you."

"Don't worry, Imperator. If the Mogwa sit with us, we'll get the best service in the house."

We stayed standing while the aliens approached. Drusus was alarmed. He'd been standing at a distant table.

He followed in the wake of the two aliens, waving his hands toward a variety of conveniently empty tables. The Mogwa ignored him.

"McGill-creature," Sateekas said. "I was told you wouldn't be present at this event."

"Well, Grand Admiral sir, sometimes plans change."

Sateekas seated his mate like a human gentlemen. Had that behavior rubbed off on him, or had the Mogwa brought it to us long ago? I wasn't sure.

Drusus arrived at the table. He was left without a chair, as the table only had room for four seats. Galina stepped away from her chair. "Praetor, perhaps you'd like to take my place. I was just—"

"Nonsense," Sateekas interrupted. "I'm tired of Drusus. He's dull and uninspiring company. Besides, Nox and I are mates. It's only fitting that we dine with slaves in a similar relationship."

"Um…" Drusus said, uncertain as to what to do. At last, he sighed. He looked at me, and his eyes were pleading.

I gave him a smile and a little reassuring wave in return. "Don't you worry about a thing, Praetor, sir. Our guests will be well cared-for."

Swallowing and nodding, he slipped away to another table. From there, he watched us with frequent worried glances. Lots of the diners were doing that.

Leaning back, I threw my big arm out to rest on Galina's chair. "How'd you know we were… uh… involved, Sateekas?"

Galina looked alarmed. Under any other set of circumstances, she would have hissed and clawed at me, but she didn't dare. She only spoke one quiet word of warning: "McGill...?"

"It is a gift of mine," Sateekas boasted. "When I first met my Lady Nox, for example, I knew that no other male possessed her."

It was Nox's turn to become embarrassed. "That is inappropriate talk. These beings are inferiors."

"You see?" Sateekas rumbled and farted as he laughed. "No one else would dare scale her walls."

Apparently, this was some kind of Mogwa idiom. I got the gist of it, and I chuckled politely. Galina wore a pasted-on smile.

The Fleet waiters showed up then, saving an embarrassing situation. They began to dump food on us like there was no tomorrow. I accepted every morsel and chewed with gusto. Everything was delicious.

When we came up for air, I found I was the first to finish. This wasn't surprising, even given the fact that I'd eaten twice what anyone else had consumed.

"Mm-mm," I said. "That was some good eating."

"Yes," Sateekas agreed, while bits of meat dripped from his feeding spikes. Watching a Mogwa eat was kind of a horror show, but I was used to the process. "I am sated," he purred through his translator.

Galina politely stood and bowed to the Mogwa. "I must excuse myself."

"Why?" Sateekas demanded. He was suddenly all business.

"I... I must visit the facilities."

"You what? What facilities? Are we under attack?"

"No, no, your lordship. I'm sorry if I'm being unclear. I must relieve myself."

Sateekas looked baffled, and Nox laid a hand on him. "She wants to eliminate wastes, Sateekas."

"What? Oh... why not do it in your uniform?"

"Um..." Galina said, looking flustered. "Our formalwear isn't equipped with mobile facilities."

"Why wear clothing at all, then? Such an odd species... Very well, be quick about it."

Galina stopped to lean down and kiss my cheek. That surprised me, and I almost turned to sneak one on her lips in return, when her hot breath sounded in my ear. "This is your chance, James. Don't blow it."

Then, she scampered off. I turned back to the Mogwa and frowned.

Was Galina right? Was this the moment of truth? Was I about to gun these two down?

It would be easy. I had my pistol on my hip, and all I had to do was pull it out and aim it under the table while they smacked their mouthparts and chatted. They didn't even have their bodyguard marines with them tonight. They'd left them outside the restaurant.

They must be beginning to trust us humans—a grave mistake.

-11-

Reaching under the table, I loosened my gun in its holster. Then I took a long look around the dining room.

Everyone seemed to be watching my table. They tossed glances my way often, and they spoke to one another in hushed tones.

That didn't mean they were onto me. Not necessarily. The Mogwa were our honored guests. Every human present had to be wondering about them.

Turning my attention back to the Mogwa couple, I felt a pang. They looked happy. That was really saying something, because I'd hardly ever encountered any of the Mogwa when they were enjoying themselves. They were usually bitterly lamenting their fate about some imagined abuse and blaming others for it.

Sateekas really wasn't a bad sort. He'd had a rough time of it out on the frontier. Nox, on the other hand, was a cast-iron witch most of the time—but she seemed to have mellowed out somewhat as well. Maybe motherhood had agreed with her.

That thought struck through the rest: where was the baby?

Dropping my eyes, I watched her hands without seeming to. There—in her pouch. I caught movement. Just a squirm, a ripple under her hooked fingers.

She had her kid in there again. Even tonight, while dining. Jeez...

My hand slipped away from my gun, and I leaned forward. I told a rude joke about Galina, and it got them both laughing. The ghastly baby bounced inside Nox's pouch.

A moment later, Galina reappeared at my side. She had her hands on her hips.

"What's so funny?" she asked.

Sateekas took it upon himself to answer. "McGill has shared some of your unique sex-noises with us, Imperator."

The Mogwa attempted to imitate a hooting owl, but he did it poorly. The two aliens went off into another gale of laughter.

I snuck a glance at Galina's face. She didn't look like she was enjoying the joke all that much. As I watched, she moved her fine right hand from her hip down to the butt of her gun. Her teeth were showing.

"Uh…" I said, trying to get her attention. "Maybe if you gave us a bit more time…"

She glanced down at me. She smiled, but there wasn't any humor in the expression. "You take all the time you want to, McGill."

Galina walked out then, straight out of the restaurant and into the dim-lit passages beyond.

I frowned after her. Call me paranoid, but I could tell when that woman was up to no good. I stood up and excused myself, just as Galina had.

Sateekas made more enthusiastic hooting sounds. He seemed to have mixed up our various bodily functions, but I didn't bother to correct him. He and his girl were having too much fun.

"Heh…" I said. "That's right. Laugh it up, guys."

Stepping quickly to the doorway, I stood to one side near a row of fake fish tanks that glowed and bubbled with such a deep blue light it looked purple.

Two men entered the dining room. They lifted their weapons—morph-rifles, set to assault mode. All over the restaurant, officers dove for cover and clawed out their weapons.

The two Mogwa, taken totally by surprise, just sat there and looked stunned.

71

I stepped behind the assassins and chunked my knife into one man's neck. The other guy caught three rounds in the back of the skull.

The man I'd shot went down fast. He didn't even have time to fire his rifle. The man I'd knifed squeezed the trigger and a wild spray of power-bolts flew all around the dining room. Drusus was hit, and he went down, spinning. Three other officers, two tribunes and a primus, died as well.

The fish tanks took the worst of it. Big glass sheets shattered, and sludgy purple-blue liquid gushed out. Fake fish flopped rhythmically on the deck, looking even more real than they had in the water.

I pulled my knife out of the second man's neck, and I gave him a shove with my boot. Graves walked up to me, staring at the horrific scene.

"McGill? What have you done, man?"

I pointed at Sateekas and Nox. "I've saved a family, sir."

Graves formed a tight line with his mouth. He didn't answer, but instead called for security and medics.

Wading through the confusion, the flapping fish, and the human bodies, I stepped up to the table. The two Mogwa stared at me.

"Where did our security detail go?" Sateekas demanded.

Nox was hunkering low. She eyed the scene warily. "I thought they were in the passageway—but I don't see anyone. Not a single marine."

That's when I got the idea that their bodyguards had been purposefully waylaid somehow. Thinking hard, I rubbed at my stubbly chin with the back of my pistol.

The Mogwa eyed me as I did this.

Nox spoke first. "I told you we should never have come here. These beasts are too feral. Too full of themselves. Troops of this nature will always buck the collar. Just transporting them into the Mid-Zone is a violation of Imperial Law.

"No it isn't," Sateekas said.

"Well, it should be. What if our offspring had been hit? We don't have duplication facilities for someone so young. We might have lost him."

72

"Yes, yes," Sateekas said impatiently. "You there, McGill-creature."

"Yessir?"

"How did you know to strike? How did you spot these assassins?"

I shrugged. "Just dumb luck, sir. I stepped outside to take a piss, as I said earlier, and I saw these two come in with rifles. I'm sure they're just some unpaid slackers who have a grievance over their paychecks or something."

"A grievance? Paychecks? Absurdities. You're deadly, but hopelessly naive. I suspect these men were paid handsomely to kill my wife and I."

"Uh… I guess that could be. But how would the Skay pay humans to attack you on one of our own warships?"

"What are you talking about?"

"Here, I'll show you." I walked over to the two dead men, and I made a quick circular slash with my knife on their arms. Then I dragged the bodies closer to the Mogwa.

Nox shrank back from the dead, but Sateekas was braver. He leaned forward.

"See here?" I made a show of cutting away their uniform sleeves. I displayed the circular cuts I'd just made. "That bloody circle is a marker. A symbol of their loyalty to the Skay."

"What new outrage is this?" Sateekas demanded.

I managed to pretend I was surprised. "What? Haven't you heard? Skay agents are infiltrating Province 921. After you guys pulled out our battle fleet, they've been causing all kinds of trouble."

Sateekas looked intrigued, but Nox looked suspicious. Sometimes, I suspected she was the brains of the outfit.

"Why would they cut at their own skins like that?" she asked.

"To show their loyalty to the enemy AI. They aren't even human, not really. Skay sympathizers must be hunted down and exterminated. Every last one of them."

Nox looked around at the crowd. Armed humans were everywhere. She put three hands on Sateekas, who had begun demanding an inquiry.

"Our marines are almost here. We must return to our ship."

At last, he listened to reason. The other officers were cleaning up the place. Most seemed to be baffled by the events of the evening, but a few like Graves—they were glaring at me.

The Mogwa Marines arrived and encircled their masters. They marched them off our decks in a tight security circle. I waved after them, but they didn't wave back.

When they'd gone, Galina appeared again. She'd been lurking somewhere, and she'd waited until it was safe to reappear.

Her knuckles rapped me on the chest. "Did you actually kill my men? Why'd you interfere?"

"Well sir, I had no idea you were planning anything dramatic. I went out to take a piss, see—"

"And when you saw two armed men walk into the restaurant, you killed them without asking any questions?"

"They pulled out weapons, Galina. Should I have let them shoot everyone?"

She shook her head. "I can't believe it. You're an imbecile, just as my father always said you were."

"I can't argue with you there."

"This will be so much harder now. They're onto us. We may never get another shot."

I shrugged helplessly. She stalked away, and I got the feeling that all chances of a fine evening spent in her apartments had evaporated.

Graves approached me when she and the Mogwa had left. "You really stepped on your dick this time, McGill."

"How so, sir?"

He gestured after the others. "Half the Fleet is plotting to kill the Mogwa and throw them overboard. The rest of them *want* to do it—but they're chicken. Only you seem to be sweet on them. Why is that?"

"Well sir, we swore an oath of allegiance to the Empire. It doesn't seem right to backstab them when they come to ask for help."

He eyed me. I was using his own brand of logic on him because I knew it was the only thing that might be effective.

74

"I get that sentiment, as uncharacteristic as it seems for you but, McGill, these people didn't ask for our help, they demanded it. What's more, they aren't from the Core Systems. They're outcasts from the Mid-Zone."

"Yeah... but they're still technically Galactics, right?"

"They're Mogwa, but they aren't the important kind. The truth is that I don't know how they rank in the Empire's hierarchy."

Throwing my hands high, I felt I'd made my point. "Don't you think we ought to know details like that before we go and execute guests while they're enjoying a banquet in their honor? Huh?"

Shaking his head, Graves muttered that he didn't know what to think. He retreated, and he left me alone after that.

Pretty much everyone else did the same.

-12-

I was pronounced a pariah after that night. No one wanted to be seen with me—much less share my bunk. Galina wouldn't answer my texts, and Kivi wouldn't even look me in the eye. I was an outcast.

For a few days, it was sweet bliss. Sure, the brass was pissed. Sure, Kivi figured I'd pulled a fast one on her, and Galina was flat-out enraged after I'd blown our best shot at killing the Mogwa—but I didn't much care.

To pass the time, I worked with my troops. We drilled and practiced and cleaned our kits. By the second day, I'd pretty much forgotten all about the Mogwa and assassinations and dinner parties full of screaming guests.

When someone finally did contact me about the situation, four solid days had passed. The call came through on my tapper, and at the time I was leading 3rd Unit in some heavy PT.

Physical training wasn't easy to arrange on most transports, but *Dominus* had huge decks and wide corridors. These advanced accommodations were due in part to the fact the ship had been designed to support near-humans from Blood World. They were big folk, some of them three times the height of a man.

Left with plenty of room to maneuver on the oversized decks, we used the passageways as jogging paths. It was a common sight to see troops trotting all over the ship. I made sure that 3rd Unit never missed our slot of running time.

When the fateful call came in on my tapper, we were nearly finished with our daily run. Puffing, I lifted my tapper and eyed it. The thing kept buzzing, even when I shook it.

"Is it Primus Graves?" Harris asked. He'd caught up with me just to snoop, apparently.

I lowered my arm. "Looks like it. I'll take the call when we get back to the module."

"It's your funeral, Centurion."

Harris fell back. My tapper continued to buzz for a while, but it finally stopped. I felt some level of relief, as I didn't feel like getting reamed right now. The run was a good one, and we'd almost completed it.

Then my tapper began buzzing again. I winced. After the third ring, I glanced at the name. It wasn't Graves this time. It was Imperator Turov.

Gritting my teeth, I decided to let this one go, too. Damnation, couldn't these people check my logged itinerary? I was in the middle of an exercise routine, and *Dominus* was nowhere near enemy space, and—

"McGill? What is this? Are you swinging your arm around on purpose? You're making me ill."

Lifting my arm to my face, I faked a surprised grin. "Imperator? Did you just force a call through? We're on the last leg of a 5K run, sir, and—"

"Shut up and stop running."

Suppressing an urge to grumble and curse, I stepped out of the formation. I ordered Harris to lead the troops to the finish line. He gave me a wave and a grin, and I gave him the finger.

"What's up, sir?" I asked, breathing hard.

"You are. You've been given a second chance by providence."

"Uh... what?"

"The Mogwa want to see you aboard their warship. They've ordered us to transport you to their battlecruiser—only you."

I thought that over for a second, and I found I didn't like the sound of it. "All right, I'll head down to the docks and catch a shuttle to their—"

"You'll do no such thing—not yet, anyway. You're to report to Blue Deck first. You must be properly fitted."

"Huh?" I said in confusion, but she was gone.

Lowering my tapper, my mind worked on the problem. I thought I knew what she was hinting at—and I didn't like it.

The last time I'd been "fitted" before meeting an important alien, the alien had been Squanto, and I'd been fitted with an internal bomb by Claver.

Could this be the plan today with a couple of different players mixed in?

Compressing my lips tightly, I came to a fateful decision. I didn't feel like dying in a fireball to kill a few Mogwa. Not today.

Although I'd been running for an hour, I picked up the pace and ran some more. When I reached the lifts, I didn't head to Blue Deck as ordered. Instead, I shot right past that profane place and reached the shuttle bay instead.

Clamping a helmet into place, I switched on my magnetics and marched out onto the flight deck like I owned the place. Walking to the first shuttle I saw, I climbed into the cockpit, startling the pilot.

"Centurion? What are you doing aboard my bird?"

Ignoring her, I tapped at my tapper. I called Sateekas directly. I wasn't even surprised when he answered immediately.

"McGill? What is it? What's the delay? I can't abide delays."

Tilting my tapper toward the pilot, I let her see the Mogwa's face. Her eyes flew wide.

"Sateekas, sir?" I said. "Could you help me out? This pilot doesn't know what her orders are. She's confused."

His weird, numerous eyes scowled in unison at the pilot. "Human debris. You are a poor slave if you would dare question the McGill-creature. Transport him to my ship immediately, or face immediate expungement."

The pilot swallowed hard. "We'll be right there, sir."

Satisfied, the Mogwa cut the channel, and I smiled at the pilot. She wasn't half-bad looking, but she seemed kind of freaked out about something.

"Let's fly," I said. "The Mogwa hate waiting."

"We don't have clearance to fly anywhere, sir," the pilot protested.

I shrugged. "Okay…" I said, making a show out of working my tapper again. "I'll just have to tell Sateekas he can't have his way today. What's your nametag say…? Lt. Patel? Don't worry, somebody will take care of sending your scraps home to your momma—if there are any scraps left."

After seething and cursing for several seconds, Lt. Patel contacted traffic control and requested emergency clearance to lift off. It was granted after a few complaints, questions and lies on her part. She said something about her engine overloading and being worried her ship would blow up inside *Dominus'* guts. That worked. They lowered the big bay doors, and we flew out into space, sliding sideways a bit with too much acceleration.

Once outside, we were bombarded by serious radiation. The ship was tiny, and the cockpit had some lead-lined shielding, but there was no doubt we'd gotten a dose.

The trouble was we were in a warp bubble, and we were crossing over to another ship inside the same bubble. That was a dangerous thing to do under any circumstances—but Lt. Patel made it look easy.

I grinned at her as I climbed out of the ship onto the Mogwa flagship's shuttle deck. "Hey, I need you to sit here and wait for a bit, okay?"

"Why not? I won't live beyond a week with that dose of rads we just got. I'm not in any hurry."

"Such pessimism. We'll be fine… probably."

I left her in a sour mood and marched across the deck plates. I took a small passageway and followed it until it led to a bigger one. Repeating this process, I soon located the main passage that interconnected with all the others. After several more minutes, I found the bridge.

Countless Mogwa Marines swarmed me when as I entered. They took my weapons and ran wands all over me—this would have been a fun moment to blow myself up if I'd been wired—but I wasn't.

Sateekas and Nox were nowhere to be seen. They stayed clear of the bridge until I'd been poked and prodded thoroughly. I realized right then that Galina's cheesy plan to turn me into a human bomb had been doomed to failure. There was no way the Mogwa were going to let me get that close without a thorough examination. They were way too paranoid for that—especially after recent events.

At last, Sateekas appeared alone. He seemed concerned, but I sensed he was willing to give me a chance.

"McGill? Is this the real, actual McGill-creature?

"I'm the one and only, sir."

"Hmm..." he had a few medical types show him data from a biochemical scan they took of me. At last, he seemed convinced. "My apologies for your poor reception. We've had to take precautions due to the irreversible bloodlust inherent in your species."

"I completely understand, sir. What are your orders?"

"You will listen, and then you will obey. Your Fleet officers and legion tribunes must all swear personal allegiance to me. Their mates and offspring will be transported to this ship to be kept as hostages. Upon the conclusion of this glorious campaign, the chattel will be returned."

"Uh..."

"Further," the Mogwa went on, "the criminal known as Drusus will be deposed. He will no longer command this mission."

I blinked a few times. "Who will command in his stead, sir?"

He shuffled closer. "Me, of course. How can a being so large and seemingly functional be so great a fool?"

"People have been asking me that my whole life, your worship. But say... can I make a suggestion?"

"The very concept is offensive, but I will allow it. Consider it a gift for having defended my person during the banquet."

"Very generous, sir. My suggestion is this: if you could only tell us a bit more about the mission, we'd probably feel better about it and become more willing to accept your orders."

"This should not be necessary! Mogwa do not explain themselves to slaves!"

"I know that, sir. I know it oh so well. But… we're kind of out of our territory, here. My leadership—the humans, I mean—they aren't certain about your legitimacy."

"My legitimacy?" Sateekas boomed indignantly. "Who dares question my celebrated authority?"

"Uh… no offense, but you said yourself that you were from the Mid-Zone. Doesn't that make you a different breed when compared to the Mogwa from Trantor?"

Sateekas looked like his head might explode. He sputtered and walked around for a bit, but at last, he deflated a little and made a sad blatting noise.

"I see it all now. My status has leaked out—even to the humans. Yes, we were exiles. Nox and I now live on a planet full of exiles, and no one on Trantor cares about us. They think almost as little of Segin as they do of your world. What's the name the name of it again? Dirt?"

"Earth, sir. We call it Earth."

He flapped a limb. "Whatever. Segin is a separatist colony world. Ninety percent of the Mogwa populace live on Trantor, but not *all* of them do. There are splinter groups, those who fell out of favor, who eschewed orthodoxy. Segin is one of those unfortunate enclaves."

"Huh…" I said, thinking hard. "So after falling out of favor on Trantor, they sent you to Segin?"

"Yes, we were cast out and sentenced to live in abject solitude. Segin has barely twelve billion souls living upon it—a pitiful few. The single-city colony apes Mogwa Prime, but it only covers a fraction of the surface of the planet. It's an embarrassment, really, but pleasant enough by Mogwa standards. Standing in the midst of the place, you can almost believe you are in a true hive of activity."

"Doesn't sound all that bad…"

Sateekas snorted wetly. "The Mogwa who were born there would agree with you. Raised in obscurity, they don't find their lives to be depressing. They've never slithered on the walkways of the one true city."

"Hmm, that all sounds well and good, sir," I said, "but I still don't know why you need Earth's help. Why do you need a fleet and an army? You aren't planning to invade Trantor, are you?"

The Mogwa released a long, farting gale of laughter. "What an absurdity you are, McGill! We would stand no chance against the might of Trantor. We'd be outnumbered a thousand to one."

"What's the trouble then, sir?"

He was about to answer me when another voice interrupted. Nox had prowled onto the deck, daring to show her nose at last. I suspected that she'd been quietly listening at a safe distance to see how the interview went before revealing herself.

"Segin is under siege, McGill," she said. "We're under attack by barbarians."

"Really? A Mogwa colony is fighting some lower-tier beings? Won't Trantor consider this a great insult? Won't they send one of their vast fleets to defend a Mid-Zone province?"

"One would think so. But the Mogwa leadership considers us to be shameful. An officer on the borders, a fleet-commander or a governor—such officers are necessary. But the people of Segin have dared to emigrate of their own volition. They're considered untouchable. Low class—disgusting to even think about."

"Wow... so they don't care what happens to you guys? Just because you aren't in the Core Worlds?"

Nox crawled a little closer. "Segin is technically an independent state living under Mogwa rule," she said. "But our overlords consider us to be a colony of rejects and renegades. Many of them would enjoy watching us perish, if only to justify their own prejudices."

"Okay, I get it... that's why you came to Earth for help, right?"

Sateekas ruffled. "Help? That is an inappropriate term. We've come to commandeer. To seize power and lead gloriously. To elevate your grunting species by allowing them to die at our orders."

"Sure, sure... but one thing you haven't explained is who your attackers are. Do we know the species?"

Nox and Sateekas exchanged glances.

"Yes," he said. "I believe you do."

"Really? Let me guess: It's the Skay, right!"

Sateekas flapped his limbs in the unhappy negative. "Sadly, no. If it was such an enemy, the homeworld fleets would come to our defense. No, instead it is those awful bears you speak so much about. The tiny beings who refused our generous offer of servitude."

That brought back memories. I recalled one of the last times I'd seen hoary old Sateekas. It had been at Storm World—a messy planet inhabited by salamanders and which orbits M244-H.

At the time, Sateekas offered the Rigellians the job of becoming local enforcers, taking over Earth's job. Squanto had refused. In a rage, Sateekas had reinstated Humanity as the local thugs of the empire.

"Uh…" I said. "Can't you guys fight them off? I mean, they don't have much tech compared to the Mogwa."

Sateekas glowered at me. "Must you mouth an infinity of insults whenever we meet? I just got done telling you that Mogwa Prime has no interest. Segin has a defensive force, of course, but it consists of little more than thirty aging escort ships, along with this single battlecruiser. The enemy forces have chased off our fleet, and even now they lay siege to the Great City."

"Huh…" I said, giving my neck a scratch. "Did you say your ships ran off? Well then… how is it a siege? I mean, how didn't you already lose this battle?"

"Segin has a dome of force over it, protecting the world up to an altitude of eight kilometers in your measurements. The enemy has encircled this dome, and they continue to bombard it. They seek ways to penetrate our defenses with regularity. Sometimes, we discover agents in our midst. We fear they will figure out a way to sneak in a teleport bomb or some such thing. We think it's far more likely, however, that they mean to invade with infantry after they weaken our shielding sufficiently."

"Well sir, I know what you need to do right off. Go to Praetor Drusus. Talk to him. Get Earth to commit our fleet—

but make it our choice. Together with your forces, we should be able to chase them away easily."

"Normally, your humiliating suggestion would be feasible. Possibly, as a final solution, we will choose such a path of abject horror. Today, however, the governors of Segin will not allow such a thing. They even objected to my idea of gathering help against the invaders. I intend to do it anyway. I refuse to be further burdened with the task of explaining my reasoning to slaves and beasts."

I shrugged, not much caring. "All right, I'm willing to help you. But I can't do much in regards to making a decision of this magnitude. I'm a pretty low-level officer. It's time to level with Drusus."

"No! I won't have any more direct communication with that fop! Drusus must be one of the villains plotting my assassination. I'll talk to you—only you, McGill. You will carry my orders back to your wretched, conspiring officers."

Sateekas often seemed to forget that I didn't rule Earth. Just because I sometimes committed diplomatic breaches and struck deals with aliens, that didn't mean I had any real authority.

I sighed and scratched myself thoughtfully. "I'll do my best, sir."

Sateekas swept away then, and half the marines in the room followed him. When he was gone, Lady Nox took another step closer.

"Drusus is a tool, McGill," she said. "He's a fingernail on the hand of a servant. You must go above him to the real authority that presides over Earth."

"Uh... who's that?" I asked.

Nox looked shocked. "Why, I'm speaking of myself, of course. I am still the official governor of Province 921. It's true, I'm no longer allowed to retreat to Trantor... but my offices and titles are still intact, shoddy though they may be."

"Oh, of course! I was thinking you meant another human that I know about..."

Nox narrowed her many eyes. She was a smart one—easily smarter and more perceptive than Sateekas. "Are you thinking of that civilian oldster? The one in the robe which poorly apes the color of space?"

I blinked. She'd pegged it. I *had* been thinking about our esteemed Public Servant Alexander Turov in his long, black robes. He was more powerful than Drusus, there was little doubt of it.

"Hmm..." Nox said, reading my reaction correctly. "All right then. We will trust you in this instance. You will carry our words to that den of pirates, and you will convince them to follow us into battle. Do you have any questions?"

"No, sir. Not really."

"Excellent. I hate questions."

That was it. They kicked me off their ship, and I boarded the shuttle with Lt. Patel. She gritted her teeth and flew us back into the radiation storm.

"How did it go?" she asked, noticing I was quiet and sunk in deep thought.

I shook my head. "I don't know... it seems like the Mogwa expect the impossible out of me every time we meet."

She smiled. "You are infamous, you know. A man reputed to be the craziest in your crazy legion."

Forced to agree with her, I nodded my head. "I can't deny that rumor."

We landed a few minutes later, after getting another dose of wild cosmic rays. A posse waited to greet us on the flight deck.

"Let me do the talking," I told her.

When the hatch opened, and the little metal stairway unfolded, I stepped down to greet the navy pukes who were waiting there with their short-barreled guns pointed my way. Behind me, the pilot lingered in the doorway.

"Hey guys! Glad to see a welcome-home color-guard has been issued. Don't worry about a thing, every supposed violation against me will be dropped, then eventually an apology will be issued. It always ends that way, see, when misunderstandings—"

"Are you Centurion James McGill?" an unsmiling naval officer demanded. He had a short-barreled automatic carbine like the rest, and he was standing in front of the group.

"Yep, that's me."

They fired. All of them did, all at once. It was a regular ambush. Their guns were loud, but the power bolts didn't hurt

85

that much. I don't think my body really had a chance to register anything other than shock as dozens of burning holes ripped through it.

Spinning around, I stumbled down the steps and fell on my back. Behind me, I saw Lt. Patel go down. She'd been blasted to death, too.

I had just enough time to regret getting her involved in all this—then I died.

-13-

The first thing I heard was a beeping sound. That's all. Then, as my consciousness improved, I sensed bright lights and muttering voices. It seemed like an argument was on-going.

"…and he should have stayed dead. I want you to recycle this mistake, and this time, leave him permed."

"The Mogwa declared McGill their liaison. We have no choice but to bring him back."

"Liaison?" the first guy laughed bitterly. I recognized him now: it was Tribune Winslade. "He's a turncoat. A renegade. A serial miscreant who—"

"All right sir, you're in command," said the second man. I had him placed now as well. Rough voice, uncompromising: he was Primus Graves. "I'll notify the Mogwa immediately. They'll have to accept your decision. After all, this is your legion."

"Lower your tapper immediately, Graves, or I'll have you shot down like a dog, just like McGill."

"What's the problem, Tribune?"

"This nonsense of me countermanding the Mogwa is unacceptable. You'll tell them no such thing."

I thought about opening my eyes at this point, but I passed on the idea. At this stage of a revival, the lights in the average medical chamber were painfully bright—even when your eyelids were squinched shut.

The two men were having a stare-down, I figured. They'd never been pen-pals, and that situation hadn't improved recently when Winslade had been promoted over Graves to take control of Legion Varus.

"All right," Graves said finally. He was lower ranked, so I wasn't surprised that he backed off first. "I won't tell anyone. You can grind him up feet-first if you want to—I'll even help."

"No, no... I've reconsidered. I'm not giving any such order. You'll only shirk the blame and point a finger at me as your commander."

"Honesty, sir. It's called honesty."

Winslade made a rude, pffing sound.

At this point I decided to stage a wake-up. I coughed and finally opened my eyes a crack. I squinted up at them. There I was, lying naked on a gurney between two ornery officers.

"Damn, boys," I said. "I didn't realize both you fellas asked me to the prom. This is embarrassing."

Winslade glanced down at me in disgust.

"We'll finish this later," he said, and he stalked away.

Graves watched while I struggled to sit up, but there wasn't anything like love in his eyes.

My muscles were still floppy, but they were getting better every minute as my new brain knitted up with tingling nerves to operate the latest version of James McGill. Finally, I managed to prop myself up with an elbow.

"Primus Graves, I owe you my heartfelt thanks."

"Why's that?"

"Because I listened in on that lovers' spat you just had with Winslade. I got the feeling you were trying to keep me breathing."

"Then let's straighten you out right now. In my opinion Winslade should have you executed. You disobeyed orders in a manner indicating you're working against the interests of Legion Varus and Earth in general."

"Uh... so then how did I catch a revive at all?"

He flicked at his tapper, tossing a text in my direction. My tapper caught the message, and I squinted at it. The note was from Sateekas, and it was full of flowery threats and demands. I didn't bother to read it past the first sentence.

"They want you to be their spokesman," Graves said. "Our officers are required to communicate through you—and only you. How the hell did you manage to bamboozle every Mogwa on that battlecruiser, McGill?"

He seemed honestly curious, so I dredged up a good-sounding lie for him. He deserved my best.

"Well sir, it goes like this: Aliens are kind of like women. At first, they seem complicated and even inscrutable to the average Joe. But given time and careful study, I've come up with ten simple rules that apply equally to—"

He put a worn glove into my face. "Save it. There's a briefing in the command center in fourteen minutes. Get dressed."

I took the time to shower up and finger my hair into place. Nineteen minutes later, I reached command center on *Dominus*' sprawling Gold Deck.

"You're late," Graves said, giving me a flat, disapproving stare.

Unconcerned, I looked around the room. I saw Graves and a pack of other primus-level officers. But the big boys were missing.

"Where's Imperator Turov? Or Drusus? Or—wait... not even Winslade is here?"

Graves shrugged. "We've been directed to attend this meeting in the tribune's place. We'll evaluate your message from the Mogwa and determine if it's worth forwarding to flag officers."

"Oh... so the brass doesn't want to listen to the prattling of an old warhorse like Grand Admiral Sateekas, is that it? I'll have to put this insult into my report."

"What report, McGill?" Graves demanded.

I looked up at Graves in surprise. "Why sir, you must realize that as the formal liaison to the Mogwa, I have to give both sides reports on these interviews."

"I realize no such thing. May I remind you, Centurion, that you're an Earthman first, foremost, and always."

"That's true sir. And as such, I have a duty to the Mogwa who rule all Humanity, as well as to Earth herself."

Graves chewed on that for a second or two. He didn't look happy—but then, he rarely did. "Why can't you give me the report?" he asked. "I'll forward it to the other officers personally. No insult need be registered."

I shook my head. "The first rule the Mogwa insisted upon was that I operate as their one-and-only liaison. If I give the report to you as a go-between, that makes *you* the mouthpiece, not me."

Graves and I had a brief stare-down. Lesser men might have pissed themselves and changed their tunes, but not me. I went the distance, and he gave up on intimidating me at last.

The trouble for Graves was we both knew I was right. He could order me around, but if any Mogwa countermanded anything he said, that was the end of the story.

Technically, Sateekas outranked all of us.

Graves stood up, and the rest of the officers looked at him wonderingly. "Excuse me," he said. "This meeting is on recess until I return."

He walked out then, never sparing me another glance. That was just fine with me. He wasn't in a good mood, anyways.

"Recess, huh?" I laughed after he'd gone. "I think I'll go swing on the monkey bars."

The rest of the officers looked at me like I was a turd on the sidewalk—except this specimen was one they wanted to step on.

One of them stood up. He was a big-boned, old guy. I squinted at him, recognizing who he was. Captain Merton was the name. He commanded *Dominus*, and he'd often led super-boring meetings like this one. I groaned inwardly as he began getting his laser pointer all warmed up.

"Rather than waste our collective time," Captain Merton said, "I've been authorized to proceed with our Order of Battle report."

My eyes squinched up. They did that naturally when I saw something I wanted to unsee.

Working in a slow-motion monotone, Merton laid out our impressive roster of ships.

"In the forward squadron we have three heavy cruisers, the *Lexington*, the *Kabul* and the *Mekong*. They are supported by

90

fifteen destroyers and smaller ships. In the main body of the formation we have two carriers and two battleships. These ships, known as the Mars Division…"

He kept on going like that for seven long minutes. I knew it was seven minutes, because I was working on my tapper the whole time, and the ticker on my arm crawled with pulsing numbers.

I'd stopped listening to Captain Merton's speech partly because I was bored, but mostly because I needed to think of something to say when Graves came back. Sure, I was the liaison from the Mogwa battlecruiser, but that wasn't enough to go on at this point. Graves might very well come back with someone important in tow, someone to whom I'd be forced to tell everything I knew—even though I didn't know anything.

Pretending I already had information—and that it was critical in nature—had been part of my charade from the start. Without that imaginary, secret knowledge, Winslade could have kept me dead for a lot longer. Now was the time to put up or shut up.

Texting back and forth with Sateekas was never easy. He hated texting, and he hated giving his subordinates clear instructions even more.

In his texts, he basically bitched about all kinds of things. Among his numerous complaints, I gathered just a single factoid of actionable importance.

Tell them that my flagship must lead the others when we return to Segin.

"Uh…" I said, lifting a hand and waggling fingers at Captain Merton.

He paused to frown at me. He lifted one chunky hand and pointed at me. "What is it, McGill? I'm just finishing up."

"Sir, I'm so sorry to interrupt, but it occurs to me that one element of your plan must be changed to fit with the Mogwa demands."

A wave of grumbling went up from the other officers. "What is it, McGill?" Merton demanded.

I looked around, and I almost played my single card, but some smarter part of my brain stopped me.

91

Shaking my head regretfully, I threw my hands wide. "I think I've already said too much. We'll have to wait for Drusus and the others to get here."

Captain Merton leaned forward on his bony knuckles. Eyebrows like lobster-spines glowered at me. "Now see here, McGill. This game has gone on long enough. You are a centurion. Everyone here outranks you. If—what are you doing?"

I held up my tapper, which I'd been poking at. "I'm recording your refusal, sir. I have to document every act of insubordination for Sateekas. Nox will probably want to know about it too, now that I think about it. Please continue."

Merton clammed up immediately. He stayed standing, leaning on his knuckles for several more seconds. Finally, with a growl of frustration, he sat down again.

"Lost your train of thought, sir?" I asked. "Not a problem. I'll catch the rest of it whenever you're ready."

The meeting fell into a grumbling silence after that. I sensed that no one in the room was a happy camper—except for myself, of course.

By the time Graves returned, I was raiding the snack trays on the side-table. After all, I hadn't had time to eat since they'd brought me back to life, and I was famished.

When Graves walked in, he didn't come alone. I was impressed. Behind him walked Winslade, Imperator Turov, and—surprise, surprise—Drusus himself.

"Whoa!" I said, scooting away from the snacks with two skinny plates in hand. After saluting until the brass took their seats, I shoved some little finger-sandwiches into my mouth and swallowed hard.

They all looked at me expectantly. I pointed toward Captain Merton helpfully. "Our excellent captain, here, has been briefing me on our order of battle. Quite an impressive fleet we've assembled."

"Yes," Drusus said, "sixteen capital ships, nearly a hundred screens—we've probably never fielded such a large force and committed it to battle. Not since the Clone World campaign, at least."

Merton stood up again. "Praetor," he said, "this centurion has done everything possible to delay these proceedings and defy authority. I suggest—"

"I suggest you consider your every word very carefully," Drusus said, interrupting him. "We're recording, and we're going to transmit the final copy to the Mogwa flagship as has been requested."

That stopped old Merton in his tracks. He swayed there, not knowing what to say next. "Ah… all right. Let me continue where we left off."

Merton was flustered, but he handled it well. The threat in Drusus' statement about recording and transmitting the recording to the Mogwa was a serious one. Nairbs might pore over every word spoken and every gesture made. If they found an obscure violation of a regulation, they might well demand the perpetrators be put to a violent end.

The old bastard rattled away, listing his ships and formations again. It was like replaying a file—I swear, the man was part machine. When he got to the part about the organization of ships and which ones were to arrive in what order—I raised my big hand high.

"What is it, McGill?" Drusus asked.

"Sirs, I've been instructed to inform Fleet that the Mogwa flagship must arrive in the system first and foremost."

That took them all by surprise.

"Are you sure?" Imperator Turov asked, speaking up for the first time. "That's not like the Mogwa. They don't usually lead from the front lines."

"True, but those are his demands."

Drusus nodded. He stepped up to the battle planning holograms and slid the Mogwa battlecruiser up from the back of the formation to the front. It joined the three heavy cruisers.

"They'll get their wish," he said. "I see no reason to deny them."

Merton was annoyed, but he kept his mouth shut. He must have been thinking about the recording that he'd been threatened with.

When the meeting finally dragged to a close, I was almost drooling. Just keeping my head up was a challenge.

At last, Drusus declared we were finished. I wanted to stand up and whoop, but instead, I took my third plate of snacks and slid toward the door. I was the second man to lift a boot over that threshold.

"Not so fast, Centurion."

Shit.

Being the only centurion in the room, I couldn't even pull any tricks of mistaken identity. Instead, I stepped out of line, watching longingly as everyone escaped the room except for me.

Drusus was standing at the battle maps, poking at the ship icons. They flickered at his touch. We were the only two left in the room.

"Are your recording devices turned off, McGill?" he asked me.

I glanced down at my tapper, and I did a double-take. "Oh no... I must have forgotten to turn this thing on. I'm mighty sorry about that."

Drusus nodded. His expression didn't change. He was wise to my tricks by this time. "In an amazing coincidence, I failed to record the proceedings as well."

His fingers ran over the battle table, and a file was flicked to the trashcan. I got the feeling he'd deleted some evidence, but I wasn't a snitch. Not usually, anyway.

Drusus relaxed somewhat. "Okay. You're our official liaison to the Mogwa. What are you going to tell them?"

"The plain truth, Praetor. We've got a big fleet, and they can lead the way into the Segin star system. That star, by the way, is part of the constellation of Cassiopeia from Earth's point of view. I looked it up."

He looked at me expectantly, as if he thought there would be more. "That's it?"

"Yessir. I believe in brevity."

"Indeed you do... All right, McGill. Make your report, and put a good face on it. Keep in mind that your transmission will be recorded and monitored."

It was my turn to be startled. "What transmission, sir?"

"You're reporting this to the Mogwa, aren't you?"

94

"I surely am. But my instructions are to report the facts to them in person."

Drusus showed his teeth. He began to pace. He always did that when stressed. For some reason, he was stressed a lot when I was around.

"Okay," he said at last. "Have it your way. But don't screw-over your home planet. You can manage that much, can't you?"

I grinned. "Don't I always handle diplomacy like a pro, sir?"

He shook his head. "No. Not always."

"Well sir, you've got my heartfelt assurances this time. There will be no embellishments, hyperbole or braggadocio on my part. You can take that to the bank."

"Outstanding... How do you propose to deliver your report? With another radiation-laden ride through our warp bubble?"

"Oh... I was hoping you could spare me a teleport harness, sir."

He frowned, but at last he agreed. After that, he finally let me go, and I trotted out of there like my shoes were on fire.

-14-

Out in the passages, I slowed down to a walk and whistled a tune. I was in no hurry to do anything other than eat and shower. Accordingly, I did just that. My report to the Mogwa could wait until I was in a proper state of mind and body.

On impulse, I checked in on the lady-pilot I'd gone to the Mogwa ship with. She'd popped out of the revival machine less than an hour ago. They'd taken her down to the brig for questioning. Eventually, someone had figured out she was an unwitting bystander in my schemes, so she was allowed to return to duty.

I approached her with high hopes and a warm smile—but it didn't go well. After getting gunned down, revived and interrogated, she just wasn't in the mood for a date.

Rejected but not dejected, I moved on to my own module. People there gave me sidelong glances—even more than they usually did.

Leeson came walking up to talk to me first. "Centurion? We were told you were reporting to the Mogwa ship, sir. We were told not to expect you back tonight."

"Really? I planned to go over there tomorrow. Don't worry about it. The suits are always getting it wrong."

Frowning, he nodded and walked away. Harris approached me next.

"Sir? This is going to sound strange... but I was hoping you might see fit to leave me in charge of the unit this time out. I mean... it's usually Leeson, but..."

I made a show of thinking this over. Finally, I nodded to him. "You know what? I do usually leave Leeson in charge because he's senior. But you've convinced me. I'm going to spread the love a little."

He brightened, but then I pointed over his shoulder and beckoned to Erin Barton. She came over at a trot.

"Adjunct Barton, as I understand it, the only other legion in this fleet is Victrix—is that right?"

"Sort of, sir. There are two support legions as well."

I shook my head. "Zoo legions aren't important in this instance. I want someone backing me up on this campaign who has been a centurion in the past, and who knows a lot about Victrix. Do you know anyone like that?"

"Um..." she said, "well sir... I fit that description. I used to be a centurion when I served under Victrix."

"Oh yeah! That's right!"

By this time, Harris was glaring at us both. He had his big arms crossed, and he looked pissed. I ignored him.

"This time, I'm handing command over to Adjunct Barton when I'm away from my duties. She has acting command over 3rd unit in my absence. We have Adjunct Harris, here, to thank for this suggestion."

There was some scattered clapping, but it soon died out. Harris never stopped fuming and glaring at everyone. He finally marched away and slammed the door to his tiny cabin. The thin metal door rattled in the frame behind him.

After that, I retreated to the showers and my bunk. I felt pretty good after a solid nap, and I came out yawning at around dinnertime. Heading to the mess hall, we ate well during our slot of time. I ate with the enlisted troops, which always brought smiles to their faces.

Winslade showed up unexpectedly as I was tossing my tray into the recycler. He had four goons with him, and he pointed at me without so much as an introduction.

"Arrest that man," he said.

The goons were navy security types, shore patrol, they used to call them. I thought about killing a few of them, but I held off. I was in a pretty good mood, after all.

"Uh… what's this all about, Tribune?"

"It's about *you*, McGill. We intercepted your new orders from the Mogwa, and we've decided we don't like their instructions."

Confused, I looked down at my tapper. The hog-like guard holding onto my left arm was pulled around to face me as I brought my tapper to my face for viewing. I had it silenced and everything—but Winslade was right. There was a new message from Sateekas.

"Says here we're to be used as target practice? By Mogwa marines?"

"Not exactly. Keep reading."

I did, and I frowned as I did so. "A 'hand of hands' of primus-level officers are required. They will be issued weapons deserving of their primitive roots. After they're exterminated in a blood-ritual, their meats will be sampled, and they will be revived to serve the Mogwa again. Hmm…"

Winslade was glaring at me. "What do you have to say for yourself?"

"Uh… not much. I'm glad I'm not a primus, though."

"Why's that?"

"Because of the numbers. A Mogwa hand has six fingers. A hand of hands… that's thirty-six, if my math doesn't fail me. If we take all the top officers from both our legion and our support legion, plus some of those wanker staffers on Gold Deck, that should just about—"

Winslade thumped a small fist on the nearest mess hall table. "That's not going to happen."

My eyes widened. "Whoa… you're not saying they want Victrix men too, are you? That would mean you'll all have to hop into the grinder. No one less than a primus rank… are you guys going to draw lots or something?"

"McGill, this has the stink of revenge written all over it."

"Uh… how exactly do you write stink on something, sir?"

He snarled. "You're accusing me of mixed metaphors? I'm not going to accept this boondoggle of yours, McGill."

"Mine, sir? How do you think this is my idea? I hadn't even read the text until—"

"Some years ago, you manipulated events to get all the officers in this legion killed—I won't go along with another of these schemes."

I smiled, recalling sweet memories. Winslade had been the last one to die on that fateful day, having thought to ambush me in the final moments. He hadn't liked dying back then, and he certainly didn't seem to have sweetened on the idea today.

"Okay," I said. "Just let me dig out my teleport harness and pop over there to deliver the news."

"What news?"

"I have to relay your refusal to comply, sir. It won't take more than a few minutes. You want to escort me down to Gray Deck?"

"No, I want to shoot you again."

Nodding, I made a sympathetic clucking sound. "I get it. I truly do. But executing the Mogwa liaison a second time might not look good on your record, sir. I'm just saying."

Winslade did some pacing then. He did some cursing, too.

"I've got it," he said, stopping and snapping his fingers under my nose. "We'll send them forty officers—more than they asked for. I'll issue everyone in your unit a plastic badge identifying them as a primus. You can choose who the lucky souls will be."

"Forty, huh?

"That's right. Gentlemen, unhand Centurion McGill. He has work to do."

The shore patrol let go of my arms, and they grinned at me. They seemed to like the sound of my coming fate.

Winslade got into my face. "Report to Gray Deck—unarmed—in ten minutes. Bring whatever vagabonds you chose to take to the slaughter with you."

They left then, and I turned around to see a whole bunch of unhappy faces. Barton looked worried. Harris looked angry, and Leeson looked amused.

"Who's gonna die tonight?" Leeson asked me.

"Forty…" I said. "That's quite a few… Well, Barton's off the hook. She's got to hold down the fort here on *Dominus*."

Harris went from frowning to outright smoking-mad, but I ignored him.

"I'll need a second officer," I said, "a man with experience in this kind of dirty-fighting."

"Why does it have to be dirty?" Harris demanded.

"Because we're talking about the Mogwa, here. Do you really think it will be a stand-up fair fight?"

He didn't answer me, he just shook his head and spit on the deck.

"I'll take that as my first volunteer," I said, pointing at Harris. After that, I proceeded to select a mix of troops with good hand-to-hand skills, and all my weaponeers. It wasn't clear how we'd be armed and armored—if at all. I needed men who could be effective even if they were buck-naked.

When we'd assembled and stripped down to our spacer suits, we looked unarmed and harmless. Being a long-time Varus man, I knew neither of these two things was true. Everyone probably had at least one weapon secreted on his or her person. Besides that, Varus legionnaires were always ready for a fight. We'd use our teeth if we had to.

Marching to Gray Deck, we were met by a smiling Winslade. True to his word, he had fake emblems for our shoulders. We were christened as primus-ranked imposters while Winslade and his staffers laughed.

"What about nameplates?" Harris asked. "Shouldn't we have names printed on our uniforms? These are all wrong."

"It won't matter," Winslade assured him. "The Mogwa don't know one human from the next. Even Sateekas will be fooled. McGill will be just one more ape in the grunting pack to him."

Knowing he was probably right, we took our harnesses and put them on. I ordered my men to give a cheer as we ported out, and they did so with gusto.

The blue wavering light throbbed and flashed every time one of us vanished. Soon, the chamber was empty.

-15-

Two squads of hand-picked men teleported out together. They were all from my unit, and I'd officially "volunteered" them.

Moments later, we were all transported to the Mogwa battlecruiser. We didn't know what to expect, so most of my troops had their eyes open and their hands balled into fists. Knees bent and muscles tensed, we jumped back into existence ready for anything—or so we thought.

To our surprise and dismay, we found that none of us could move. Very slowly, my eyes traveled to see what was happening around me, but it took a long time.

We appeared in a large empty chamber surrounded by stasis field projectors. These things kind of looked like X-ray machines—freaky ones. They had flexible, telescoping arms and heads with glowing conical tips. Together, these projectors cast a field of force that prevented movement.

We'd used such systems before to trap criminals such as Claver, but I'd never liked the way the stasis effect felt on my skin. It was like a thousand electrified ants were crawling all over me.

As I was at the front of my unit, a team of Mogwa nerds approached me first. They went over my body with instruments. At last, I was freed.

Stumbling and almost pitching onto my face, I looked behind me. My men were still frozen, looking alarmed and baffled.

"Why'd you do that?" I asked. "You can see we don't have any rifles."

A Mogwa lieutenant approached. He looked me up and down. "You're a loud beast. Do you always offend your masters with that bleating voice?"

"Yes, as a matter of fact, I do. Can you answer my question, Lieutenant?"

The Mogwa lifted one of his many hands. He flicked two fingers in the direction of my men. "We're checking for explosives. We suspect some or all of you might be assassins."

"Oh... I get it."

Their reaction made perfect sense. After all, they hadn't yet forgotten about how they'd been treated at the banquet. Galina's gunmen had made a lasting impression.

I watched as the Mogwa scanned and released my men one at a time. We were all wearing fake officer emblems, and as I considered this, a new worry struck me.

Sateekas and Nox knew there were Earth officers who were disloyal. By demanding everyone above a certain rank come to their ship, the Mogwa were placing themselves in a position of power...

Could it be the Mogwa leaders wanted a pound of flesh for the insult the assassination attempt represented? Maybe they thought that by pulling this prank, they'd be able to purge the very officers who'd dared to order them assassinated a few nights ago.

Hmm... if that was the case, then we imposters were in for a rough time of it.

"Name?" the lieutenant demanded when he got back around to me.

I almost slapped my nametag and called him an idiot—but I stopped myself. I wasn't supposed to be James McGill, and Mogwa couldn't read Earth languages anyways. "Uh... Primus Smith, sir."

He made a note on his tapper. "Smith seems to be a popular name among your incestuous herd of animals. We've already encountered three Smiths so far."

"Very popular, yessir."

The lieutenant let me walk out of the chamber ahead of the rest. A set of glowing yellow arrows appeared on the deck, and we followed them. This was typical of Mogwa directives. They rarely told you where you were going or why. They expected us to travel through their winding passages without asking any questions, like trained hamsters in a maze.

Leading my team of hamsters, we eventually reached a much larger chamber. Upon our approach, this otherwise featureless cargo hold flickered, and it became something new.

"Wow, this is nice!" I said.

The others walked in behind me and made similar appreciative comments. We were in a lush tropical garden. There were fruits and trees and flowers—even rushing water and bare rocks.

Harris moved next to me. He looked at every bush with great suspicion. He touched the fronds of a large fern plant and plucked a huge orchid. He walked over to me, frowning and tapping the bloom on my chest.

"How's this even possible? I thought it was all a projection—but everything seems solid. It even smells nice."

"I can only think of two ways they might have done this," I said, kneeling and putting my hand into a rushing stream. Lifting my fingers, I watched as cool water ran down into my sleeves. "Either they imported it all by teleportation from a real planet, or they created it with some kind of matter manipulation."

"I'll give you another idea," Harris replied. "This is a mind-fuck. Some kind of psychotic projection. They're in our heads, Centurion. We have to be on our guard."

"You're right about that part no matter how they performed this miracle."

Right about then, a loud clap of thunder rang out. We all turned in place, looking upward. A tropical rain began to fall. A moment later, a disembodied voice spoke like the Almighty himself.

"Attention, beasts," the booming voice said. "You are in a Mogwa entertainment center. This chamber has been programmed to recreate a suitable environment for your species. There are countless places to hide and obscure yourselves, just as any prey animal might find in nature."

Harris and I exchanged glances. Neither one of us liked the way this sounded.

"You will be allowed to roam and explore for a short time. Do not waste these precious moments of existence. The hunters are coming, and they will not be merciful to those who stand about aimlessly."

"What the fuck…?" Sargon said, coming up to me. "Sir? The doors we came through—they're gone!"

We rushed to the spot, seeking any seam or crevice. There wasn't even a wall there at the limits of the cargo hold. It felt as if the rock growing up the sides of the chamber were as solid as granite back home.

I stepped back, breathing hard and looking upward. The walls of the place had to be twenty meters high. The sky projected up on the ceiling—it looked so real. It might be a screen or something else, but whatever it was, it seemed flawless. The rain stopped just as suddenly as it had begun, and a yellow sun rolled out from behind silver clouds, making us blink and squint.

"What if they teleported us to some alien planet?" Sargon asked. "Someplace with an Earth-like pit full of plants and shit. Maybe we could scale that wall and get out of here."

"Maybe," I said, trying to think.

"I've got another idea," Harris said. "How about we make weapons as fast as we can, hide, and brain these Mogwa hunters when they come in here?"

I pointed at him. "That's the best idea I've heard yet." I turned on my tactical broadcast channel. "Troops, everyone arm yourself with anything you can find."

"Like what?" Carlos demanded. "Sticks?"

"Yes. Make clubs, grab rocks. Find a bush and squat behind it. Sargon, you take three men and lie in ambush right here where we walked in. It's the only entrance we know about."

"Sir?" another man asked, trotting close. It was a big weaponeer I recalled from Edge World.

"What is it, Washburn?"

He pointed into the trees. "When we first walked in, I saw something close up over there. Another door, I think. On the far wall."

I nodded. "All right, it's worth a shot. You come with me. The rest of you, spread out and arm yourselves. Hide deep in the forest. Kill anything that's not human."

Washburn hustled to follow me through the jungle. After a few minutes, we reached another wall that looked like a natural rocky outcropping. It was covered in vines and leafy growths.

As we reached the edge of the forest, we saw the terrain waver. A large door appeared and opened.

Behind that door was a column of Mogwa with bright metal tubes. The tubes had bulbs at one end, and triggers at the other.

The group that led the column was made up of obvious Mogwa marines. They didn't have their powered armor on, fortunately. Just more of those strange-looking rifles.

Putting a hand to Washburn's shoulder, I signaled we should go to ground. We both hugged the dirt, peering out from under the leaves of a large bush.

After around fifteen marines had entered and spread out, another more regal figure entered. I knew him well.

It was Sateekas himself.

-16-

"Release the canines!" Sateekas ordered.

To our surprise, a rush of dark, furred figures came out from behind the Mogwa. I recognized their type in an instant: they were the dogmen that Clavers like to breed and sell.

I hadn't seen their type since Green World. They were an ape-dog hybrid, hairy guys with long dark snouts and bad attitudes. They didn't talk much, but they were strong, mean and highly protective of their masters.

Eight of the dogmen advanced toward the edge of the forest. Two approached our bush. Their snouts were already up and casting for a scent. I thought they must have caught our trail already.

"Fools!" Sateekas shouted. "Don't piss on every bush. I want four to run down the north wall, and four to run along the east. When you find the humans, don't attack, instead fall back and report to the hunters."

Casting evil looks toward their Mogwa masters, the dogmen shifted their course to follow their orders. They lifted their dark lips to show wet fangs. I got the idea they weren't entirely happy with their soft Mogwa masters, but they were obedient enough.

The marine leader then turned toward the Grand Admiral. "Sir, what about the forest? Will the beasts be hiding in there?"

"Possibly," Sateekas admitted, "but they won't do so until a few of them have been slaughtered. I've studied this species. I would expect them to first attempt to escape the walls. Only when they realize their fate is inescapable will they try to prolong their wretched lives by hiding in the trees."

I thought about that, and I was fairly impressed. Sateekas was right—our first instinct had been to escape.

Now however, I knew the truth: there was no escape from this arena. We were to be hunted down and killed. That left us with only one option, to my mind.

The Mogwa hunters didn't spread apart and follow their dogs. Instead, Sateekas worked at his tapper and his headset. "I've got a location on the herd. Most are still near their entry point, chattering like monkeys to one another on their radios. It's almost disappointing. I'd hoped for better sport."

I tapped Washburn's shoulder, and we slipped away into the dark forest. Once we were clear, we moved at a dead run back to our men. Along the way, I ripped loose my microphone and signaled for Washburn to do the same. Once I was close to the main body of my troops, they were laughing and hefting rocks and sticks.

"What's so funny, Adjunct?" I asked Harris.

"You should have seen it, sir. A pack of dogmen just came running at us from both directions. We threw a few rocks at them, and they ran off like curs!"

I grabbed his shoulder and plucked the microphone off his helmet. "The enemy just reconned us, and now they're listening to our radio transmissions. Shut that shit down!"

"Yessir! Yessir!" he said, and he raced away. Smacking helmets and cursing, Harris soon got everyone who was chattering and wandering aimlessly back onto a war footing.

"Where should we deploy, sir?" he asked.

I pointed at the forest. "Into the trees. I think they're going to come in two groups, one on each wall. We must mass up and destroy one of the two groups."

He nodded, and the troops were soon moving out. We spread into the forest and gripped our makeshift clubs and rocks with determination.

We seemed to be closer to the group coming from the north, so we decided to ambush them first. We were only fifty meters or so from the wall—some were closer than that—when the hunting party came walking along the perimeter.

"Where are the beasts?" the marine commander complained. "Are these canines defective? This is the spot where we pinpointed them."

None of the other Mogwa had an answer for him. The marine commander was the same one I'd seen before, talking to Sateekas. The wily grand admiral himself wasn't in the group. Apparently, he'd gone the other way.

"They've stopped transmitting as well..." the commander said in disgust. "I'm annoyed. This farce will probably end up wasting hours."

The dogmen prowled around their masters, and they proved to be our undoing. One of them caught our scent and plunged toward the nearest hidden recruit.

Snarling and baying, the rest charged into the trees as well. They launched themselves onto a hidden soldier and began to tear him apart. He threw one dogman off himself, but his arms were already torn and bloody. The enemy had teeth and claws, along with superior strength. Rocks and training could only do so much.

"This is it," Harris said. "Can I give the order, sir?"

"No. Let them come into the trees."

He showed me his teeth, snarling like one of the dogmen, but he waved down the troops that wanted to stand and charge.

The Mogwa hunters approached cautiously. Their strange rifles were up and ready. When they saw the sorry heap of mangled meat my man had been transformed into, they laughed and shot him repeatedly.

The guns were of a strange variety. They fired black pellets—tungsten, if I had to guess—that seemed to explode upon impact. Each round was powerful and deadly. The man was shredded before they were through.

Turning back toward the wall, the hunters congratulated themselves on their first kill. Their dogmen had snouts high and sniffing, but the Mogwa weren't paying any attention.

"Now. While their backs are turned, take half the troops and charge in quietly!"

Harris was up and slapping heads. Each man he touched launched himself in a head-long sprint toward the enemy.

The dogmen spotted us first. They became alarmed and agitated.

"What is that racket?" the marine commander demanded, turning around.

What he saw was two dozen men charging at him. We weren't shouting and carrying on, either. Varus men know the power of an ambush. We could be silent killers, when it suited us.

The Mogwa leveled their strange weapons, and they cracked and boomed. Eight men were knocked flat in the initial volley—then we were in among them.

The dogmen each tackled a single man. These contests weren't even, so I ordered my second squad to rush in to support the first. I hadn't wanted to commit every man I had until I saw if we could win, and I now knew that we could.

Letting a war whoop escape my lips, I led that second charge. We reached the dogmen who were mauling my troops, and we beat them down. Rocks crashed into skulls. Sharpened sticks jabbed into bellies, and the dogmen all died.

"Keep going, let's help Harris!"

We rushed closer. It was a grim thing, charging at aliens armed with deadly ranged weapons. We had to get into hand-to-hand fighting to win this.

Most of Harris' men were dead. The Mogwa were individually weak, but then so is any hunter when he's fighting a bear in the woods. The advantage of the gun is huge.

The strange rifles cracked and boomed. The forest around me popped and branches exploded. A spray of splinters—or maybe it was shards of tungsten, I couldn't be sure which—struck my shoulder and left cheek. I ignored the blood, the pain and the danger and plunged on in a primitive fury.

We closed with the Mogwa, and we tore them apart. In the end, every one of their weird skulls was cracked with a rock. Every one of their ugly legs and bulbous bodies were dented and lumpy from a thorough beating with stout clubs.

Standing tall and breathing hard, I looked around. My grin faded quickly.

"Harris?"

"He's gone, sir," Sargon said.

"Flores?"

Sargon shook his head. "She didn't make it. She caught one of those mini-rocket things straight in the chest when you charged in."

I rubbed at the blood on my cheek and shoulder. It wasn't serious, but I was wounded too.

"Sound off! How many do we have left?"

The men reported in, and the news was grim. We had lost over half our number, and half the rest were injured.

"Pick up these guns. Let's figure them out."

We tried. We worked the rifles, pushing and tapping on everything. Nothing we could do made them fire.

"Biometrics, sir," Sargon concluded. "They must have them programmed to only operate for a Mogwa soldier."

I cast down the gun in my hands, disgusted. They didn't even make effective clubs.

It was at that moment that I heard a baying sound. More dogmen were coming—it had to be them. The other hunting party had discovered us.

-17-

"Into the trees!" I shouted. "Sargon, take six men and setup an ambush. I'll get them to chase us."

"Yessir!"

We set off into the trees, the majority of my troops on my heels, with Sargon setting up a smaller group in the thickest brush. My group made no effort to hide ourselves, we ran through the trees and hooted like apes. The Mogwa veered and ran right after us.

Their strange rifles cracked. All around, the trees splintered and popped. Some of my men fell. A few got up, but most didn't. When these bullets hit an unarmored man, they tore him up inside.

Excited, the dogmen charged after us in a wild rush. The Mogwa hunters found their slaughtered comrades, and they chattered and clicked in a rage. They set after us in a blind fury.

This was exactly what I'd hoped for. I wasn't disappointed by their charge—I'd counted on it. Sateekas was just like all the other Mogwa, they were an arrogant, haughty people. They often overestimated their relative strength.

Still, the situation was desperate. We'd taken too many losses in our first encounter. We were still basically unarmed and outmatched by the enemy firepower. Only if we managed to get close, into hand-to-hand, could we hope to kill the hunters.

Sargon's group performed beautifully. I was almost sad I wasn't there to participate. They waited until the Mogwa overran them, then sprang up, chasing after the Mogwa hunters like charging gorillas.

The Mogwa's growls of fury—or glee when they shot one of my men down—quickly changed to bleats of dismay. Sargon himself grabbed a stray foot-hand appendage and lifted a marine high into the air, beating him senseless with his other bare hand. The rest of his team did the same, engaging the Mogwa in close-quarters. Rocks crushed their thin skulls, and improvised clubs broke their stick-like bones.

The rifles stopped shooting at the rest of us, so we turned toward our dogmen pursuers.

"Let's finish this," I told my panting troops.

There were only nine left in my squad, but we weren't interested in body counts. We were down for the fight. The dogmen, to their credit, rushed in and struck powerful blows with their leathery hands. They soon had muzzles that dripped with blood—some their own and some ours.

I rushed one, throwing a punch at his snout. It landed, but it didn't put him out. He slammed into me, and he bowled me over. We rolled in the grass and the leaves, with me tearing at his black, wet nose and him trying to bite my neck.

Reversing the positions with a wrestling move, I got my arm around his throat. He growled and gurgled and heaved under my weight, but he couldn't break free. I lost most of a finger and had tears in my uniform and my skin, but he lost consciousness eventually. I let him slump to the forest floor.

After delivering a final kick in the ribs, I staggered away, panting.

"Report in," I said. "Sound off."

"Wilson."

"Washburn."

"Torres."

I waited a few seconds, but that was it. Four of us were left standing. We'd beaten all the aliens, but I'd lost most of my troops.

Limping back toward Sargon's group, I found them hiding in the brush and took stock of the situation. It was grim for both sides. Sargon was dead, and only two of his men had survived. All of the Mogwa were either dead or squirming in a twisted pile of limbs.

"McGill...?" a weak alien voice spoke.

That voice! I stood up and looked around. Under a massive, leafy fern I found one more injured Mogwa. He was the only one of his kind I'd ever liked.

"Grand Admiral?" I said. "Is that you, sir?"

"McGill...? What have you done?"

"Well sir, what we did was have a great time today. I truly hope we gave you Mogwa boys a run for your money. We died, sure, but we took a few down with us. I surely hope you aren't disappointed in our performance."

The old Mogwa breathed for a few seconds, chewing this over. If he had a single weakness that stood out from all the others, it was his sense of pride and honor.

"I gather from your statements," he wheezed, "that you believed this exercise to be one of comradery and challenge?"

"Absolutely, sir! And I must say, you guys really impressed us. Mogwa marines are nothing to sneeze at. Your boys showed great guts coming in here without their power armor. All my men remarked upon it. You made it so fair and all, what with using primitive weapons and giving us lots of room to run around. Why, I'd go so far as to—"

"Silence! This exercise is finished! You are commanded to help me stand."

I signaled my final handful of troops to help me. Forming a litter, we carried Sateekas and two other Mogwa who were still breathing to the walls.

Suddenly, the stone sheets parted and slid away. A fire team of six Mogwa marines rushed in. They were wearing full powered armor and combat rifles. They leveled the muzzles of their guns, and I expected to die in a hail of power bolts.

"Stop!" Sateekas grunted. "Stand down, Marines. Help me exit this cursed chamber."

Washburn leaned close. "You think maybe we should jump them right now, sir?"

"No, no," I said. "Hold your horses, boys. Grin and try to look friendly. Talk about how great the Mogwa are."

113

"Huh? Great at what, sir? Getting rolled by unarmed humans?"

A few of my men laughed, but I cuffed them. That earned me angry looks, but I didn't care.

"Try to think, boys," I whispered. "These aliens have all the cards. Just follow my lead."

The humans did so, but with poor grace. Eventually, we were all allowed to exit the chamber and marched up to nicer, more modern decks. Given some salves and basic bandages, we patched up the holes in our skins. Mogwa flesh-printers were incompatible with our biology, so we did the best we could with what we had.

Some hours later, after we'd come to realize that our "waiting area" was really a prison cell, the Mogwa returned. Looking a bit banged-up, Sateekas himself stood behind a fire team of fully armed and armored marines. The Mogwa troops looked at us like they wanted revenge.

"McGill," Sateekas said. "I'm glad to have met you on the field of honor. I'm baffled, however, as to how you might have come to be here on my ship?"

"Uh... how's that, sir?"

"I stipulated in no uncertain terms that only humans of primus rank were to be transported to my ship. Imagine my shock at discovering you among these other, less accomplished beasts."

"Oh... maybe there was some kind of a mix-up. We were just told to report to your ship for some friendly war games. My boys, here, they were bored and spoiling for a fight, so I volunteered the lot of them."

Sateekas swiveled one of his few working eyes over each of us in turn. Only a handful of humans had survived.

"You're telling me this gaggle of apes is made up of enlisted men?"

"Why of course, sirs. Our officers challenge each other all the time to duels and such-like—but they don't normally fight in person. They send in champions." I faked a look of shock and smacked myself on the forehead with the palm of my hand. "That must be it! This whole thing was a big misunderstanding.

A cultural difference that neither side completely got the gist of."

"Hmm..." he said, pacing around with at least two bad limps among his six legs. "Things like this have happened before. It is possible... but then again, it might be an example of abject cowardice on the part of you humans!"

"Truth well-spoken, sir. I *believe* it was an honest mistake—but I can't be certain because I can't read minds. Maybe the brass on my side did a little weaseling by sending us in their place. It's hard to know. But the good news is, after we broadcast all this fun action back to our ship for everyone to enjoy, the rank and file of both armies are bound to pull together, men and Mogwa alike."

"Broadcast?" Sateekas sputtered. "You'll do no such thing, McGill! I'll not have a single frame of such a sick embarrassment transmitted to your fleet or to mine. I'd rather destroy every vessel in the armada."

"Uh... okay. Sorry, sir. Don't worry, we'll delete our recordings right now."

I waved to my men, and I made a show of removing files from my tapper. My troops were bewildered, but I saw them deleting things as well. In my own case, it was all a pretense, but the trick seemed to work. Everyone bought it, even the Mogwa.

After a lot more grumbling and complaining about our lack of proper slave-love for him, Sateekas kicked us off his ship and sent us back to *Dominus*.

-18-

Once I was at home again in my unit's module, I broke out the beer and the flesh-printers. Those of us who'd survived the Mogwa hazing ritual were in good spirits. We howled with laughter as we played vids of the hunt, over and over, on the wall of the ready-room. Even Harris, who wandered in from the revival chambers with an awful look on his face, started smiling. He did a little griping at first, of course, but he finally took a beer and plopped himself in front of the show.

"Play that part again where you're beating on a dogman with that palm frond," he said, and I happily obliged.

We were still playing recordings and hooting at them half an hour later. Some of my troops had managed to recover their deleted files, and we were already editing up a compilation of the best moments for the ship's social media sites.

Winslade and Graves came down to talk to us as we were in the middle of an upload, but they didn't seem to find things as humorous as we did.

"McGill?" Winslade said. "Did you publicly accuse the officers of this legion of duplicity?"

"Uh..." I said. "You mean, like, sending ringers into the Mogwa blender instead of your own skinny asses?"

Winslade's hands moved to his hips, and Graves pursed his lips and frowned with disapproval.

"McGill," Winslade said, "you know we couldn't send our entire upper-tier officer corps to the Mogwa. That would have been irresponsible."

"I get it, sir. I get it. Some people are more important than others, and some people are just plain chicken. Anyway, what can I do for you gentlemen? Maybe you'd like to see more of our troops beating these dog-ape hybrids to death?"

Right about then, Winslade noticed our vid, which was playing behind his head. He stared and cringed. His eyes crawled all over the wall screen as the vivid, bigger than life action played out.

"Is that one of the dogmen? I've never encountered such a beast in person."

"Sure is, sir. They were all over Green World, and now they're all over that Mogwa flagship. Quite a coincidence, huh?"

Winslade turned back to look at me thoughtfully. "Are you suggesting the Mogwa bought these creatures from the Clavers?"

"If it walks like a duck and quacks like a duck—it's probably a duck, sir."

"Baffling... How did these Mogwa from the Mid-Zone end up encountering Clavers and doing business with them? At the very least, it's disturbing." He went back to watching the screen again. "What's happening there? Are you abusing that animal?" He pointed up at the screen, where I was, in fact, braining a dogman with a big rock.

"They aren't animals, sir. They're hybrids. Part people and part butt-sniffer."

"Hmm... I don't understand this, and I don't like what I don't understand. Your unit is hereby suspended from all activity outside your module for the time being, McGill. I'm going to sort this out properly."

"What?" Harris had the balls to exclaim. "After a beat-down and a near perming on your behalf, we're confined to quarters?"

"That's exactly what I said, Adjunct. Have a care. I like my junior officers to have a civil tongue in their heads."

117

Harris crossed his arms and glared at everyone. He wasn't a happy camper.

After telling us we couldn't post our recordings publicly, the officers walked back to Gold Deck. My men were fuming mad in their wake.

"What a nutless wonder," Carlos complained. "Winslade should be shot in the face for sending us over there in the first place."

I signaled Harris, who chased the bio specialist out of the room. We kicked all the enlisted men out, and decided to have a meeting of our own.

"What are we going to do?" Harris asked. "That was plain unfair, and I don't think we should stand for it."

"Yeah, sure," Leeson said. He hadn't gone with us to be one of the hunted, but he'd enjoyed the recordings. "What do you have in mind, Harris? Mutiny?"

"No. I'm not that dumb—or that crazy. I say we have ourselves a little accident."

Leeson leaned forward. "Oh yeah, this is going to be good."

Barton stood up suddenly. We all looked at her. Of the four officers in 3rd Unit, she was generally the quietest. She hadn't said anything since she'd walked into the ready-room. She'd watched the vids with mild interest, but she hadn't laughed much.

"Centurion McGill? Can I be excused?"

After a moment, I nodded, and she walked out in a hurry.

"Is she late for a date?" Harris asked, watching her go.

"Nah," Leeson responded. "You're not thinking, Harris. Legion Victrix is here, flying along with us in this same fleet. That's her old outfit. She doesn't want any more of our kind of stain on her record, that's all."

"Huh... she's too good for us, is that it? You think she still wants out? You think she's longing for her snobby old home legion?"

Leeson nodded. "I'd say so. Can you blame her?"

For my own part, I held my thoughts in check. Leeson might be right, and he might be wrong. I decided I needed to find out. If one of my officers was applying for a transfer right before a campaign began, that could spell serious trouble.

I followed Barton to her private quarters, and I tapped on her door. She popped it open and gestured for me to come inside.

Stepping into the tiny space that had been allotted to her, I put on a happy face—but Barton didn't meet my eyes. Right then, I knew. She was trying to leave Legion Varus.

"Bugging out, huh?" I asked her.

She glanced up at me for a second, then studied the deck plates again. "It's that obvious?"

"Yeah. Leeson figured it out pretty much instantly."

She rolled her eyes and sighed. "Don't worry. They probably won't let me back in—and I'm not going to even try until this campaign is over and done with."

"Oh... I get it. You're avoiding all the dirt you can during this operation, so your record looks clean at the end of it. Well, good luck with that."

She finally looked up and met my eyes. "What do you mean, Centurion?"

"I mean nothing about Legion Varus is acceptable to those prigs over in Victrix. They're going to sneer at you no matter what. Worse, your own actions can't possibly fix a reputation as low as the one we've got. If you don't do something off-color the rest of us will. And you'll get blamed for it."

Erin sighed. "I suspect you're right..."

"Why do you want to leave so badly, anyways?"

She shrugged. "It's partly the nature of our missions. Each campaign takes a long time, they take us to places we can't even talk about... The secrecy is the worst part."

This kind of surprised me, as I would have thought that any sane person would have hated the part about dying all the time in heinous ways—but there's no accounting for taste.

"Uh..." I said. "What's so bad about the secrecy?"

"When you have to deploy, people who care about you want to at least know why you're leaving."

"Ah... I get it. You were engaged a while back, weren't you?"

Erin shrugged.

"You think that if you'd gotten a Victrix gig—something where you spent a year following a royal family of Skrull around—things would have been better?"

Erin frowned and thought about that. "I don't know... maybe it's the legion life. I can't have a solid home this way. I can't have a family."

"Oh... that. It is hard. My daughter is older than I am now, isn't that a kick? Physically, she's over thirty. It's kind of weird when I scold her for something."

She pointed a finger at me. "Yes. That kind of thing... right there. Our lives aren't natural. It's bugging me."

"Okay. I get it. That's totally normal. You want to leave the legions. To become a civvie. That's okay, recruits do it all the time."

"No, I was talking Victrix..."

I laughed at her. "Come on, girl! You don't really mean that! You're tired of the legions. You can't take the life anymore. That's no sin—but switching to Victrix isn't the answer. You'll have to become a hog—or leave the service entirely."

She looked stunned. "But it's all I know..."

I stood up, and she did the same. I gave her a light hug. "You've got some tough decisions to make after this deployment is over. But you don't have to make them today. Forget about all that. Be my reliable officer one more time. If you still want to quit when we get back to Earth, I'll sign off that you served with distinction."

She gave me a fluttering smile. "Okay..."

Walking out of her quarters, I saw Carlos. He must have spotted me going in. He made an obscene gesture with his fingers, and he raised his eyebrows questioningly. I flipped him off in return. Then I contacted Moller and had her assign him some extra cleaning duties.

-19-

About four hours after Winslade had issued the confinement to quarters order, I found myself wandering the vaunted halls of Gold Deck. I'd been ordered to stay with my unit in our module—but I got bored.

Every time someone dared to ask my business, I gave them some horse-hockey about being the eyes and ears of the Mogwa. This earned me plenty of frowns and sneers—but people sure got the hell out of my way real fast.

Finally, someone who really knew me spotted me hanging around the back of a briefing room. It was Gary, the adjunct who had shanghaied himself into going on this mission at my suggestion.

"McGill...? What are you doing on Gold Deck?"

I smiled at him. "I might ask you the same question. I thought you were planning to fly that desk back at Central all the way to an early retirement check."

"Imperator Turov listened when I told her she needed me on this mission. I was surprised she did, actually... anyway, you still haven't answered my question, sir."

I pointed into the briefing room. I wasn't an invited guest, so I was just haunting the doorway. The meeting wasn't marked confidential, or anything, so I figured it was open information.

121

"I'm learning a lot," I said, lowering my voice. "Did you know the Mogwa gave us some tech before we left Earth? Something to help us make this mission work?"

Gary looked kind of shifty. "Like what?"

"Like a new kind of gateway posts. These new models work continuously. They allow a constant flow of materials from one end to the other."

"So what?"

"Imagine there's our fuel tank at one end, and a pipeline going back through space and time that connects our fuel tank to a bigger one back on Earth."

Gary gaped a little. The diagram on the screen behind the pretty centurion who was giving the briefing depicted exactly what I was describing. The truth was I'd stopped by and peeked in because I saw a nice face doing the presentation, but I'd stuck around for the briefing itself.

"That's awesome new tech..." Gary gasped. "We could fuel our whole fleet with that. We could go anywhere!"

I nodded. "Exactly right. It still takes a long time to fly a long distance, but we no longer have to worry about running out of gas or starving."

"Impressive... so, who are you here to see, exactly?"

I glanced at him in annoyance. I'd dodged that questions twice, and I'd done so artfully. But Gary, bless his little heart, he just wasn't about to let go. He still wanted to know why I was here, and what I was up to.

A dozen quick lies sprang up into my mind. The trouble was, I needed one that he'd believe. At last, I pointed a finger into the room again.

I pointed at Galina Turov. She was in the front row, listening intently to the briefing.

"She called me up here for a date," I said flatly.

A cloud went over Gary's features, but he didn't call me a liar. He didn't get mad and stalk away, either. He just nodded.

"Right. Of course, I should have known."

After that slam, he walked away in defeat.

"Hey, Gary," I called after him. "If we get into some serious action down on the target planet, you want me to request your presence at the front lines?"

That stopped him. His eyes were wide with shock. "Why would you do that?"

"Just to help out an old friend. What's the point of you having come all the way out here if you don't at least get your feet wet? Have you ever shot anyone with that gun on your hip?"

"Um... once. Back in basic, of course. We were all shooting, and the guy went down. Everyone in the squad said it was their kill, but I'm pretty sure it was mine."

I smiled at him like I was impressed. "That's good enough for me. I'll request you personally if any of my officers are taken out."

He wandered off, looking bemused and a little bit worried. I knew he wouldn't sleep tonight, and I felt I'd done my good deed for the day.

When the meeting broke up at last, I waited until everyone filed out. The pretty centurion who'd done the talking came out first, and it took some serious willpower on my part not to follow her down the passageway. Fortunately, I managed to exert an unusual degree of self-control and waited for Galina herself.

Galina wasn't a disappointment when she finally put away her notes and came walking out the door. She looked at me quizzically. "McGill? Are you waiting for someone?"

"Bingo!" I pointed at her and gave her my best smile.

She frowned in return. She glanced up and down the passageway—could she have been looking for someone? It was my impression that she was.

"You want to go to dinner?" I asked. "I'm famished."

"You're always hungry. But... all right."

We found the finest officer's mess on Gold Deck and ate like kings. Everything was fresh and delicious. I had smoked salmon on rice, a roast beef sandwich, a bowl of spaghetti and two beers. Galina ate a fancy salad.

We got to talking afterward, and she admitted she'd been quite impressed by the vids of us playing whack-a-mole with the dogmen and the Mogwa. Everyone aboard the ship by now had heard about it, as we'd gone ahead and posted our recordings using a hacked account.

The two of us were hitting it off pretty good, in fact, when a certain professional cock-blocker named Winslade came to find me.

"Centurion McGill? What are you doing on Gold Deck?"

"He's having dinner with me," Galina told him. She was an imperator, and she outranked old Winslade.

He flashed her a scowl of disapproval. "Imperator, I'd appreciate it if you would allow me to discipline lower ranked officers in my own legion as I see fit. This man was confined to quarters. He's under investigation for disrupting diplomatic protocol with the Mogwa."

"Disrupting it? I thought he was our liaison with respect to joint operations."

Winslade appeared smug. "That is no longer the case. We took the recordings, which McGill here insisted on making public. Sateekas took a grim view of his actions and rescinded McGill's absurd post."

I stood up, shocked. "You did what?"

Winslade turned in my direction. We had a face-off right there in the restaurant, and I knew it wasn't going to go well for Winslade if I got too riled up.

"That's right," he said. "Did you think I was going to allow all this insubordination? You're a constant troublemaker. From now on, professional diplomats from the xenology team will handle our interactions with Sateekas."

"They'll screw it all up! They've got no idea how to talk to a Mogwa."

Winslade shrugged. "You had the job, but you blew it. You just couldn't keep from having a laugh, could you?"

Galina cleared her throat. We both glanced at her. "Who made this decision, Winslade?"

"Praetor Drusus himself, after I explained what McGill did. He was horrified."

"Aw, come on," I said. "It was really funny."

"Sit down, James," Galina told me. "Winslade, you're dismissed."

With a sly smile tossed in my direction, he walked away. I flipped him off under the table.

Galina watched me. "Are you happy now? We've got fools from Xenology doing our diplomacy. How long will it be before Sateekas flays one of them alive?"

"Not long, I suppose. I guess Winslade is right. I went too far. But he shouldn't have dressed me up as a primus and sent me and my boys over there in the first place. The Mogwa demanded that high-ranked officers participate. We did all the dying, so we felt like playing a few tricks of our own."

Galina nodded. "Mistakes were made all around. Legion Varus is a disorganized mob of people. None of us are qualified to handle sensitive diplomatic interactions. Everyone should have known better. I'm just glad Drusus is in operational command of this mess, rather than me."

I thought about that, and I realized she seemed unusually calm. I guess she could be pretty chill when disasters couldn't be traced back to her desk.

The rest of the night went very smoothly from my point of view. I ended up spending the evening in her apartments, and it was a nice change of pace.

-20-

After losing my status as a liaison, I felt relieved. It wasn't easy for a shiftless scoundrel like myself to hold an important job—unless the job involved killing someone or stealing something.

Talking nice for a living? That kind of job wasn't for me, at least not long term.

Five long months went by. We spent the time training, killing each other, screwing each other and getting into trouble. I was flogged twice, and once I was left for dead nine whole days. All in all, I had myself a pretty good time.

One day in what people back home would have called February, we finally arrived at our destination. The funny thing was, the exact moment was kind of a secret. Even the Mogwa seemed uncertain until a few hours before the big arrival happened.

"This is weird," Leeson kept saying. "I've never been this far from home. How do the techs even know where the hell we are?"

I pointed at Natasha and gave her the nod. She was our resident brainiac. I figured she could do the briefing herself.

"Well… it's kind of hard to explain. I'll try, however. When we go into a warp field, we're blinded."

"I get that," Leeson said, crossing his arms. "The only thing we can do to detect our whereabouts is measure nearby gravitational forces."

"Right. But you see, that's not an exact science. There's a lot of astrophysics and calculus involved. We're traveling faster than the speed of light, and we're doing so into regions we've never visited. Everything we know about the Mid-Zone is thousands of years old."

"Uh..." I said. "How can that be? We can see the whole Milky Way galaxy from Earth, right?"

"No," she said, bringing up some star charts. A holographic vision of our local galaxy appeared with billions of stars spinning in space above us. She reached up and manipulated the image. Like a god on a stormy mountain, Natasha reached toward the Core Systems, a massive spheroid of stars at the center of the whole thing. "This is where Earth is—relative to the Core."

She touched the map, and she made a green dot blink. That was Earth, two thirds of the way out from the center.

"From our point of view, there's a zone of stars we know nothing about. These are on the opposite side of the Core. The stellar density in the Core is so great, we can't see through it from Earth."

"Oh... keep going."

"Okay," she said, lighting up the Mid-Zone again. It was a soft blue band between Earth and the Core. "The problem we're having now is navigational. We've flown so far from home that the reality of these stars, of their real positions, isn't the same as what we've seen from Earth."

"Huh?" Leeson asked. "How the hell does that work?"

"I'm trying to explain. You see, the speed of light is relatively slow on this grand scale. We've only seen these stars as they were thousands of years ago. Some have moved. Some may have gone nova. Some might be affected by dark objects, like black holes, and end up moving somewhere unexpected."

"Oh... I get it," Leeson said.

"Well then, explain it to me," I asked.

"It's like this, we've been looking into the past with our telescopes. If you go out a thousand lightyears to examine a planet you've been looking at, that planet will be a thousand years in time further on. Since we're trying to navigate by gravity, well, we might make mistakes. Our guesses as to

127

where stuff should be a thousand years from when we last saw them might be off."

Natasha pointed a finger at him. "That's exactly right. We've been looking into the past since Galileo first invented the telescope. Until now, we've never really flown out here to record definite information. We've been working with old images and mathematical models."

"Okay, okay," I said, pointing to the Mid-Zone. "Where are we headed? Best guess."

Natasha hemmed and hawed, but she finally isolated a set of about fifty stars in a ball that she figured held our target.

"Cagey Mogwa," I complained. "They love to be secretive. They don't even want to tell us where we're headed. Is it a hot planet or a cold one? You'd think they'd give us a clue."

"Those who control us always have secrets," Leeson said in the tone of a man imparting a great wisdom. Maybe he was.

"Okay, so how long until we arrive, and how far off might we be from our target?" I asked, turning back to Natasha.

"I don't know... but I'd say it'll be less than a week before we get there. I know the techs are being asked to do regular location math now. Several times a day. They're guesstimating like mad."

"We should just come out of warp, take a quick peek, then go back in," Leeson said. "This business of plowing our way all the way to the target star is dangerous and plain nuts."

I pointed a finger at him. "There must be a reason why they're doing it. I think they expect a hot arrival."

He looked startled. "Enemy ships?"

"Has to be. Why else take these risks? There has to be a reason."

"Aw, damn. I hate space battles."

Leeson wasn't alone in that sentiment. We were ground-pounders. When ships blasted away at each other, we were helpless cargo.

We broke up the meeting about an hour later, and I went back to my quarters to freshen up. Galina and I had a date planned this evening, and I didn't want to be late. I was already hoping the date would come with some fringe benefits later on tonight.

As it turned out, I never made it to her door to knock and pick her up. The first clue I had that something was wrong came in the form of a lurching gut-punch. The ship's internal gravity generators had all been switched off then on again.

I knew enough to throw my hands in front of my face. That was all I had time to do.

Slam! I did a facer on the deck. They'd done something to *Dominus*, something sudden and dirty. We'd either been hit, or we'd performed a hard turn in space.

When I was lifted up again, sent flying into the air and slammed against the starboard wall, I knew it was the latter of the two options. We were maneuvering under emergency power.

Belatedly, a half-dozen klaxons and spinning lights began to play. It would have been nice to have a warning before the fireworks began—but then again, maybe the fleet pukes were as surprised as I was.

Less experienced crewmen and soldiers climbed awkwardly to their feet when the violent motion stopped—but not me. This wasn't my first rodeo.

"Everyone! Stay down on the deck! Crawl!"

The legionnaires within earshot did as I'd ordered. A few of the fleet pukes did too—but not all of them. Some gave me a sneer and began to trot toward their battle stations.

Slam!

We spun around again. A few more people did facers, and one ensign didn't get up. She flopped over the deck like a ragdoll.

We scrambled on all fours after that, crawling over the walls half the time, to get to a safe spot. Soon, the all-clear was sounded, and a familiar voice boomed over the ship's public address system.

"All hands," Captain Merton said, "we've arrived at our target world. We're coming out of warp in a hostile situation. Proceed to your battle stations."

My mind was full of questions. Why hadn't we gotten an earlier warning? Why had we done those sudden, vicious maneuvers?

129

But there were no easy answers coming. There was no time for explanations. As combat troops we had one duty, possibly two, to attend to. One job was to cover all the ship's vital systems, in case there was a boarding attempt. The second was to make ready to land on the target world, if we were within range. Accordingly, I rushed to my module and marshalled my troops. We scrambled to pull on combat gear and arm ourselves at the nearest armory.

I barely knew what was happening, but I was sure of one thing: This war had just become real.

-21-

Once I'd reached my module, I found my troops were already hopping. Everyone was shrugging on gear, yelling at each other and checking weapons. We'd been armed since earlier this week, but we didn't have a full load-out of supplies and ammo.

"McGill?"

My tapper was talking to me. It was Primus Graves.

"Sir?"

"Get your unit to Red Deck. You're dropping on the target if we can clear a path."

"Uh... got it, sir. But... why should we have to clear a path? What's in the way?"

"That doesn't matter to a ground-pounder. Follow orders."

That was it, he was gone. I scrambled my troops as fast as we could, racing down the passages following blinking arrows under our feet to Red Deck. The arrows were sophisticated these days, even telling us to halt and wait when another unit was charging by. They were like a smart traffic-control system.

When we got to the chaos and noise that was Red Deck, we were packed onto a lifter. Excited and uncertain as to what we faced, we chattered and checked our gear yet again.

A half hour passed—but nothing happened other than a few hard swerves to port or starboard. *Dominus* was clearly on approach—going somewhere and avoiding something.

At last, I got tired of waiting. I summoned Natasha.

She arrived and Leeson was edged out of his seat at my side. She had a sheepish look on her face.

"I know what you're going to say, James… " she said, not meeting my eye.

This came as no surprise. I'd often asked her to hack stuff for me, to find out what they knew up on Gold Deck. I naturally assumed she'd figured a way into the feeds... She lifted her tapper and flicked a feed to mine.

"You already hacked the bridge?" I asked, impressed. "Did you know I was going to ask you?"

"No, I just couldn't stand the suspense myself."

Laughing and shaking my head, I examined what she'd captured. It was an eyeful.

A reddish planet, kind of like a big Mars but with some silvery oceans dotting the land, came into view. Two things besides the planet itself I found impressive.

First off was the big-ass dome on one side of the planet. It was huge and shimmery. It had to reach all the way up to the clouds. Underneath this dome was a massive city. The city was so big it covered a lot of the world. If I had to guess, I'd say it was about as big as my beloved Georgia Sector back home.

"Wow… that's one big town. That dome, too… it's…"

I trailed off, frowning. "What do I see there? What are those sparklers above the big city?"

"Those aren't sparklers, James. They're falling debris."

Frowning, I squinted. The screen was small and the images were odd. I couldn't make heads or tails of it.

"I don't get it. What am I looking at?"

Natasha leaned closer. I immediately liked her smell. It wasn't perfumey, it was light and clean, with a hint of hot nervousness underneath.

"There are ships bombing the dome. They're sieging the only city on the planet."

"Oh… I get it. Sateekas said the bears from Rigel were out here. Is that who we're facing?"

"They don't know for sure yet."

"Why are we sitting on this lifter, anyways?" I demanded, coming to the next obvious question. "There's no way we can land on a planet that's under bombardment."

"I don't know. Maybe they plan to attack and drive the raiders away, then land. I just don't know."

I stared at the feed for a few minutes more. It looked like our fleet was organized now and making a serious approach. We were obviously on an attack vector.

That said, the enemy ships weren't paying any attention. They just kept bombing the big city, as if they couldn't even see us. It was kind of weird.

"Are we in stealth or something?" I asked Natasha. "What are the people on the bridge saying?"

She looked at her boots. "I don't know."

"Liar. Hook me up."

She sighed and relayed an audio feed to my helmet.

"...the enemy force still isn't withdrawing," said a voice. I recognized it as Captain Merton. "The Mogwa are gleeful. They're racing ahead with their lone battlecruiser. I don't like it."

"Shall we maintain our formation, sir?" asked a fleet flunky.

"Drop our engine output by ten percent. We'll fall back a little. After all, we're flying a transport here, not a battlewagon."

"Engines dropping ten percent."

I looked at Natasha. "Old Merton is cagey. He smells a trap—but why?"

"I don't know exactly. I've only got audio feed. But as I understand it, all they can see is a squadron of enemy tugboats. They're unarmed."

"How are they bombing the city dome, then?"

"They seemed to be dragging asteroids to the planet and dropping them down into the atmosphere."

Thinking that over, I was impressed. "That might be all they have—a few tugboats? We'll smash them."

Natasha shrugged. "That's what Sateekas seems to believe. He's rushing in to destroy them."

Thinking things over, I frowned. I wasn't totally getting it. Sure, it made sense that a planet with no fleet to protect them could be abused by nothing more than a few tugboats. But then, on the other hand, those same tugs should be running the moment they spotted warships on approach. It was really the behavior of the tugboats that didn't make any sense.

With a decisive finger, I moved to turn off the feed. This whole thing wasn't my problem. It was fleet business. In my experience such things might take hours to play out. It was time to consider catching a nap while I could.

My finger hovered over my tapper, but I hesitated. Sighing, I decided to doze while I let it play. Maybe something interesting would happen.

A few minutes later, Natasha jostled me. My eyes snapped awake.

"James!" she hissed. "James—there are ships. More ships!"

I lifted my tapper into view again. We were a lot closer to the Mars-like planet now. It was unmistakable. Finally, at long last, the tugboats were goosing their tiny jets. They were accelerating away from us—but it was too late for that. We were almost on top of them.

"Looks like we've caught these bastards red-handed."

"No, no," Natasha said, impatiently. "Look over here—at the horizon!"

I squinted, and I thought I saw some more plumes. Exhaust trails? They were coming from the far side of the planet.

"Uh-oh…"

It turned out to be the understatement of the campaign. A dozen large warships were now flying around into view. Already, *Dominus* and the rest of Earth's fleet was coming about, bringing their broadsides to bear.

"We're about to be treated to a space battle."

There were few things a ground-pounder liked less than sitting in a tin can while fleet-types tried to kill each other. We were like kids strapped into car seats, hoping our drunk parents were going to make it home this time out.

Each side blazed with fire. Big guns were going off, and I felt the kick from ours. *Dominus* had launched sixteen fusion warheads toward the enemy.

Sateekas' battlecruiser, ever seeking glory, had insisted on leading the charge. Now, he was spinning around in a panic, firing every gun he had, and I wondered if it would be enough.

On the red planet's horizon, more ships kept sailing into view. We were already outnumbered, and the odds kept getting worse.

Missiles, fighters and smart-shells flew in both directions. It would take a few minutes for all this destructive firepower to land on target, so we had some waiting to do.

It was kind of weird, knowing that my death was possibly out there in space somewhere, hurtling toward me at a hundred thousand kilometers an hour.

We were glued to our screens, and soon all my officers and most of my noncoms joined us on the pirated feed. I couldn't blame them. The news of the battle outside the thin hull of *Dominus* spread like wildfire through the lifters.

All of a sudden, the Mogwa battlecruiser's salvo struck the attacking vessels. Two blew up—then five more. Moments later a cloud of enemy fighters flashed close to us, engaging our protective screen of ships and force fields.

The fighters chewed on Sateekas' ship more than any of the others, but they couldn't get through her defenses. Point defense cannons all over *Dominus* began to blaze away, setting up a hammering sound that rang throughout the hull. You could feel the vibration in your boots.

"Looks like we're gonna win!" I shouted.

War-whoops echoed all down the rows in the lifters. Everyone was watching the action now, whether it was sanctioned to do so or not.

Then the enemy heavy salvos reached our ships. Fusion shells came pouring in, having taken a while to reach our lines. The big Mogwa battlecruiser took the worst of it, a vicious pounding. Worse, our own cruisers and destroyers were being pelted. A few gushed fire, venting a mix of lavender gas and flame into space.

Our initial wave of excitement quickly died, and we began to wince and gasp. It was less than a minute later that we saw Sateekas' battlecruiser veer away. She was retreating, having taken too much punishment. We felt our stomachs lurch and heave as we felt *Dominus* turn away, too.

I felt pretty sick. Could this actually be happening? Was Earth's grand fleet defeated? Were we going to have to retreat after having come so very far across the heavens?

-22-

"Legion Varus," Tribune Winslade's voice was broadcast to our headsets. His tone was a bit tremulous, as if he was shaken up. Not even I could blame him for that. "We're switching tactics. It has been decided that *Dominus* will jump past this conflict and unload her most precious cargo onto the target planet. Good luck to you all."

Harris turned to me with huge eyes. "Don't tell me they're going to dump us? McGill, tell me this isn't happening."

"Sounds like we're being hot-dropped into Hell itself," I admitted.

"You've got to do something, Centurion. Work some of your crazy magic."

I blinked at him, wondering what the hell he thought I could do to change the course of a pitched battle. I was a glorified grunt in fancy armor. "What's happening today is whatever the brass wants to happen, Adjunct. Get a grip."

Harris bared his teeth and stared straight ahead. He no longer wanted to peek at my tapper, or anyone else's. I could tell he'd seen enough of the savage battle raging outside the hull of our transport.

Not ten seconds after Winslade's announcement, we felt a sickening, wrenching sensation in our guts. The world went white—and we knew we'd gone into warp. That lasted for about five seconds, and during that short span of time we all got a heavy dose of rads. There had been no time to set up the ship's shielding properly. Every safety protocol had been ditched.

Dominus jumped and came out of warp again moments later. Every light on the lifter changed color, going from our red running-lights to brilliant green. The lifter's ramp dropped open, falling down to the boarding decks with a tremendous clang.

Graves overrode all our confusion. His voice rang in every helmet in our cohort. "3rd Cohort, your lifter's ramp is down. Move out of the vehicle! Proceed to the drop-pod cannons on the double! Move, move, move!"

We were surprised, but we hustled to obey. We scrambled, slapping at our harness release buttons and ripping at oxygen hoses. Many men, including myself, slashed at these obstacles. As a result, I was one of the first men to get to his feet.

"Let's go, let's move!" I shouted, charging for the exit. Fortunately, it wasn't all that far away. 3rd Unit had been one of the last to board the lifter.

Hundreds of troops poured out of the ship. We hadn't been properly released, and every safety protocol in the book was being broken—but that's how things went sometimes. This wasn't a drill, this was go-time. For all we knew, *Dominus* had been hit hard and was going to be vaporized in the next few minutes.

Pounding over the deck plates in heavy boots, we rushed to the drop-pod cannons. These were also built into Red Deck, an improvement in modern transport design. Taking a glance at my tapper when the mass of men was pressed together into a traffic jam at the cannons, I saw some of the lifters were launching. Half of them had taken flight.

I knew right off what the plan was. We'd drop half our men in pods and half in lifters. One group might fare better than the other, but without good intel on the target we were hedging our bets.

Overall, I wasn't sure how I felt about being slated for drop-pod delivery onto a hot LZ. In the lifter, it only took one lucky hit to wipe out the entire cohort. On the other hand, drop-pods were tiny flying coffins that were much harder to target individually. They were more likely to land, but there was no way *all* of them were going to land safely. Which was better? I supposed it depended on whether you were one of those who died or not.

As luck would have it, our group got to the cannons relatively quickly. We didn't have to worry about much. We just stepped out into open space and dropped into a chute, which slammed a pod around us. The pod was then spun around and aimed at the planet.

A massive jolt struck the bottom of my boots, and fortunately I was set for it. My knees didn't buckle or crack. In an instant, I was sent headfirst on a screaming dive toward the target world.

My modern officer's helmet allowed me to "see" outside the capsule virtually as my pod dove into the atmosphere. This was a mixed bag, both a blessing and a curse. Although it allowed me to satisfy my curiosity, it also allowed me to glimpse my doom.

The space battle was still raging. If anything, it was more chaotic than ever. Earth's fleet was now split, with the two transports delivering legions over the world, having jumped past the defenders.

The defending ships were now between our warships and our more vulnerable transports. They would have to choose between chasing down our retreating fleet or turning around and destroying the ground forces we were dropping on the target world.

Was that the true purpose of this mad maneuver? Had the brass decided to feed Varus and Victrix to the enemy? Were we only doing this to provide cover for the retreating ships?

It was a grim thought. For a few moments, as the enemy slowly reacted to the changing battlefield, I was in suspense.

The planet itself was a glory to behold. It was a reddish world, perhaps heavy in iron content like Mars back home. The Mogwa city was a soap bubble of light on the eastern flank of the world, stretching over a big chunk of land. Eventually, I knew, if the Mogwa were allowed to build and breed indiscriminately, they'd cover every meter of the world's natural surface. It would transform into a single conglomeration, a City World of epic proportions.

But Segin wasn't quite there yet. Although they'd built a city big enough to contain billions, a true Mogwa City World could hold *trillions*.

All around my capsules, hundreds of others rushed toward the atmosphere. Some struck the smoky surface of it, blazing alight immediately. Every capsule became a burning meteor, a shooting star in a vast shower of shooting stars.

Just before I plunged into the troposphere, I swept my field of view up to see the fleet again—and I felt a jolt of alarm.

The enemy fleet had decided to follow both options. They'd split their fleet. Two cruisers now stalked our transports, while the rest of them pursued our warships, chasing them from the field of battle.

Even as I watched, I saw pinpricks of flame blossoming near *Dominus* and the Victrix transport. For a moment, I was baffled—then I realized what I was seeing. Those explosions had appeared below the transports, between the transports and the planet itself.

They could only be one thing: lifters. They were shooting down our lifters.

Right about then, I hit Segin's envelope of atmosphere and plunged into it. A blazing inferno encompassed my drop-pod, and all communications were cut off. I could no longer see anything outside the capsule.

Blinded and screaming down toward the planet surface, I experienced the most gut-wrenching part of the drop. This was when anything could happen. My pod could fail in a thousand ways, each of them fatal. The enemy could shoot me down. Anything could happen.

At times, men in my situation had sunk into lakes of fire and been cooked. They'd smashed down too hard into the ground, every bone crushed to jelly. They might even die from simple causes, like a failed oxygen pump. This was when every splat earned his nickname.

Gritting my teeth, I found the blindness to be the worst part. Somehow, being locked into a space tighter than an Egyptian sarcophagus was worse than watching the enemy shoot at me. Not knowing your fate was tougher, because there was nothing to occupy an active mind.

To pass the crucial time period, I watched the clock count down. I should reach ground zero in less than two minutes...

With thirty seconds to go, the pod inverted itself and the retros fired. I was now flying feet-first instead of head-first. That switch around was a relief, really, as it meant the pod was still operating properly.

Just before touch-down, however, I felt a shock. My pod was knocked to the left. It was a hard blow, and my helmet thumped into the side of the capsule. This was followed by a screeching sound of metal being torn up.

Was it anti-air fire? A sharp gust of wind? Or maybe I'd hit some cliff face on the way down and caromed off a wall of stone. I wasn't sure. I didn't even really know where I was landing. No one had bothered to tell us.

Whatever the cause, the rest of my descent was done at an angle. As the pod landed I tried to set myself, to be ready for anything. The pod landed and flopped over on its side. I was left lying in my coffin now, and I was faced with some choices.

I could study my environment, using cameras and transponders—or I could get the hell out of my pod. Deciding to risk everything to get out and on my feet, I blew the explosive bolts. The pod split in two, with the smoking husk of the top half blowing away from the bottom.

Rolling out to my left, I levered my morph-rifle up with my right arm. The moment I came out of my pod, I was struck by a spray of projectiles.

At first, I thought I was under fire—but it wasn't so. Another pod had smashed down very close to me, spraying up stones and debris.

Scrambling away from more falling pods, I sought cover. Once I found a small indentation scooped out of the earth, I huddled in a ditch and took a second to look around.

My surroundings were uninviting. The land was indeed reddish brown. There were some greens, but they were muted and dark. The leaves on the various twisted plants were purple in most cases. A deep color like that of plum trees or eggplant.

Craning my neck and looking back toward my crash point, I saw a strange thing—a shimmering wall that resembled liquid glass. The wall shot up into the sky, merging with the brown-orange clouds themselves. It rippled as I watched it, and after a second, I understood what I was looking at.

My drop pod had come down at the very edge of the force dome that protected the great city. I'd slid down that dome, and I was lucky I hadn't been smashed to a pulp. Only the fact that my capsule had been decelerating hard and had enough smarts to reroute to a new LZ had saved me.

-23-

Once I had my bearings and no longer believed I was going to die instantly, I got into the game. "3rd Unit, this is your centurion. Sound off!"

They began reporting in. Not everyone had made it to the ground safely. Leeson was dead, as was Natasha. I counted the missing and dead carefully. Twenty were gone. Exactly twenty.

All and all, it wasn't a bad start. I'd definitely seen worse.

"All right, let's try moving into that dome."

"Sir?" Harris called. "I already made an attempt to penetrate. No dice."

"Not even at walking speed?"

"Nope. It's like trying to walk into a glacier. That dome is solid."

Internally, I cursed. It made sense that the Mogwa would have built something that didn't allow invaders or bombs to enter—whether they were moving quickly or not—but I knew of other domes that worked differently.

"All right. I'm not in communication with Graves yet, so we don't have operational orders other than to survive and hold whatever ground we've landed on. Let's do a tactical scan and look for something defensible."

At the moment, due to the sheer chaos of the pod-drop, I was in charge of my own unit. We hadn't really had time to draw up sophisticated invasion plans. We'd simply arrived in the middle of a space battle and been dumped on Segin.

Apparently, they'd seen fit to put us at the very edge of the city's dome. That was fine—if we could get in, and if the Mogwa inside believed we were friendly.

Outside the dome, it was a torn up landscape. Bombs had clearly pockmarked every inch of the territory surrounding the force field that protected the great city. I was mildly surprised that the Mogwa defense batteries hadn't fired on us in our drop-pods. Maybe all the pillboxes had been destroyed already. Maybe the ones inside the dome didn't dare to drop their protective cover long enough to take a shot at us—or maybe, under the best circumstances, the defenders here knew we were landing to help them.

It really didn't matter much which theory was right. We had to get into that dome to help the defenders before we were annihilated by the enemy ships in orbit.

"Barton, you find us a bolt-hole to crawl into. A bunker, a tunnel, a sewer—I don't care. Take your lights and scout the area."

"On it, Centurion." She raced away, whistling and calling for her light platoon. They scrambled over jagged rocks and crusty surfaces that had obviously once been open dirt. Whole regions had been blasted by terrific heat and were glassy in spots like frozen puddles.

Buzzers flew as well, searching the land from the air. About ninety seconds later, I made a discovery.

"Harris! I see a good piece of defensive ground about a half a kilometer to the west."

He cranked his neck and looked skeptical. "That's a crater, sir. Should we really shelter in a spot the enemy has already zeroed?"

I waved a big arm, indicating the whole fried landscape around us. "You see something better? Feel free to make a suggestion!"

He shook his head, and we took his heavy platoon and Leeson's support teams to the spot. With Leeson dead, I was commanding the auxiliaries myself. Every bio, weaponeer and tech in the unit looked freaked out. It was never good for troop morale to know your direct commander had died right off the bat. The trick was not to give them too much time to think about it.

We hustled for the crater, struggling to carry our heavier pieces of gear. As the specialists were trained for that, I had the heavy troops help by stripping the dead and taking their gear with us. You never knew how long it would be before you got resupplied—especially since our fleet seemed to be bugging out in the skies above us.

Kivi was helpfully sending me texts and streams still. They were snatches of the action, really. Things caught from the skies above and captured by her com gear. I saw ships burning, some winking out as they warped away, and others exploding as they succumbed to too many fusion shells. It was depressing, so I didn't spend too much time studying it.

The glassy dome, on the other hand, looked intact. Inside you could tell the landscape was untouched. I could see regions that were unspoiled and purple-green. The ground in there wasn't as red or as burned. For a moment, I studied the land under the dome, seeing this planet might have been beautiful once. Maybe, out somewhere on the opposite side of this globe, everything was lovely and peaceful.

Farther in, of course, the great city loomed. Tall buildings stood like mountains. They weren't as rectangular as human construction. Instead, they were more jagged and angular. Most of the biggest were massive pyramids, like Central back home.

Like a vast mountain range seen from a distance, I couldn't see the far side of it. All my eyes could grasp was the side facing me. The tops of the tallest buildings in the center were bluish and indistinct due to the distance.

"Centurion?" It was Kivi, and she looked worried. I didn't take this too seriously, because she practically always looked worried.

"What do you have, Specialist?"

"Rads. We've gotten a lot of them, and we're getting more every minute. This land is hot, sir."

That didn't overly surprise me, but it was a concern. The human body could suck up a lot of radiation for a while, but eventually those tiny particles popped too many of your cells and you began to die. It was like being hit by thousands of tiny

145

bullets every hour. Eventually, we would begin to bleed and turn to sludge inside.

"How long have we got?"

She shrugged. "In a few hours, we'll start to taste metal. Then, we'll become fatigued. After a few days out here we'll have difficulty fighting. That is, if we don't find shelter from the radiation."

"Have you seen any lead-lined bunkers out here?"

She shook her head and bit her lip. "Not so far, sir."

"Wonderful."

Kivi walked away, and I stared after her, but I didn't really see her. I was thinking about my entire command—actually, all of Legion Varus. We were stuck on an unfamiliar world without support or shelter. The deaths were going to come fast and hard—and possibly be permanent. We didn't know yet if any lifters had made it down with revival machines.

Taking stock of our supplies, I soon noticed we didn't have much food. The air however was breathable, and the water could be filtered and consumed. We even had a pretty good supply of ammo—but so far, there wasn't anyone to shoot.

My gaze drifted upward. I couldn't see the ships up there with my bare eyes. The sun was too big and bright for that. But I knew they were up there.

Checking my tapper, I watched until all the feeds from the sky fizzled out. That could only mean one thing: The fleet had retreated, and they'd left us down here to die alone.

-24-

We hunkered down in the crater until darkness fell. I was kind of waiting until Graves contacted me and established operational command of the cohort—but he never did. I was following orders to maintain long-range radio silence until relieved, but I didn't like it.

The word from nearby units indicated the lifter with our direct commanders aboard had been taken out on the way down. This was being whispered among the techs from other units in the vicinity. I didn't dare tell my troops, because morale was low enough already.

Instead, the line I gave them went something like this: "If we can hold out until dawn, we'll be fine. Relief will come."

It was all a lie, of course—but a good lie. Half the troops seemed to believe it, or at least, they wanted to.

When night fell, it was a thick velvety kind of darkness. There was no moon, and the sky was overcast. The only light was from fires in the distance, and the shimmering bluish glow of the streetlights from the massive Mogwa city.

Although we were right up against their dome, we weren't all that close to the city itself. There had to be at least ten kilometers of open land—farms and forests—before the buildings began. I guess that made sense, as they had to eat somehow. Back on Trantor, they'd paved over all the oceans with streets. They used the sunless seas underneath as a vast farm, growing algae and fish to consume.

Here, they hadn't progressed so far with their utter remapping of the natural environment. They were still tilling fields and harvesting food the old-fashioned way. Call me a hick, but I liked this world better than Trantor.

"McGill!" Kivi said, crawling to my position. We were all lying in the crater, trying to keep our heads down.

"What's up, Specialist?"

"I've got word from 7th Unit. They're under attack."

"From what?"

"I don't know. It's total confusion. Listen." She flicked at her tapper and strange sounds came into my headset. I heard screams, grunts, whirring noises and the rapid fire of power bolts.

Standing up, I lifted my head over the rim of the crater. Everyone else was keeping low.

To the north stood the glassy dome. It was blue-green in the night. It looked like an upside down salad bowl of gigantic proportions.

Off to the west... yes, I saw a firefight. Something was up—a vicious struggle a few hundred meters away.

Unlike my unit, Manfred had taken his 7th down into a gully. A crack in the ground. I could see bolts spraying up into the sky and flashes going on down in that gully.

"We're moving out!" I announced to a hundred upturned faces. "Light platoon, head for 7th Unit's position. Move quick and spread out. Look for trouble. Heavies, follow them when they're fifty meters out from the crater."

"Centurion?" Harris asked. He'd appeared out of nowhere and now stood at my elbow. "Is that wise? Maybe we should send relief, but not by charging everything we have over the landscape into god-knows-what."

I looked at him sourly. He was a man who always saw the safer path as more inviting.

"Sir," he said, interpreting my expression correctly. "I know Manfred is your friend and all, but—"

"Harris... you're right this time. I'll leave the specialists here. You take your heavies and follow Barton. I'll hold down the crater."

148

Harris swallowed and nodded. He didn't give me any more grief. He led his men in Barton's wake, and they crossed the open dirt to the gully where Manfred's unit was still engaged.

I zoomed in using both aerial buzzers and my HUD's optical powers. It was as if I was with them, watching over their shoulders as they raced toward the gully.

When they reached the edge and looked down, it was a scene of chaos. Bug-like things were moving among Manfred's troops, slaughtering them. The firefight had turned into butchery.

"What are those things?" I demanded.

As I was using Kivi's buzzers, she answered my question. "They appear to be... yes, I think they're drones, sir. Land-crawlers. About the size of a man, or a large dog... they have six limbs and walk like insects."

I studied them for a few seconds. My troops lined the wall of the gully, looking down. The mass of struggling human troops had merged up with the drones.

"Heavy platoon!" I shouted. "Harris, give the survivors supporting fire."

"It will be hard, sir. There's bound to be blue-on-blue."

"I know it—fire!"

They opened up, pelting the crawling machines with power-bolts from above. Some of them were knocked out—but not many.

The enemy drones turned their nozzle-like weapons upward, toward the rim of the gully. They fired plasma beams that resembled a gush of flame from a flamethrower, but this flame was more ghostly, and more carefully projected. Some of my heavies were struck, and they were all forced back.

"Not working, sir!" Harris called out to me.

I squinted at the scene, knowing there were still some of Manfred's troops down there, struggling to survive. I came to a hard decision.

"Light platoon," I said. "I want every other squad to toss in grenades. Aim for concentrations. Everyone take cover."

Barton was on the ball, as usual. She had her troops toss in grenades, all at once, less than thirty seconds after I'd given the order.

The results were dramatic. Dozens of blue-white flashes went off. They kept going and going, like sparks in a fusion generator. Brilliant points of light blinked again and again, blowing apart clumps of men and drones alike.

This time, the effects were clearly visible. The enemy had been damaged—but so had the human troops. After crawling around for a moment, stunned, the enemy realized Manfred's unit had been effectively destroyed.

Although many of the drones were damaged as well, that didn't deter them. They turned as one and began to scale the walls of the gully—they were moving up to attack my troops, now that 7th Unit had been annihilated.

"Harris! Barton! Full retreat! Return to the crater!"

They needed no further encouragement. They began bounding over the rough terrain in our direction.

Sargon loomed close. "What are we going to do, sir? Those things will boil up out of there and destroy us just like they did Manfred."

"I know it. Have we got any mortars?"

"No sir... no 88s, either. But... we've got some indirect-fire missiles. They're built to land on top of armor like that and destroy it from above."

I nodded, and I got my techs online and grilled them. I found out they had a few special EMP grenades.

"Unscrew the warheads from the rockets. Load in the EMPs and fire them into that gully."

Fortunately, most of our gear was Imperial. They'd long since designed frontier weapons to be as interchangeable as possible. This design goal came from the Galactics themselves. They tended to build weapons and gear that fit humanoids of various sizes and types. Since there were countless different kinds of aliens in the Empire, it only made sense to build stuff that a lot of different species could use.

The effort to achieve widespread compatibility had both positive and negative effects. As a benefit, we humans could usually pick up any piece of foreign equipment and use it. But there was a price to pay for that extreme flexibility. All our weapons tended to not fit us precisely right. Uniforms often had patched up tail-holes in the back, or extra finger-holes in the gloves—but all the gear was rugged. It all worked, and it was designed to be simple to operate.

Our modifications to the indirect-fire missiles were easy to make. In less than a minute, the first rockets streaked high, then did a ninety-degree twist and roared down into the gully. The EMP blasts did their work, and the drones in the gully were electrically disabled.

Unfortunately, not all the enemy drones had been in the gully when we'd unloaded on them. A number of them were still coming, chasing after Barton and Harris.

Barton and her lights made it to us first. They scrambled up the rim of the crater and threw themselves into it. Once on our side of that earthen barrier, they directed fire downward, spraying snap-rifle rounds at the approaching machines. This seemed to have little effect, but I didn't tell them to ceasefire. Maybe it would distract the enemy, or somebody might get a lucky hit now and then.

Harris and his men came next. These were the troops I was worried about. I watched as thirty-two heavy troopers were chased toward me by twenty alien machines. Speed-wise, the race was going badly. The aliens were catching up.

After we'd fired our indirect missiles into the gully, the drones stopped coming out of it. This indicated our gambit had been successful. I considered doing it again, landing an EMP volley right in the midst of Harris and his men.

The trouble with that idea was the armor the men wore. Heavy armor is *heavy*. It was far worse than the star-stuff I was wearing. It required servo motors and computers for most men to be able to move with speed. An EMP would blast all that circuitry, despite our shielding. It was designed to do exactly that.

I couldn't afford to disable the core of my heavy infantry. Barton's troops were already outgunned, and who knew how many more of these drones were running around. No—I was going to have to find another way to win this.

The drones buzzed and clattered, their six metal legs churning as they raced after Harris and his men. It occurred to me that the enemy machines were rather similar to Mogwa marines—but smaller. These things looked just like the mobile power-armor the marines wore, but they were empty, instead of being full of angry Galactics.

None of that mattered. These things were running down my men, and if they took out Harris, they would wipe out the rest of my command just as surely as they'd annihilated Manfred's.

"Weaponeers!" I shouted, standing up and shouldering an extra belcher. "Stand up and move out. We'll advance to contact. We can't let Harris face destruction out there alone."

Sargon and the others stood with me. They were startled, but they were game. The enemy had caught two of Harris' men already, and they were fighting to the death with force-blades flashing in the night. We didn't have enough time to let Harris' platoon reach the safety of the crater. Most of them weren't going to make it.

"Barton, snipe for any weakness you can find. Just don't hit us in the ass."

"Roger that, Centurion."

The storm of chattering snap-rifle fire quieted, turning into a steady crack of sniper fire. Meanwhile, every man with a belcher rushed downslope to meet the enemy. Seven of us in all charged together.

Harris stopped running when we reached his line. His men weren't going to be able to outrun their pursuers anyway. It was always better to turn and fight a pursuing enemy face-to-face than to be run down like stray dogs.

I was wearing my special armor, spun of Vulbite spit and stardust. That made me the man in the lightest kit, so I reached Harris and his ragged line of troops first.

The combat was wild, with the drones behaving like tiny tanks. They were as tough and fearless as only machines could be. Up close, their turrets spun and their nozzles gushed plasma. A man—even an armored man—was cooked alive when he took a full blast from that strange weapon.

My weaponeers with belchers on their shoulders helped even things up a lot. Dialing down the aperture to a single narrow beam that was no bigger around than a baseball, but which hit as hard as a truck, we lanced single machines down each time we managed to get a dead-on hit.

152

Harris' men were, in effect, pinning the enemy drones and giving my weaponeers the opportunity to aim and release deadly beams into their midst. Sometimes, the beam struck cleanly and destroyed a crawling mini-tank without a human being touched. Other times, we burned them both down together into a confusing slag of man and machine.

Right at the end, the enemy seemed to comprehend who their real enemy was. Two of the tanks turned their swiveling nozzles onto Washburn, who'd moved close to me and had a habit of whooping whenever he destroyed one of the enemy.

Two streams of liquid fire struck him at once, from two different angles. He went to his knees, trying to lift his belcher for one last defiant strike—but the power of the enemy weapons overwhelmed him, and he sagged down, burning alive. Even the heaviest armor we had, that worn by weaponeers, wasn't enough to stop the enemy's attack.

In revenge, the rest of us cooked the two drones, and they were left smoldering and glowing red with heat.

After that, it was soon over. The drones kept falling until none were left.

We staggered, panting with exertion. Men called for the bio techs, who rushed down from the crater to patch them up while they lay on the smoking earth in the darkness. No one among the wounded was going to be slated for a recycle today, because we didn't know if there was a single revival machine on the planet that could print out a new human.

We'd won a battle, but I'd now lost close to half my men—half my heavies, that is. The men that counted the most.

-25-

In the aftermath of the battle, we didn't lounge around. No one knew if the drones were coming again with a fresh wave of machines. We hustled up the crumbling slopes of our home crater, and we threw ourselves into it.

While the heavies and weaponeers took a breather and nursed their wounds, I ordered Barton's lights to retrieve the wounded, rob the dead, and collect every scrap of useful gear we could.

"At least we won't starve now," Harris said. He'd taken a hit in the leg, and he was limping. Normally, I might entertain the thought of a recycle for him—but tonight, that was out of the question.

He hobbled to my position and threw himself down with a grunt.

"How's that leg?" I asked him.

He eyed me coldly for a moment. It was only natural to suspect your commander of grim things when you were wounded on the modern battlefield. But after giving it a moment's thought, he shrugged.

"I think it's pretty much cooked. I took a shot from one of those plasma gushers—only a few seconds, but a few seconds in a blast furnace can do all sorts of damage."

"Yeah… your armor is metal, so it probably carries the heat better than my stuff."

He eyed my black flexible armor thoughtfully. He reached out and pinched the arm, which was thick and rubbery.

"I wish we had more of this stuff," he said.

"You know who just got a suit? Direct from Central?"

His eyes narrowed. "Who?"

"Tribune Winslade, our finest."

"Shit…"

We both knew that Winslade rarely took to the battlefield in person. Even now, he'd probably bugged out with the fleet.

"Sir?" Harris asked. "If those metal monsters come up here in strength, well… we're toast."

"Agreed. What's your point, Harris?"

He pointed to my tapper. "What about contacting Graves? Or whoever is in fucking charge of this cluster?"

I heaved a sigh. "We're supposed to maintain radio silence until command—"

Harris forced himself up on one elbow. "Sir, I don't want to rain on your parade, but we just got our asses kicked by unknown assailants. We might not last until dawn. Manfred didn't."

I thought that over. I counted my men again. If you thought about it as Manfred's unit and mine combined, we'd lost around seventy percent of two units. That was rough.

"Kivi?" I called out. "Get over here."

She hustled to my position and flopped down opposite Harris, who'd rolled onto his back to nurse his burned leg. He was opening up the armor and poking at it, spraying on foamy new skin cells, disinfectants and salves.

"Yes, centurion?" she asked.

"What's that pack of techs doing over there? They've been poking at something big they dragged up from the battleground."

"That's a dead drone, sir. We're trying to figure out how it ticks."

I thought that over. "You pulled an alien machine into our camp without telling me?"

"Yessir."

"What if it wakes up, or explodes, or sends out a distress signal or something?"

She shrugged. "Then we're slightly more screwed than we are right now, sir."

I nodded, unable to counter her argument. "What have you learned so far?"

"Not much," she admitted. "It's a drone, and it's advanced in design, but not insanely so. The basic construction is similar to a Mogwa marine's power-armor. The weaponry is unusual, however. Those plasma cannons are unknown to us. Designed for antipersonnel use, I figure."

"Damned good at it, too," grumbled Harris. He was still grimacing and poking at his leg.

"Wrap that thing up or cut it off, Harris," I told him. "Can you walk or not?"

Those words were a bald threat when they came from your commander, and Harris knew it. He finished fussing with his leg, slapped the plates closed over his shin and bared his teeth as he struggled to his feet. He walked around gingerly for a moment, testing it.

"Right as rain, Centurion."

"Good. Go count your heavies and patch them up. We're moving out within the hour."

"Moving out? To where?"

"You have your orders, Harris."

Grumbling, he limped away and started shouting at his men.

Kivi watched him go. "Where are we going?" she asked me.

I stood up and brushed my suit off. "That drone you're dissecting is Imperial-made, right?"

"Yes. I guess it must be."

I pointed toward the dome. "Where do you think it came from? How do you think it got into the middle of Manfred's gully without him expecting it, or seeing it coming?"

She stared at me for a moment. Then she stood with me, looking toward the dome, which was a shining glassy bubble in the night. Then she looked toward the gully where Manfred and his men had perished.

"You think there's a tunnel or something? In the middle of that ditch?"

Nodding, I looked over the landscape. The more I thought about it, the more I wanted to move out right now. If the enemy really was coming out of there, we didn't have much time to lose.

Contacting Harris and Barton, I spoke into their headsets directly. "I'm canceling that last order, Harris."

"Ah, jeez. That's great news, sir. You had me worried."

"What order?" Barton asked.

"The centurion was talking about marching out of here," Harris asked. "I'm glad you've come to your senses, sir."

"You might want to hold back on that feeling, Harris. The part I'm changing my mind on is the bit about waiting for an hour. We're moving out right now."

"Um…" Barton said. "Where to, sir?"

"The gully. Let's find out who killed Manfred, and how they got in there in the first place. With any luck, we'll find some of them are still alive and squirming down there."

"Seriously?" Harris exclaimed. "Why don't you just shoot me right now?"

"That can be arranged, Adjunct."

He fell silent for a few moments. "Sorry, sir."

"Apology accepted. Barton, advance with your lights. Scout Manfred's pit. When you sound the all-clear, I'll move up the rest to support you. If you encounter stiff resistance, skirmish and fall back to this crater. Don't expect support."

"On it, Centurion!"

She bounced up and began kicking her lights into order. Wide-eyed recruits scrambled to obey her. A minute or two later, Harris and I watched from the crater rim as they raced off into the dark. No one was running suit lights, but they had their night vision faceplates engaged. If they ran into more machines, they'd be sure to take the worst of it—but that was the job of light troopers in the legions.

It always had been, even back in Roman times.

157

-26-

To tell the truth, I half expected a firefight to erupt out there in the darkness. If it did happen, I knew Barton's team would be slaughtered.

Breathing shallowly, tense and watching, we gave it five minutes. Then five more.

I wanted to call out to Barton, but I didn't do it. At this range, radio silence was impossible. We could dampen and hide our signals at close range, especially when in line of sight, but there was a limit to that stealth tech.

"Kivi," I said at last, "get ready to send up some buzzers again. Have them fly nap-of-the earth, and—"

"Sir!" Harris called out, pointing downhill into the dark. "I see movement."

I turned up my night vision, and I saw it too. Our uniforms were designed not to emit much heat, of course. They were as thermally neutral as the environment around them, reflecting whatever was on the opposite side of any point on a troopers' suit. But with light-gathering turned way up I saw what Harris was talking about. Figures were racing in our direction.

"What are those things?" he asked.

"Kivi, send the buzzers now."

She released several, but by the time they reached the approaching targets, we were able to identify them ourselves.

It was Barton's platoon, running for all they were worth over the broken stones and ashes.

When she sprinted up the slope and dove between Harris and me, we grabbed her, expecting she was wounded, but she was hale and whole.

Harris flopped down on his back, breathing almost as hard as Barton was.

"Damn, girl, we almost lit you up. What were you running from, anyways?"

"Sir," she said, addressing me between puffs. "We spotted another of the machines. It was poking around, coming out of the gully. It seemed to be scouting the area, counting the dead."

"Just one machine?"

"Yessir."

I nodded, thinking that over. It confirmed all my suspicions. If the machines really had come out of that hole, they were clearly thinking of doing it again.

"Dammit," I said. "Why isn't anyone from headquarters talking to us?"

Harris and Barton looked at each other.

"What?" I asked.

"Uh… sir?" Harris said. "I don't think there *is* a headquarters. I think 3rd cohort is all out here, huddling in the dark, waiting for Santa—but he's not coming."

I eyed them both. "All right… Kivi!"

She came hustling over. She'd been poking at her dead drone again.

"Get out the com gear," I told her. "We're going to start transmitting."

"Wait a second," she said, scrambling with her equipment. "How about I send an automated buzzer—no streaming back data—to every landing spot we know of? They'll come back in thirty minutes, and we can count the number of dead in the cohort."

"What if those spots are overrun?" Harris complained. "What if the unit assigned to each position has found better ground, or retreated, or—?"

"Shut up, Harris," I told him. "Launch your buzzers, Kivi. It's a good idea."

She arranged the flock and set them off, one at a time. Soon a dozen of the little things were skimming over the landscape in every direction. They were programmed to fly to a certain set of coordinates, scan the area, then return and download their video. That was much safer than broadcasting our position to everyone in the region.

We waited tensely for ten minutes. Then fifteen. Finally, the first of our automated scouts returned.

Kivi caught it out of the air and drained the scans into her computer. I huddled with her to watch it play out on her pack-computer screens.

The video was disappointing. The unit had found troops—but they were all dead. Apparently, less than half of the 4th had made it to their rally point. They'd then been destroyed by someone or something.

The next buzzer came back a moment later. It was damaged, barely able to fly.

"It's been shot," Kivi told me.

"By what?"

"Snap-rifle fire, if I had to guess."

We reviewed the vids, and sure enough, we saw what was left of a hunkered down unit. They were in a building of sorts, a ruin with the roof blown off of it. They fired at the buzzer first, asking questions later.

"A least most of them are alive," I said.

In the meantime, Kivi had caught two more. I finally found something interesting when the sixth one came back.

"Is that…?" Kivi asked. "Oh, no."

"Yeah… it's a crashed lifter. That's headquarters, right there. Now, give me your com-pack. I'm calling in."

She licked her lips, then nodded and handed it over. No one was ever going to call us. Not if the lifter carrying the brass had been shot down.

"Wait!" she said, putting her gloved hand over the pickup. "How about this? How about we fly a buzzer to a bullshit location and transmit from there?"

I nodded. "Make it quick."

She rigged up what she could, and I recorded a message. It was in code, and it reported our status, coordinates and casualties. Then I fired the buzzer off away from the dome to a position we knew was lacking any known formation of troops.

160

I included a quick explanation concerning how we did the deception to hide our position.

The buzzer flew, it transmitted, and we listened to our own message in silence. No one responded for a long time. After ten more minutes, I was about to try something more drastic when a message came in from someone else.

"I might have known that Centurion McGill of 3ʳᵈ Unit would be the first to lose his nerve and transmit an SOS," said a familiar voice. It was Tribune Winslade, our legion commander. "Graves is dead, so I've taken over command of his cohort for the time being."

I sighed in relief. Sure, I kind of hated Winslade—everyone did. But it was better to have a bad living commander than no officer in charge at all.

"Lest I get more of these panicky transmissions, be it known that although 3ʳᵈ cohort's lifter crashed, it was not entirely destroyed. Key members of the command staff—such as myself—are still alive and sheltering in a large complex of buildings near the reservoir to the southwest."

We all craned our necks around and gazed in that direction. Checking the coordinates he gave us next, we were surprised. It was quite a distance from the crashed lifter.

"They must have high-tailed it a long way from the wreck," Harris commented.

"Further," Winslade continued, "we have a single surviving revival machine in our possession. Here's my new orders, to all units: withdraw under the cover of darkness and move to my position here. Winslade out."

That was it. Everyone clapped me on the back and congratulated me on stirring the pot. Harris in particular felt expansive.

"That was a smooth move, McGill," he said. "I couldn't have done better myself. Your one message kicked Winslade in the pants and made him start doing his job."

Shrugging, I didn't comment. I was thinking hard. There was at least one of those automated mini-tanks in the area. If we moved out in the open, we might be reported and inviting an attack.

"Okay," I said, coming up with a tactical plan. "We're moving out in ten. Barton, put one squad on each side of us, and one out front."

"I don't have that many troops left, sir."

"Right, right. Let's see… you've only got one veteran left? Take Moller. She'll run a flank with a fire team. Send another team to the other side with your vet, and you command the front line."

Barton rushed away to follow my orders. Harris looked after her wonderingly. "I don't think I've ever seen anyone more eager to die on a shit-hole planet than Adjunct Barton."

"She gets the job done."

"You think she's still trying to earn brownie-points? I mean, to get out of Varus and return to Victrix?"

I didn't meet his eye. During the long flight aboard *Dominus,* Barton had suggested she was doing just that.

"What's it been?" I asked him. "A decade since she joined our unit? How long is she still going to be the new girl you suspect of everything?"

"A decade…? Really?" he said. "Huh…That's crazy, but I think you're right."

He finally shut up, and we got the heavies and the auxiliaries up and marching. I had to shoot seven soldiers who couldn't stand. Harris was limping, but he could keep up.

Now that we knew we had at least one revival machine in service, I felt comfortable about recycling the wounded. It wasn't a nice job, but someone had to do it. As the unit commander, the task fell to me. It was just another day in the life of a centurion.

-27-

On the way, things were dicey. We saw another unit about a kilometer north of us, and we signaled to them. It was the 9th.

Just as our two groups were moving together, planning to merge up, something went wrong.

"They're getting hit," Sargon said. "Are we going to rescue them, boss?"

I stared and used my HUD to zoom in. A squad of the enemy machines had found them. The Lord only knew where they'd come from. We couldn't do anything from this distance, we'd have to get in close to be effective with belchers and missiles.

Gritting my teeth, I shook my head. "We wouldn't get there in time. If we rush over there, it will be several minutes. We might help, but it will probably be over before we reach them."

"Yeah, but what if—"

A heavy gauntlet fell on Sargon's shoulder. It was Harris.

"The centurion has made his call, Veteran. Let's move on. By morning, we'll meet up with whatever hot date you're thinking about from the 9th. I promise."

Sargon looked annoyed, but he didn't complain openly. "Yessir," he mumbled and wandered off.

I knew it was rough on group morale to abandon troops in need. I felt that, too. But we had orders, and we were close to reaching Winslade's position.

Less than thirty minutes later, we were ordered to identify ourselves by pickets. We moved past them and kept marching.

Winslade's complex of large buildings turned out to be a shutdown manufacturing plant. We entered and as soon as I was announced to Winslade, I was summoned to his headquarters.

Naturally, he'd set up camp in the safest spot in the region. This amounted to an underground bunker of sorts. It was really the basement of the plant, but it served him well.

"Centurion McGill, 3rd Unit, reporting, sir!"

Winslade didn't even look at me. He was frowning down at a battle table. As we watched, formations of virtual troops moved around. The group labeled with a number 3 was inside the complex now.

Winslade reached out a finger and tapped at the hologram. Another unit with the number 9 floating over it was still struggling over the rough landscape to the north of the complex.

"You abandoned the 9th, I noticed," he said without looking at me. "That was unexpected."

"Well sir, I figured we couldn't make it in time to save them, and—"

Winslade put a gloved hand up and spread his fingers wide to stop me. "Don't misunderstand. I was impressed. It was the right thing to do—it just seemed uncharacteristically sensible."

I shrugged. "Well sir, I'm half-retarded on a good day, but our whole cohort is in a bad way out here. I didn't think I could risk a rescue that was likely to fail."

Winslade looked at me at last, and he nodded. "We *are* in trouble. What have you seen?"

I gave him all our buzzer vids from the front. I showed him the downed lifter, the mini-tanks in action, and a couple of unit locations that appeared to be overrun and wiped out.

"This is startling, but it fits well with all the intel we have. You're the first unit to get here that's had a serious fight with these machines and lived to tell about it. I want you to brief all the commanders I pull together. We have to know what we're up against."

"Uh... yessir. When would that be?"

"Ten minutes, I should think. I'll summon them. We have six centurions and a primus available at the moment."

Stepping aside, I began doing everything on my emergency list. The top item consisted of getting my dead troops on the revival queue. Unfortunately, that was a long line indeed.

To my surprise, I saw several names being deleted almost as fast as I reported them.

"What the hell is this?" I demanded. "My men are getting kicked off the list?"

One of the officers had come close to look at the tactical displays. It was Primus Collins, a woman who'd never liked me. She'd argued with me more than once on Green World and Ice World, too. Today, she was yawning and stretching like a cat that had just risen from a long nap. That was irritating to me, as I'd just busted a hump coming across a wasteland to get here.

"Get used to it," she said. "Revivals are being rejected right and left today."

"Why?"

She shrugged. "We don't have enough machines for one thing. More importantly, they're being strict about it. If you don't have clear evidence that a trooper is dead—he's marked MIA."

That was a chilling statement. The worst thing that could happen to a legionnaire was to be lost, instead of found stone dead. If they couldn't verify your death, they left you off the revival lists.

I studied those who were being rejected. One name stood out in particular. "Adjunct Leeson? He's my most senior man."

"Tough break, there," Collins said, sounding like she couldn't give two shits.

"Sure, I don't have a photo of his body, but his drop-pod went off-course and vanished. From the trajectory of the drop, it's easy to see he hit the dome and was pulped. I lost a number of men that way—twenty of them."

Collins twisted up her lips and nodded slowly. She took out an apple and began chewing on it. Only a high-level officer would have something like fresh fruit in the middle of a hard campaign.

165

I felt a surge of dislike and frustration. I wanted Leeson back. I wanted all of them back.

Turning away from Collins, I marched over to Winslade and tried to get his attention.

"Yes, yes, McGill. We're not ready for your briefing yet. Can't you see that only half the centurions are here?"'

"Sir, why are my men getting rejected and kicked off the revival queue? They died hard out there."

"I'm sure they did. It's very regrettable. But if you haven't noticed, we have one revival machine in the vicinity. We might get more, or we might not."

"Yessir, I get all that. I'm not saying these men shouldn't be prioritized against the needs of the legion but they're being marked as MIA. That means they'll *never* get a revive."

Winslade sucked in a breath and let it go. "McGill, your men aren't necessarily permed. If you fight well—if all of us do—we'll chase these mini-tanks back to the dome and—"

"The dome, sir?"

"Yes, of course. Where did you think they came from?"

My mouth dropped open and stayed that way. Winslade continued to explain to me that we were on a Mogwa planet, and therefore we couldn't be caught doing sloppy things like reviving people we weren't sure were dead. After a minute or so, I interrupted him.

"Sir? Did you say the mini-tanks came from the dome itself?"

"Yes, of course. I thought you knew that. You fought them, didn't you? They came out of that tunnel in the midst of Manfred's unit. A dumb place to set up camp, as it turned out."

"But sir... we're here to reinforce the Mogwa. Why are they killing our troops?"

Winslade shrugged. "We're slave-troops, McGill. Apparently, no one yet has bothered to reprogram their machines. When they find a soldier, and that soldier fires on them, they return fire. Think about it: did you fire on them first, or did they fire on you?"

I did think about it for a moment. "Manfred was in a death-fight with them. We came to his aid."

He pointed a thin finger at me. "You see that? Hubris. Jumping to conclusions. Classic mistakes of the inexperienced. The first rule of these technological nightmares is this: if you shoot at them, they shoot back. That course of action is therefore ill-advised."

-28-

After learning that the mini-tank drones were possibly not as dangerous as we thought, I had to rethink our entire tactical situation. Without an army of robots coming for us, we were in better shape than I had assumed—but we weren't out of the woods yet. Winslade and his snotty sidekick Primus Collins made that point very clear.

"It's my opinion," Winslade said, "that our position here is untenable. We'll have to pull out and withdraw farther from the dome itself."

"Farther away? What in the hell?" I blurted out.

My outburst caused the crowd of centurions to shuffle away from me. I didn't recall farting, but they were sure acting like I had.

"McGill...?" Winslade said. He made a show of checking a timer on his tapper. "Another interruption? What? Has it even been ten minutes yet?"

"Sir, if I may—"

"If you may what? Interrupt me again?"

I closed my big yap and squinted. It was hard to be quiet. I'd killed Winslade about the same number of times as I'd felt respect for him. We didn't have what you might call a perfect professional relationship.

At last, he sighed. "All right, all right. Out with it. I can see you're about to burst and piss all over the carpet. What is it this time, man?"

168

"Sir, we're here to save the Mogwa inside that dome. We're not even inside the dome yet. How can we protect them if we retreat even farther away?"

Winslade snorted. "McGill... have you noticed we haven't been received with open arms? There are no Mogwa maidens—perish the thought—throwing flowers in our path."

"Huh...?" I said, blinking.

"I mean that we *can't* get inside that frigging dome. None of us can—not Legion Varus, not Legion Victrix, not even a single stinking Blood Worlder has been allowed to pass inside. Four legions of us, all with devastating losses, and we're being ignored like beggars by these ungrateful Galactics."

Thinking that over, I began to nod. "That makes perfect sense, sir."

He eyed me for a moment. "Why?"

"Because they're Galactics. They're better than us. We're slave troops. We might be ornery if we got into their nice dome, we might tromp on their flowers or whiz on their furniture or something."

"What are you talking about?"

"Without a Mogwa leader to speak for us, sir, no Mogwa will give us the time of day. It would have to be someone respected like Sateekas, too."

Winslade put his hand to his narrow chin. His fingers massaged his jaw, and he did that for so long that it became cringey.

"You might be onto something there. You're saying we need some kind of introduction to get their attention? They're ignoring every transmission, every—"

"That's right, sir. We're animals to them. Chattel, slaves, dogs that bark in the night."

"Well then, how do you propose that we get their attention and get inside that frigging dome?"

Pausing before I answered, I gave it a think. Then I came up with an idea. It was iffy, but then, my plans always were.

"I think I can do it. But not if we waste time pulling out and moving farther from the dome itself. We'll be left outside forever if we do that."

169

"Hmm… I suspect you've got some insane scheme in mind, yes?"

"Ah… Primus?" another voice interrupted. This time, it was Primus Collins. She'd stopped looking bored, exchanging that expression for one of growing alarm.

"Yes?" Winslade asked, turning toward her.

She pointed at me. "Tribune Winslade, I know Turov put you in operational command of this sector, but you're not seriously considering taking advice from this madman, are you? I would caution you not to listen to him—in fact, I think he should be removed from our command bunker for insubordination."

Winslade nodded thoughtfully. Then, he turned back toward me. "McGill, we have very little time. We must withdraw from this area within hours. Even now, we're making those arrangements."

My mind was full of comments about chickens and rainstorms, but I held my tongue. That kind of criticism, no matter how valid, never made anyone happy. "I think I can do something, sir. I think I can get inside that dome. But I need several hours to do it."

Primus Collins approached the table. Her hands were fists. To me, it looked like her hands were a bit shaky as well. I wasn't sure if that was from anger or fright—it could have been either, or a combination of both. She was a volatile woman.

"We've all done the math, fool," she told me. "We've lost the battle in space, and we're about to lose it on the ground. It's only a matter of time before the enemy ships return to continue dropping asteroids on the dome. Even at this distance, we'll be destroyed by the shockwave of any serious strike."

It was my turn to look alarmed. I'd kind of forgotten about all that business of the enemy fleet trying to destroy the big Mogwa City. When we'd arrived here at Segin, we'd seen them in action, but we'd driven them off and even destroyed the tugs that lingered to bait us into orbit.

But now, according to Collins, they were coming back. Winslade and she were in the command bunker, so they definitely had better intel on the topic than I did. Their command lifter had scanners and the like to paint a tactical picture of City World along with whatever was hanging above the clouds in space.

Collins altered the display, first zooming out, then adding some perspective. Segin was a globe in the center of the hologram. We could see three small vessels heading toward the planet, each of them dragging something bigger than the tugs themselves.

"Hours," she announced. "Less than twenty, if our estimates are correct. That's all we've got before the first of those rocks falls on top of us. The Mogwa dome might hold, but we will probably die."

"I get it," I said. "I understand the danger, and this isn't a happy situation for any of us. But at the same time, I'm not ready to give up on this mission. I don't think we should run off and hide, pissing our pants in a cave somewhere while this war plays out without our participation."

Primus Collins came at me then. She'd been unhappy before, but now she was steaming mad. "You'll follow orders, McGill. That's what you'll do, or I'll shoot you myself."

We faced off, and she put her hand on her sidearm. As she was my superior officer, she had the right to gun me down on the spot. If two other officers of her rank and above agreed, she could make it permanent. That was Legion Law.

But I didn't cower. I stood tall, and I stared at her—daring her to do it.

"Just a moment," Winslade said.

We both turned to look at him.

"McGill… it pains me to admit this… but I'm willing to give you a chance. How long do you need to perform this miracle of yours?"

"Twenty hours will be plenty," I said.

Collins made a squawking sound, but Winslade waved for her to be quiet. "That won't do, McGill. We do actually have to move out, you see. We have to withdraw to a safe distance. Even if—by some act of a stray deity—the Mogwa do agree to let us enter their dome it must come sooner than twenty hours."

I could see his point. I squinted at the holotable, thinking hard. It would take a few hours just to reach the spot I was

171

thinking of on foot. That would make things pretty tight for my banged-up unit.

"All right," I said. "I think I can do it—but I'll need some skimmers. Not all of them, just enough to take my unit close to the dome and drop us off."

"Insanity!" Collins sputtered. "Winslade, are you seriously considering this? I'm going to have to—"

Winslade put a gloved hand into her face, palm out. He didn't look at her at all. He was eyeing me thoughtfully and thinking hard. Collins didn't seem to like that, but she did shut up.

"You've done surprising things in the past, McGill. I hope you can pull off another miracle. You'll get one skimmer and no more than twenty minutes to use it."

"All right, I'll take it," I heard myself saying. "But sir, could you find a way to accelerate some revives for me? I'm short a lot of good men."

Winslade made a farting sound with his mouth. "We have one revival machine—one. Even if I were willing to grant your request, I couldn't get more than a single man into play before you have to leave on the mission."

"One man... all right. I'll take that. Give me Adjunct Leeson."

"No!" Primus Collins interjected. She'd been holding her water for a few minutes now, but she'd finally lost it again. "Right now, that machine is halfway done with reviving my chief of staff. It's a sick waste to recycle him without cause."

Suddenly, I knew why Collins was in here bossing Winslade around. She had her own agenda.

"Hmm..." Winslade said, checking things on his tapper. "It would seem that you're correct. Request denied, McGill. Go work your miracle with what you have."

Dismayed, I shook my head. "I need my officers, sir. I need a man who's capable with specialized gear."

Winslade shrugged and pursed his lips. He turned slowly, scanning the room. His skinny finger finally pointed into the darkest corner.

Following his gesture, I spotted a man I hadn't noticed before. It was none other than Gary, the adjunct who'd gotten Galina to land his ass on an unknown world for the first time.

"Take that man. He's an officer, and he's wasting space in my command bunker at the moment."

Gary and I looked at each other, startled. Neither one of us liked the proposal.

"Sir," I said, "Gary's a fine fellow and all, but I don't think—"

"He's all you're going to get. Take him or leave him, I really don't care. But I suggest you get going, McGill. You're twenty minutes are now nineteen in total."

"Uh… what? You've started that clock already?"

Collins made a smug gesture. She pointed at the battle planning table. She'd helpfully brought up a clock app and started a countdown.

I opened my mouth to object, but Winslade wasn't having any of it. "Dismissed, Centurion. Get out of my bunker—we've got work to do."

I was annoyed, but I'm also a man who knows how to hustle. I strode to Gary and rapped my knuckles on his chest. "Get your kit. Meet me on the landing strip."

Gary looked stunned. He reached for a bag and his cap, and he followed me out of the place.

"McGill, this is crazy. I don't—"

"Look, Gary," I said, turning on him. "Your ass is mine now. We're on a battlefield, and we're in an emergency situation." While I spoke, I drew my pistol and checked the charge. Then I snapped the breach shut. "If you're going to give me any kind of trouble, let me know immediately. I'll put you down as is my right and duty. Maybe you'll get a revive someday, maybe not, but you'll stop being my problem."

Gary gaped at me and my pistol. He'd flown a desk for decades, and he wasn't really accustomed to how things worked in the real legions.

"I'm… I'm sorry, sir," he stammered. "I'll meet you at the skimmer."

"All right. But don't be late. We're taking off in five, and you'll be marked as AWOL if you're not there."

Gary ran off like his ass was on fire. I forgot about him and began shouting orders into my tapper. Harris groaned aloud when he learned he was going to be accompanying me.

"Round up every heavy we have who's able-bodied—and that includes you."

"Sir, I took a serious injury out there—"

"My tapper says Winslade's bio people have approved you for duty. Are you shirking, Adjunct?"

The channel was muted for a few seconds. I could almost hear the awful show of cursing Harris must be putting on. When he came back on he sounded resigned to his fate. "I'm headed for the skimmers, sir."

Moving at a steady running pace, I reached the skimmer first. An irritated pilot lowered the loading ramp.

Barton showed up next with a pack of her lights in her wake. I stopped her as she rushed to board.

"Not everyone will fit on this skimmer, Erin," I told her.

"But sir, if we take two trips—"

I shook my head. "Winslade isn't even giving us time for one run. You stay here and tag along with the rest of the cohort. Get my people revived if you can. You're in command until Leeson or I start breathing again."

She looked troubled, but she didn't argue. She rarely did. I took one squad of her light troopers, the ones who looked like they were in the best condition. By the time they were all loaded up and seated, Harris was hustling up the ramp. He had a full squad of heavies behind him. They looked tired, but they were game.

Next came the specialists I'd chosen. Among them were Kivi and Sargon.

Then, just as we were about to raise the ramp and lift off, a figure in black came racing across the airfield. I didn't recognize him, but out of curiosity, I waved for the pilot to wait for thirty more seconds.

The man was wearing armor—special armor, like mine. Squinting and staring, I had a sudden thought.

"You've got to be shitting me..." I said aloud.

Then the stranger flipped up his faceplate, and I realized I *did* know him.

"Sorry sir, hard to get this kit up over your hips quickly. I guess you know all about that."

It was Gary, and he was wearing a twin suit to my very special suit of armor.

The lifter took off in a blast of exhaust and debris. The ramp was still rising, and I had to grab hold of Gary before he tumbled to the hard ground as it spiraled away below us.

It was Harris who first demanded answers. "Hey, Gary? Where the fuck did you get that kit? Do you have any idea how long I've been requesting gear like that? Do you know how many times I've been *killed* because I didn't have a suit?"

Harris was truly pissed, and for once, I couldn't blame him.

"Um…" Gary said. "I don't understand, Adjunct. Back at Central, lots of officers have them."

"Like who?"

Gary shrugged. "Like Praetor Drusus, and Praetor Wurtenburger, and Equestrian—"

"The brass, huh?" Harris demanded. "The fat prigs who never go out into the field?"

"Um… I guess so…"

Suddenly, Gary choked and gasped. He grabbed at his belly.

We all looked down. Harris had stabbed his combat knife into the man's gut. It would have been a killing thrust, but the armor had turned the blade.

Harris lifted his knife and flipped it in his hand. "Looks like it's the genuine article," he said. "Just checking for you, kid."

He clapped him on the back and walked away, muttering to himself.

Gary gaped and rubbed at his belly, which was no doubt smarting a bit underneath his fancy armor. "What the hell was that for?"

I smiled. "Lucky for you he's in a good mood. Oh, and you might consider putting some more padding under that suit of yours. Off the rack, it's good at stopping punctures, but you can still get plenty banged-up in combat."

The stunned adjunct let me steer him to a jump-seat. I told him to strap in and stay quiet. Then I opened a chat channel with my officers and noncoms. It was time to do a little planning during the ten minute flight to our destination.

"3rd Unit, we've been given a golden opportunity today. We're truly going to become the few and the proud of Legion Varus."

A number of groans could be heard, but I ignored them.

"Troops, we're returning to the site of Manfred's last stand. Unlike 7th Unit, we're not going to make the single critical mistake that they did."

I had their attention now. There was a circle of frowning faces, worried eyes and a few open mouths staring back at me.

"What Manfred did wrong, is he shot at these little drone tanks first. That triggered their software. It set them off, putting them into kill-mode. If we avoid that single error, we should be fine."

A hand was up—several in fact. I ignored Harris, and Sargon, and several other whiners. Surprised to see Gary raise his hand, I called on him. I was a little bit curious as to what he might have to say.

"Adjunct Gary Dahmen," I said. "In case the rest of you don't know, Gary is joining us as our replacement for Adjunct Leeson."

A lot of suspicious, unwelcoming eyes traveled to look Gary over. He didn't look very impressive. He was a big enough man, but he carried himself like he was a little soft or something. He was also obviously in his thirties, which made him physically older than most of us. We Varus types tended to die a lot and come back out of the machines in prime condition.

177

Faking a smile and a nod, I gestured for Gary to speak.

He cleared his throat and swallowed. "Troops, I'm Adjunct Dahmen. Our centurion asked for questions, and I have one. What if we've already permanently compromised our status with these robots?"

"What?" I asked, blinking.

"I mean... I know how these automaton brains tend to think. Once they've learned a given target is hostile it's been classified for good. Not shooting at them might not convince them of anything from this point forward."

"Whoa, whoa, whoa," Harris said, lifting his arms and pointing a bouncing finger at Gary. He looked at me. "This hog might have a point, Centurion. That *is* how machines think. We actually opened fire on those bugs. They've definitely classified us as hostile. It might not matter what we do when we reach the LZ."

I took a second to consider the point. I had to admit, Gary might be right. But then, if that was true, the mission was tits-up in the first place. We might as well fly home immediately.

I didn't want to take that step. I wanted to take the risk. I wanted to give this longshot a chance.

Accordingly, I grinned at them. Then I slapped my knee hard and laughed. "That's the dumbest thing I've heard all damned day. Weren't you guys there at the briefing in Winslade's bunker—oh yeah, that's right, you *weren't* there. Now let me tell you how this whole thing is going to go down. We're going to jump off that ramp and down into that gully. If we have any luck at all, there will be no drones, no nothing. We'll find whatever tunnel they used to get out of the dome and follow it back into the Mogwa city."

This was too much for Harris. He appeared to be having some kind of conniption.

"What is it, Adjunct?"

"Sir, we have no idea if such a tunnel even exists or not."

"Not so. It must exist. Those robots must have come from somewhere."

Harris crossed his arms and looked glum.

A tone sounded then, and yellow warning lights lit up all over the hold. We, the human cargo the skimmer was carrying, were being warned the flight was coming to an end. At the exact same instant, the aircraft tilted and slanted down toward the ground. Its jets were screaming a new tune, and we all reached out a hand to grab hold of any strap we could.

"All right, that's our cue!" I roared at them. "I want everyone and every pack of gear off this bird thirty seconds after we touch down."

The ship landed less than a minute later. The rear ramp dropped, and we hustled out into the open.

"Go-go-go!" every officer and noncom shouted together.

The troops obeyed, scrambling for the ramp.

Outside, the air was filled with smoke and soot. We walked over burnt bodies and broken machines. The gully was full of death and destruction.

"Let's go!" I shouted, leading the way.

My men trudged for the gully, and the skimmer vaulted into the air behind us a moment later. The pilot wasn't taking any chances.

"Come on," Harris shouted. "Search this dung pit. Let's find the centurion's magic tunnel."

I glanced at him, as his words didn't seem overly respectful. He didn't meet my eye.

Troops spread out and poked around. We looked high and low. We rolled over every dead, stiff corpse and shoved broken robots away from humps in the ground.

We found nothing. After about twenty minutes, grumbling could be heard—more than normal, that is.

"Centurion," Gary said, coming close and almost whispering. "I don't think there's anything down here."

"Where is it then, Adjunct Dahmen?" I asked. "Where did those robots come from?"

He pointed at the glassy dome, which stood no more than a hundred meters off. "From inside there, sir."

"Obviously. But how did the robots get through that barrier and out into our territory?"

Gary frowned, giving the question a serious thought. "Maybe they didn't use a tunnel. Maybe the dome can be crossed by these robots. Maybe they have a field, or a friend-or-foe code, or something."

179

I grabbed onto his helmet and pulled him close. "Are you telling me there's no way for us to get inside?"

"I don't know—but I don't see any tunnels, sir."

I let go of him, and he staggered back. I tried to think it through. Every sign had indicated that Manfred had been ambushed. If not from within this gully, then the source of the enemy intrusion had to be close.

"Widen the search. Let's go topside. We're going to locate and examine every nook and cranny we can."

The troops groaned.

"Sir," Harris said, "the sun is going down. If we hustle, starting right now, we might be able to reach Winslade and rejoin his forces before they withdraw. We'd keep the cohort together, sir."

He was in earnest, and he had a good point. There was no need to get stubborn and keep looking for something that wasn't possible to find.

The trouble was, I'm a very stubborn man. Just ask any girl I ever took on a date. I don't give up easily on anything.

"No. Get your men up topside and search the area."

Grumbling, Harris did so. He led a squad of heavies up into the open and swept the area. I looked at Gary, who was pretty much scratching his ass in the gully with a few specialists. "Adjunct Dahmen! Up and at 'em. Find the entrance to the Mogwa City, and I'll drink a case of beer with you when we get home."

Gary gave me a worried but determined smile. He joined the search party. I soon sent everyone looking. It was getting dark, and no one was reporting good news. We had buzzers out, soldiers marching in a pattern—the works.

Then Kivi shouted for my attention. I thumped to her side, and she lifted her tapper. She had a buzzer feed coming live from about half a kilometer out.

"They're coming, Centurion. A whole column of robots. Twenty at least."

I eyed the formation. The machines walked steadily over the broken landscape. They were marching directly toward us.

"Kivi, forget following them. Send that drone to their origin point. Where are they coming from?"

She expertly controlled the flying machine. It swooped and wobbled. Suddenly, we saw an opening in the stones. It was a doorway in the ground, with a lurid red light glimmering out of it.

"Troops!" I shouted. "Everyone move north on the double! Run for your lives!"

That order was instantly obeyed. Troops that didn't listen to their officers in Legion Varus were killed over and over until they started listening.

A minute or so later, we were all struggling over rocks and torn up buildings. We raced about a half a kilometer away from the gully and the dome.

I called a halt to our wild retreat and ordered my men to gather and regroup. Harris caught up to me then, trudging in my wake. His sides were heaving, and his eyes were shining.

"What did you see, sir? Are they coming to kill us? Are we pulling back to Winslade's position, or are we fighting them right here?"

I shook my head. "Neither. We're circling around. Kivi pinpointed where they've been coming from. While they sniff around in that gully, looking for us, we'll circle and find their secret tunnel entrance."

He looked aghast, but I pretended not to notice. I clapped a heavy gauntlet on his armored shoulder.

"Don't worry, Adjunct. We're going to complete our mission today, come hell or high water."

Harris was far from reassured, but he followed me anyway. He knew there wasn't any other choice.

It took nearly a half hour to reach the point where Kivi's buzzers had spotted the drone tanks exiting the ground. Even then, the entrance wasn't easy to find. It ended up looking a lot like a large sewer grate.

"That's got to be it," I said, pointing. "Heavies, open it up with your powered exoskeletons. Lights, dive right in."

No one was happy, but they did as I ordered. Gary lingered at my elbow. "You sure this is a good idea, McGill?" he asked me. "If there's anything dangerous in there, that squad of light troopers is going to get eaten up."

I looked at him, and my expression brightened. I jabbed him with a hard finger. "Good idea, Adjunct. Those men need leadership, and they need someone in tough, light gear leading the way, too. Get in that sewer pipe—at the front of the line."

Gary looked stunned. He stammered for a second, but then Harris prodded him from behind. "Are you refusing a direct order from your superior officer, Adjunct Dahmen?"

"No... no, sir. I'm going in."

Bravely, Gary clamped down his faceplate and was the first to jump into the culvert when we had it open. He had to bend over, being a tall guy, but that didn't stop him. Following him like a mother duck, a squad of lights went in too, disappearing one at a time.

A few minutes later, they were all gone. Harris and I watched and listened, frowning. I had Kivi send in a few buzzers to watch over them. The buzzers got to Gary just in time to witness an amusing scene.

Something had clamped onto old Gary...something in the dark water at his feet... something he couldn't see.

He set up an awful hollering. "I'm caught! I'm trapped!"

"Cut your foot off," Harris suggested over the tactical radio. "It's the only way!"

He put his hand over his mouth, stifling his belly laugh. I slapped him. "You know he can't cut his foot off in that suit."

"He can try!"

Shaking my head, I had Kivi circle the buzzer around him. "I see what's wrong. You've got your fool foot twisted into a grate—another grate, under the water."

Calming down, Gary twisted and tugged. At last, he freed himself. It had been a false alarm.

The group continued on, deeper and deeper into the pipes. They widened out to about two meters in diameter, enough for the troops to stand and walk freely.

"Harris, you're going next," I said, turning to the heavy platoon.

"What? Are you kidding me? Let's at least wait until something eats that moron."

I shook my head. "We don't have that kind of time. For all we know the drones are coming this way right now. We've encountered no resistance, so we're all going in."

Grumbling about getting permed and crazy rednecks, Harris led his team into the pipes. I took the specialists in last. They weren't much happier than Harris had been.

Soon, we were all underground and walking into the unknown. I'd been in this situation before, and it was never pleasant. Harris was right. This was an easy way to get yourself permed. Sewers tended to be lined with metal and earth. They blocked signals easily, and if things went badly, the unlucky victim of circumstance could experience an unconfirmed death—the worst kind.

But I didn't care about any of that. We were either going to find our way into that dome, or we were going to die trying.

It was the Legion Varus way.

-30-

Eventually, we reached another barrier of an unexpected sort. It wasn't a wall of glassy force. It wasn't a sealed metal door, either. Instead, it was a torrent of water.

It gushed down into our faces, blasting like a fire hose. The flow was accelerated by a tilt in the land.

"We can't get past this," Harris declared. "No frigging way."

"Kivi, send a buzzer up there—how far does this pipe go?"

She did as I asked, and we found it was a fairly short distance. "It looks like it's less than twenty meters, with a ten percent grade. That's not much, but when you're slogging in water, it's enough to knock anyone off their feet."

"Hmm…" I said, thinking it over. "We need someone to get up there to the top and toss down a line. We can pull ourselves up if we can get it attached firmly enough."

I looked around at my thin roster of troops. I thought about Gary—but I passed on the idea. Sure, he had lightweight armor, and he was a fit enough man, but he was too green. He'd end up falling and breaking his neck or something.

Next, I considered Harris. He was already scowling at me in glances. He must have suspected my scrutiny.

But again, I passed on the idea. I only had three officers, and Gary didn't really count. Flicking through my tapper of names again, I stopped among the specialists.

"Cooper?" I said aloud. "Cooper, are you with us? How come I haven't seen my best ghost all damned day?"

Cooper answered, and he was surprisingly close. "A ghost that's easily spotted is a dead ghost, sir."

His words were sullen and resigned. I smiled.

"Good enough. It's time for you to earn your pay."

"Sir, I'm not strong enough to do twenty meters uphill in the face of a thousand liters of water pressure. Maybe if you sent up some beefcake, like Sargon over there—"

"Hey!" Sargon objected. "That's not cool."

I shook my head. "Nope. It's going to be you, but you're not going to slog uphill into the blasting water, you're going to climb over it. See those handholds on the roof of the tunnel?"

"Those notches?"

"Yep. Take a line and get hopping, froggy."

Cooper did as I commanded, but he didn't seem happy about it. One mistake, one slip-up, and he'd come tumbling down that chute. He'd probably break his neck too—but I didn't care. He hadn't done a damned thing to help my unit so far on City World.

He passed us up and kept going. He took his stealth suit off, but I didn't object. A man who was asked to kill himself could do it in his own way, in his own time. That was a legion axiom.

Dragging a thin line behind him, he struggled to hang over the torrent of water. I could imagine his painful, hand-over-hand effort. He had some gear to help—his hands being equipped with climbing pads and the like. But it wasn't much.

Now and then, he slipped a little. I saw a foot dip down into the white gushing flow twice. Each time, everyone watching the stream from Kivi's buzzers gasped and showed their teeth—but he didn't fall in.

"See that?" I said. "He's skinny, he's sneaky, and he's annoying, but he's a Varus man."

"He's a perv, too," Kivi added. "I suspect he hangs around the showers for hours. Have you ever seen him show up late for breakfast, all prune-skinned with a big smile?"

"Uh... can't say that I have. But look at that! He's almost there!"

185

Cooper grunted and struggled that last few meters. He was getting tired.

"I found something," he said, with puffing breath. "A metal loop, or something. I'm attaching the line to it."

He hooked the line we gave him onto the loop and tugged. It held.

"What now, sir?" he asked.

"Test it with all your weight."

He leaned out and yanked hard—too hard, as it turned out.

The loop was a pull that lowered a heavy metal grate. Cooper was caught under that, and he was pinned.

"Shit!" I said. "Let's go get him."

Sargon surged forward. He was a good man in a tough spot. He naturally wanted to rescue his comrades. It was an enviable trait, a rarity in our outfit.

Clanking upward, he used the exoskeletal strength to take steady steps. With the line to pull on, he was able to use his arms as well as his legs to keep his balance. The water rushed over him in a blasting spray, but he made steady progress.

At last, he reached the grate and threw it upward. A moment later, Cooper's lifeless body came sliding down to the rest of us. He was as dead as yesterday.

"Record it," I told Carlos, who was our only bio. "The rest of you, get up that chute. Heavies first. Sargon will help pull you up."

Sargon set himself and worked his powerful arms. His suit whined and strained. One at a time, we were all dragged up to the top. We took about a minute to rest—then we pressed onward.

"What's the frigging hurry now?" Harris demanded. "We're all going to end up like Cooper if we aren't careful."

"Those drones might be coming back at any minute. They're a patrol, and they've got to return to base at some point. Say... I've got an idea. What do you think about staying here and playing rearguard? You can get all the rest you want that way."

"I'm not feeling tired anymore."

"Good to hear. Let's move out!"

We continued, but soon the pipes forked—that wasn't good.

"Scout each way," I ordered Kivi.

She didn't answer right away. She was looking at her tapper and checking her instruments. Techs had a pack with a much more powerful computer and other gear.

"What's wrong?" I asked her.

"I left a buzzer behind us, to watch our rear… but it's gone dead. I think they're coming back, McGill."

She looked at me with big eyes. I stared back for a second or two, thinking hard. I turned in each direction, peering into the hanging darkness.

"I think this way is going upwards a bit… look at the water flow. We're going that way—on the double."

The troops complained, but they picked up their feet. We jogged down the pipes until we reached a circle of light in the ceiling. "Lights, climb up there and open that exit. Move!"

While the lights grunted and sweated above, I thought I could hear the whining of servos and the scraping of metal claws on metal pipes behind us.

Soon, the sounds became distinctive. There could be no mistake. The drones were coming after us.

Goaded into hurrying, we soon had the grate open. We climbed out of the pipes and stood in an open field.

Looking all around us, we gaped and stared. It was morning now, and the light had us blinking and squinting.

"It's beautiful," Kivi said. "What is this place?"

"Some kind of farmer's field, I think," Carlos said, coming near. "These plants aren't terrestrial, but they're clearly a cultivated crop."

Plants reached up to our hips. They had thick stalks, a lot of triangular leaves, and a purple flower at the top. Spines protruded from each bloom. Insects buzzed around these flowers—big ones.

In the distance, the city stood tall in the morning sun. The monstrous buildings cast long shadows that seemed to reach all the way to the horizon.

"McGill," Kivi told me, "those drones are still coming."

187

"Yeah… Sargon, put the grate back and seal it with your belcher. Melt it closed."

He knelt and went to work. Brilliant light and smoke flared up from the tip of his weapon. Soon, the grate and the pipe were fused together.

"That might hold… or it might not," Sargon said.

"Let's move out," I ordered.

Everyone hustled through the field of odd plants. Lacking direction, we headed for the only building that was nearby. It was weird-looking, a round structure that slanted up on the sides.

"Looks like a bunt cake," Gary commented.

"I hate cake," Harris said. "Who's going to scout that structure, Centurion?"

I halted and eyed my crew. There weren't all that many of us… we couldn't spare anyone. I pointed at Gary. "Take two lights and knock on the door."

"Seriously?"

Harris laughed. "Is that a piss-stain I see on your fancy armor, Adjunct?"

He gave Harris a sour glance, then slapped two recruits. He did this decisively, just as I would have done. The man was teachable.

The trio trotted to what looked like an entrance. We all saw the door spring open as he approached. Gary tried to play kiss-ass with the Mogwa at the door. He bowed and talked expansively.

In response, a gout of blue fire hit him in the belly. He was knocked flat, and the door was thrown closed.

Harris laughed until his gut hurt. Gary climbed painfully to his feet. He wasn't seriously injured due to his tough armor, but his pride had been stung. He walked away in defeat.

Sargon came near, and his belcher rode his shoulder. He looked purposeful. "Shall we light-up this farmer's shack, sir?"

"What? Hell, no! We're supposed to be rescuing these people, remember?"

Sargon retreated, and Kivi took his place. "Centurion, I've been trying to reach someone—*anyone*—on the public grid. I'm being ignored and cut off. You have to have a password or something to get access to any kind of communications. We probably look like invaders to them."

"Damn that Sateekas," I complained. "He just had to lead the attack and get his battlecruiser smashed-up. If he hadn't been forced to run off, he could have told these people we're friends, not enemy troops."

No one argued with my logic, they just looked glum. Unsure of what to do, we stood around approximately a hundred meters from the farmer's home. We could have blown the place up and killed him, sure, but that wouldn't have accomplished anything like "making peaceful contact" with the Mogwa.

I realized about then that we'd come here without much of a plan of action. Sure, we knew we had to get under the dome in order to make contact with this splinter colony of Mogwa, but now that we'd met up with one of them, we didn't have a clue as to how to establish a meaningful dialog.

Kivi, Carlos and Harris all made unhelpful suggestions as to how to proceed. I took off my helmet and gave my head a scratch. It was quite a mess we were in.

Before we could think of anything intelligent to do, a strange-looking truck came trundling down the road from the city. It never touched the road, and it didn't fly higher than a meter off the ground. The air under the truck was kind of blurry and wavering. It ran on antigrav plates as far as I could tell.

"Who's that?" Harris demanded, pointing and crouching lower among the plants.

"I don't know..." I said. There was something purposeful about the vehicle. Someone official. "Everyone hide in the flowers until we see what's what."

Sargon had his belcher out again, and I didn't complain this time. After all, this truck looked like it could be dangerous. The exterior was all flat planes of metal. There weren't any windows or even a windshield to see through. It could have been an armored assault vehicle.

My weaponeers naturally wanted to blow it up, but I ordered them to stand down. Soldiers weren't the best diplomats in the world.

We watched as the truck came down the road at speed. It didn't seem like the driver was in a friendly mood. The vehicle stopped in front of the farmer's door, and two Mogwa got out. The farmer opened his door promptly and pointed out into the fields—directly at us.

All three of the Mogwa looked in our direction, and they produced some odd-looking gear. Then they approached the field we were squatting in.

It took me a moment to recognize what they were carrying. They were shock-sticks with nooses hanging from the tips.

-31-

Harris was alarmed. "Uh... McGill? Are we going to let these dog-catchers round us up and put us in that truck, or are we going to shoot them?"

I blinked at him for a second, then I laughed. He was right. They were dog-catchers—or slave-catchers. Something like that.

I'd been to Trantor, the Mogwa homeworld, just once. That was many years back. They'd been big on collars for humans back then. They hadn't been keen on the idea of us wearing clothes, either. They saw all aliens as animals. We were chattel to be owned and kicked around at will.

"Put your weapons down," I ordered the group. "Stand around and look dumb."

"Seriously?" Harris asked, disgusted. "That's our plan? To get captured by these losers? I could kill all three with a piece of pipe."

I knew he was probably right. I'd seen humans tangle with Mogwa in hand-to-hand combat in the past. The Galactics had never stood a chance. They were physically weak and generally poor fighters. If they had vehicles or starships, sure, they could give us some real trouble. But just walking around with shock-sticks? No, that wasn't going to cut it.

"Drop your weapons and look docile, dammit," I ordered.

Reluctantly, my troops finally listened. The Mogwa continued to approach cautiously.

191

The leader came near and used his foot-hand things to gesture furiously. He seemed to want me to step forward and put my head in the noose hanging off his shock-stick.

With a sigh, I walked up and turned on my translation app. Fortunately, these guys spoke Imperial standard. They had an accent, but it was understandable to my tapper.

"Beast-leader," the Mogwa leader said. "Approach and be neutralized."

"Hey, your overlordship. It's great to meet you. I'm a legionnaire from Earth."

All three of the Mogwa reeled back in horror. "Improper! Foulness! Beasts should not speak the high language!"

"Uh... I think there's a misunderstanding. We're here to help. Grand Admiral Sateekas brought us here. We have thousands of troops outside your dome, ready to fight for your safety."

That was too much for the Mogwa. My words only seemed to make them angry. The leader trundled up and extended his shock-stick in my direction. He shook it at me.

"Place your upper protuberance into this noose. I don't know what beast-collector you might have escaped from, but you will be controlled and then disciplined."

"My upper protuberance? Do you mean my head?"

"Yes, ignoramus. I command you. I demand instant and total obedience."

This was usually the way things went with any Galactic. They were as predictable as they were arrogant.

"Look sirs, we don't mean any harm. We need to talk to your military commanders. We're a military force, and we're trying to help you guys."

"Your words and your very existence are offensive enough. I demand obedience. Will you comply, or will you be abused?"

Heaving a heavy sigh, I walked forward and let the leader Mogwa try to drop the noose over my neck. It crackled with power, and I knew I couldn't let him do as he wished.

With a grunt, I yanked the stick out of his hands and dropped it in the field. I then walked another step forward, standing heavily on the stick. It cracked and stopped sparkling.

"What's this? You've destroyed my device!"

192

"What? Oh... I'm real sorry about that, sir. I didn't understand. We're off-worlders, see. We don't—"

My bullshit didn't get me very far. The second Mogwa dog-catcher had circled around on my six and was trying to get his noose into position.

Harris intervened. I hadn't told him to act, but he took the initiative. He yanked the stick out of the second Mogwa's hands and broke it over his knee. Then he tossed it back at the owner. The stick still seemed to have some juice in it, because it sparked once, sending the Mogwa skittering like a dog with his tail on fire.

My men laughed. They couldn't help it.

That was enough for the three Mogwa. Shaking with rage and fear, they raced away toward the truck. They all piled in and sped away.

I turned on my troops, glaring at them. "That could have gone better."

"It was funny as hell," Harris said. "You've got to admit that."

Throwing an arm up and pointing after the retreating truck, I shouted at all of them. "They'll come back with marines. You know that, don't you?"

Harris shrugged. "Isn't that what we wanted? We made contact. That's all we're supposed to do. We found the way in here, and we met with the Mogwa. I say our mission is a success."

I glared at him for a bit, but then I started blinking and thinking it over. Harris had a point.

"I like it," I said at last. "Let's go back and report in. We've done what we set out to do. Let's give this bag of shit back to Winslade."

Taking video of everything we could, we marched back to the culvert we'd come from and burned our way back inside. We were worried that the drone mini-tanks might be lurking down there, but we didn't meet up with them.

Hurrying back the way we'd come, we quickly exited the dome and stood in the open again. I was the first to contact Winslade.

Once he answered my transmissions, I gave him the short version of what we'd done. Even with a lot of candy and lipstick slathered on top of my story, he didn't like it very much.

"McGill, are you telling me you assaulted Galactic officials in the pursuit of their duty? Again?"

"Uh... no sir. Not exactly. It was just a couple of dog-catchers and a farmer. There weren't any duchesses or archdukes around."

"That's not the point, McGill. You were supposed to establish a diplomatic channel. You weren't supposed to upset them, or challenge their authority in any way."

"Well sir, if you want tea ceremonies and top hats, you sent in the wrong man."

Winslade began to pace on my tapper. "Evidently... All right, what's done is done. I'm uncertain concerning my next move. My instinct is to retreat from this fresh disaster and hope it will all be forgotten when the Mogwa finally let us into their dome."

"Who's going to negotiate that miracle?"

He flapped a hand at me. "That's none of my affair. I shouldn't have sent you in there in the first place. In truth, I didn't think you'd manage to find a way in."

I grinned at him. "Well sir, you thought wrong. I'll tell you what, I'll just report this up the line. There's got to be an imperator or an equestrian who will know what to do."

Winslade showed me his teeth. "You'll do no such thing. *I* will report it, and you will stay silent. Standby."

The screen on my tapper went dark, and I grinned, waiting patiently. It didn't take very long, because I'd already sent a message to several of Winslade's superiors. Everyone in the legion had given up on communications blackouts. They'd realized they weren't doing us any good.

Transmitting the contents of my call to Winslade to everyone, even Legion Victrix, I had nothing more to do but stand around and grin. The calls soon began coming in to my tapper in a torrent.

194

First up on the roster was Primus Collins. She looked shocked. "Centurion McGill...? You're inside the dome? And you're alive?"

"Last I checked, Primus, sir. I'm doing fine. We're out in the east quadrant—"

"Shut up. I need you to tell me what happened when you talked to the Mogwa. Is there any chance that... ? Hold on— I've got another call." She frowned at her tapper and looked concerned. She put me on hold, but she forgot to turn off her camera.

I watched as she manufactured a pleasant, business-like expression. She spoke to someone, and her face crumbled. At last, she cinched up her pretty mouth into a tight pink rosebud. She nodded, as if being shouted at. Then, she merged up the two calls.

I saw Drusus on one half of the screen and Collins on the other. I smiled at them both, and the truth was I was as pleased as punch to have them both on the line at once.

"McGill? It was you?" Drusus demanded. "Oh my God... how many Mogwa did you murder? Were there any children involved?"

Blinking and frowning, I felt my jaw drop. "No sir, you've got the wrong idea. I went in as a diplomat, not a marauder."

"But you must have killed someone. Right?"

"No sir!" I said, slapping my right hand over my heart. "I swear it before the Almighty. I'll send you my suit-vid if you want proof."

"All right, I'll review that later. There's no time now. The enemy invasion ships will be landing shortly. Just tell me how you got inside."

"Uh... enemy invasion ships? What's that about? I thought tugs were coming to drop more asteroids or something."

"No. We saw ships up there, and some theorized that's what they were—but we've since gotten better intelligence. Assault ships are coming down from orbit. They'll be on the ground within hours."

I chewed that over, and I didn't like the taste of it any more than Drusus did. Our forces were trapped outside the domed city, and we would eventually be short on supplies. There was no fleet on our side to destroy these invaders. We'd be caught fighting them out in the wastelands.

"Huh…" I said. "That does put a different light on things. I can understand now why all the brass are answering my tapper calls tonight."

"So far as I know, your unit is the only force that's been able to penetrate that dome. Now, for the last time, how did you do it?"

I told him then, and it was a tale to be remembered. Instead of a sordid affair trudging through sewers and running from drone tanks, my version of the story was one of heroism and ingenuity.

Drusus suspected I was laying it on thick, but he didn't seem to care much. He wanted the essentials, and he managed to glean them from my bullshit.

"So… you backtracked the drones to their logical exit from the dome and forced your way inside. What are the welcoming Mogwa forces like?"

"Uh… the what, sir?"

"The Mogwa officers you mentioned—or whoever it was you met with inside the dome. Did they offer you any promises about allowing the rest of us inside?"

"Oh… uh… no," I said, and I scratched at my neck. I was suddenly itchy, and I was wishing I hadn't told such a glowing tale a moment ago. "The city defenders can't drop the dome, see. They said we have to all go in the same way I did."

"Seriously? Tens of thousands of troops are supposed to wriggle through a tunnel? Even the Blood Worlders?"

I shrugged helplessly. "The Mogwa aren't always a reasonable people, sir."

"No… no, they're not." Drusus sighed in defeat. "All right. I'll spread the word. We'll get every man inside that we can. There must be more of these ditches buried in the landscape. We've certainly seen enough drone-tanks to support the existence of a dozen such secret entrances. All right, I'm getting off this call. Collins, you and Winslade know what to do. Drusus out."

He vanished, and Primus Collins, who'd wisely been listening quietly this whole time, regarded me with suspicion.

"McGill, you aren't bullshitting this whole thing up out of nothing, are you?"

"No sir! I got into that dome, and I can get more troops in there the same way. I am kind of worried about the Blood-Worlders, however. They're too damned big to fit in those pipes. They'll have to crawl on their hands and knees."

"Don't worry about that. Now that we've pinpointed the coordinates of one of those entrances, we're sending engineering teams to swarm the location. We'll dig in and shorten the tunnel to a minimum length."

"Oh... heh... that's great." I tried to sound enthusiastic, but I think I failed.

Fortunately, Collins didn't seem to notice. She soon dropped the call, and I was off the hook for further explanations.

I was slightly concerned that when they did finally get inside... well... I didn't think they were going to get the warm reception they were hoping for. But that was someone else's problem at this point, so I tried not to think about it.

-32-

After crawling out of the sewers and giving my reports, I considered myself to be a modern day hero. To my mind, I'd saved the lives of four legions worth of troops, and I deserved some R&R—but that wasn't in the cards for old McGill.

I was, in fact, marching my ragtag group back toward the rear lines when my tapper started talking to me.

"McGill? What are you doing?"

It was Graves this time. He'd apparently called my tapper and forced it to answer.

The fact he was calling me at all only slightly surprised me. He'd been certain to make any revival list, as he was an important person and all.

"Hello, Primus, sir! Great to hear from you. Are you calling to congratulate me?"

Graves' face twisted up. "Hardly. I'll congratulate you when our troops are safely on the inside of that dome."

"Oh… okay. That won't be long, take my word for it. So… what's this call about then, sir?"

"I saw your unit moving away from the dome, and I wanted to know what the hell you were up to."

"Uh… I thought maybe we'd have time for a hot meal and maybe a few hours of shuteye before we went back inside the—"

"Forget it. Do an about-face and help the engineering crews pinpoint the site. After they've done their work, you'll function

198

as a guide. We're on a time-schedule here, McGill. This isn't a vacation."

"Don't I know it..." I said, but I was talking to a blank screen. He'd cut the call short.

When I relayed our new orders to my unit, the news was met with a chorus of groans and curses, but no one was all that surprised. There was no rest for the weary, the wary or the wicked in Legion Varus, and we all knew it.

We turned our marching column around and headed back toward the dome. It began to rain as we did so, and the ashes under our boots turned into black mud.

Vehicles converged on our location as we drew near the site. I was stunned by the number and variety of them. There were skimmers like the one we'd rode in on, plus all kinds of ground cars and trucks. I was impressed, and I walked up to the engineering officers.

They were sappers, and I held some respect for their sort. They weren't frontline troops, mind you, but they died often enough in the service by setting off bombs and building temporary structures that got blown up on alien worlds.

"How deep are you going to dig this tunnel?" I asked the first centurion I saw.

His nametag said he was Centurion Roth. He rounded on me, frowning hard, but his face softened when he saw I was the same rank as he was. He squinted, and then his face lit up as he read my nametag.

"McGill? You're that crazy, shit-for-brains who crawled under the dome, right? That was impressive, Centurion."

"Thanks, but it's nothing compared to the work you boys have ahead of you. What's your game plan?"

Roth looked thoughtful. "Well, we started off by laying out EMP traps. To disable those mini-tanks. They're heavily shielded, but a burrowing buzzer and a quick jolt in the wire-harness seems to take care of most of them."

"Uh-huh," I said, uncertain as to how the drone-tanks would take to such behavior. It might trip their AI into marking all humans for death—but again, it wasn't my problem, so I kept smiling.

"Next, we're going to drill about a hundred meter long tunnel. It will be ten in diameter, twenty deep. A quick run down and up again, like a dog digging under a fence."

"Sounds good," I said, using a convinced tone. "How long do you think it will take?"

"Ten hours, more or less."

Frowning, I shaded my eyes and studied the skies. They looked quiet, but that wouldn't last long.

"Uh…" I said, "did anyone mention to you guys that there are hostile ships approaching this planet even now?"

Centurion Roth waved a big gauntlet at me. "They sure did. That pesky Winslade of yours brings it up every few minutes, seems like. We'll have this trench done long before that."

"Yeah, but did you calculate how long it will take our column to get through the dome?"

"Of course. There shouldn't be a problem, as long as everyone lines up neatly and hustles."

I was frowning more deeply now. "But… what if the Mogwa on the other side don't understand? I mean, what if they want to scan our tappers, or search our rucks for contraband?"

The engineer eyed me strangely. "You went in there, right? You're the one that knows how they're going to react."

I was feeling itchy again. That happened sometimes when one of my frequent lies caught up to me. I opened my faceplate and scratched. "I have some idea…"

"Were they officious? Uncertain?"

"Yeah, well… they didn't greet us with open arms. Don't expect to be hailed as liberators. They kind of… well… to a Mogwa, humans are all like trained seals, see. Or dogs, maybe. Stray dogs that barely know how to do tricks. They're more likely to worry about us pissing on the carpet than to give us a treat, to be honest."

Roth stared at me in disbelief. "You're telling me there might be a delay? An interruption to the flow of personnel? This is critical information. Why wasn't I told about this?"

I wagged a finger in the air. "I think you know where the trouble comes from. You already mentioned him by name."

His face brightened in recognition. "Tribune Winslade… right. Okay, I know what to do on that score. I take my orders from Drusus directly. We'll remove the bottleneck. In the meantime, is there anything else you'd like to tell me?"

I thought of a dozen grim realities that this man was about to face once he got under the dome. To my way of thinking, that was when his real troubles would begin. But I didn't want to tell him any of that, so I just grinned and spread my hands wide. "Can't think of anything right now. Maybe something will come to me later."

"All right. I'll contact you if we run into anything… unusual. Thanks for all your help, McGill."

The engineer turned back to his digging, but he seemed to be moving faster now. I skedaddled out of there before anyone else could start asking me questions. At this point, stacking up any fresh lies was liable to make me feel bad.

To make shirking easier, I led my team back to the crater we'd occupied when we first landed. That wasn't popular with the group, but they were bone-tired and didn't much care where we went as long as we stopped marching.

"Damnation," I told them. "Does anyone here need to have a good cry? How about you?" I grabbed Gary and shook him. "Are you going to soil that armor you don't deserve?"

"Me, sir? I didn't say anything." Gary looked sheepish. He'd been one of the chief complainers, and I knew it. That was unacceptable in a supporting officer.

Naturally, I knew what the trouble was. Marching around night and day with no rest could wear down a weak man. Gary wasn't a real Varus soldier, and it showed. He'd earned his rank by kissing unmentionables, not by slogging through mud and blood.

"All right then," I said, letting him go.

Harris had been standing behind Gary pantomiming murder. When I let the adjunct go, he stalked away in disappointment.

My unit proceeded to lounge and snooze in the crater. Along about noon—or whatever passed for noon on this rock—the brass finally caught up to me.

"McGill? McGill!"

My tapper was buzzing and bitching at me again. It was Tribune Winslade, and he was all fussed-up about something.

"Hello, sir!" I said, answering with the most cheerful tone I could muster. "Is it time for us to march into the dome to receive our heroes' welcome?"

"What? Hardly. I'm calling because we've had difficulties. Are you *certain* the Mogwa officers knew what you were saying when you met with them?"

"Both sides spoke Imperial Standard, sir. If there's a misunderstanding, it's probably on the head of your tunneling crew."

Winslade shook his head and tsked. "It must have been some breach of protocol, then. That engineer—what's his name? Centurion Roth? He's been complaining all afternoon about everything. No matter, I've come to expect incompetence at every turn. I'll handle it—Winslade out."

Disconnecting with a happy touch of my index finger, I sat back in the mud and smiled. Now *that* was how you handled a difficult situation. You diverted the attention of two antagonists so that they focused on each other, rather than the real weasel in the mix. That way they would get more deeply involved with the problem and end up owning it.

By the time the officers figured out that the Mogwa were huge tools, and that there was no way their plans were going to work out, it would be *waaay* too late to blame one James McGill.

This time out, it wasn't going to be easy for Winslade and his sidekicks to point the big stick of shame at me.

Closing my eyes again, I managed to nod off after a few minutes.

-33-

Access tunnels were constructed all around the dome, with our engineers and sappers working night and day. When the following dawn came, I awakened to an unpleasant development.

Looking through the glassy dome itself, I could see an army of mini-tanks had assembled. Walking around in front of each squadron of drones was a real, live Mogwa marine. These bad hombres were just as threatening as the drones themselves, and they looked kind of similar, too.

"Huh…" I said, eyeing the standoff. "Doesn't look like the Mogwa are interested in being rescued."

"It sure doesn't," Carlos said. Somehow, he'd managed to sidle up to me and poke his nose over the rim of the crater. "So far, they haven't allowed anyone other than a few engineering officers in there to talk to them. The funny part is they grabbed the engineers with those shock-noose things."

I frowned. That seemed to me like the Mogwa were going too far. After all, Centurion Roth was a hard-working fellow. He didn't deserve to be outright abused.

"What about Winslade? Any word?"

Carlos looked furtive. "Well… Kivi might have tapped into the local grid."

"She might have, huh? What happened?"

Carlos leaned forward grinning. "We think Winslade went in there and got his ass arrested, too."

"Huh... That's funny, but not good."

I craned my neck, looking up at the sky. It could have been a moon or some local planets... but I thought I saw a number of small bright objects hanging over us. I pointed up at them.

"What are those things?"

"We thought they were tugs bringing rocks to bombard us—but there's no such luck. We're not getting off easy, dying clean and catching a revive next year when some investigation declares this mission a wipe—no, we're going to have to fight for our supper. Again."

Staring upward, I thought I saw some streamers dropping from the bottom of the lowest craft in orbit above us. Whatever they were, they weren't acting too friendly.

"Invasion ships..." I said.

"What?"

"Winslade said they're enemy troops. They're dropping on us right now."

Carlos gaped and twisted his neck this way and that. "Holy shit... I think you're right. What are we going to do, McGill?"

"Lock and load. I'll report the sighting—even though they have to know what's happening."

When I reported in, I wasn't too surprised to get Primus Collins on the line instead of Winslade. Apparently, what Carlos had heard about him being captured inside the dome was true.

"Primus Collins? Are you in operational command of this zone now?"

"That's right, McGill. You fucked up."

"Uh... could be you be more specific, sir?"

"You heard me. My staff has informed me that you've been trying to get Winslade permed for years. Now that you've succeeded, you'll find me to be your worst nightmare."

Frowning, I tried to puzzle out what she was saying. "First off, what happened to Winslade?"

"As if you didn't know... He went inside that dome and was captured and abused by a pack of enraged, ungrateful monsters. I don't know why we pay homage to these aliens. They're no more honorable than any of the rest—possibly worse."

"If you're talking about the Mogwa, sir... well... you've got the right of that. But as to me somehow engineering this whole thing—"

Collins cut me off, and she seemed to be speaking with growing anger no matter what I said. "Stop! Just stop right there with your lies and nonsense. You pretended to penetrate that dome, then—"

"Pretended? I handed in my vids, sir. Have you reviewed them?"

"A very well-edited sequence of shots. I admit, it *looks* like you made it to some farmer's field on the inside. But you didn't negotiate anything with the Mogwa. Show me that vid, McGill. Show me the one where you talked to these bastards and made friends with them."

I began feeling itchy again. That was the trouble with smart people, they asked questions. I naturally had vids of my interaction with the Mogwa, but I'd erased them and hid them. I didn't want to show any human, alive or dead, how we'd taken their shock-sticks and run them off. That would be hard to explain.

Dammit. Why couldn't Winslade have managed to fix this on his own? Did I have to do everything?

Heaving a sigh, I decided I was somewhat responsible for this impending disaster. "Okay. I'll go inside that dome again and see what I can do to help."

This statement seemed to take Primus Collins by surprise. She was just winding up for a fresh set of accusations, but she deflated somewhat. "You will...? All right. Hold your position until after the immediate area is clear, then you'll go in and do what you can. I'm already suspecting I'll regret this, but I also suspect it's the best chance Leonard has. Try to set aside your natural hate for him, McGill. Your little joke has gone too far. "

"Uh..." I said, but I trailed off. She'd disconnected.

Flumping back against the crater wall, I frowned upward. There were a lot of mysteries packed into that conversation, but I was beginning to sort them out in my mind.

For one thing, I now believed Winslade had been playing a little grab-ass on the side with Primus Collins. That was kind of a shocker. He rarely got anything from the ladies, even though he tried now and then.

The clues were all there as I reviewed her words. She'd talked about his best chance, and how he'd been screwed over, and she'd even called him "Leonard" instead of Winslade. That, right there, was a dead giveaway.

Collins wasn't exactly a beauty queen, but her main problem came in the form of a heinous personality. Apparently, that hadn't deterred old Winslade. He'd gotten her attention, and she seemed to care about him.

To my misfortune, I realized I now felt a little guilty about Winslade. Collins was right, I'd passed the buck and then some. "Leonard" was very poorly equipped when it came to any kind of diplomacy. The idea he was going to talk his way into that dome—that was plain ridiculous. I'd let my hopes for a clean dodge affect my good judgment.

There were other things to think about, too. What had Primus Collins said? Something about going into the dome after the current action? What was that all about?

"McGill!" Harris said, thumping over to my position. "What are we going to do about the drop-pods? Some of them are coming down right here. Kivi says so."

He pointed into the sky, and I followed his gestures. The trails I'd noticed before had grown in number and in size. I knew what they had to be—enemy drop-pods, falling down on us from orbit.

"Centurion?" Harris continued. "I know you've been talking to headquarters. What are our orders?"

I glanced down at my tapper. Sure enough, the damned thing was chock-full of maps and tactical schematics—but there wasn't time to dig through all that stuff now.

Collins must have figured I was wide awake and reading everything she sent me. That marked her down as a weak commander in my view. Graves would never have made such a mistake.

Grunting, I jumped to my feet and began shouting orders. We positioned ourselves, guns ready, to meet the invaders, whoever they might turn out to be.

-34-

Having drop-pods scream down to fall on your head is alarming. I'd experienced this before, but not often. Once, Saurians had invaded Machine World and landed right on top of us. Another time Legion Varus had landed on an island on Green World...

This time things looked different. The drop-pods themselves weren't the same model. They slowed down as they approached the ground, firing jets to reduce speed. I squinted up at them, trying to figure out why they looked wrong somehow...

"They're small, and they have shielding!" Harris shouted. He pointed a gauntlet up into the sky and released a large amount of explosive pellets from his morph-rifle.

Letting the gun aim itself, he tracked and chugged out pellets. These pellets were made of black tungsten, a metal with a high melting point. The pellets weren't smart, not exactly, but the guns were. When approached by an object in an open sky, they could track it and fire accordingly.

As we watched, the pellets popped into spinning sprays of tiny fragments. These jagged flying knives were designed to wreck missiles or other unarmored targets.

Watching the pods fall, I calculated that everything I'd heard from Sateekas was true. These guys were Rigellians. There weren't too many other species around who were small, brave and mean.

Flashes like sparklers showered around the descending pods. I could see at a glance our antiair pellets weren't working on the targets. They were shielded by weak force-fields—just enough to ward off small arms fire from the ground.

All around us, Harris and his men were filling the sky with showers of pellets. I reached out a hand and pushed Harris' gun down.

"You're wasting ammo," I told him. Then I raised my voice to a shout. "Heavies! Forget the anti-air fire. Switch to armor-piercing rounds, and move to the rim of the crater."

They glanced at me in surprise, but then quickly hustled to obey. The chattering fire ended and transformed into clacking sounds as they reconfigured their rifles. I busied myself doing the same.

Soon, we were ready to dish out some pain. Our morph-rifles were newly designed to have an armor-piercing mode. This allowed our guns to fire specially coated rounds at very high velocities that were designed to punch through hard targets.

"You think there are drones in these pods?" Harris asked me as the first smoking capsules came in for a landing. "Cause these guns aren't going to get through shielding and a drop-pod's shell."

"Nope," I said. "I think there are infantry in there."

Harris pushed his head up over the rim. "I see the first one in our vicinity. About two hundred meters south-by-southwest. Permission to fire, sir."

"Hold on. Let the trooper climb out. We don't want to have to root them out of their pods if they decide to hide in there."

I scooted up next to Harris. A dozen other troops were all along the rim of the crater, aiming in the same direction. Two other pods came in, firing their landing jets.

The first pod popped open. One half of the pod fell away and a figure climbed out.

Harris gave a cry of inarticulate rage. "What the fuck? That thing is tiny. Is that what I think it is?"

"Focused fire, people," I ordered. "Take him down!"

Streams of bolts showered the enemy soldier, the pod and the smoking dirt all around. The figure spun around, fell, but

208

got up again. He scrambled to get behind his pod and take shelter.

"No you don't!" Harris shouted, holding down the trigger on his rifle. He hammered the target in the ass and back, and it seemed to work. Having taken dozens of hits, the soldier fell and crawled feebly. We kept pecking at him until he lay still.

By then, everyone had recognized what we were shooting at. Harris turned to me as more pods landed and popped open, and still more fell from the sky.

"Bears, sir?" he asked, his eyes wide with alarm. "The bears are dropping right on top of us? This is crazy."

"Armor-piercing rounds," I shouted, calling to all neighboring units. "Use only armor-piercing ammo, or you'll get no joy."

My com channels buzzed and chirped with acknowledgements. It was confirmed officially. We were fighting bears again, bears from Rigel.

These guys were small, but they were tough and strong. Worst of all, they had armor as good or better than the suit I was wearing right now. In my whole unit, only Gary and I had a kit that could match this enemy.

It was going to be a rough day.

The firefight continued without a break, and it was mostly one-sided. When the bears landed nearby in their drop-pods, we could usually take them out in the first minute or two. A few managed to crawl away to safety and find cover.

The ones that worried me much more were those we didn't see land. Pods were dropping all over the rough land, and they were steadily disgorging fresh troops that were out of range. We killed a dozen of them, maybe—but the rest managed to find cover and slink away.

Finally, the shower of drop-pods stopped falling in our vicinity. After that it fell quiet out there in the open, beyond the rim of our crater. I couldn't see them, but I knew the bears were gathering strength and numbers, organizing into units. Soon, they would assault our strongpoint—they had no other choice.

"They didn't counterattack," Harris said. "That's weird."

I shook my head. "No, it's not. They would have been killed if they'd charged our position. They're grouping up somewhere. This land is so pockmarked with holes and craters, they could be hiding anywhere."

I turned to Kivi, who was working her equipment at the bottom of the crater. "What have you got on track? What are the buzzers reporting?"

She shook her head. "I've lost half of them already. I can't fly more than five meters off the deck without getting them blasted."

"Huh..."

Crawling to the rim of the crater, I used my HUD to look around. I didn't see any anti-air systems set up, but maybe the bears had managed it.

All around our position, we could hear firefights in progress. Bears and men struggled in knots here and there on the landscape. My tactical maps showed where these hotspots were, but it hardly mattered. When you're in the middle of a battleground all that matters is the men at your back and the enemy within range.

While we waited, we got another call from Primus Collins. She was quickly becoming my least favorite officer. "McGill? Why are you still squatting in that crater? Get up and get moving. Head for the dome breach point—now!"

"Yessir, Primus!"

Heaving myself up, I ordered my lights to charge out first. I told Barton the heavies would cover her men—but really, they were going out there to see if they could attract any fire.

They ran like rabbits, terrified and almost helpless. Wearing thin spacer suits and carrying snap-rifles, they were no challenge at all to any bears they might run into, and they knew it.

Not one of them was shot down, however. The moment they'd made it a hundred meters or so, I ordered Harris and his heavies to advance behind them, then brought up the rear with the specialists.

In this kind of situation, luck was as important a factor as anything else on the table. The only way I knew of to increase our odds was to move quickly. The shorter the timespan we were out running around in the open, the less time the enemy had to zero us and attack.

So, we ran for it. Three waves of troops hustled over the broken landscape. Boots slapped in mud and crunched on pulverized gravel. We got halfway to the finish line before we ran into trouble.

The lights discovered the bears first, just as they were supposed to. Snap-rifles chattered and cracked. They threw themselves to the ground and threw grenades into an abandoned ditch.

Blue-white flashes glowed all along the trench. Barton had trained her troops well. They couldn't do much to a bear, but they were giving it their all.

"Lights, go to ground, and stay there," I ordered. "Harris, advance to that ditch and finish the job. My weaponeers will be there as soon as they can."

Harris marched right through the lights and moved up to the ditch. They hosed down the place—but the bears still had some fight left in them. Six of them cracked shotguns into my heavies, then charged close with force-blades. A fast-moving, vicious fight broke out.

In the end, our superior numbers won the day. We killed all the bears, a full squad of them, and lost only four men.

After taking a minute to patch the wounded and catch our breath, we were up and running again. The breach, which was unrecognizable now with all the digging and machines parked there, came into sight.

A company of scared engineers were hunkered down there, hiding behind drone dozers and automated walking machines we called pigs. They welcomed us in relief.

"McGill?" asked the man in charge. I recognized the sapper, it was Centurion Roth.

"Hey, Roth. I heard you got captured by the Mogwa. How'd you get away?"

He shook his head. "That's kind of a secret... well... I got mad when they kept shocking me with some collar on a stick— so I ripped it off my neck and ran off."

I laughed. "I would have done the same thing."

211

Roth pointed out to the battlefield all around us. "What the hell is going on? We had two units here to cover us, but they were called away."

"It's chaos. These crazy bears like to drop right on top of our positions—they've done it before."

His face went blank. "Bears? You mean like, from Rigel?"

"That's them."

"What the fuck...? How did they get here? What are they doing in the Mid-Zone?"

The question was a legit one. Rigel was pretty far from this place. The bears hadn't fought a hot war with us for years, but they'd always been our enemies. Now, somehow, they showed up all the way out in space, thousands of lightyears from their homeworld. It didn't entirely make sense, unless...

I had a sudden thought, one that I didn't like too much.

"What if these bears decided a while back to bypass Earth?" I asked Roth. "To go around Province 921 and just plow right into the Empire's belly? Here in the Mid-Zone, it doesn't seem like these people are accustomed to fighting off invaders from the frontier."

"Huh..." Roth said. "I don't like the sound of that. It makes sense, though. The Mogwa must be weaker than we thought."

"Yeah..."

I told him then about my new orders—that I'd been directed to enter the dome and talk to the Mogwa about Winslade.

Roth wished me luck, but he didn't seem to hold out much hope for my chances. "Those Mogwa are crazy. They don't seem to get that we're here to help them. They have a terrible attitude."

"You've got the right of that. Galactics are always ungrateful and cock-sure. Don't worry, I've dealt with them before."

With that confident statement, I left Roth at the breach site and walked through his crude, still-narrow tunnel under the dome. A hundred steps later, I led my unit out into the open. We found ourselves standing in fields under the glassy dome once again.

212

-35-

The first thing I did was huddle-up with my troops and tell them their new rules of engagement. Legion Varus boys tended to shoot first and ask questions later—that wasn't the way I wanted to do things here today.

"You mean we're supposed to take it up the butt if these guys start shooting at us?" Carlos complained. "Why don't we just nuke the lot of them? Ungrateful pricks."

"They're all that and more, Carlos. But this is a diplomatic mission. We're supposed to fight side by side with these guys, not against them. Let me do the talking. Keep your guns slung!"

They grumbled and milled around, tossing angry glances at me and the towering buildings of the city in the distance.

"Hey, Sargon!" I shouted. "What are you doing with that belcher?"

He had it on his shoulder, and he was sighting on the nearest building with it. Startled, he turned to me and lowered it sheepishly.

"I was just using the optics to scout, sir."

"Well, knock it off! Aiming at things with your weapon tells folks that you're an invader trying to blast a farmhouse. You've got your cock out at a funeral, Veteran."

"Yessir."

He reluctantly slung his belcher, and we began marching toward the nearest signs of habitation. It didn't take long for us

213

to walk smack into a nest of Mogwa marines in their power-armor.

Lifting a hand and throwing them a grin, I hailed them as friends. They encircled and advanced, turrets at the ready.

"Lay down your arms and surrender, animals," a booming voice said in standard. "Your invasion has failed. There will be no plunder, no orgy of blood."

"Uh... hah..." I said, walking forward with my hands up. "Can I talk to whoever's in charge here, Mr. Mogwa sir?"

One of the six-legged armored troops separated from the rest when he saw we weren't causing a fuss. He advanced toward us.

"Silence, slave!" he said with an external speaker that was punishingly loud. "You have failed in your mission. You are now a possession of the Empire."

"That's not failure to us, sir," I said. "We always have been servants of the Empire. We're the local enforcers from Province 921."

The squinty-eyed devil in the machine advanced a few paces closer. He didn't look terribly trusting, but then, I'd never met a Mogwa that was.

"What are you talking about? You're barbarians from—"

"Yessir. Barbarian troops. Levies, mercenaries, whatever you'd like to call us. Grand Admiral Sateekas is our military master, and Governor Nox is our civilian leader."

"Nonsense!" he said, suddenly turning angry. "Sateekas is nothing. He is a failure. He commandeered our best warship and flew it away without authorization! We've been under threat of extinction ever since!"

He shook an angry limb up at the sky. I glanced upward, following the gesture, and I began to understand the true nature of our situation.

I felt a sudden sickness in my gut. Sateekas was an impetuous, overbearing, overreaching blowhard. He often took the initiative when commanding armies and navies—and just as often he got them wrecked. He had his heart in the right place—for a Mogwa—but he wasn't terribly good at his job.

The real nature of our diplomatic problems was now apparent to me. Whenever we'd invoked the name of Sateekas, we hadn't been doing anyone any favors. We'd been pissing off the locals.

The situation obviously required some hard maneuvering. I was going to have to switch my tactics and my approach. Fortunately, the Good Lord had seen fit to equip me with a highly flexible mind.

"Mr. Mogwa, sir? Are you saying Sateekas didn't bring that battlecruiser out from the Core Worlds?" I asked this with my best look of shocked ignorance.

"Hardly. He stole it from Segin. He is a scoundrel, and a poor leader."

"Oh... then who *is* the rightful commander of your armed forces here on Segin?"

"As far as you're concerned, I am that individual."

At that point I made a big show of kneeling and lowering my helmeted head, like he was the pope come to dinner or something. "Please accept our apologies and our fealty, Mogwa Overlord."

The Mogwa was no lord. He was a marine officer. But I'd never met an alien yet that didn't like to be told he was a bigger deal than he was.

His power-armor's mechanical legs squeaked and churned. He came quite near. He squinted at me, studying me and my reaction. At last, he spoke again in a more thoughtful voice. "It's wrong I should speak so long with a creature that is so low in both caste and value—but I will finish this conversation, as it intrigues me. You are implying things we have not yet considered."

"Uh... like what?"

"That your claims of serving the Empire might be in earnest. That you might have been duped by that scoundrel Sateekas just as surely as we have been."

I pointed a finger at him, and even though he was wearing walking power-armor, he recoiled a little. Maybe he thought I was going to shoot him with my finger-gun or something.

"That's exactly it!" I said. "We didn't understand. We serve the Empire, not Sateekas. But he told us you guys were his slaves in turn."

"What? Such wild impudence—!"

215

"That's right. He said he was the local king out here, and he needed us to come out and put down a little rebellion—he wasn't too specific, see. He also mentioned the dome and the rebels dropping rocks on it... But now I think we were misled. If you are the Overlord here, sir, I'm here to declare there are over forty thousand ground troops outside this dome, ready to swear fealty specifically to *you*."

The marine officer's eyes lit up a little, and I couldn't blame him. After all, who doesn't like the sound of a personal army?

"You will submit to my instructions?"

"Damn straight we will. If... that is... you truly serve the Empire. You're not some crazy rutting beast like Sateekas, are you?"

"Certainly not. My credentials are bona fide and beyond reproach." I threw my arms wide, and he backed up a step in alarm.

His turret aimed itself at me while I grinned like an idiot.

"This is a display of happiness, sir," I told him. "We are at your command and eager for glory. Thousands upon thousands of us stand ready. If you want us to stay outside the dome and perish under the blasts of a thousand falling rocks from space, so be it. We'd be happy to sacrifice ourselves in any way you might imagine."

"Sacrifice? What is this nonsense?"

"Well sir, our fleet got run off—you know that, right?"

"We witnessed a battle and a shameful retreat, yes."

I nodded vigorously and got back to my feet. I pointed upward and stared at the clouds like I could see the battle from here. "It was a glorious struggle, but Sateekas chickened and ran out on us at the end."

The marine followed my gesture. "Yes... I'd heard such reports. It's hard to credit his behavior."

"Mighty strange," I agreed. "So, now that you command the biggest land army on Segin, what do you want us to do? We're cut off, no fleet, no food, running out of supplies, but we'll kill a few of those bears, don't you worry. I bet we'll drop ten percent of them before they burrow in here and slaughter every baby-Mogwa they can run down. Hell, your streets are going to be painted with blood soon, but don't you—"

"Shut up, mindless human. Listen to me, and heed my orders. I demand that you withdraw into the dome as quickly as possible. You will not spend your strength in a pointless struggle outside the protective shell of force. Such a strategy can only have come from the idiot brain of Sateekas himself."

I gave him that slack-jawed stare again. "I'm sure you're right, Commander. Now, how do you want to do this?"

"I must talk to the Council. Every border command unit must be compliant. It can be done—it *must* be done."

He began to hustle, and soon countless messages were relayed to the City and to the outside world. Less than an hour later, the beleaguered troops of Legion Varus and Victrix, along with their auxiliary legions, began to march into the safety of the dome.

-36-

Now, any right-thinking person would assume that I would be hailed as a hero by one and all once these arrangements were made. After all, we were facing certain destruction out there in the open, outside the dome.

But noooo, you would have thought wrong. Dead wrong.

"Seriously, McGill?" Winslade complained. "This is the best you could arrange?"

"You're not a captive any longer, sir," I pointed out. "The Mogwa have accepted you as an officer of Legion Varus and everything."

"Yes, as a *slave* officer. A slave who leads other slaves, at best."

I shrugged. That sort of status just came with the territory when you were dealing with the Mogwa, or any other Galactic for that matter. I was almost sympathetic with the Mogwa in this instance. They'd taken a big chance. They'd invited thousands of unknown barbarian soldiers into their city, and they'd allowed us to camp out along the outskirts in the pig-shit fields and whatnot. They were even letting us eat off their land. To their minds, they were making huge concessions every which-way.

"Well sir, you can go ahead and negotiate better terms for us anytime you like. The City is thataway." I pointed off into the distance, where the buildings stood like mountains.

Winslade sniffed. "I would, but you've spoiled everything. The deal has been struck, and once that step has been frittered away, renegotiations are a thousand times more difficult. I suppose there's nothing for it—we'll have to live with these humiliating conditions... for now."

He stalked off, and I frowned after him. Just what had he meant? Saying "for now" indicated he might be harboring some dark plans of his own. I tried not to think about it, and I soon dropped these questions from my mind entirely. That was easily done, as I really didn't care much, anyways.

Whistling as I walked out of our new headquarters bunker, I headed back to my unit. Coincidentally, the Mogwa had seen fit to clear the ornery Mogwa farmer off his land. My unit had been there front-and-center, so we'd confiscated his farmhouse.

As it turned out, our farm soon became prime real estate out here on the fringe of town. I couldn't even tell you how many primus-level scoundrels tried to come and chase us out of it. Most people didn't even have a hole in the ground with puff-crete poured over it yet. An honest-to-God building was considered luxurious.

Each time, however, I employed a foolproof approach. First off, I made a big show of dialing up the marine commander and the City Council on my tapper. I explained that I couldn't possibly give up my position without letting the Mogwa brass know they'd be disappointed when they came out here to consult with their Earth liaison.

While I made my bullshit call, pretending to wait on hold, I quickly invented a list of imaginary alien dignitaries in robes who were all marching out here from the big City like the wise men coming to meet Jesus. That got the sweat popping out, let me tell you.

Whatever snooty officer had come along to steal our accommodations soon began to urge me to stop the call. The next step in my script was to pretend to blink in confusion, but at last, I let myself be convinced.

That approach quickly turned away all but the most stubborn thieves. As a case in point, only one primus dared argue with me after I'd made the scenario clear to her.

219

"I want you to know I'm not buying any of this, McGill," Primus Collins said. She had her little fists all balled-up on her hips, and she was glaring up at me with her eyes slitted. She looked like a cat with a freshly pulled tail.

Throwing my right hand high and placing my left on my heart, I looked at her with deadly seriousness. "As the Almighty is my witness, I will not tell anyone who it was that ordered me to desert this post, sir. I will let you meet with the Mogwa and explain things to them yourself. No one at Headquarters has to know what happened out here today, either."

"What do you mean by that? Is that some kind of threat?"

I huffed. "It's the opposite, sir. I'm pledging to cover for you. As a fellow officer of Varus, I feel the comradery. It will be our little secret when the dust settles. Now, if you don't mind excusing me, I've got to gather up my boys and find a new place to sleep tonight."

Primus Collins licked her lips. She looked troubled. She watched as I made a show of gathering gear and shouting orders to my startled troops. My adjuncts asked what was going on, and I made vague gestures in Collins' direction.

They glanced at her and nodded. Soon, everyone was packing and grumbling.

My tapper made a tone, and I looked at it expectantly. "Just a false alarm," I said to Collins. "I'm still on hold with Mogwa Command. I guess they're busy, what with the invasion and all."

Collins watched me, her teeth bared and clenched in her mouth. Despite the fact I was complying with her demands to clear out, she didn't seem happy. Damnation if some people weren't nigh-on impossible to please.

After about four minutes—that's all it took, I know because I'd marked the time on my tapper, which was set to make a beeping sound every minute—she caved.

"Damn you, Centurion!"

I turned in her direction, looking as surprised and innocent as possible. My jaw sagged, and I snapped it closed again. "Uh... what's the problem, Primus?"

"Just forget it. You're staying put—and you're dismissed."

She spun on her heel and walked out of the place. A few of the noncoms looked like they were going to snicker at her, but they controlled themselves after a stern warning look from me.

At the door of our place, however, there was a chance meeting. As Primus Collins was marching out, Adjunct Barton was walking in. They almost walked into one another.

Both girls pulled up short, and Barton dodged away, being the lower-ranked. But then, Collins stopped and cocked her angry head.

"Barton?" she asked. "Didn't you get drummed out of Victrix?"

"Ah… no sir, I was reassigned."

Collins gave her a dirty laugh. "Sure. Everyone wants to bail on Victrix of their own free will. Well, whatever you did, rest assured the recommendation you asked me for has been rescinded. I think you deserve to be serving with these animals in 3rd Unit. I'm surprised you haven't quit your commission yet."

Poor Erin didn't answer. She just studied her boots, and mean-assed Collins brushed past her on the way to the door.

"Aw now, that wasn't right," Harris said. He gave me a nudge on the shoulder. "Go comfort her, McGill—but not with your dick this time."

I gave him a reproachful glance but then walked up to Erin. She was a nice enough girl. She was also very business-like and effective as an officer. Her private life, however, had always been an unmitigated disaster.

"Hey Adjunct," I said. "Have you heard the good news? We're not camping out in the fields again. Not even the sewers. No, sir! Tonight, every officer in this unit will get a bed to themselves."

"Right sir. I'll get right on it," she said. She didn't seem to be hearing me.

"Uh…"

She went outside and put field goggles on. She was using them to study the surrounding land.

Walking slowly, I came up next to her. I couldn't help but notice her cheeks were a little wet under the goggles, but you

221

couldn't really tell if she was crying or not. The goggles were a good cover.

"Hey, Erin," I said. "You want me to go ask Collins if she'll trade this farm for a recommendation letter?"

That got her attention. She lowered her visor so I couldn't see her face inside her helmet, and she shook her head. "That's a really nice offer, sir. But it won't work. Collins isn't flexible like that. You managed to threaten her and push her today—and now you've made a fool of her in front of the troops. She'll just be even angrier if you admit you were bullshitting her in the first place."

"Huh…" I said, giving myself an idle scratch. "Yeah, I can see that. Ah well, you don't need her approval anyway. If Victrix wants you back, you'll find a way. Don't worry."

She nodded, and I left her out there, stewing and pretending to do a tactical survey of what was pretty much a flat, featureless stretch of land.

-37-

Primus Collins left us alone after that single visit, and a few days passed by pleasantly. Almost all of my troops were revived and returned to duty during that time span.

It was kind of nice to be lording it up on a for-reals Mogwa farm. Honestly, I never thought I'd experience such wonders.

Unfortunately, our happy state of affairs didn't last long. New orders came in on the third day when the bears made their first serious attack.

Just like I'd predicted when I talked to the Mogwa marine captain, the bears didn't appreciate us humans retreating under the safety of the dome. They tried to follow us. They began burrowing under, just as we'd done.

Now, don't go thinking that our engineering folk were total morons. They filled in the holes we used with puff-crete and crystallized steel—but that didn't mean much. The bears had gotten the idea from us, and they decided to run with it. Digging in new spots, they came up like sappers inside the sewer systems.

"The bears are breaching in your sector, McGill," said a familiar voice. It was Winslade, and he was in as sour a mood as ever. "I'm sending the coordinates and the tactical sitrep to your tapper. Move your unit into the defensive position stipulated. You have twelve minutes to get there."

"Twelve minutes?" I demanded, spitting out a mouthful of bootleg brew. I'd put my bio people to work fermenting things all over the Mogwa farm, and they'd finally produced something that didn't taste like formaldehyde. At least, not *entirely* like formaldehyde. "Sir, that's a kilometer off, and my people aren't…"

I stopped talking because Winslade was gone. He'd dropped the call and gone off to hassle some other subordinate.

Cursing, I stood up and pulled my boots on. While I was hopping and cursing, I gave the all-hands scramble order, sounding the alarm. People began racing around pulling together their gear and rushing to the road.

Once they were eighty percent assembled, I began to trot. Very quickly, I increased my pace to a ground-eating run. Soldiers who were still taking a crap or making out together somewhere would have to catch up on their own. This was go-time.

Ten minutes later, we arrived at our designated rally point. Behind me most of my troops were bent over grabbing their knees. They were huffing and puffing. I frowned to see that. Sure, we'd brought a lot of gear, and we'd been traveling at a dead run for more than a kilometer—but a true legionnaire wouldn't let something like that knock the wind out of him.

"We're going to start practicing wind-sprints if you guys don't stop that embarrassing gasping and groaning."

They straightened up and hid their pain after that. Harris and Moller walked among the group, cuffing people and lining them up.

Winslade met us a few minutes later, stepping out of a ground car that looked like it had been polished to a chrome shine.

I whistled long and low. "Damn, sir. That's one fine piece of equipment. How'd you manage to wangle that?"

He gave me a pursed-lip shrug. "It's courtesy of the Mogwa. All our upper-tier officers have been provided with personal transportation—hey, get out of there!"

I'd ducked my head in to feel-up the seats and admire the instrumentation. The rear buckets were shaped wrong, mind you, but I didn't think a human Winslade's size would be too uncomfortable.

"That's some kind of leather in there," I commented. "The real deal."

"Forget about it, McGill. I recall what you did to Praetor Drusus' air car years back."

I looked up in disappointment. "He still talks about that when I'm not around, huh?"

"Incessantly."

Jerking a thumb over my shoulder at my unit, I faced Winslade squarely. It was time for business. "So this is where you want us to set up camp? Really? We're all just standing around on a puff-crete road."

"You've failed to grasp the obvious yet again. You're to deploy in that ditch—on the city side of the road."

Squinting in the sunshine, I eyeballed the ditch in question. "That's not much cover, sir."

"No. But it's one of the most likely surfacing points of the Rigellian digging machines."

"Huh…?"

He looked at me sourly and crossed his skinny arms. "Don't tell me you haven't been looking at the latest intel?"

"Well sir, we've been hard at work shoring up our defenses at the farm, see, and—"

"Shut up. 3rd Unit is working now, not loafing. You'll cover this stretch of road for about a kilometer span. The bears will probably emerge somewhere in one of the culverts that come out of the sewers. Either that, or they'll surface in one of their digging machines in that field to the west."

I eyed the landscape unhappily. "How long have we got? Until they get here?"

"If they actually *do* choose to breach here, you'll see them in the next half hour. Attack them immediately then report the contact. Hold them until you're annihilated. That's your purpose—to give our real lines a chance to form up and envelop the invasion."

"That doesn't sound—"

But I was talking to his back. He climbed into his car—the backseat, of course—and tapped the shoulder of a pretty adjunct with severely short hair. They drove away without giving me a second glance.

"Fuck me," Harris said, coming near with his hands on his hips. "How in the hell are we supposed to defend a stretch of road this long and open?"

"We're not. Not really."

I told him what our real orders were, and he didn't get any happier. In fact, he looked like he smelled shit.

"That's just grand, sir. How do you want to do this? Break up in to squads, or...?"

I ordered Kivi to do a buzzer survey before I answered him. It turned out there were seven culverts. Seeing those as the most likely exit points, I placed a squad at each location, then took the rest of my men—mostly specialists—and pulled back from the road a ways. There was a hillock with some rocks around it. We set up in there.

"Now listen-up," I broadcast over tactical chat. "If your squad draws the lucky ticket and bears start boiling up out of your ditch, start shooting and call in. We'll move to support you. Throw grenades into the hole immediately to keep them ducking. We'll come save your bacon in ninety seconds flat after that."

This was a bald-faced lie, of course, but it did help with morale. Grim-faced soldiers squatted in a circle about ten meters off from every opening. Every squad was pretty much staring at the mouth of a pipe, swallowing hard and checking their rifles every minute or so.

"Kivi, I want half your buzzers zooming over that field. Run patterns, scanning for any changes in the landscape. The second a dirt clod moves, tell me about it."

She did as I ordered, and I sat back to wait. I was tense, but not too tense. After all, thousands of troops were watchdogging nowhere roads like this one on the city outskirts. The odds that we would be the ones—

"Sir!" Kivi shouted in my headset. "We've got underground vibrations to the west."

"Show me."

She sent me a live feed. All kinds of technology had gone into projecting some red triangles on my tapper. The vibrations were depicted by dozens of these triangles, which kept appearing in new spots and indicating a northern course. The

226

last of about ten triangles faded out the moment a new one appeared.

I called in the contact and gave the coordinates and direction. Winslade called me back less than a minute later. "That has to be one of their digging machines. You've got one of our first sightings, McGill. Congratulations. If they surface, give them hell. Winslade out."

My first thought was to pull my unit together and abandon the culvert watch-parties, but I held off on giving that order. What if the bears were doing both strategies, running troops through the tunnels and riding in digging machines? I just didn't know enough yet.

"Dammit, Kivi. I need intel. What's happening? What are the other units seeing?"

"To our north and south, no sightings. All we know so far is there's a machine tunneling along in the earth on a course that's parallel to the roadway."

I thought about that. I thought hard. "They're reconning us. They've spotted us, somehow, and they're deciding what to do about our formation, just like we are eyeballing them. Keep looking."

"Yessir."

Ten long minutes went by without further incident. The digging machine moved north and into the next unit's territory. No doubt they were giving Manfred a heart attack about now.

"How fast did that thing move, Kivi? Have you got a speed measurement?"

"It's steaming along at about ten to twenty kilometers an hour. Not very fast—but fast enough for a digging machine."

"That's crazy... where did they get that tech?"

Kivi came to my position and squatted next to me. In situations like this, your tech noncoms were like honored guests for any centurion.

"I'd say they had to know about this dome and how it could be penetrated. Maybe they planned all along to breach this way—if their business of dropping rocks didn't work out for them."

227

"Huh… yeah, I guess. The rock-dropping seemed crazy, anyway. I mean, if you want to capture a city, it makes no sense to blow it up."

"They weren't doing that," she said. "They were smart about it. They dropped their rocks on one section at a time, trying to destroy it. The shield isn't a single wall of force, you know. It's far too big for that. It's a series of reactive fields that overlap each other, like shingles on a—"

"Yeah, yeah. That's real interesting, Kivi. How did you come to hear all these tech details, anyways?"

She shrugged and avoided my eye. "There have been certain briefings for the upper tier officers. We techs share, you know."

I laughed. I did know all about that. Techs were like birds on a wire. They buzzed and gossiped almost as much as their buzzers did in the sky above.

"Okay… so you hacked some briefings. What else did they say?"

"Well… our fleet did do one thing right. They destroyed a lot of those tugs. That stopped the rock-dropping effort. The enemy gave up on knocking down a pie-slice of this dome and decided to invade on foot when we showed up. That's how things got to this point."

I stared out at the open field again. The drilling machine that had given us all a good scare was long gone by now. It was a kilometer or two to the north, still refusing to come up for air.

Leaning back with a grunt and a sigh, I tipped my helmet's sun shade over my eyes. "Wake me up when something happens."

In the end, it wasn't Kivi who woke me up. It was the crack and boom of gunfire.

-38-

"Bears, sir! Zillions of them! They're pouring out of the ground!"

That was the report that came into my earpiece, word for word. The speaker was Johnson, a veteran I'd placed in charge of a squad at one of the culverts.

Even before I heard Johnson's fateful words, I heard the rattle and boom of a firefight in progress. As I'd ordered, the troops fell back, using grenades and encircling fire to keep the bears at bay.

"I'll tell you one thing, these bears aren't pussies," Harris said. "Look at 'em, charging right into our guns."

He'd appeared in my circle of rocks somehow, probably sneaking in while I was taking a catnap. I got up and frowned at him.

"Harris, gather up a reserve squad of heavies. Move to Johnson's position to support him. Maybe we can keep them contained."

Harris looked startled. "Say what? You really want to commit our reserves already? You really have been sleeping, haven't you Centurion? Check the cohort-wide sitrep."

Annoyed, I did as he suggested. Harris' point was immediately made in stark graphics. All along our cohort's covered ground, the bears were making probes like this one.

"They're poking at our defenses, checking our lines," I said.

229

"That's what I see, sir," Harris said. "They're harassing Manfred's unit next door, and everyone else down the line. They might pop up anywhere in real strength."

"Hmm… okay, we'll hold tight and see if they retreat or come on full-strength."

The gunfire died down after a few minutes. The bears had surged, killed a few men and lost five times as many themselves. Then, they pulled back into their hole and disappeared.

"You want to send Barton's lights after them to scout? Or at least a buzzer?" Harris asked.

I looked at him, but I shook my head. "No. That might be what they want. They're checking out our responses, our readiness. Let's just hope that our link in this chain isn't the weakest one they find."

Things quieted for a bit, but we were on edge now. Everyone knew the enemy was coming back. They were going to hit us somewhere, and they were going to hit us hard.

When the next attack finally came, it was almost an hour after we'd first spotted their digging machine. All of a sudden, there was lots of squawking on our radio headsets.

"McGill! McGill? Are you there? Dammit, man!" It was Winslade, and he sounded kind of upset.

"What's happening, Primus? It's all quiet here."

"Well, that's dandy. It isn't quiet a few kilometers up the road to the north. I'm sending support up there to help out."

"Uh…" I said, paging through the tactical maps. "Sir… that sounds too far off. Our cohort isn't responsible for—"

"Yes, yes, you idiot. I know that. We're at the very edge of our territorial zone. But this dome is our responsibility to defend in its entirety. Up there, you'll find a regiment of Mogwa marines. Just past that, Victrix has their troops deployed."

I thought that over for about a full second. "So… the enemy decided the Mogwa themselves were the weak link?"

"Apparently so. Mogwa Command is panicking. They're demanding we rush to their aid."

I thought that was funny, and I began to laugh, but old Winslade wasn't in a jovial mood. "Listen to me. Every other unit in the cohort is rolling north to patch up this breach."

"Every other...?" I said, looking to the north. It did seem like there were some fireworks going off in the distance. Black smoke was rising, and flashes could be seen on the horizon.

"That's right. You're marching north with the rest. Get going immediately. Manfred will fill in from one side and Singh from the other."

"That's going to make a thin line even thinner, sir."

"Don't I know it. I'm going to command the remainder personally. Primus Collins will command the relief force. Please don't antagonize her unnecessarily."

My face fell, and my heart sank into my boots. Primus Collins had never liked me—she didn't outright hate me, unlike some of the others—but she wasn't my fan. I opened my mouth to protest, but Winslade was moving on.

"You have your orders. Move out!"

Grunting, I got to my feet and began to pinwheel my arms. My nap was over, and the pain was just beginning. We were on the march again.

The unit walked out onto the road, and we began to trot northward. I ordered the troops in the rear of our stretched out column to run, while the ones in the middle jogged and the farther north boys walked. Soon, we were moving in a more coherent formation.

As we passed by the boys in the trenches in Manfred's zone, we heard hoots and catcalls. Nothing seemed to amuse a Varus man more than seeing a comrade get chosen for hazardous duty.

Harris growled and snarled at every one of our tormenters, while I studiously ignored them. He never seemed to catch on to the idea that acting upset only garnered more teasing, especially when the other unit's commander didn't give a shit about your feelings.

Manfred even hopped out of his trench and trotted after me. He fell into step and grinned up at me.

"What are you smiling about?" I asked. "You boys having a circle-jerk party again?"

"Even better," he said, still grinning. "We're cheering on comrades. I can only hope that you won't hog all the glory up there and shame Victrix."

"Victrix? We're marching to save some lame-ass Mogwa marines."

"Right, right. But you know full well those ingrates will fall apart after ten minutes of facing those bears. Then you'll land on them, and Victrix will hit them in the other flank. You'll meet in the middle and kiss, I wager, in an hour's time."

I wondered if he could be right. The Mogwa Marines weren't a joke force, but they didn't have the experience or the self-sacrificing nature of human mercenary troops.

"Well," I said, "don't you think you ought to run off and hide with Winslade and the rest?"

"All right, all right. I can tell when I'm not amusing someone. Good luck, McGill."

He offered me a gauntlet to shake, and I took it. We often razzed each other and played mean tricks, but we were friends underneath.

Harris hustled up to walk at my side after Manfred had faded away behind my fast-moving column.

"That was it, huh?" he asked. "A few jokes and a handshake? Manfred is a real piece of work."

I shrugged, not caring what Harris thought. "He's got his orders, and we've got ours. Move back to your platoon, Harris. You'll take the middle position, behind Barton's lights. Let's make this look like we mean business."

The unit became more professional as we approached the newly-forming front lines. There were already several units there, hugging the back of a ridge. It was only about twenty meters tall, but anyone who's been in battle can tell you any cover is welcome.

Ahead of us, a food-processing plant lay in the middle of the battle zone. Maybe that was on purpose. It occurred to me that the bears might not be attacking a weak spot, but rather a strategic installation. All the farms in this area fed this plant, which produced food for the Mogwa in the big city off to the north. If they captured it or destroyed it, the siege would be brought closer to an unhappy conclusion.

Primus Collins took personal command when there were four units assembled. "You took your sweet frigging time getting here," she complained at us. "Normally, I'd wait for the last unit to get here, but we can't do it. Intel says the Mogwa are losing the battle over at that big food plant. We're going to have to go in there and save their asses."

I opened my mouth to ask a few questions, but she wasn't in the mood.

"Line up your troops, Centurions. We're going over the top of this ridge of dirt in three minutes. I've marked your starting spots and your target waypoints on your tacticals. Get moving!"

That was it. Her entire briefing, her planning session—that was the whole thing. This battle felt rushed, and it was. That could only mean one thing: the Mogwa marines were losing.

Losing badly.

-39-

A few minutes later, Primus Collins ordered us to charge up and over our ridge. We rushed up the dirt slope, with rocks and strange-looking alien weeds crumbling under our boots. It occurred to me that every planet I'd ever been on seemed to have weeds—at least the habitable ones did. I guess weeds were a universal constant of the living universe.

Our first waypoint was a pipeline that led from the big city down to the plant itself. The pipe was partially above ground and about two meters high—good cover for an advancing force. It was probably full of slime, or sludge, or whatever these Mogwa ate during a siege—but that didn't much matter as long as it blocked a bolt from a power-rifle.

I sent Barton's lights in the lead, as usual. They fanned out and raced ahead. Next came Harris and his heavies. Last, behind me, were Gary and the specialists. Their kits were bulky and tended to slap them in the ass as they ran, making them the slowest of the lot. I didn't give them a second glance.

It was the situation ahead that had my unwavering attention. The battleground was obscured in smoke, but what I could see of it didn't look good. I counted six drilling machines, long caterpillar-like things that had fired up out of the ground and beached themselves. The forward nose of these machines was spread open, and they'd clearly disgorged all their troops in a surprise attack.

None of that was the disturbing part. What I didn't like to see was the number of destroyed Mogwa vehicles strewn in front of these caterpillars. Dozens of drone tanks and dead marines in their walking machines were burning and broken. They'd probably massed and counterattacked against the bears when they first emerged—but they'd obviously been driven back.

Now, the Mogwa were holed up inside the food plant. That building was a mass of pipes and silos. All of it was battleship-gray and unadorned. Mogwa architecture was generally like that—they were engineers, not artists.

I couldn't see the bears from where I was, because Collins had positioned us to approach the plant from the city-side—the safer side. That only made sense if we could get into the plant without taking fire—

"Incoming!" shouted one of Barton's recruits. "Look out!"

Looking up and toward the plant, I saw spinning vapor trails. A flock of mini-missiles was descending on our location.

No one needed to be told what to do. We raced for the pipe, diving for cover the moment the missiles reached us.

They were smart little flying drones, really. Driven by propellant rather than propellers, they discharged a shower of bomblets that sought out flesh like swarms of angry wasps. The bomblets made hissing, burning sounds as they came. That sound was familiar, and it made every man on open ground feel his balls cinch up tight.

Just as automatically, our countermeasures went off to protect us. The specialists in the rear of the formation had counter-missiles and jammers. Kivi's own buzzers even turned suicidal, diving to intercept the missile-flock.

Some of that worked. Maybe half the missiles didn't reach us before they detonated—but that wasn't good enough to save all of our sorry asses. Before the barrage died down, eleven troops were dead or incapacitated.

"This sucks," Gary informed me as we hugged the food pipe, breathing hard. "Is it always like this, McGill? We're just targets out here. We haven't even spotted the enemy."

"Don't worry," I bullshitted him. "Once we get in close on those bears, we'll give them some payback."

235

This, of course, was an outright lie. The bears were at their most dangerous when you were in close with them. They had advanced armor like only Gary and myself did, and they were mean as hell when you finally got one in a clinch.

None of that would raise morale, so I left it out. Slamming a gauntlet on his shoulder, I grinned into his freaked-out face. "Speaking of which, I've got your next tactical mission all lined up for you."

"How's that, sir?"

"Primus Collins wants our weaponeers to sight on that building—that's right, the long low one off to the west. You're supposed to melt it with combined belcher fire."

His breathing hadn't slowed down from our run yet, and he looked a little sick. "Is that where the mini-missiles are coming from?"

"I think so."

"But if we light them up, won't they fire everything they have at us?"

I clapped him on the shoulder again. "Nah, probably not. They'll duck and cover. Bears are awful cowards on the battlefield. Not everyone knows that, but it's true."

"Really?"

I almost didn't have the heart to bullshit the kid any further, but I could tell he needed some hopeful words. "That's gospel. Now, get your weaponeers lined up. Don't fire until you can do it all at once."

"Uh… where are your guys going, Centurion?"

Apparently, he couldn't help but notice that we were all crawling away from him and his weaponeers. Harris and his heavies were on their bellies like worms—and Barton's lights, well hell, they were slipping under the food pipe itself in places.

"Just follow orders, Gary. Have your boys aim and fire their belchers all at once!"

Breathing hard and blinking fast, Gary directed his troops. The men shouldered their weapons, cranked their apertures down to make tight, narrow beams, then unloaded on the target all together.

236

The building lit up white-hot inside of seconds. Around about the eleventh second, the response came from the enemy. They'd finally noticed us.

A familiar hissing and burning sound began. The enemy had fired their mini-missiles back at us. From the size of this new incoming flock, it looked and sounded like they'd fired everything they had.

"Other side of the pipe!" I roared at everyone. "Dive over it and take cover!"

The weaponeers scattered, but they did so in slow-motion. They looked like lumbering two-legged turtles in their heavy armor and massive kits. Some dropped their belchers, but most held onto them by instinct.

One man, a big boy taller than the rest, grabbed Gary by the scruff. He shoved him down on his face, then sat on him and aimed his own belcher upward into the missile swarm. Somehow, he'd managed to crank his weapon's emitter wide open, from the tightest beam to the widest, and at the last possible instant he blazed upward into the oncoming swarm.

The mini-missiles had targeted him instinctively. There he was, a big target, immobile and right in the dead center of ground zero.

It was Sargon. It had to be. I knew in my heart he was as good as dead, but I dared to hope he would pull through somehow. Even if he didn't, he'd made one hell of a valiant last stand. One we'd remember when he eventually caught a revive.

The missile-swarm swooped for the kill and met his cone of fire. He held that trigger down, burning for a long time—too long. There was no way the internal coil wouldn't be burnt out after this—but I understood. It was his only option.

The missiles formed a point and they were burned away like a flock of sparrows flying right into a hot furnace. Flashing explosions blinded all of us who gaped at the scene from a safe distance. The flashes seemed to go on and on—but I'm sure the whole thing took less than ten seconds of real time.

Finally, it was over. Men crawled and groaned in the dirt. Some of them were missing limbs and had scorched black holes in their armor. Others began to stand and shake themselves off.

Miraculously, Sargon managed to heave himself onto his feet. He looked kind of stunned, but functional. Using one long arm, he reached down and lifted Gary, standing him up like a ragdoll.

"There you are, Adjunct," he said. "Orders?"

Gary was open-mouthed and wide-eyed. Harris might have shouted at Sargon. Leeson might have thanked him. Gary did neither, he just kind of gawked. Then suddenly, he opened his faceplate and puked on the smoking ground.

"Uh… Centurion?" Sargon asked, turning my way. "What next?"

I looked downslope again. The bunker I'd ordered to be destroyed was indeed a smoking, flattened pile of puff-crete.

"Good job, men. See to your wounded. We'll ask Collins for our next objective."

I reported in, and I was immediately given fresh commands. I didn't like them much. I liked them even less, in fact, than our last orders.

-40-

Primus Collins didn't bother to answer my private requests for directives. Instead, she just overrode tactical chat and talked to me and all the other units at once.

"Brave soldiers of Varus," she said. "Our new mission is to infiltrate that factory in any way we can. Get inside, engage the enemy, and save the Mogwa before it's too late. Reports from our allies indicate they're being hunted down inside."

We grimaced and got to our feet. These new orders were far from ideal. Infantrymen like to work their way toward the enemy, moving from one scrap of cover to the next. The last thing any of us wanted to do was charge into an unknown building without scouting or planning.

Worse, this huge building wasn't going to be friendly inside. It was a tangle of unknown equipment. Some of it was bound to be dangerous. I knew aliens rarely had safety precautions built into their industrial sites the way humans preferred. They were as likely to lay bare wires carrying heavy voltage over the floor or along a wall as not. It seemed like aliens didn't much care if incompetent workers lived or died.

"All right," I said, "you heard the lady. We're going in hot and fast. Lights first. Keep your eyes peeled and your asses tight. Go for it!"

Adjunct Barton needed no more encouragement. She took off at a run, and her startled light troopers followed her in a rush. There were only about two dozen of them still breathing,

239

but they raced away along the pipes and fences, jumping over obstacles such as the hexagonal barrels we saw all over the plant.

Scattered enemy fire came from the direction of the factory, but it wasn't much. By knocking out that bunker with the mini-missile company in it, it looked like we'd gotten rid of much of the local resistance on our side of the factory.

"Looks good," I said. "Harris, you're on deck."

"Are you kidding me, sir? Can't we even let Barton get across that open area and into the plant first? Let the lights show us the way."

Normally, I'd have taken his advice. It wasn't unreasonable—but it was against our orders. I shook my head and pointed after Barton.

"Move out right now, or I'll relieve you of command, Adjunct."

Grumbling, Harris bellowed at his heavies. They trotted after Barton. When they ran into fences, they cut through them with their force-blades rather than hopping over. The hexagonal barrels suffered a similar fate, being kicked over roughly by metal boots.

I turned to Gary next. "You're up. Move with me, we're bringing up the rear again."

Gary was white-faced, but he was game. He nodded and followed me without complaining. He did spit and swallow a lot, though. Sure signs of a nervous man marching through alien dirt.

As the most awkward gear to carry was on our backs, the specialists took the easy path. They hustled in the wake of the heavies who'd hacked their way in a straight line toward the biggest open gate that led into the factory.

It was a mad dash, but we received very little suppressing fire. Apparently, Collins had made the right call by having us nail that bunker where the mini-missiles were coming from.

Still, we were all breathing hard by the time we made it inside. The factory was dim-lit, with only a few high grungy windows covered in soot and grime to let any sunlight in.

The big doors were the primary source of air and light, and they were wide enough to let aircraft come in.

"We're in some kind of warehouse," Harris told me. "We reconned the whole chamber. There's nothing here but those hex-shaped barrels and some dead Mogwa workers."

I reported in to Collins, telling her we'd made it inside the building. She ordered me to sit tight and cover the next unit that was hustling in from farther away. The other two had gone in another direction, and they were meeting some resistance.

"There they are!" Harris said, pointing out the doorway.

We all peered into the glare of the sunlit world outside. It was dusty out there, and a wind had picked up. The wind caused the various burning buildings to obscure the landscape with drifting black smoke.

Jogging in our direction was a full unit. They weren't as strung out as we'd been. All three platoons were hustling in a single mass. They were going to make it or break it together.

"Harris, line your troops up on the other side of that door. Prepare to lay down suppressive fire. Kivi, have you got buzzers out there?"

"They haven't been going down as fast after we knocked out the bear's strongpoint," she told me. "I've got plenty of eyes in the sky now..."

She surveyed her data, but she frowned suddenly. "Bears spotted, sir! They're coming out of the factory—there's some kind of side door. They're lining up about two hundred meters to the west."

I took two steps toward the open doorway. "Put them on tactical."

About then, the supporting unit that was coming our way must have gotten the message that they weren't alone out there. Instead of jogging in an organized fashion, they began to hump-and-bump. They raced toward us.

"Barton, send out a squad of snipers. Put down fire on those bears before—"

She began to move even as I said it—but it was too late. A volley of fire came from the bears. Worse, their squadron had swollen to a platoon—maybe more. They shot at our troops, hitting them in the flank. The running troops split up, sending their lights in toward us at a dead run, while their heavies slowed and fired back at the bears.

241

Barton's squad of snipers joined in, contributing to the chaos outside. Bolts were flying everywhere, punching holes in every barrel and chipping at the puff-crete walls of the factory.

I gritted my teeth, wanting to order Harris out there to support her—but maybe that's what the bears wanted. Maybe they were coming in for the kill. Right now, I had my unit inside, under cover and safe. Collins's plan had worked, and I didn't feel I had the right to second guess her and screw everything up at this point.

So, I held back.

The lights racing our way took heavy casualties on the way in. The ground was just too open, and they were too lightly armored. Half of them didn't make it—probably more than half. It was hard to watch another unit taking hell while you looked on from a safe position.

When the lights finally came close, dragging their wounded and screaming for help, I had Harris rush out and grab anyone who was kicking. His heavies turned their armored backs to the bears and hustled the survivors inside.

"Who are you guys?" I asked one of their noncoms.

He was gasping and grabbing at a bubbling spot on his side. It looked like he'd been lung-shot.

"Are you from 4th?" I demanded.

"No, sir. We're from the 7th."

My heart sank. I knew 7th Unit. Their commander and I had once had a fling. Her name was Jenny Mills, and she was in serious trouble. The 7th had gone from "taking cover" to being pinned down by enemy fire in a matter of thirty seconds. More bears had shown up on the opposite side of the first group—another platoon of them. Jenny and the 7th were caught up in a crossfire.

"Gary, get your weaponeers over here. Sargon? Fire on those damned bears."

"We're not supposed to expose ourselves, Centurion," Harris reminded me.

"Shut up and help out."

He did so, and Gary never even complained. He lined up his remaining weaponeers—although most of them were limping after the mini-missile barrage—and he nudged them out into the sunshine.

They sighted and beamed the bears. It wasn't a very effective attack, but it distracted the enemy.

Seeing this was her chance, Centurion Jenny Mills took it. She ordered her heavies to rise up and race toward our position at a dead run. The last hundred meters or so were wide open. Nothing but a few barrels and wire fences were between them and the bears—but she was going for it anyway.

In the end, my whole unit got involved, blazing away at the bears. They ignored us and fired at Jenny's exposed troops. About thirty heavies from the 7th made it to our doors, and we dragged them all inside. The specialists behind them broke and ran for it as well—but there were more bears than ever out there now. The lighter troops were cut down to the last man.

Jenny's heavies fell on their backs, gasping and groaning. Some were calling for medics. Others gaped like fish. Our bio people wandered among the stricken, delivering what aid they could.

I joined the medics, and after a few minutes I found Centurion Mills. I helped her pull her helmet off, and her blonde hair spilled out. There was some blood in her mouth, but she was still breathing.

"Hey, girl! Fancy meeting you out here! It's like fate brought us together again."

She grinned at me with red-rimmed teeth. "Forget it, McGill."

I grinned back, and we talked for a bit. I fed her some water—but then I saw her vitals on her tapper. I frowned. She was in a bad way.

"What is it?" she asked. Her voice was kind of raspy.

"Nothing... uh... you want some whiskey?"

She sucked in a few painful breaths and tried to get up—but she couldn't. At last, she gestured for the whiskey. I helped her tip my flask up to her lips.

A few moments later, she stopped drinking. The booze ran out of her mouth, and her eyes glazed over.

Rolling her over, I saw there was a big hole in her back. The damned bears had punched right through her back plate.

243

She'd been bleeding out the whole time we'd been talking, and the automatic medical systems we all had in our armor hadn't been able to stabilize her.

Carlos landed a gauntlet on my back. "Tough break, but we're short on time for grieving, Centurion. What do we do now?"

I looked up at him. This was Carlos' way of waking me up. He was trying to get my head back into the game. I stood up with a grunt and slammed my gauntlets together repeatedly, demanding attention.

"7th Unit, I'm formally assuming command of your survivors. Heavies, you're under Adjunct Harris. Lights, follow Adjunct Barton. The rest of you follow me and Adjunct Dahmen. Form up! Let's go!"

Those who could stand struggled to their feet. The rest were executed and their deaths were reported to headquarters.

No one argued. It was time to move out.

-41-

With two units compressed into one, I had about a hundred and fifty troops to lead. We soon located a door that led deeper into the factory. We advanced, hearing gunshots echoing ahead of us in the dimly lit passages.

Cooper and Della were my ghost specialists—scouts who could camouflage themselves with the aid of a high tech stealth suit. I sent them in first, racing ahead of us. Then I sent in a squad of Barton's lights to back them up.

Things got hot pretty quickly.

"Centurion? Centurion, sir?" It was Cooper, and he was whispering. "I've got eyes on the enemy. We made contact just a hundred meters west in one of the main passages."

"Give me a visual, Cooper."

He linked my tapper to his head camera, and I got an eyeful. Cooper was lying on his side, apparently, in a pile of debris. Part of the roof had collapsed, and he'd crawled right into the mess like a good ghost. The angle was an odd one, but I saw bears scuttling down the passages in our general direction.

Then, before Cooper could ask permission to withdraw to a safer spot, gunfire erupted. Two Mogwa marines with a few supporting drone tanks rammed down a wall and began blazing away.

Cooper was in the middle of an ambush, and no one even knew he was there. A hail of streaks cooked the air right over him, going in both directions. He began worming backward toward shelter, whispering, "shit, shit, shit..." over and over again. I couldn't blame him for that.

Sucking in a deep breath and getting a positional fix on this firefight, I came to a quick and fateful decision. "Barton, advance to contact. Support the Mogwa that are hitting those bears. Harris, rush them with your heavies. Let's take them out."

Harris didn't argue for once. Barton never argued, so we were left following in her wake.

The light troops hit the bears in the ass, flanking them. Her troops couldn't do much with snap-rifles, but they were certainly throwing a confusing blur of fire downrange.

The bears, caught in a crossfire between two forces, must have figured the ambush was bigger than they'd believed at first. They threw themselves on the deck and tried to crawl back out the way they'd come. When I reached Barton's people with a platoon of heavies, I brushed her troops aside and charged right through.

"We can't let them escape," I told the troops. "Get close while they're busy ducking. Gut them with force-blades."

When Harris and I reached the action, we'd only lost two light troops. The bears were mostly firing at the Mogwa tanks, figuring they had the firepower to knock them out.

They hadn't counted on force-blades at close quarters. We rushed in among them, and a vicious struggle began.

The Mogwa tanks and marines, for their part, seemed stunned by our arrival. The tanks reared up, swiveling turrets in our direction. After a moment's hesitation, the Mogwa officer urged them to stand down. His own troops extended blades from their multi-legged power armor. They came forward like metal spiders, and they helped us slaughter the bears.

A few men and a single Mogwa died. All the bears perished.

Standing tall and breathing hard, I hailed the Mogwa officer, who's name was Elgu. "Sir, I'm Centurion McGill of Legion Varus, reporting for duty."

"You are slave-troops?" Elgu asked.

"Mercenaries, sir. Enforcers from Frontier 921."

"But... you serve the Empire?"

"Yes. We serve the Empire."

Looking pleased, the officer came forward and pointed an appendage at the dead bears. "You must destroy all these rebels. Find them in the rubble. Root them out and kill them all."

"Uh... okay, sir. We're working on that. Do you have more troops behind you? Where is the rest of the local garrison?"

Elgu gestured toward his handful of drones and marines. "We're all that's left of the garrison. We attacked these wretches as a final act of desperation. Fortune has smiled upon us, providing you to aid in our righteous cause. I should not have doubted Mogwa superiority."

"That's right. You always want to put your money down on the Galactics."

He stared at me for a moment, listening to his translation. "Pointless babble... but one cannot argue with the ferocity of your species. Perhaps Sateekas was arrested prematurely."

That made me blink in confusion and doubt my translator. The app on my tapper assured me it was ninety-seven percent sure it had gotten every word right.

"Uh... did you say, Sateekas, sir?"

"Yes. I do not like to repeat myself. Are you weak-minded?"

"Uh... no sir. I'm right as rain. I was just wondering if you've got any information on where Sateekas is now?"

The Mogwa was annoyed already. That wasn't unusual. Anything beyond two questions started to piss them off.

"He's in the City. He's under arrest, of course. I was merely questioning our judgment in his incarceration, not his existence or his motivation."

"He's here? In jail?"

"That's what I said, human. Apparently, you apes can speak glibly, but your oversized auditory organs are dysfunctional."

"That's right. We're a pack of retards on a good day. Anyways, according to my tapper more human units are entering the factory, and the bears are in retreat. Mind if I accompany you? I'd like to meet the Victrix pukes with you guys at my side."

"Nonsensical. I gather you wish to guard my person, and that is acceptable."

He let me join ranks with him, but he was huffy about it. Normally, any Mogwa marine figured he was worth any thousand barbarians in a fight—but this fellow had clearly had his bell rung. He'd almost died, and he wanted a bodyguard, whether he would admit it or not.

I took my time setting up defenses. I had my troops make an effort to look like we'd been hanging around bored with the Mogwa for a long time.

I talked to Elgu for a bit while we waited, and we'd watched buzzer reports coming in. With human troops converging in strength, the bears had decided to withdraw. That was only temporary, I figured. Bears never gave up on an objective easily. You always had to pry it out of their hairy paws in the end.

I was sipping some hot caff—fake coffee—when a Victrix unit arrived at last. They walked into our camp in the rubble, looking aghast.

"There you are, ladies," I said, calling to them and waving. "Good of you to show up and give us a break here on the front lines."

The Victrix legionnaires weren't well-known to me. Mostly, I'd met them in the Mustering Hall. Their armor was definitely less dented and shinier than ours was. Their banners and patches displayed crossed swords and a big V emblem, just like they'd done in ancient Roman times.

"Varus?" the centurion in charge asked. "Seriously? You beat us down here? How?"

"Uh... mostly by walking and fighting. We lost a unit's worth of men, a cheap price to pay to save just one of our beloved masters. This here spider-monkey-Mogwa—excuse me, this high overlord of fantastic worth—his name is Elgu. Leastwise, that's the closest I can come to pronouncing it."

"Elgu..." the Victrix man said, squinting. "I'm Centurion Tran, sir. This is quite an honor, sir. You're the first Galactic I've ever had the pleasure of meeting in person."

Elgu turned on Centurion Tran. His numerous eyes narrowed in suspicion, and he peered at the gauntlet the other had offered. After looking it over with distrust, he ignored the hand and eyed Tran. "You are substandard in performance parameters." He pointed at me. "This oversized ape arrived first, and he fought as would any beast to save his master. Where were you during this critical juncture?"

Tran looked stunned. I knew right off what the trouble was—up until this moment, he'd never known what card-carrying tools all the Mogwa tended to be.

"That seems like a poor attitude, Elgu," Tran began. "After all, we've sacrificed—"

"Uh…" I said, loudly, interrupting. "What Centurion Tran means to say, Elgu, is that he's embarrassed for his piss-poor performance and near cowardice on the field of glory. He'd further like to profess his slave-love for you and yours, and he hopes you can find it in your heart to forgive him."

"That's not—" Tran began angrily, but I waved a hand in a spinning gesture, suggesting he should shut the hell up. He caught on and sulked, crossing his arms.

Elgu eyed me disgustedly. "This one's words weren't conciliatory in any way," he huffed. "But still, under the circumstances, I'll let this instance of insubordination pass. I'm in need of every soldier Earth has in the region today."

"Yeah? What for, sir?"

"Why, to drive these bears back into their holes—and to push them off the planet after that. Servants, gather your grunting forces and assemble them. You will march in the forefront. The Mogwa will bring up the rear in case your troops fail me."

"Hmm…" I said.

Tran's mouth fell open, and he looked like he was going to have kittens. "We just got here. You're planning a counterattack so soon? What if the enemy is waiting outside in strength?"

"Then your forces will flush them out. We'll soon know the truth. You will march in the lead, Tran. Make a brave example of yourself in order to inspire your army of beasts."

The Mogwa was technically in charge, so Tran and I didn't have much choice. We formed the spear tip of Elgu's counterattack.

I, for one, found this exhilarating. "This is cool, isn't it?" I asked Tran. "Did you hear Sateekas is alive? This guy Elgu claims he's right here under the dome with us. They arrested him or something—but that kind of thing never stopped old Sateekas. He's one tough old bird."

"Please shut up, McGill," Centurion Tran pleaded. "You're giving me a headache on top of everything else."

"A headache? Are you serious? What are you, twelve years old? The only headache a human gets to have in this army is punched through his skull by a power bolt."

"What is this prattle in the ranks?" Elgu asked sternly. "Further insubordination from the beast called Tran?"

I raised a glove to calm the angry alien. "Never, sir! Don't worry about a thing. I'm just helping this man get his head clear before we meet the enemy again."

Elgu gestured with his arms dismissively. I was happy to note he didn't dare heap more threats and insults upon us humans. It had to be due to the fact we were in a combat zone, side by side, and we humans outnumbered the Mogwa significantly. The Mogwa were as arrogant and as mean as all get-out—but they weren't stupid.

Tired and injured, the troops readied themselves for another assault. We had linked up with Victrix and the Mogwa garrison, which meant it was time to turn the tables and push the bears out.

-42-

After we retook the center of the factory and gathered our troops together, we had about five hundred soldiers to work with. Primus Collins herself had finally arrived, and as the highest ranked officer in the area she began directing the counterattack. I had to give her credit for that. Winslade wasn't down here in the combat zone, after all. He'd sent her as a sidekick to do the dirty work.

We massed-up and pushed outward, heading for the bear positions to the west. Our advance was relentless. We met light resistance, recapturing much of the factory within minutes.

When we finally came out under the open skies again, we were surprised. The bears had retreated. We shot after a few hairy figures on the horizon, but they slunk away into the gathering night.

Apparently, once Victrix and Varus had managed to link up and support the garrison, they'd called off their lightning assault on the factory.

We'd won the day. Once that sunk in, we did some hooting and hollering. The Mogwa Captain Elgu sneered, referring to all humans as barbaric ape-descendants. Centurion Tran and Primus Collins did their best to look calm and dignified, apologizing in particular for the overly enthusiastic Varus troops.

I didn't care. We'd fought hard, and we'd won. That's what mattered. How a man celebrated his victories—that was up to him.

Primus Collins came around to talk to me after the battle was over. She'd decided not to pursue the retreating bears, in case it was some kind of trap.

Collins gave me a strange look right from the start. It was the kind of look a person might give a suspicious person found in their backyard. Was this a neighbor? A burglar? A friend or a foe? She wasn't sure.

"McGill? I understand your unit was the first to reach the Mogwa garrison. Is that true?"

"It sure is, sir. After we toasted that bunker with mini-missiles, we never looked back. Hard-charging, that's what 3rd Unit is known for. Hell, if I had—"

Collins put up a gloved hand to stop me. "Yes, yes. I've heard plenty of your boasting already. But... in this case I have to admit some of your self-congratulatory talk is warranted. You did well. I thank you for your efforts, Centurion."

That was it. She turned and walked off. I didn't give her any guff about cutting me off. She'd thanked me, and that was good enough. This little moment of comradery didn't mean we were engaged or anything, but it was certainly better than trying to get each other killed by any means possible.

The next thing I knew I had a call pinging in on my tapper. It was old sourpuss Winslade. He seemed as surprised by the results of the battle as Collins herself.

"Collins actually *took* the factory? With less than a thousand men?"

"Uh... I'm not rightly sure how many Victrix pukes were involved, but a thousand sounds about right, sir."

"Amazing... too bad it's all for nothing."

I blinked a few times. Then I squinted. "For nothing?"

"Yes, sadly. We've been pushed back everywhere else. The bears have taken several key locations around the perimeter of the City."

That alarmed me. I hadn't really considered the idea that this attack wasn't the only one. The way it sounded, it wasn't even the biggest.

252

Checking on my tapper and linking up with the strategic command feed, I browsed through the latest reports from every front while Winslade continued to talk.

"McGill, since Primus Collins has been victorious in the zone, people have taken notice. The Mogwa High Command is requesting that the 'crack' combat team involved in the factory recapture be elevated in stature. It is truly her day to shine."

"Uh... what? How's that, sir? We're not even a combat team. We're half Victrix and half... "

"Yes, yes. Of course, I know. But for now, you'll operate under Primus Collins and you'll pretend to like it. The Mogwa are panicking after losing the outskirts of their City in every direction."

Frowning fiercely, I ran to the nearest tall gray silo. I found a rickety Mogwa stairway and began taking them two at a time. Every time I found a door, I kicked it open. Higher and higher I climbed.

While I ran, Winslade kept talking. "In order to capitalize on this diplomatically as well as militarily, you're going to be transferred."

Huffing and puffing, I kicked open the last door. I walked to a railing and gazed out to the north, then south and at last to the east, where the City skyscrapers stood tall. High up above the factory complex, a dozen floors above ground level, I was able to get a pretty good picture of the landscape.

In the distance, I saw the vast city center. Massive buildings were clustered together like a mountain range of oblong shapes. Most of the buildings were lit up, but not as many as there should be.

Arching over the urban landscape, I saw the protective shell of force had survived intact thus far. It hadn't been taken down yet. That dome took fantastic amounts of power to maintain, and I knew the generators were located in the heart of the metropolis.

But looking lower, toward the edges of the dome, things were clearly not secure. There were fires, for one thing. Massive plumes of oily black smoke hung over lurid flickering flames.

"...are you listening, Centurion?" Winslade demanded. "Is there some kind of cock-up in communications?"

"Uh..." I said, my eyes roving over the scene in dismay. My hair fluffed up with a dry wind that came in from the east. "I'm here, sir. I'm outside, looking at the damage. How bad is it? How far have the bears pushed into the dome?"

"Far enough. They're threatening every sector. We're pulling back all troops into the Mogwa City itself."

"What? We're surrendering our position here at the factory?"

"Yes. Collins has her orders. You're going to retreat to the center of the city and help shore up the defenses at the location the Mogwa most fear to lose."

"Yeah? Where's that?"

Winslade shrugged. "There are plenty of vulnerable targets. Take the power generators, for instance. If power is lost, even briefly, the dome will flicker out. I don't need to tell you that such an event would be disastrous, or possibly even fatal, to everyone involved in this grand struggle."

"I've got it, sir. We'll do our best."

"I need more than that, McGill."

Confused, I stared at my tapper. Winslade looked back at me. His expression was cagey.

"Uh... what else can I do for you, sir?"

"I understand that Primus Collins and you haven't always gotten along. In this coming struggle, there might possibly be... an opportunity to be considered."

He'd lost me entirely at this point. I was thinking of nothing other than how we could stop the bears from winning this fight.

As I considered the campaign in its entirety, it occurred to me that we really couldn't win by hiding under the dome. We would have to go on the offensive eventually. The city was too big, too hungry, and too thirsty. Sure, the Mogwa had all kinds of advanced recycling systems—but there were limits. You really needed a lot of support to keep billions of souls happy and functional.

Along about then, I realized Winslade was still talking, and he was sounding increasingly shrill.

"Are you listening to me at all, you ignoramus?" he demanded.

"Huh?"

Winslade controlled his temper with difficulty. "Do I really have to spell it out, McGill? Collins is hogging all the credit for this battle, and she'll do the same for the next. We can't have that. Do you understand me?"

"Uh..." I said, and I gave myself a scratch.

The funny thing was, I *was* beginning to get a glimmer of what he was hinting around about. He'd originally sent Collins out here to get rid of her—or at least that was my impression. To his surprise and chagrin, she'd performed all too well—with my help. We'd taken the factory and held it. For Winslade, this was a terrible turn of events.

I knew this kind of petty officer rivalry was more important than anything to him. He'd gladly risk getting permed in order to leapfrog ahead of another officer and scoop up the credit for a victory. That's just the kind of guy he was.

Seeing my dumbass expression, Winslade closed his eyes and shook his head. "McGill, let's put this as simply as I'm able: I want you to make sure there are no more dramatic victories in your immediate future. That's all. Winslade out."

He closed the channel, and I lowered my tapper to gaze out into the night sky again. The fires were everywhere now, and that wasn't all. I saw streaks of heavy fire rattling and roaring in the distance. A few kilometers away to the north and the south, the bears were pushing back the Mogwa and the legions alike.

Then, I turned toward the city center in the east. Those big buildings weren't pretty, but they were impressive. The city was larger than anything humanity had ever built. It was massive, hulking, blocky. In the night it looked more impressive than it had in the daytime, as most cities did. The countless lights that lit up the massive buildings shimmered in the distance.

My tapper soon buzzed again, and I answered it. This time, it was Primus Collins.

255

She had a strange tone in her voice. She was suspicious, I could tell. In my overly long lifetime, I'd heard that tone from the throats of countless women like her. She didn't trust me.

"Centurion McGill?" she said. "I see that you've been talking to headquarters."

Innocence and hardcore ignorance sprang to mind. It was my first and only defense. I went hard with it right from the beginning, using a cheery and matter-of-fact tone to counter her paranoia. "That's exactly right, sir. Tribune Winslade called me just now."

"I find it strange that Winslade would talk to you and not to me. What was the nature of this discussion?"

"He told me to congratulate you on your victory. He said this factory was the only win on the front lines today."

"So... why did he call you, then?"

"Huh... You know, I'm not rightly sure about that... I guess he thought you were too busy talking to the Mogwa High Command."

Her expression shifted from one of deep suspicion to bafflement. That's right where I wanted her.

"What? Why would they contact me?"

"I don't rightly know, sir. All I know is they requested this combat unit to be reassigned to the center of the City to coordinate their defenses. They seem to see you as some kind of a glorious hero, sir."

"They... what? Are you blowing smoke up my ass, McGill? I've heard rumors about you. If this is some kind of trick to get a date, or something, let me assure you that—"

I cut her off by transmitting a snippet of my conversation with Winslade. I'd been working on trimming that piece of audio from the recorded talk since she first contacted me.

She trailed off and listened to Winslade for a few moments. Naturally, I cut off the feed the moment we stopped talking about how cool she was in the eyes of the Mogwa.

"I had no idea!" she said. "Why didn't Winslade tell me about this himself?"

"Like I said, maybe he thought that the Mogwa were—"

But then, Collins made an impatient gesture with her hands, fluttering her fingers at me. "They're calling right now. Collins out."

Her finger stabbed down at my face, and the image faded.

Smiling, I lowered my arm and gazed out into the night skyline again. That's how you handled two cottonmouth snakes. You tied their tails together and watched the fun.

My smile faded as I watched the battles that were ongoing all over the horizon. The war wasn't going so well. Sure, I'd dodged a bullet and won a small victory—but the struggle was far from over.

-43-

Things moved quickly after that call from Winslade. A lifter came down—I didn't even know they'd managed to get some of them through the dome, but go figure... It landed right next to the factory. We loaded up every Victrix lamer, Varus man and a handful of Mogwa from the garrison. They even had room for a few dozen of those drone tanks of theirs.

The whole kit-and-caboodle was hauled off toward the big city. Ten minutes later, we landed on top of a large flat building—one that was obviously designed for large craft to squat on. Marching down the ramps, we found that we'd been placed on top of Mogwa Command headquarters. This was the very center of the city's defenses.

Primus Collins and I were directed to go straight down into the inner sanctum, which was just under the flight deck. Mogwa marines and human troops were running all over the place. There were sirens and alerts. It was damn near chaos. There was a real energy around the place—but also one of impending doom.

When I finally reached the big row of tactical planning tables, I was impressed. They had some real nice tech gear at work. We humans had good battle computers, don't get me wrong, but you could tell right off that the resolution was higher, the sensor input was more sharp and detailed—everything was a cut above our usual fare.

Primus Collins and I weren't friends—we didn't even like each other much—but we stood together anyway. Winslade wasn't even present, so we couldn't stand with him. Together, we were the lowest-ranking people in sight. Looking around with big eyeballs, we could tell everyone else in the room was more important than we were.

After a minute or two of gawking, I spotted Tribune Harold Kraus. He was the vaunted commander of Legion Victrix. Among all the tribunes and legions, Victrix was probably the most famous. They'd been the first commissioned legion in Earth's history. They'd saved our world back in the old days, when we didn't have a trade good worth spit. In a last ditch attempt to not be erased as a species, we'd come up with the idea of sending mercenary troops to the stars to serve the highest bidder. Victrix had served those initial contracts, and they'd brought home the bacon. Everyone on Earth felt they owed Victrix a personal debt as a result.

Tribune Kraus looked the part. His kit was immaculate. There wasn't a dent or a scratch, and I'll be damned if his armor wasn't more than just shiny. It seemed to glow a bit, as if somehow it was lit up by an internal source of holy power.

"He probably paints that breastplate in radium," Primus Collins remarked.

I glanced down at her. She was at my elbow, and she didn't look any cleaner or fresher than I did. We'd both just come from the front lines, and there wasn't a streak of soot, grease or filth that hadn't found its way onto her scratched-up armor. My own armor was that impenetrable black kind, so it looked better than hers did at least. It was, however, no less stinky when you got up close and personal.

Kraus beckoned to us, and we bellied up to the battle table. Kraus gave us a critical eye. Was he faintly disgusted? He might be.

"Ah," Kraus said. He was Austrian and had a sonorous voice with a German accent. "Can this be our conquering heroes from the front lines?"

"Primus Collins reporting, sir... and this is Centurion McGill. His unit was the first to reach the Mogwa garrison."

"Excellent! You saved the day at that one point along our crumbling front lines. How did you do it?"

One of the Mogwa high command officers ruffled up at his words. The Mogwa had about the fanciest outfit in the room, being all dressed up like a peacock complete with feathers and fluff. The Mogwa idea of high officer costumes was... strange.

"Again with the implied insults, Tribune Kraus. You try our patience."

"No insult was implied, I assure you, Field Marshal."

The field marshal guy looked unconvinced. "First, you insist that these animals be dragged up from the front to our planning tables. Then, you proceed to insult our intellect by suggesting it was these grunting humans that saved the factory, not the glorious Captain Elgu."

"Well, let us hear their report and judge accordingly."

Primus Collins and I hadn't been happy campers before, and now we were even less thrilled about being here. Apparently, we were pawns in some sort of interspecies pissing contest. That was just grand.

"Um..." Collins began. "There isn't much to say. Perhaps some vids clipped from the action will tell the tale more succinctly."

So saying, she tossed a few glittering images from her tapper to the tactical table. With poor grace and angry gestures, the Mogwa guy in the feathered boa allowed the vid to be displayed.

Highlights of the action were played out. The edits were quite well done and dramatic. Most of all, I was impressed that Collins had had the foresight to put together this collection of clips. Maybe she'd had an inkling of what we were walking into.

The vids clearly showed we had fought our way inside and destroyed the bears, even while the Mogwa garrison was getting its ass beaten soundly.

Tribune Kraus smiled all the while. He glanced now and then at Collins, and I realized right about then that the two were in cahoots.

Finally, the field marshal fellow threw in the towel. He reached out with a foot-hand thing and slapped away the vids, tossing them to the dumpster in the corner of the big screen.

"All right, all right. You've made your point, Kraus, as offensive as it is. Your apes were critical in the defense of this single point on our front lines. They have, however, failed us at every other juncture imaginable. The barbarians are frothing at the mouth to consume our young. What do you propose to do to stop them?"

Kraus nodded sagely. I could tell he had been waiting for this exact opening. He stepped forward and took command of the tactical table himself. His shining gauntlets cut traceries over the table, conjuring up the terrain of the great city and its surroundings.

The Mogwa field marshal looked annoyed. He reluctantly shuffled his numerous limbs a pace or two to one side.

"You see here?" Kraus asked, tapping at a point along the city perimeter. "This is where they will strike next. This is where we must stop them."

"Why this factory? There is no critical technology there. No repository of weapons. No—"

Kraus cut him off with a flourish. "This installation is the key to your city's water distribution. It produces nothing—but it controls the flow of liquid needed for life. Any city can take a disruption in food, or power—but none can withstand thirst for long."

"Hmm..." said the Mogwa thoughtfully. "How do you propose to stop them from conquering this spot?"

"We will not try. Instead, we will strike with a full Blood Worlder legion, pushing them back from this point to the wall of the dome."

The field marshal looked troubled. His eye-groups traveled to look at Collins and me. "And these filthy apes? Why are they here? Move your genetic mutant armies to the spot and push the enemy back. You don't even have a representative from their number here."

Kraus laughed. "And happy you are that we don't. If you find these disheveled humans offensive, you would find the Blood Worlders intolerable. But still... they are not here

261

without purpose. I want them to command the near-human legion on this mission."

Alarmed, Collins gave a squawk and raised her hand. Kraus gestured for her to speak.

"What is going on, sir?" she said. "Don't we have an imperator, or perhaps even an equestrian for this level of—?"

"No," Kraus said. "It is unfortunate, but I, a lowly tribune of Legion Victrix, am the highest rank among the human forces. Praetor Drusus, along with several imperators saw fit to leave the system via teleportation. Our best decided to run off and hide, so to speak."

That's when my hand shot up. No one seemed happy to see that. Not Kraus, or any of the sneering Mogwa brass.

Kraus, in fact, ignored me. "To further answer your inquiry, Primus Collins," he continued. "I see that Winslade was placed in command of Legion Varus in the place of Galina Turov. That is unfortunate, and it also means he must remain with his forces to provide leadership. The other support legions are poorly led by various near-humans and Blood Worlders. I am, however, working to repair that situation."

"Repair it? You mean... you're removing officers from command?"

Kraus shrugged, his metal epaulets flashing like two mirrors. "To be precise, I had all non-human top officers shot."

"Shot...? But...?"

"It's a temporary measure, one I felt was necessary. They aren't permed, merely replaced by more reliable personnel. This is an important mission, Collins. I don't like to leave incompetence in place. You are only a primus, but you proved yourself on the battlefield. You have gained my confidence."

Collins looked shaken, and she'd finally figured out she should shut up.

All this time Kraus was speeching, my hand had been raised high. At this point, I began to waggle my fat fingers.

Finally, with a heavy sigh, Kraus waved for me to speak. "What is it, Centurion McGill?"

"What about Sateekas, sirs? Isn't he here someplace? He knows human and Mogwa forces. Why isn't he at this planning table?"

262

All the Mogwa officers stumped from foot to foot in irritation. Kraus looked alarmed.

"That is not widely known information, Centurion. I think it's best if we leave such internal affairs to the Mogwa. They're responsible for determining who shall lead them."

"Yeah, but—"

"That's enough, McGill."

Reluctantly, I fell silent. I've been told to shut my damned pie-hole more times than I can count, so I knew the drill.

Kraus turned toward the field marshal. He spread his hands. "Well, sir? What do you think of my plan?"

"It's quite mad," the Mogwa replied. "I would never have come up with such a thing... My instinct is to withdraw our best forces to the center of the city. To protect the important personages first and foremost. But... your plan is intriguing. It is bold. It involves counterattacking, and I feel it has merit."

"Excellent. Is it agreed upon, then?"

The Mogwa huddled and made funny noises in their own language at one another. I didn't bother to listen in and translate.

"McGill?" Collins hissed at my side.

I looked down at her, and I thought she looked kind of agitated. "What's up, Primus?"

"What's wrong with you? Why did you bring up Sateekas? He's not even that great of an officer, and they clearly hate him here."

"Well sir, the truth is no Mogwa I've ever met was a great tactician. Sateekas at least takes the job seriously."

"Whatever. Don't surprise me like that again."

I made no promises. I just fell silent.

After a few squawky minutes, the Mogwa commanders finally agreed to Kraus' plan. Just like that, Primus Collins had been promoted to acting sub-tribune and placed in charge of a Blood Worlder legion. The big shocker, however, was that I was going to be her acting exec.

-44-

We took a short flight on a local skimmer. It was a military flier, and it was Mogwa-made. As one might expect, the aircraft was utilitarian and crisply functioning—but it was more than that.

"Wow," I said, feeling up the seats. "These chairs are comfy! The Mogwa really know how to treat their hindquarters, even when they're just going cross-city."

Primus Collins glanced at me, then back to the cityscape that was swooping by the windows.

"Such a strange place," she said. "The architecture consists entirely of oblong shapes with sharp edges... there really isn't any artistry to this metropolis. It's just a pile of rectangles heaped onto one another."

"Oh now, I don't know about that. I see nice triangles up at the top. Triangles and cones both."

She glanced at me like I was some kind of idiot. I took no offense, as I was used to such looks from people. "Those are rooftops, James."

James? It had to be the first time I could recall where this woman had used my first name. What's more, she'd done so without adding in a curse word or two. That was significant. It had to be.

"Uh..." I said. "How is this going to work out? Between the two of us, I mean?"

Collins gave me a questioning stare. "What are you talking about?"

"I mean... what about command structure? I'm supposed to be your sidekick. Are you thinking chief-of-staff, or...?"

She laughed out loud. "Hardly. You'll be given a few units of grunts to order around. I'll put you on the front lines."

"Okay."

Again, she gave me that quizzical look. "No objections? No complaints?"

I shrugged my shoulders. "I'm a Varus fighting man, Primus. I'll probably do the most good on the front lines."

She seemed to think about that for a while. Finally, she heaved a sigh. "I think I've spent too much time hating you, McGill. You're right... we should cooperate."

"That's a good idea, sir," I said, studiously ignoring her offhanded comments about hating me. She'd always seen me as a random crazy-man from 3rd Cohort. To her, I was a punishment from the Almighty himself.

But now... maybe she was beginning to see the good side of old McGill.

She nodded again, half to herself. "Since you're willing to follow my orders, and you obviously have skill as a tactical commander and small-unit leader, I should use that. I understand from your records that you have operated as a cohort leader commanding Blood Worlders in the past."

"That's right. Back on Edge World, Foam and I stopped an army of Bright Siders."

Collins frowned. "Foam? The same squid that eventually became our tribune and attempted a mutiny?"

"One and the same, sir."

"Huh... all right. You must know something about squid—I mean, Cephalopod psychology. I want you to take command of a cohort and set up pickets to slow down the bears—if they really are coming to attack this water plant."

"You doubt Tribune Kraus' logic on that point?"

"Yes. I don't think he has much of an idea what the bears are going to do next. I think he just used that to take command of the meeting. I was surprised the Mogwa let him get away with it."

265

I considered her words while she stared out the window some more. Soon, we spiraled down for a landing. She might be right, I decided. Kraus was a political animal, after all. He reminded me of a smoother, less-drunk version of Armel.

When we piled out of the lifter, we were met by a crowd of non-human officers. Their tribune had been arrested and executed—apparently just for the crime of being born a squid. At least, that's how they thought about it.

As a result, there wasn't a kind eye in the bunch as we disembarked and walked toward the line of angry squids—and squids have a whole lot of eyes.

After smoothing out some ruffled tentacles, I soon took charge of a cohort and marched their sorry asses toward our destination. The former sub-primus was flustered and irritable. His name was Trickle, and I was already having a hard time not making jokes.

"I find this process humiliating," he said.

"You don't like it, huh?" I asked him. "Would it be better if I chopped off those slimy limbs of yours? They're kind of flopping around and creating an eyesore."

The squid seemed surprised. "That would not be a preferable outcome. I was referring to… "

"That's right it, wouldn't be. Listen up, Trickle. You don't want to be dismembered and executed as a coward. You don't want that at all. Accordingly, you're going to shut that big beak between your legs and take orders the first time I give them."

My abusive attitude would have been the first lesson I'd have given Primus Collins if she'd come along to learn the fine art of squid-wrangling. Cephalopods didn't understand kindness, they considered pleasant talk to be an invitation for deviltry.

Even worse, in their eyes a nice guy was just openly demonstrating his weakness. Using squid-logic, nice people who were in charge of anything were begging for someone to take them down.

That's how you moved up in Cephalopod social structures—by bringing superiors down. Consequently, you couldn't give a squid anything without demanding more in return.

266

On the other hand, if you built up some impressive wins while operating as a tyrant, they would eventually give you the respect you'd earned.

My hostile attitude worked wonders from the get-go. The mean guy behavior pattern changed the attitude of my squid sidekick just as it had Foam himself back in the day.

Soon, I had all my squid officers slapping around the place with their nasty tentacles, humping this way and that to meet my demands. Within hours, I'd packed up a cohort that consisted primarily of heavy troopers. We marched toward the shimmering dome along the outskirts of the City, which was enemy territory these days.

Within hours we reached an abandoned zone. It wasn't open ground like the farm we'd started at, but it wasn't entirely industrial, either. For the Mogwa, it was a kind of local suburb. Effectively, it was a district on the outskirts of the main urban center.

On Earth, however, the neighborhood would have been top-tier. There were massive buildings, wide streets and far-flung archways everywhere. We found the widest thoroughfare and marched down it, forming a column twenty troops abreast.

"Uh…" I said, as we came to a region that was smoky and had torn-up streets. "Have we reached the front lines yet?"

Trickle looked at me carefully. His eyeballs were bulging. "I am allowed to speak?"

"Yes, dammit. That's why I asked you a question."

"We have passed the front lines. We are in territory captured by the enemy."

"Huh…" I said, pulling out my morph-rifle in a seemingly casual way. I knew right off it was time to do some lying and ass-covering. "That's what I thought. This is far enough. Spread out into these buildings and the neighboring blocks. We'll wait for enemy contact right here."

Trickle didn't dare go up against me. He clacked his beak and relayed orders. All around us, about a thousand troops took cover.

It was just in time too, as it turned out. A single power bolt spanged off the puff-crete at my feet. The bears were around—or at least their snipers were.

267

Shouts and return fire erupted, breaking the quiet of the streets. The environment was among the worst for infantry combat. There were huge buildings with hundreds of windows all around us. Snipers could perch up there and peck at us all day long.

Scrambling, we moved off the streets and into the soot-stained puff-crete structures. I took to a building that had once been a crematorium—at least, that's what my translator told me.

Climbing up steps that were wider and more shallow than I was used to, I passed ranks and ranks of ovens. These grim machines were crusty with ash, just as they always were on Earth.

"Why the hell does this city need so many crematoriums?" Primus Collins asked me. Rather than choosing her own ground, she'd decided to run up the same steps I'd taken. After a moment's thought, I decided not to make any remarks about that. Instead, I answered her question.

"The Mogwa populace all use revival machines."

"So what?" Collins asked, not getting it. "If they live effectively forever, why would they—? Oh… the bodies are still left behind, right?"

"That's it. Unless you want to bury them all or recycle them for regrowth, you've got to burn them. The Mogwa like fresh materials when they kickoff new lives. They don't reuse the stale stuff."

Collins stopped asking questions. Instead, she ordered me to scout the upper floors. I ran up about two dozen flights before I found a spot that seemed to be a little above the level of the enemy snipers.

That's when the fun began. I had slavers with me for the most part. They were tall, skinny guys about twice the height of a man. They did a lot of the extra jobs in Blood Worlder legions, like scouting and sniping.

Setting them up in windows, we plinked away at the bears, and they fired back at us. Even when hanging out the windows, we found it was hard to take out a bear with nothing but a single round from a rifle. Even a direct hit didn't do the trick because of their armor. At the same time, they often killed one of my men.

After exchanging fire for several minutes, I was getting nothing but curses and a few deaths on my side.

"Sir?" I said, calling Collins over command chat. "This isn't working. We're getting whacked."

"Keep it up anyway," she said. "You're distracting the enemy. I've got men climbing the buildings to get to them."

I didn't like having my slavers getting chewed up, so I came up with a way to improve our odds.

"Here," I said, grabbing onto a big man's harness. He stank, and he looked scared, but he was shooting his rifle at the enemy, so I couldn't fault him. "Here's what I want you to do. Lean out, real sudden like, take a pot shot, then race away to a different window. Take another wild, quick shot from that window, then run away again."

He looked baffled, but when I asked him if he understood, he nodded. Without questioning orders he no doubt considered insane, he began to follow them.

I passed the same instructions to a dozen squid noncoms, and they soon had the entire unit doing it. Instead of taking careful aim and pegging bears, they began popping off wildly inaccurate shots and running away. Each time, a storm of fire came back the other way from the bears, but the end result was no one was hitting anything.

Trickle eventually oozed up next to me and stared at me with his big, scaredy-squid eyes.

"What is it now, Trickle?"

"Sir, are you aware that our men haven't hit a target in several minutes?"

"Yep. What about it?"

"They're missing, sir—they're all missing."

I began to frown. "That's right. We're supposed to tie up the enemy, not kill them. That's someone else's job."

Trickle wandered off, no doubt baffled as to what we were up to, but too cowed to complain about it openly. I liked that state of mind in my subordinates, so I let him stew over it.

After several minutes, the heavy troopers finally managed to climb the stairs and ambush the bear snipers from behind.

They rushed them, moving close and fighting them in the windows.

"Cease fire!" I ordered my snipers. Then I contacted the unit commander in charge of the heavy troopers that were hitting the bears. "Hey, 2nd Unit! Don't shoot the bears! Don't sword-fight them, either!"

"What alternative would you suggest then, commander?" came back a snotty-toned question from the squid in charge.

"I'd suggest you grab their little furry butts and throw them out the windows they're shooting from. If they hold on to your troopers, just tell the men to jump and take the bears down with them!"

The squid had more to say, but I closed the channel. As far as I was concerned, he had his orders.

To my mild surprise and amusement, it soon began to rain bears. They were trapped, as the heavy troopers were under them and driving them to the rooftops. When a given bear seemed to be winning a fight, sure enough, he found himself taking a header out the nearest blown-out window and tumbling into open space.

Trickle came to stand next to me. He watched the scene with lots of eyeballs. Again, I noticed that his eyes seemed to bulge and weep a bit more than was usual for a squid. Maybe that's why he was called "Trickle" as he seemed to be almost crying most of the time.

"Impressive, sir," he said. "I'm learning from you already."

"That's right. Stick with me, squid, and I'll teach you all kinds of tactics you never even dreamed of."

After the interlude with the snipers, we counted up the dead. The numbers came out about even, with us ahead by maybe a dozen splattered corpses on the street.

As the bears weren't here in strength, they didn't hit us back for a while. The streets fell quiet, and the skies reddened. It was going to be dark soon.

It was at that point that streaks began to shine in the skies. They were odd projectiles, coming from the enemy's side. At first, we ducked and hunkered—but the streaks went right over our heads. They rose and fell on a slow arc.

270

"Trickle?" I demanded. "Any idea what they're firing over us?"

"No, Commander. We have reports of strange vapor trails from these launches, but when they impact there is no explosion. They appear to carry no discernible warhead."

"Huh... I don't like it. Keep me apprised of things. The bears aren't launching duds into the city for nothing."

Trickle signed off, and I demanded better intel from my cohort. That didn't go over so well.

In a normal human outfit, we'd use buzzers and scanners to learn of our surroundings. But the Blood Worlders didn't utilize that kind of sophisticated equipment. Most of the near-humans were too damned dumb to count all their fingers without losing track.

As I complained and demanded better recon efforts, I became aware of something I'd never suspected: my cohort had a dedicated platoon of techs as an auxiliary group.

That was a shocker. I demanded to meet with them immediately.

My order was relayed down the chain of command. It was grunted over and muttered about and clacked at by the squids. The Cephalopods were the backbone of my lower level officers and noncoms—but they seemed to not want to obey me in this instance.

Finally, as the day waned into night, I demanded to see Trickle again. While I waited, the bombardment of silent, seemingly harmless projectiles continued above us. I was determined to get to the bottom of this mystery and the one about my missing techs.

Trickle finally came to the top floor of the building I was squatting in—the twenty-fourth floor, as it were. He looked like a hound-dog who'd been kicked a few times.

"What's going on, Trickle?" I demanded. "Where are my techs? I know your cohort has them."

"Yes, sir. That is correct."

"Well then? Why are they so shy? Are you hiding them from me?"

He looked furtive. That was a bad sign. When one of your squid underlings looked sneaky—well sir, that could only

271

mean he *was* being sneaky. And that usually meant he was plotting your assassination.

Accordingly, I jumped up and rushed close to him. I held a combat knife up to one of those leaky, dribbling eyeballs.

"Talk to me, Trickle. This is your last chance."

"Sir, you don't understand. The tech platoon—they don't want to meet with you. They see you as a danger."

"I'm going to be a danger to *you* if you don't start explaining."

The squid inked himself a little, and he made a flapping motion with one of his back tentacles. A signal? I thought that it was, and I prepared myself to drive home my blade. Even if they did manage to take me down, there was going to be a pile of chopped-up calamari to clean up afterward.

To my utter surprise, I wasn't rushed by a gang of squids or renegade heavy troopers. No, sir. Instead, I saw an army of tiny creatures approach. They came from every nook and cranny, every doorway, every windowsill and attic access that allowed entrance into this penthouse. Once gathered, they formed a full platoon of creatures of a sort I'd hoped to never lay eyes upon again.

They were gremlins. Little guys who looked human, but were wiry with stringy arms and legs. Each was less than a meter tall, and most wore nasty grins. They were a special type of near-human from Blood World. I'd rarely seen them serve in Earth's armed forces.

The gremlins slunk into the room and surrounded me like so many feral cats. Lowering my blade from Trickles' eye-groups, I began to understand his hesitancy.

I had a long and unpleasant history with this kind of near-human, and our meetings had never resulted in anything resembling happiness.

"Gremlins…?" I said. "They're the ones running the buzzers? Ah, right. I get it—they're technically competent, unlike most Blood Worlders."

Coming to a decision, I turned back to Trickle. "Why didn't you tell me I had gremlins in my cohort? These guys are the best at spy-work and technical gizmos."

"The big-man speaks the truth," one of the gremlins said in a weird, hissy little voice. "This is surprising. I thought this big-man never spoke wisely."

I turned back to him, and I grinned at the little bastard. "Your type has never understood me. I don't hate you guys— we were just enemies back in the old days, that's all. Now we're all working together on the same team. I'm glad to have you aboard."

The gremlins gurgled and whispered among themselves. They were creeping up all over the place. I already had the idea they might have decided to rid themselves of old McGill tonight—and they had good reason to feel that way.

You see, I'd gotten a bad rep after slaughtering hundreds of their kind back on Blood World and Ice World. But they didn't attack immediately. It seemed that I'd thrown them for a loop what with all the compliments and the lack of instant hostility.

After I let them grumble and fuss for a while, I walked to the open, glass-free windows. I gazed down at the city. There were no lights in the streets. I could use a few buzzers out there, scouting around.

Turning back, I found no less than a dozen gremlins had snuck up close behind me. They were no farther away than I could kick, and they were all crouched like they were about to jump me—but they froze when I faced them again, because I had a new toy in my hands. Their tiny faces registered shock.

I smiled, and I bounced a plasma grenade up and down a few times. They watched it, mesmerized. A few began to backtrack, but I raised a finger and placed it on the firing stud.

"Ah-ah," I said. "No running off now, my friends. It's too late for that. This fuse—well, there really isn't a fuse on this thing... Anyway, it will go off in an instant if I want it to."

The gremlins looked kind of freaked out. I glanced around, and I saw that old Trickle had wisely vanished.

"Now," I said, "any death of mine will only last about thirty minutes or so, after which I'll be back here making sure whatever is left of your pile of little corpses is polished off with a bonfire of stick-thin bones. I think you should start listening to me."

They didn't say anything. They were staring and baring their teeth under quivering lips—that's about it.

I made a show of putting my hand up to my ear and cupping it. "I don't hear anything."

"Speak, human!" one of them whispered at last.

"All right, then. Remember, when I execute ornery subordinates in this legion—that means they're permed. On the other hand, I'll only be inconvenienced and pissed off if I die."

"More threats!" one shouted angrily.

"All you do is make idle threats to us?" another demanded. "How is this useful?"

"Because we're negotiating right now," I explained, "and my threats aren't idle. We're going to come to a mutual understanding—you'll see. Just you guys and me. Just us, up-front and personal."

They carried on and whispered crap for a bit, but at last they settled down.

"Tell us what you require."

I smiled. "To start with, I require a modicum of respect and obedience. No more working with Trickle or any of his kind to overthrow my leadership. Don't blindly follow any squid and do his dirty work for him."

"You insult us. We have our own plans. No Cephalopod rules our kind—not anymore."

"That's right. And that's because of *my* kind. We're the basic model—the very thing that made you. Even your genes are offshoots of mine."

"Insulting…" several of them muttered. "…more insults."

"…but still, it is the spoken truth!" shouted several others. "The big-man speaks with the weight of facts behind him. We owe no squid anything more than a prolonged death!"

I could see I was getting through to them. The gremlins could be reasoned with—to a degree. Of course, you could never fully trust any of them—not unless you held a loaded gun to their baseball-sized heads.

"Well?" I asked. "Do I have your support?"

"You have our ears. What would you ask of us?"

274

"I want you to do your duty. You must send out your buzzers and your scouts. Inform me concerning the position of our joint enemy—the Rigellians."

Lots of them laughed then.

I squinted and looked around. "What's so funny?"

"Big man, you evoke pity," one of them said. "You are so blind, despite the fact your eyes are as big as fists."

I spotted the speaker, and I fixed on his glass-like eyes with my own. I'd come to suspect he was their leader.

"Explain yourself, gremlin."

He laughed again. "The bears are already here, you see. They encircle us, and the circle grows tighter with every hour. Before dawn, they will kill every living creature trapped in this region of the city."

This was news to me, and unwelcome news at that. But I didn't let on.

Instead, I sagely nodded my head. "Very good," I said. "You've passed my first test."

"What? You test us? What trickery is this?"

I laughed, long and loud. "You really think I didn't know the bears are surrounding us? I command this cohort, fools. I just wanted to see how big of a pack of traitors you are. As I said, you passed the test."

They hissed and squeaked a bit. It was like being surrounded by a mass of oversized, ornery rats.

"What do you propose to do for us?" the leader asked. "We are all about to perish here. Why should we not avenge ourselves immediately upon the fool who led us to our deaths?"

"You won't do that. You're no pack of heavy troopers. You're not that dumb."

"This is true, but your meaning is still unclear."

"What I mean is I have a plan. I'm going to beat the bears, and you're going to help me do it."

They looked at each other. They still seemed unhappy. Being sneaky tricksters themselves they were harder to fool than the average fellow.

But after complaining about me for a bit, they finally peered at me with curiosity. Was that a sliver of hope? I thought that it was.

"What is the nature of this plan, big-man?"

Right then, I knew I had them. I put my gauntlets on my knees, and I leaned close just like I'd seen them do. They leaned in too, looking at me with big, hungry eyes.

At that point I began to lie, and I went big with it.

Outside the windows, another silent shower of projectiles flew overhead. I had to wonder what they were and where they were going—but I couldn't spare the time to worry about that right now.

-45-

Old Trickles' eyes were bigger and more drippy than ever when I came down out of the building with a gaggle of whispering gremlins in my wake. No doubt Trickle had figured he'd gotten rid of one ornery James McGill—but he'd thought wrong.

When you're in a bad tactical situation, and doom is clearly impending, it's best to give a whole bunch of orders. Accordingly, I got everyone hopping and skipping around, preparing for the coming assault.

As soon as that was underway, I got on the horn to talk to Primus Collins. I relayed my situation, but failed to mention that I'd driven too deeply into enemy territory and got myself encircled.

"You're requesting reinforcements? In advance? They haven't even hit you yet."

"That's true, sir. But we're in a bad way. We can't hold back the numbers we suspect will be hitting us by morning—before that, even."

"What are you—?" she asked, and I saw her consulting maps. "You're too far forward, McGill. I hereby order you to conduct an orderly withdrawal toward my position."

I smiled and nodded. "That's a great idea, sir. It would have been even better if it had come a few hours ago. But I think it's too late now. My gremlins have buzzers, and they tell me we're surrounded."

She fussed and carried on about this for a bit, and I let her get it out of her system.

"I was a fool," she said, talking mostly to herself. "I shouldn't have given a gorilla like you an open-ended operational command."

"Uh... we can still solve this, sir."

"How?"

"Well, you can come to me—or at least move toward me. Then I can probably break out of this trap."

Collins shook her head so hard her hair did a little dance. "That's not happening. We've been charged with holding this water plant. I'm not leaving it to save a cohort that's gone rogue."

"Sir... you ordered us to go on a deep patrol. We're in the middle of that action now."

She looked sour. "I see where this is going. You're going to write an after-action report hanging me out to dry, aren't you?"

"I hope not, sir. There are other ways to fix this."

She showed me her teeth, but at last, she gestured impatiently for me to keep suggesting things.

"Well, you could fly a lifter out here—or maybe a fleet of skimmers. We could rush aboard and pull out."

She considered that, but finally she rejected the thought. "Too risky. I don't want to lose aircraft on top of manpower. The risk isn't justified."

It was the typical calculus of war in the legions. There was nothing cheaper than troops. We were only blood, sweat, bone meal and protoplasm to the brass.

"All right then, we'll have to hold out—with some artillery support, perhaps?"

She narrowed her eyes. "Artillery? You're in the middle of a city, McGill, in case you haven't noticed."

"That's right. But Varus and Victrix have a lot of star-falls. And this city doesn't belong to Earth. The area surrounding us isn't even inhabited."

She showed me her teeth again. With a wild grunt of unhappiness, she threw one hand to her forehead and rubbed at her face. "All right. I'll try to get approval to call in a heavy barrage all around your position."

"That would be greatly appreciated, sir."

"Fuck you, McGill," she said with real feeling. "Collins, out."

That was it. I tried to contact her a few more times over the next hour, but I was unsuccessful.

Finally, in the middle of the night, the skies lit up. We all gazed upward and gaped.

This time, the bombardment wasn't all in one direction. Yes, we could see more of those strange canisters flying—quiet projectiles from the Rigellian side arcing high and landing deep in the city.

But there were things flying in the other direction as well this time. Streaks of light sailed overhead, moving away from the city center and toward the outskirts and the dome beyond.

They were balls of glowing hot plasma, and they seemed to move in slow-motion. The flickering spheres were white in color, with long, bluish tails behind them. It looked like the planet was being showered by a hundred comets at once.

But I knew this was no natural phenomenon. The star-falls had launched a volley. From the look of it, every artillery piece Earth had on City World was involved.

"Incoming!" I roared over the cohort-wide channel. "Everyone, this is your commander. Take cover! We're under bombardment!"

The star-falls weren't targeting us of course, but the gunners could still miss.

Men shouted, heavy troopers croaked in dismay. Soon, the ground began to shake as the impacts rained down. The buildings we crouched within swayed and rumbled. One of them, the very building we'd chased the snipers out of, cracked at the midpoint and toppled. After the dust cleared, only a jagged spear of puff-crete still stood where it had once been. A hundred lives had been lost, a full unit that I'd stationed there.

Farther out in the night, things were much worse. The artificial comets crashed down upon the buildings surrounding our neighborhood, destroying many of them. After a full minute of this abuse, the volley ceased to fall. We climbed to our feet, dug our comrades out of rubble, and called for medical aid.

That's about when the sky lit up once again. The second volley was on the way.

Before that wave crashed down upon us, a new threat emerged.

"It's the bears, big-man!" one of my gremlin friends reported in. "They've figured out that our zone isn't under fire. They're rushing us!"

"Troops, get your guns out! Shoot them as they come in!"

Outside in the streets, short dark-suited figures raced toward us. There were hundreds of them. Some were injured, while others dragged their wounded comrades.

The crack and whine of rifles began to rip up the quiet night air. In between artillery volleys, the night grew dark again—but not for long. The star-falls themselves were virtually silent until they landed and caused great destruction. In each interim, we filled the air with bullets and power-bolts.

Caught in the open and desperate, the bears were knocked flat. They scrambled up and kept running, only to be blasted down again. Some had horrible injuries, and we didn't make things any easier for them.

By the time the enemy reached our buildings, I'd already set up a hot greeting at the doorways. Each bear that rushed into our strongholds for safety was grabbed and harshly dealt with.

Power-blades were driven into their guts if an opening could be found in their armor. When it could not, the attacking soldiers were buried under a falling tower of rubble. These towers, built up by my men during the long night of waiting, crushed the life out of them—armor or no.

They squirmed and growled and died snapping at us. There was no mercy, as we knew there would be none for us if the tables were turned.

Eventually, it was over. Six full volleys had come crashing down out of the skies onto the neighborhoods that surrounded us. The buildings were wrecked, and the skyline was a lurid red. Flickering flames danced in a thousand broken windows.

After the last volley and the last desperate charge by the bears out of the darkness, we waited, tense and sweating in the still night. But they didn't come at us again.

Soon, dawn broke, and the near-humans set up an odd, warbling cheer. It was a primitive sound, the kind of thing that hadn't been heard on Earth for tens of thousands of years.

The Blood Worlders were celebrating. They'd survived the night, and this was their way of welcoming the dawn.

The bright light of morning found me and my men in a good mood. We ate and drank in our makeshift bunkers—most of which were piles of overturned furniture. The bears were nowhere to be seen. Soon, I found myself fielding calls from various officers.

"You're still alive?" Primus Collins asked. She seemed both amazed and pleased.

"That's right. It was a little rough out here, I'll admit. Pretty touch-and-go just before dawn, but it was nothing a tough band of fighting men couldn't handle. These bears have a rep, sure, but it's mostly hype."

She laughed. She'd finally come to understand when I was bullshitting, and today she seemed to appreciate it. "Whatever, McGill. I'm glad you're still among the living. Now, I need you to return to the water plant. We've got new problems."

"Uh... what kind of problems, sir?"

"Brass problems. There's been a shuffle at the top of the Mogwa commanders. I don't understand it, but when I call headquarters, there seems to be total confusion. They keep talking about mass casualties, but I—"

"Mass casualties? How? On what front?"

She sounded rattled. "I—I don't know. Last night, things began going wrong in the center of the city. The Mogwa command center sent out a few confusing messages. Something about poison, disease... I really don't know. I don't understand it."

My mouth fell open, and my gut fell away from me. I pulled my helmet off my head and let it fall to the floor. Inside it, I could hear Collins' voice still squeaking my name.

I didn't care. I felt sick, because I thought I understood what was happening. I'd been watching it happen for a full day now.

Standing up, almost reeling, I staggered to the doorway of the smoldering building I was sheltering within.

My eyes rose up to gaze into the sky. There, high above the skyscrapers, strange projectiles were flying again. Every now and then, one sailed by overhead. In the daylight, I could see them more clearly. They were trailing something... vapor, perhaps? Or dust?

What I suspected—no, what I *knew* in my heart of hearts—it was a terrible thing.

Those streaks in the sky... they were projectiles. They were canisters, probably. Canisters full of poison. A formula that had once been secretly stored on Earth in an old, old book...

It was a bioweapon. A terrible compound designed to kill only the Mogwa.

And if I didn't miss my guess, it was killing them right now. All of them.

Billions of them...

-46-

"McGill? McGill!"

I found my way back to my helmet and put it on. I listened to Primus Collins as she ripped me a new one, but I didn't really process anything that she said.

"Sir," I said when she took a breath, "I know what's wrong and how to fix it."

When she finally broke off her tirade, I explained. I told her about the Mogwa bioweapon and how the spooks at Central knew they had it. I never mentioned my own prominent role in distributing it, of course.

Collins didn't believe me right off. She called in to headquarters, and she talked to Tribune Kraus. After hearing that I'd given her this grim warning, Kraus contacted me personally.

"Centurion McGill?" he said. "What kind of dark fantasy are you spreading rumors about?"

"I wish that's all it was, sir," I said. Then I began to explain.

I'd first discovered the formula back during the Home World campaign, decades ago. Various players—including the Cephalopods—had been seeking it even then. Over the years, it had been traded and lost and burned and rediscovered. One of the last homes it had found had been with the Rigellians and the Skay.

283

Tribune Kraus was horrified. He was also pensive. "If you are correct... then they must have manufactured it in massive quantities. Then they came here to use it—to massacre the Mogwa wholesale."

"Yes. That's what I think happened. This planet is the perfect proving ground. The test case to teach them how it might be applied on Trantor, the Mogwa home planet."

"Stunning..." Kraus said. "All right. This puts us at a historic juncture. So many of the Mogwa commanders are out sick—even those who've managed to struggle into this planning center look unwell. I see their roster is full of those who are either gravely ill or deceased. The population at large has been affected as well. We've seen them falling ill, collapsing in the streets... it's diabolical!"

"That it is, sir. The stuff is completely inert for humans and near-humans. Squids too, I'd wager. Can you warn the populace? Can you get them to shelter in their homes and filter their air?"

Tribune Kraus didn't seem to hear me. He was too busy talking the whole thing through. "It makes sense now why the enemy pressed so hard to gain control of food and water supplies. They planned to poison them. That approach might have been even more effective than this aerial spread."

I blinked and thought that over. I figured Kraus was right. The bears had been pushing for targets that fed and supplied the great City. All along, we'd figured that was because the situation had devolved into a siege, and they wanted to starve the people into submission. Sadly, their real plans were far more grim.

"Tribune? Who is in command there on the Mogwa side?"

He shook his head. "The field marshal is gone. I think he's probably dead. There are some subordinates around, but most of them are ill. They should be—"

I stood up and snapped my fingers in his face. He blinked at that, then he frowned. He wasn't accustomed to my particular flavor of disrespect.

"Sir, you need to take command," I told him. "You have to do it *now*. Without leadership, the city will fall for certain."

Kraus chewed at his lower lip. "How am I going to get Mogwa citizens to listen to me? They refer to us as animals with regularity. They'll see me as we might see a dog that's trying to drive a car."

"You're right about that... you need a stamp of legitimacy... I've got an idea."

I told him my plan, and he wasn't keen on it at first. As time was short, and he didn't have anything else in his head to pull out and save the day, he eventually agreed. He sent a skimmer to my location for pickup.

Swept up aboard the aircraft, I stared out of the rearmost window and watched the streets fall away and shrink to vague lines. From the air, this sector of the City we'd fought so hard over didn't look like much. It was an island of damaged buildings inside a blackened ring of destruction. I hoped Primus Collins and Trickle would do all right on their own. Part of me didn't like leaving the Blood Worlders down there in the midst of a burning patch of rubble—but it wasn't up to me.

Turning myself forward, eyes-front, I gave myself a shake. This was big. This was a mass extermination. The Mogwa were in real trouble, and I'd had a hand in their demise. As much as it pained me to admit it, I owed them whatever help I could give. Sure, they were annoying prissy assholes most of the time, but they didn't deserve to be erased from the cosmos.

When I landed back at headquarters, I was sent a message summoning me to the main nerve center. I ignored this order and went downstairs, going deeper into the big building.

A few sickly Mogwa tried to interfere, but I brushed past them. One Mogwa Marine coughed and fell out of his chair as I swept past, and I continued without breaking my stride.

In the darkest, most isolated cell in the prison underneath the city's military headquarters, there was a cell block distinctive from the rest. Walking into the place, I saw a few Mogwa who were dead on the floor. A few others were crawling around, wheezing. I picked up the pace, worried that I was too late.

At last I found him. Sateekas was huddled inside one of the last cells on the right. I thought maybe he was dead already, but he stirred at my approach.

The doors were all open, as some AI script had recognized this was a legit emergency and opened the cages to release the inmates. Sateekas, however, had chosen to stay in his cell. He hadn't come out to escape or find help.

"Sir? Grand Admiral, sir?"

I stood over him and eyed him critically. He lifted bloodshot eyes in my direction. He took a breathing device from his mouth for a moment, and he whispered to me.

"Gas…" he said. "I think everyone is affected."

"Not me, sir. But you keep that breather up to your face. Don't pull it away until we can get you into an environment-controlled suit. Don't worry. You'll be right as rain in a moment."

Then, without asking permission or even telling him what my plan was, I scooped up the Mogwa in my big arms and carried him the hell out of there. A few alarms sounded, and a light or two spun and flashed—I ignored it all.

A few flights up I'd seen a locker with emergency gear. As we were on a comfortable planet, there wasn't much in the way of spacer suits, but I got a fire suit out instead and pulled it over Sateekas. He complained as I nearly broke his thin bones while stuffing limbs into the numerous armholes.

"Sorry sir, sorry. Don't worry. You'll be feeling better soon."

I put him on the floor of the elevator car and propped him up. He had to at least look upright and functional. Who would follow an emergency interim leader who looked like death warmed-over?

On the long ride up to the headquarters room, I explained the situation as best I could. Sateekas was aghast about the application of a bioweapon to a peaceful planet.

"These barbarians…" he said. "I didn't think they would have the gall to do something so… final."

His voice sounded kind of raspy. I was worried about it.

"Look, sir," I said. "The Field Marshal is dead. The revival systems are overwhelmed and unmanned. I think you have to declare that you're in command of the Mogwa defense forces."

"Hmm..." he said, thinking that over. "It may have escaped your attention, McGill-creature, but I'm quite ill. I might not survive the day myself. Only my isolation in that accursed prison saved me from a more decisive dose of the bio agent."

"I'm sure that's all true, sir. But it doesn't change anything. The people need a leader. They need that leader to tell them what to do—to warn them about the danger. Down deep in the city, in the lower levels, the people haven't been touched yet. Billions might still be saved."

He finally agreed to do what he could. He had me walk him onto the floor of the headquarters. There, he was met with snarls of displeasure.

Various Mogwa officers approached us. They were all coughing and sweating, but they were united in their hate and distrust of Sateekas. It made me wonder about how, exactly, he'd come to possess that battlecruiser he'd flown to Earth. It was pretty obvious to me he had commandeered it without permission from anyone and flown it to the Frontier provinces to seek aid.

That made me smile. This old bastard Sateekas was the only Mogwa I'd ever met that reminded me of myself.

"Listen, citizens of the Empire," he told the circle of unhappy faces. "We're faced today with extinction. With utter annihilation. I'm not just talking about here, at this ignoble splinter-colony. I'm talking about all Mogwa everywhere. Even those who huddle in the Core Systems at Trantor are endangered."

They shouted at him. They accused him of all kinds of misconduct. Sateekas shrugged this off.

"I, among all of you present, am the only official from the Empire itself. I am not only an ex-Governor of a neighboring province, but I was once a grand admiral leading a border fleet a thousand ships strong."

One of the exec officers dared to step forward. "You did nothing but lose fleets, Sateekas. You failed the Empire every time it trusted you. You failed us as well, bringing back these insolent slave-troops to protect us. They've done nothing!"

"Not so!" Sateekas boomed, forcing himself to stand tall—or at least as tall as a Mogwa could stand. "Note this specimen here. This is the McGill-creature. A loyal servant of the Empire. He has slain countless Rigellians and even a few Skay."

This was scoffed at, but Sateekas made a signal in my direction.

"Uh…" I said. For a long second, I didn't get it.

"Your records, fool!" Sateekas said. "Play them, as you once did for me!"

Brightening, I searched on my tapper for nearly a full minute. That's a long time when a muttering, angry audience is watching you. At last, I found some vids of the Skay dying at Clone World. I flicked this to the planning table, and I let it play.

The Mogwa officers tried not to look impressed, but they failed. There were shots of Sateekas and his broken fleet in the vids as well.

"You see?" asked one of the officers—it was the exec again. I figured he had ideas of taking command in the field marshal's place. "All Sateekas does is die and fail."

"Could you have broken two Skay?" I demanded of him. "You heard me right. Sateekas lost his fleet, but he did so while destroying two Skay. Then I used commando techniques to take out the third—on his orders!"

Sateekas carefully gauged how this was working on the Mogwa commanders. He could tell they were uncertain. "Let me ask you, who else here has fought in such vast battles? Who here among you will take the blame for this loss of Segin? Who will be labeled a failure over this desperate last stand?"

They didn't want to meet his eye-groups. They studied the deck, and they scowled and muttered.

"Yes," he went on after a coughing fit. "We must have a new leader, and that leader shall be me."

"By what authority?" demanded the exec guy. He was a stubborn dude.

"By the authority of the Empire!" Sateekas declared. "No one on this planet wields greater credentials than I do. What's more, I command the human forces on this world."

This line kind of stunned me. I glanced around the place—but Tribune Kraus was nowhere to be seen. Either he was off running his legion, or he'd decided to ditch the Mogwa headquarters entirely. Either way, I was glad he wasn't around to hear this.

Standing tall, I loomed over the sickly aliens. "That's right. We came out here under Sateekas' command, and we still answer to him first and foremost. It's high time we executed the lot of you fops, and I'll start with you."

Saying this, I put a pistol muzzle into the exec guy's earhole. His eyes widened, and he peered up at me with vast hate.

I turned to Sateekas. "You just give the word, Grand Admiral, sir."

"Who gave this beast permission to bring a weapon into our headquarters?" the exec demanded.

Sateekas shuffled closer. "I did. Do you have an argument with that?"

The officer's eyes rolled in his head. He finally grunted when I pressed the gun barrel closer, bonking him in the skull. Mogwa have thin skulls, so I didn't do it too hard.

"I have no argument," the officer said sullenly.

"Good!" Sateekas said, as if he'd been given a hearty endorsement. "Brothers! Sisters! Put aside your petty jealousies and join me! The Mogwa army is broken, but we still command this rabble of slaves. Do not surrender to your fear or to the barbaric enemy. They are ruthless, and they will show you no mercy… and neither shall I."

Slowly, one at a time, the surviving leadership of the Mogwa military swore allegiance to old Sateekas. He was sick, and he was trembly, but he seemed to enjoy the process.

Finally, as they finished this ceremony, he turned to the communications booth. He slithered inside and gave a stirring address to the populace. Say what you will about his command skills, he was a cagey politician when push came down to shove.

He told the Mogwa people about the bio agent, and how to take precautions to avoid it. Then he gave the Mogwa troops orders. By this time, they were buttoning up all over the City, getting every kind of protective gear, gas-mask and suit of power-armor they could get their foot-hand things on. Sateekas insisted that no able-bodied soldier could allow themselves to be exposed to the air and the wind—these elements had become their enemy.

Grimly sick but determined, the Mogwa and the four human legions prepared for a struggle to the finish with the Rigellian bears.

This all came none too soon, as the enemy was reportedly advancing on all fronts.

-47-

After Sateekas had established a shaky hold on the command center, Tribune Winslade suddenly showed up.

I'm not a believer in conspiracies, but I don't like amazing coincidences either. It seemed to me that someone had tipped him off. Either he'd planned it this way—to step in when the Mogwa coup was finished—or he'd been in hiding until things settled down. Whichever was the case, he was bright-eyed and bushy-tailed, striding around the place and making loud "suggestions" to everyone.

"McGill?" he said sternly when he spotted me. "Centurion? May I have your undivided attention, please?"

I turned to old Winslade and gazed at him with a cautious eye. "What's up, Tribune? Where's Kraus?"

Winslade made an airy gesture with one hand. "Tribune Kraus has been arrested, I'm afraid. It was decided that he lacked subservience."

"Ah, I get it. That's where you come in."

He tossed me a clouded look, but then seemed to think the better of it. "Regardless… with no one running around above the rank of primus, I thought it would be for the best that I step in. After all, I am the acting commander of Legion Varus."

"Who's the acting commander of Victrix?"

Winslade made that same fluttering movement with his fingers, dismissing my words. "I don't know, and I don't care. Whatever the case, he's not here—and I am."

"I get it. You want to run the human side of this battle. Don't worry, I won't step on your glory-hounding. Not today."

Winslade came near and lowered his voice. "That's good to hear. I thought I could count on you to see reason. These Mogwa are insufferable—as we know too well. Kraus wasn't used to their odd ways. He insulted them or something when they started getting sick. They arrested him and tossed into some kind of dungeon."

I thought about the Mogwa prison cells far below us, where I'd found old Sateekas. Those cells were all empty—but I didn't figure it was worth telling Winslade about that.

"Okay. So what do we do now?"

Winslade licked his lips, and I squinched up my eyes.

"I'm concerned about Sateekas. He's too weak. He did a good speech, and he got everyone on the same page, mind you, but he's about to fall over."

I glanced in the direction Winslade was looking, and I had to admit the weaselly primus had a point. Sateekas was definitely looking poorly.

Getting a sudden bad vibe, I turned back to Winslade. "Now look, I'm not going to follow along with any further coups and purges. We've had enough of that."

"Don't worry your simian skull, McGill. That's not what I had in mind. I *need* Sateekas—um, we do, that is. We need a figurehead. I'm just concerned about his status. A figurehead isn't much good if he's wheezing and falling out of his chair."

"Uh… oh." Taking several quick strides, I moved to Sateekas' side. With a grimace of disgust, I pushed his floppy body back onto his seat again. He was passing out—or close to it.

As I moved to walk away, Sateekas suddenly grabbed at my arm. I bent down and listened to his weak voice.

"McGill. You must aid me. I must be recycled. I must be renewed—but no one can know of it."

Thinking that over, I leaned over the old buzzard. "Don't worry, sir. I think I can arrange things."

Leaving him crouched on a command chair, I returned to Winslade. "We need a working revival machine."

"What? There are only a few still operating on this miserable planet. Did you know the anti-Mogwa poison seems to attack the revival machines that are attuned to their biology? I guess it makes sense…"

"That's diabolical! I guess we'll have to use one of our units."

Winslade eyed me critically. "What did you have in mind, Centurion?"

"Give me your blessing, sir. I need the one that's used for nonhumans."

"Hmmm. There are only two of those in service in this city. One for each of the near-human legions. Right now, I'm sure they're queued up for weeks."

"I'm sure they are, but you just told me that you're in nominal command, and that we need Sateekas as a figurehead. He's not much of a figurehead now, he's more like a sad-sack."

Winslade eyed the sagging wreck that was Sateekas. Anyone could tell he wasn't going to make it. He'd survived the bio agent through sheer determination and grit—but that could only take a fella so far.

"All right, all right," Winslade told me. "There will be breakage over this, McGill. Countless squid noncoms and adjuncts are going to be very annoyed."

I snorted.

"Go to the lifter parked outside," Winslade told me at last. "Get him aboard, and I'll aid you with overriding orders."

A few minutes later I was wheeling Sateekas out of the command chamber on an office chair. That elicited a lot of confused stares.

Trying to stare straight ahead and move with purpose, I wheeled the dying buzzard out of the place. To my irritation, the Mogwa office chair had one squeaky wheel, just like every human chair seemed to. Whenever anyone asked me what the hell I was doing, I told them the same damned thing, whether they were, human or alien. "He has to use the facilities. Step aside and give the Grand Admiral some room."

That seemed to do the trick. Mogwa upper class types sometimes wore diapers and crapped in their clothes—but that wasn't as common of a practice out here in the Mid-Zone.

When I finally got Sateekas out of the command center, I dropped all pretenses. I picked up his squeaky chair in my arms and trotted off with him.

If he'd been protesting, I'm sure some Mogwa marine would have stopped me. But Sateekas was with it enough to wave them off and wheeze something like, "make way!" now and again.

Taking the Mogwa to a skimmer, we were whisked into the skies by a pilot with an upraised eyebrow. She kept glancing at us, and she finally had to ask.

"Um... Centurion? Is that Mogwa officer okay?"

"Nope. He's dying. But we're going to fix that. Get me to lifter NC-7, pronto."

She hit the gas, and we went into a spiral, then a dive. Some anti-air flak was flying around even in the center of the city.

That was a bad sign. I took a moment to leave Sateekas and look out the skimmer's windows.

The city was engulfed in smoke, fire and ruin. The dome was down—that was a shocker. When had they lost the power plants that kept their force field up? The lights were still on, but that took a fraction of the power the dome required.

Maybe they'd decided the resources weren't worth the effort, seeing as the city was crawling with bears anyway. I hadn't even been aware of these setbacks, but they made sense. The bears were pressing the attack on all fronts, and as they captured critical services the city shut down.

Turning away from the scenes outside, I turned back to Sateekas. He was reaching for me. He had a pleading look in his eyes. His nasty mouth worked, but I couldn't hear anything intelligible coming out of it.

Sliding over the seats, I came close to him. "Hey now, don't you go dying on me, Grand Admiral." I always used that outdated honorific with him, and I still believed to this day it was part of the reason he was sweet on me.

"McGill..." he wheezed out.

Again, he reached out with a trembly arm. I didn't know what he was trying to do. So I took that leathery foot-hand thing of his into my gloves, and I tried not to look disgusted.

"What's the trouble, you old... oh."

Sateekas wasn't looking at me. He was looking at our joined hands. He struggled weakly to lift his hand from mine, so I let him do it.

Watching in befuddlement, I saw him make a tremendous effort to reach farther. To take that worn-parchment looking hand and reach...

At last, I saw a flicker on my tapper. All at once, I realized what he'd done, and what I'd forgotten to do. He'd touched his tapper to mine, transmitting his engrams and body scans into the bio-computer on my wrist.

"Ah-ha!" I said, laughing. "I get it now. You're just trying to make a backup of your data. No need to worry, sir. Once we get to the Blue Deck on that lifter I see ahead of us, the bio people will take care of all that. If you could just... uh..."

Sateekas didn't look so good. After struggling mightily to touch tappers, it was as if all the starch had gone out of his thin bones.

As I watched, he went limp and slid off the skimmer's seat. He flopped on the floor. I checked his vitals and made a fuss—but I already knew the truth. He was stone dead.

-48-

We recycled the old buzzard with Winslade's blessing from headquarters. The bio people were rude about it, of course. Nonhuman revivals were more complicated than the ones we legionnaires required—and needless to say, they took longer. On top of that, the grumpy bios didn't like dumping a gestation they'd been working on for over an hour.

"Do you know this latest grow is a Cephalopod officer?" one of the lady-bio types asked me. She had her arms crossed and a nasty scowl on her mug. "We just dumped it. Just like that. Crap like this sets us back nearly ninety minutes. People think that a revival for a large alien is the same as for a human, but—"

"Excuse me," I said, and I touched my cap to her as I walked out. She flipped me off in return, but I didn't care. I'd decided I was late for the commissary.

After getting some good grub and a beer for each hand, I returned to the revival chamber. Sateekas was out of the oven and struggling to sit up. He was almost as floppy as the last time I'd seen him, but his color was better. His carapace had a shiny black sheen to it, and his eye-groups were nowhere near as loose and unfocussed.

"Well, looky-here!" I declared from the doorway. "The rightful planetary overlord of City World is doing fine. You losers should all bow down and kiss his slimy butt."

The revival team avoided my eye. The bio-lady in charge of the place was human, but the others were not. They were saurian types—imported labor with arms big enough to lift half-ton carcasses off the deck.

One of them stood in the back, but he still didn't look like the rest... I squinted... was that a saurian with a distinctive blue shade of scales on him? Yes, yes, I think it was.

I grinned. I hadn't laid eyes on old Raash for a long while. We hadn't parted on the best of terms, but at least when he'd been called as a witness for the prosecution in a particular witch-trial out on Ice World, he hadn't lied on me. That made me feel a bit more respectful.

"Raash?" I said, stepping forward and ignoring the scowls of the others. "Is that you? What a surprise! Of all the flea-bitten horny toads I might have expected to meet out here—"

"You are mistaken, human," Raash said. "My name is Roark. I know nothing of this Raash creature you speak of."

"Uh..." I said, eyeing him. Suddenly, I caught on. Raash had reportedly gone back to Steel World and more or less defected. But now, he was back on the job again.

How had that worked out? I could easily imagine. He needed a new identity, since his genetics were all messed up. Way back during the Glass World campaign the Dust Worlder's had revived him from a single burnt claw.

Naturally, the revival had been a Galactic Crime due to the fact we hadn't used a sanctioned and licensed revival machine from Edge World. What's more, it had taken six weeks and hadn't gone all that well in the end.

After shocking Raash's new makeshift, 'Frankenstein's monster' of a corpse back to life, he'd come out... different. He had blue scales, for instance, which was unique for all his kind. Sort of like a human who was somehow born a bright magenta or a turquoise shade, he'd become a laughing stock among his own folk. He'd apparently decided to return to Earth's service and to do so under an assumed name.

"Roark, you say? Okay, then. My bad. I must have mistaken you for someone else, Roark."

Raash gazed at me suspiciously. His eyes were narrowed to slits of mistrust. But after a few seconds, during which I kept my mouth shut, he finally nodded.

That was a dead giveaway right there. Normal lizards who hadn't been living with humans for decades didn't nod at anyone. It was a distinctly human gesture, one that old Raash had picked up at some point or another.

Helping Sateekas off the birthing mats and onto a gurney, I followed as the bio people wheeled him out of the place. They dumped him in the recovery room, and I gathered his things and returned them to him.

"Such a messy process," Sateekas complained. "I hate dying and being revived."

"So do I, but it sure beats the alternative, doesn't it?"

He peered at me, not getting it for a moment, but then he finally let out one of those farting Mogwa-laughs. "Yes, yes. It does rank superior to permadeath. I have to thank you, McGill, for your efforts in bringing me back to life again."

"Not a problem, sir. This world needs you. That grand field marshal guy—he's dead, you know. You're in command now."

"Yes. Right. But surely the marshal must be in line to be revived, just as I have been?"

"Negatory, sir. Your Mogwa revival machines have all caught the same disease that you guys have. Only our human-run machines seem to be operating."

"Hmm… most unfortunate. Billions might be permed here. Generations, spawned and then lost." He sat up straighter and shook himself. "I must rise to this task. I must summon aid."

"Uh… what kind aid, sir?"

"Take me to a deep-link device."

That left me scratching my head. I had no idea where one of those might be languishing. I didn't even know if we had one here on City World.

Using my tapper, I talked to every tech I knew. They were pretty sure that Legion Varus didn't have such a device here on this planet. They'd all been left up on the warships, before they'd fled the system.

As we discussed this difficulty, a figure appeared in the doorway of the recovery room. He was a blue-scaled reptile, and he filled the space of the doorframe quite completely.

"Raash?" I asked.

Sateekas turned toward the saurian, and he immediately bristled. "Is this some kind of assassin?"

"No, sir. I don't think so. Hey, Raash. Come join us."

The saurian stood there, indecisive. At last, he approached and sat at the table with us. His seat creaked under him, as it had been designed to support half his weight.

"I am curious, human," Raash said. "I do not understand your actions in the aggregate. One time I meet you, and we growl and snarl like rival studs in mating season. On other occasions, I find you charitably reviving nonhuman debris, such as this being that sits with us."

Here, he indicated Sateekas. As old Sateekas wasn't used to being referred to as a scrap of debris, he scowled and told me he had work to do back at headquarters. I couldn't argue with that, so I wished him well and sent him on his way.

All the while this interchange went on, Raash stared at me. If you've ever been stared at by a large, predatory reptilian, you'll know it's not a pleasant experience. Due to my long association with aliens of every stripe, I didn't take offense or fuss about it overly much.

At last, old Raash worked out his thoughts in that big slow brain of his and started talking again. "I can only think that you've changed," he said. "That your prior bigotry and hatred of the nonhuman has abated somewhat."

"Nah," I said. "I still hate most aliens. But I have a few friends in the mix. Sometimes, I've even called you a friend, Raash."

He pointed a claw at me. "There. You changed my reference back to the old one. I have forsaken that name due to technical difficulties."

"I understand, and your secret is safe with me. You don't mind if I still call you Raash, though, do you?"

The big lizard shrugged. That was another human gesture. Maybe Raash was right. Maybe we were both picking up customs from one another. "It is acceptable, as long as you don't speak of the name around my superiors. I will pretend that the name Raash is a nickname we've concocted together."

I laughed at that. The idea of Raash and I having a nickname for each other—that was a hoot. "What's your name going to be for me, then?"

Raash appeared to give this some serious thought. "I will call you primate-excrement. Is this acceptable?"

"Uh…" I said, not liking the idea overly much, but deciding it would suffice as long as it didn't catch on. At last, I nodded. "All right. You can call me ape-shit if you want to. After all, it isn't too far from the mark."

Raash stood up after this, and he flipped his tail high. That was a sort of good-bye gesture. "Now, if we are done with this reacquaintance, I must return to my duties."

"Okay… but hey, Raash? You wouldn't happen know about any deep-link devices I could use here on City World, would you?"

The lizard's demeanor suddenly changed. When I say changed, I mean it did a one-eighty.

He snarled and threw the chair he'd been crouching on across the room. Then he flipped the table over as well.

Without even thinking about it, I had my combat knife out, and I was on my feet. Raash threw a couple of swipes my way, his big claws whistling through the air.

Now, if I'd been in a less charitable mood, I might have taken one or the other of those scaly hands off at the wrist. As it was, I had half a mind to do it.

"What the fuck is wrong with you now?" I demanded. "Don't tell me you're still a bad grow? With murderous tendencies baked-in?"

Raash wasn't listening. He was talking to himself instead. "Again, I've been duped by the master of lies. Why can I not learn that a human is never a friend? That nothing with ancestors that squatted in trees can ever be trusted?"

Despite my new moniker, I figured it was Raash who'd suddenly gone ape-shit on me.

All around us, the room emptied out right-quick. No one seemed to want anything to do with this giant crazy lizard, or the knife-wielding Varus man who'd squared off with him. In a few minutes the MPs would arrive, but that would probably happen too late. By that time, one or the other of us would be dead—possibly both.

Banging on that dormant organ that slept most of the time between my big ears, I tried to understand what had set the saurian off.

"Hey, are you going nuts because I mentioned a deep-link machine?"

"Do not even attempt further obfuscation. Such efforts will not be successful. You knew very well what you were saying."

"Uh…" I said, dancing back and ducking two more swiping sets of claws.

I was clueless and then some. To give myself more time, I took a poke at him with my knife. I scored a jab on his left shoulder. Blood welled up, but he took no notice of this. Saurians weren't the sensitive type.

Finally, I thought of something. "You *do* know where a deep-link machine is, don't you? That's why you're going four-star crazy."

"Further discussion is useless, human. I shall take you with me into the embrace of the final sleep. We shall endure everlasting desolation as a pair, and I will at least be rid of your chattering nonsense."

"Hold on, hold on," I said, jabbing now and then to force him to take a step back. "Listen, I need a deep-link to use myself—secretly."

Raash stood swaying, but at least he stopped lunging at me. "That is the nature of your proposal? You wish to force negotiation upon me?"

"Not exactly. I want you to help both of us. This planet is doomed. The bears are going to overrun the place."

Raash shrugged, as if he was unconcerned. "As a noncombatant, I will doubtlessly be allowed to return to Earth with the fleet."

"But the fleet isn't here. And the bears aren't known for their charity."

He still seemed unconcerned, and this made me a mite suspicious. If he had a deep-link, and he wanted to keep that a secret… what might he be doing with it? Spying? For who? The bears, maybe?

Could that be why he wasn't worried about losing this war?

Giving my head a shake, I tried to push all that aside. Right now, I needed to calm Raash down and get him to let me have access to his deep-link.

"All right," I said, flipping my knife in the air and thunking it into the table where we'd been so recently at peace. "Let's sit down and talk about this. We can always kill each other later on. Take a seat, Raash, old buddy."

The lizard stood indecisively. He was never as good as I was at switching mental gears—not unless he was switching into a murderous rage, that is.

When the MPs finally arrived, I had to shine them on with some laughing bluster about us practicing our combat skills. Only then did Raash grudgingly sit down with me again.

He sulked until the cops left, then he finally fixed me with a baleful eye. "I have such a device. It is as you described—capable of communications between the stars."

Nodding, I smiled at him. "I kind of figured…"

I was getting ideas all of a sudden. All sorts of ideas.

-49-

Once I had Raash in less of a crazy-lizard mood, I managed to get him to show me his secret communications device. Only the obvious fact that we were all about to get our collective asses permed down here on City World convinced him to cooperate. After twenty long minutes of cajoling and false praise, I got him to allow me access to his secret spy gear.

I'd always suspected Raash was a saurian spy. He'd told me as much on a few occasions, usually when he thought he'd beaten me and was in a position of power. In such moments, his sense of pride had exceeded all caution, and he'd crowed like a pre-dawn rooster.

Today was different. Today, he wasn't proud or boastful—he was worried.

"The device was sold to me by an elderly earthling," he said. "I barely know how it operates."

"Uh-huh…" I said, ignoring his nonsensical cover-story and poking at the machine.

Raash was a terrible liar. Even now, when my hands were on his spy-machine, he was still trying to pretend a little old lady had sold it to him. Next, he'd probably complain that he'd been swindled by the imaginary old bat.

"This here looks like the transmit button," I said.

"Yes. Don't touch it."

"Hmm…"

The device wasn't much of a puzzle. It had very little in the way of controls. There was an input microphone on a wire—an honest-to-God wire—and that's about it other than the single transmit button.

"But..." I said, lifting it up to look underneath. There was nothing to see there, either, except for a power cable that was warm to the touch and about as thick around as my Johnson on a Saturday morning.

"Raash? I don't understand how you change the channel on this thing."

"The what?"

"Every deep-link device has a unique ID. A station number. That's how you know who you're talking to."

Raash looked evasive. "That is not how this machine operates. I was a fool to show it to you."

"Nah... it's okay. I know someone who can get it to work for us."

Raash looked curious. "Who might this be? A man from Central? An intelligence officer?"

His big paws were up again, and the big poky things on the ends of his gnarled fingers were working the air. I got the feeling he was wishing they were working on my neck.

"No, no, no. I'm talking about Natasha. She was dead for a while, but I can get ahold of her. I'm pretty sure I can find her and get her to help."

"Natasha... I recall this one. Female, but oddly capable. Yes. She helped with my revival, didn't she?"

"Yes. That's the girl. Let me talk to her—hey, time to back off, now."

He had a few of those pointy claws on my wrist, but I pulled away and worked my tapper. I could tell I was blowing all sorts of violent plans old Raash might have been entertaining in his scaly head, but that was just too damned bad. We didn't have time to fight and kill each other right now—fun though that might be.

"Natasha? Hey, girl. You'll never believe—what? No, no, this isn't a booty-call. Far from it. See who I've got here with me? You remember this nutzo blue lizard, right?"

Natasha was never eager to join in on my schemes, but then she never said no to me in the end, either. In less than an hour, I had her down in the lower decks of the lifter with Raash and myself, working on the miniature deep-link.

"This thing is ingeniously designed," she said. "Streamlined to a single purpose."

"What's that, exactly?" I asked.

"It transmits, and it doesn't receive. Further, it only transmits to a single station. The receiver, you see, is larger than the transmitter on these devices. All you have to do is connect this baby to a big power source, and you can send anything you want to the preordained address."

"Uh… okay. It sounds like we need two things, then. One, a power source, and two a way to change the target station ID."

Natasha laughed. "Yes. A tall order, as you would like to say."

"False," Raash declared suddenly. "I have a power source. I have linked this device to the lifter's engines."

We both looked at him in concern. "How did you learn to do that?" I asked.

Raash shrugged. "I believe I was born with the knowledge innately. It is a gift of mine."

I snorted, and Natasha rolled her eyes, but we didn't argue with him. Obviously, he'd been trained by his spy-masters to do such nefarious things.

"All right, we've got the power to transmit," I said. "How about changing the destination ID?"

Here, both Raash and I looked at Natasha. She appeared alarmed. "Seriously? You want me to figure that out using a strange alien device? I barely know enough to tell you what this thing does."

Raash lifted one blue-scaled finger. "I will aid you."

Together, the two of them went to work on the device. Raash knew how to take it apart. He knew what every piece did, too. He soon led her to the parts that controlled the station ID.

It was more than obvious that Raash hadn't gotten this gear in any innocent way, but Natasha and I both made a point of not pressing him on the topic.

By midnight, the jury-rigging of the device was done, and we sent a fateful message. I had no way of knowing if the message had gotten through or not, as the machine only transmitted, it could not receive.

But it didn't matter. We'd done what we could to call for help. I'd sent the message to Galina, aboard her flagship in Earth's Fleet. It had to be out there someplace, and as those ships were the only source of aid we could hope might rescue us, I'd chosen her as the recipient.

Once the deed was done, the night closed in. The roar of artillery outside took a break along about midnight, so I made a play for Natasha's attentions. I offered her a warm spot on my bunk, which I accounted as a plus—but my offer flamed out. Disappointed, I decided it was okay, as I was pretty tired anyways.

Long before dawn, I was startled awake by sirens and a booming announcement that blared from every tapper in my unit.

Our sector of the great City was under attack.

-50-

Rushing to join my unit, I found they'd been given orders to hold at the water plant. A big attack was expected. I managed to wangle a ride on a skimmer and headed toward the front lines.

In the meantime, after getting his revival, Sateekas had taken up his station at headquarters. He and a few dozen others worked with the human commanders to coordinate the city's defenses.

Sateekas had left me in the feed that was normally only shared with top brass. Things looked bleak. Based on the chatter and colored maps laying out the tactical situation, we'd already lost a third of the city. That was mostly the outskirts, sure… but the bears were pressing ever onward, moving deeper into the central neighborhoods with every passing hour.

Joining my unit in the buildings circling the water plant, I waited for the predicted enemy rush—but it didn't come. After an hour went by, my troops and the other neighboring units began to celebrate. Manfred even came by with some hooch.

"Hey McGill," he said, lifting a disgusting concoction fermented in a ration pouch. "You want some rot gut? We've got plenty."

"No, thanks. We haven't won this yet, Manfred. Not by a long shot."

"Party-pooper," he grumbled, and he wandered off to pester Jenny Mills who was commanding the next unit down.

Becoming increasingly concerned, I finally logged in and checked the feed again. Where were the enemy, if they weren't hitting us?

The answer was soon apparent. The bears had circumvented our location entirely. Legion Varus—or a good portion of it—was deployed to defend the city's water supply. According to their profile so far, it was expected the bears would push hard to gain control of the region.

But that was only if they wanted to do more poisoning of the population. Maybe they were out of bio agents after days of aerial spread. Or maybe they didn't care anymore because their dirty-work had already been done.

Watching the crawling colored lines and blocks, I could see their plan. They were avoiding human-defended locations. They were driving right past us, pushing where the Mogwa marines were supposed to stop them. As a result, our lines were crumbling. Soon, the headquarters itself would be surrounded. It was only a matter of time until we were cut off from one another. Then, we'd be destroyed and swallowed in small, bite-sized chunks.

"Manfred!" I bellowed until he came back to me.

"No need to yell, mate. I've still got some hooch for you."

I knocked the slop from his hands. "We've got to move out. They're surrounding us. All our flanks are threatened. The Mogwa are collapsing on every side of us right now."

His mouth hung open for a second, but I showed him what was happening on my tapper, and he soon became as alarmed as I was. He ran off and alerted everyone he could.

The first thing I did was try to contact Sateekas—but it was hopeless. As the grand-poobah in charge of this war, no one within shouting distance of his office would give me the time of day, whether they were Mogwa or human.

Next, I contacted Primus Collins and Tribune Winslade. They were two rule-followers, two people unlikely to stick their necks out if it was so much as drizzling outside, but I got them to see reason by sharing the tactical feed from headquarters.

"Dammit!" Winslade squalled. "This is so typical. Absolutely typical. The vaunted Mogwa marines—bah! The finest soldiers of the Empire, we're told. Any ten of them would lose a fight with a house cat!"

"What are we going to do?" Primus Collins asked.

"We have to hit them as they flow past us," I suggested. "If we sit here, dug in, they'll surround us and pocket our positions once and for all."

"We're not going on an offensive without orders," Winslade said sternly. "Even you should know better than that, McGill. Stand down and stop viewing tacticals that aren't meant for a man of your rank. Winslade out."

He dropped the group channel, and I showed every tooth I had in my head to the video pickup.

Primus Collins was still on the line, and she frowned up at me. She looked worried—really worried.

"McGill... Winslade is wrong on this one. I think you're right. You're better than I am at getting things to happen that go against the C. O..."

"Uh... is this an endorsement, sir? Or an order?"

She shook her head. "It's nothing but a sentiment... but I think you should do what you have to. I know you'll come up with something. Let me know if I can help."

Her finger moved toward the disconnect button, which was a red circle on her tapper, but I managed to stop her.

"Hold on a second, Primus, sir. Why don't you patch me into headquarters? Through your tapper?"

She blinked a few times. "They'll think the call is from me..."

"Exactly."

"Who are you going to talk to? What are you going to say?"

I shook my head. "You don't want to know anything about that—do you?"

"No..." she said, "I don't. I'm patching you through."

Soon, I caught the attention of an underling at headquarters. It was one of Kraus' butt-monkeys, by the look of him, and only some creative talk about having critical information for Sateekas' himself kept me from getting the old disconnect.

But instead of Sateekas, I got Kraus' ugly face frowning up at me instead. Apparently, he'd managed to escape whatever trap Winslade had left for him. He didn't seem happy to see me.

"McGill? Is that Centurion James McGill? What are you doing tying up command resources? Don't you know a major battle is on-going?"

"I do indeed, sir. I happen to have critical information concerning this very situation, and I need to talk to Sateekas personally."

Kraus looked off-camera, as if glancing around the place. He shook his head. "You're way out of line, Centurion. You'll stand your post, and you'll follow orders. No Victrix man would—"

"Don't I know it, sir. I'm not fit to polish the boots of a Victrix recruit. But if you would cast your mind back to yesterday, you might recall that I personally managed to get Sateekas revived."

"Yes, yes. What of it?"

"Well sir," I continued, "during that operation, I came into contact with certain information that only old Sateekas himself was privy to."

"What information?"

I shook my head. "Now that's the trouble-spot, see? If I were to tell you about this—about something Sateekas asked me to do for him personally—that would mean I'd spilled the beans, so to speak."

Kraus narrowed his eyes down as far as they would go. "Are you loyal to Earth or the Mogwa, McGill?"

"Both, sir. I serve my legion, Earth, and the Empire—just like you do."

His lips worked for a bit. It looked like he was trying to bend his teeth with them.

"All right. Just don't do or say anything traitorous."

"You have my personal guarantee on that point, sir. That's a promise, a solemn oath. I wouldn't—" I stopped talking, as he'd transferred me over to Sateekas.

The Mogwa was shiny and fresh-looking, but he didn't look happy.

"McGill? What is this about?"

"Sir, the bears are marching right past us. They're pushing through the Mogwa lines on every flank."

"Don't you think I know that, McGill? I'm not blind."

"Yessir... but don't you think you should order all the human units to attack them as they pass by? We could slow them down, make them—"

Sateekas shook his flappy head. "It wouldn't work. There aren't enough of you. Less than fifty thousand... The Mogwa marines still number nearly that many. You can't replace them all."

"No sir, but... aren't all those men sick? All your marines?"

"Yes, most of them. The environment suits stopped the poison for a time, but it worked its way in."

"What about your drones? What about those mini-tank things?"

Sateekas made a wild gesture. "That's what we've been fighting with for days. Most of the battles have involved our drones against the bears. But before this invasion even began, we'd lost a lot of them fighting humans."

He gave me a baleful stare. I ignored this, not caring a whit. If the Mogwa had seen fit to let us into their dome without a fuss, we'd all have been better off.

"What about your power-armor, sir? Each suit is like a tank all by itself. Why not redeploy those that have sick Mogwa in them, and—"

Sateekas made a farting sound. It was Mogwa laughter. "Who would you suggest I put into these empty suits of power-armor, McGill?"

"I don't know—whoever you've got. Civvies, maybe. Or noncombatant humans."

Sateekas shook his nasty mouth parts at me. "It won't work. Humans are too large, and Mogwa civilians could never be trained to fight in time."

"But sir, I've seen how the armor operates. They aren't complicated. They fit you like a glove, and when you move they move. If they only knew how to aim and fire the turret, any citizen—"

311

Again, he shook his head. "No, it isn't that simple. We are a highly civilized people, McGill. We're not a rabble of snarling barbarians. To get any Mogwa person to fight in close combat requires a lifetime of training. A civilian would simply flee to his home. He'd use the armor to hide or to protect his person. No untrained Mogwa would stand and fight in a line against an enemy capable of harming them."

"Huh... well then," I said, getting another idea, "what if I could get you some smaller guys to man this armor? I'm talking about guys who are even more vicious than your average human?"

He shrugged. "Do your worst. I don't see how it can hurt..." he worked a console for thirty seconds or so. "There, I've given you full access to our armories. One is in your region. Now I must go attend to the last stand of my people on this planet. I appreciate your slave-love for the Mogwa, McGill. You have been an outstanding servant, even if you failed us in the end."

He disconnected, and afterward I frowned at my tapper for a moment. Things had to be really bad if Sateekas was practically thanking me for doing my job. The Mogwa never appreciated anyone or anything. Never.

A few minutes later, some strange access codes flooded my tapper. I couldn't make heads or tails of it—but I knew who could.

-51-

Contacting Primus Collins, I told her of my armory access.

"That's just grand," she said. "We've got more equipment than we need already. What we need are trained soldiers."

It was an age-old story in human history, I knew. Often, a nation that was on the way down had plenty of aircraft and other weapons systems—but they didn't have anyone left alive who knew how to use one. That was because it took longer to train people than it did to build a new machine.

This case was no exception. Still, we were curious, so Primus Collins and I found our way to the nearest armory. What we found there was amazing.

"Look, there must be two hundred suits of power-armor down here," she said. "But all the Mogwa combatants are sick—or dead."

While she prattled with her hands on her hips, I nervously watched the reports rolling in. The bears were moving around us even as we discussed the issue.

"Uh… I've got an idea, Primus. Try to squeeze into that one. Yeah, that one right there."

She looked at me like I was crazy, but she tried it. The problem was it was just too tight, even for a fairly small female human. Primus Collins couldn't weigh more than fifty kilos soaking wet, but she *still* couldn't fit in the Mogwa battle machine and close the hatch at the same time.

Climbing out and cursing loudly, she found me already tapping away on my tapper. "What are you up to now?"

"I've got a backup idea. Let's hope it works out."

She rubbed at her chaffed elbows and banged-up knees. She soon stopped that when the personnel I'd called came bouncing down the ramp that led up into the city.

I'd called the gremlin techs from the Varus support legion—and there were a lot of them. A whole unit's worth.

"Hey, guys. Good to see you again."

The gremlins hissed and burbled. They didn't seem to be in a better mood than the last time I'd laid eyes on them. That had been during the bombardment of our forward position a few nights earlier.

As I waved and smiled, they spread out and advanced.

"Uh... what's up, guys?"

"We're thinking you should dance, big-man," said one. He was standing in front of me, cocky and swaggering.

I knew these sneaky bastards pretty well by now. They liked to distract you from the front and stab you in the rear.

Whirling around, I sure as shit saw one of them creeping close with a prong and a wire. A favorite form of death they liked to inflict on humans was electrocution. They found it funny how a man jerked and writhed in spasms if he was hit with just the right current.

Kicking out a big boot, I swept the gremlin away and sent him whirling, ass-over-tea-kettle, across the chamber.

This elicited more growls and curses. I turned back to the head gremlin and spread my hands wide. The little bastard studied each hand with his eyes, looking for some weapon or trick.

"Hey now, guys. What's the trouble? Why are you upset?"

"Upset? Upset! We're not *upset*, big-man, we're in a rage. A righteous mood of vengeance and recrimination!"

"Is that so? What exactly is the problem?"

He pointed a skinny child-like finger at me. "*You* are the problem. You left us to die back there on the front. To escape, we had to lower ourselves into the Mogwa filth-rivers and wade all the way back here to safety. Now, it is happening again! Are you about to run away a second time?"

A new voice joined the discussion then. It was Primus Collins. "Hold it right there, gremlin. You're out of line. I'm the officer in charge of this cohort. McGill didn't command you to stay there—I did."

This created a stir. The gremlins circled and grumbled among themselves. I got the feeling they were chewing over her words very carefully.

Primus Collins, for her part, didn't seem to grasp the trouble she was in. She was from Victrix, after all. People in that legion lined up their ducks, counted them three times, and if they didn't get the same number they started all over again. Officers like her had no idea how the gremlins could get kind of treacherous when the chips were down.

"Now you listen to me, soldiers," she said. "McGill brought you down here to give you new fighting machines, courtesy of the Mogwa. You should be grateful to him, instead of pissing and moaning about what happened days ago."

The gremlins turned their curious attention to the machines as Collins indicated them with a pointing finger.

"Those things are useless toys," their leader said. "They won't react to the touch of a human, or a—"

To prove the gremlin wrong, Collins walked over to one of the machines and keyed open the hatch. "See? They're unlocked. The Mogwa have unlocked all of them for our use. The problem is regular humans are too big to fit inside. Would you like to try?"

Eager, but as paranoid as squirrels on a birdhouse, they swarmed the machines. Several managed to pop the hatches. They climbed inside, and they started up the engines.

"Standard controls…" said the leader, whose name was Jink. "So simple. So universal in design."

"That's right," I said. "The interface should be very natural to operate once you get used to it. Essentially, the machines intelligently interpret your body movements and move with you, just like you're wearing stilts, or something."

Within two minutes, every gremlin was marching around and laughing. At last, the leader came up to us, marching his machine like an expert. It was just like walking, after all. He did it with quick, precise motions. The gremlins were small and

315

weak, but they were very quick of mind and nimble in the body. I could tell they were going to make good pilots—too bad we didn't have more of them.

"Big-man," Jink said. "How is it that you fire this gun on top of the turret? Ah—never mind. I have mastered it!"

So saying, Jink fired the primary cannon. A boom rang out, and Primus Collins was blown clear out of her shoes. There was nothing left but some feet and fingers.

"Oh no!" exclaimed the gremlin. "What a tragedy! You must have trained me poorly, big-man!"

There was a gale of laughter from the rest of them, and they walked around me in a circle.

I put my big fists on my hips and stared them down. It was like being circled by a pack of jackals.

"Look," I said, "I get that you were angry with Collins for ditching you back on the front lines—but we've got to move on past all that. You and me—we're all about to be permed. We have to fight together to have a chance at winning."

They studied me, and they rattled at each other in their dark, native speech. I waited to see which way the winds would blow.

The gremlin leader turned back to me at last. "We will help. We will fight. We will die. But you must promise us something, big-man."

"Promise you what?"

"When you escape this planet mysteriously, you must take us with you."

I laughed. "I'm not going anywhere. I'm as stuck here as you guys are."

"It would appear so, but we do not believe it. We do not trust. You are as slippery as a sand-eel's excrement. You even managed to escape our home world when no one believed you could."

"Uh... oh yeah, right," I said, recalling a distant day when I'd slipped out a portal to Earth while pretending to take a piss. "Okay, okay. If I run off and leave this world, I'll do my best to take you with me. But first, you have to fight! Are you with me?"

"Yes," they said, all of them speaking at once in a chorus of sibilant sound. "Lead us! Lead us!"

Turning around, I stepped over the scorched stain that had once been Primus Collins and walked up the ramps into the city. I called upon my own unit and a half-dozen others.

Primus Collins was down, but I commanded in her name. I knew she would have wanted it that way.

We marched to the flanks, and we left our safe entrenched positions. We raced from building to building until we found a column of bears marching past us a few blocks away.

I started off by having all our light troops climb to high windows, five to ten floors up. They immediately began sniping at the bears, disrupting their columns.

Now, I knew bear psychology pretty well by this time. They were apex predators on their planet. They were even more naturally aggressive than humans. They were also less of an organized group of pack-hunters, so they tended to lose their tempers if you pestered them enough.

That was exactly what we did. We shot at them, not penetrating their armor, but managing to knock them off their feet so they bumped their noses on the streets. After a few minutes of this, some commander lost his mind and ordered his men to charge our light troops.

Naturally, Adjunct Barton and all the light commanders supporting her melted away.

The bears came on, snarling and rushing headlong into the dark, broken buildings. If you've had the displeasure of fighting in a wrecked city, you'll know what I mean. Torn-up buildings are dangerous places. They're perfect for ambushing enemy troops—especially if the enemy rushes at you in a disorganized mob.

I waited until a few hundred of the bears were in full pursuit—then I ordered the gremlins in.

Gremlins in power-armor advanced, forming a half-circle. They began blazing away with their turrets, which unlike snap-rifles did a fine job of destroying armored bears. They hit the Rigellians so hard, they crushed their bodies with the explosive impacts. Broken-up and bloody, they crawled and mewed— then an unexpected thing happened.

Without orders, the gremlins leapt out of their combat machines. They raced up with coils of wire, and I'll be damned if they didn't jab needles into any crack they could find and jolt the wounded bears to death. The result was grim—but also... it was kind of funny.

"They dance!" the gremlins squealed and cackled. "They dance, big-man! Watch them, don't miss a moment of it!"

I nodded and forced a smile. "That's real good killing, Jink. But hey... there are a lot more bears out there where this company came from. Let's go get them."

Reluctantly, the gremlins unplugged the bears from their idling engines and mounted up again. They wanted more killing, and I was eager to help them find fresh game.

-52-

We fought steadily for the next several hours. If the enemy bears had been more on the ball, they might have swung around and finished us—but they were under strict orders to advance deep into the city. Their commanders wanted to press the advantage they had at all costs.

The gremlins made them pay dearly. I had to ponder our disproportionate success.

For one thing, the enemy was distracted, that was a big help, but it wasn't the only factor. To my mind, the gremlins were just plain better fighters than the Mogwa marines. That was weird given the difference in training levels, but I thought it made sense. The gremlins were vicious killers in their savage little hearts. That was the real truth of it.

The Mogwa, on the other hand, were more like housecats. They'd lost their predatory edge thousands of years ago. Sure, they could be trained to fight well enough—but it didn't come naturally to them.

On top of the ornery nature of the gremlins, Legion Varus tactics helped a bunch. We were much more experienced than any Mogwa captain. Using our skills combined with the natural tendencies of the gremlin pilots, well sir, we tore the bears a new one.

After we'd logged something like five hundred kills, I got a strange call on my tapper. It was from Primus Graves.

"Hey!" I said, grinning down into my tiny embedded screen. "Fancy seeing you up and around again, sir. How did you—?"

"It's a sordid story," Graves said. "I'll talk about it later—if you can tell me how you managed to cut a wedge into the enemy positions and halt their advance in your sector."

I gave him my story, and I did it with gusto. Graves listened and nodded his head. "I thought it might be something like that. A good effort, McGill. Too little, too late—but well done, nonetheless."

"Uh..." I said, concerned by his lack of good cheer. "What's the big picture look like, sir? I haven't had time to check in for hours."

"It's not good. We're losing this battle. A day, maybe two or three—that will be it. The Mogwa troops are mostly dead or useless. There aren't enough of us to cover the whole city, and we're pulling back on every front, including yours. We'll circle up for a last stand in the center of the city."

"But sir, all you have to do is use every near-human cohort's unit of gremlins. I've got the armory codes and everything."

"I have those codes now, too. We got them from Sateekas—but it's not that simple."

"Hmm... you never did tell me how you got yourself out of purgatory, sir."

Graves chuckled. "I'll tell you. Why not? We're all doomed anyway, and it's kind of funny. Sateekas came to Winslade hours ago and asked him who the best human tactician he knew was, beside himself. Winslade gave him my name."

"Ha! Well... he's right."

"Thank you. I thought it was a nice gesture too, when I heard about it. Anyway, the funny part came when Sateekas immediately executed Winslade for incompetence, then ordered that I be revived in his place."

We both had to laugh at that. Graves always had a grim sense of humor, mind you. Virtually every time he told a joke, it was about the past, and it was always full of death.

"So... you're in charge, now? What happened to that Victrix stuffed-shirt? Tribune Kraus?"

"He was executed even sooner. Sateekas has been on a tear, gunning down anyone that fails him. As you might imagine, with our troops falling back in every sector, there have been plenty of executions."

"Oh yeah... I guess so. Say, has there been any word from the battle fleet?"

Graves stopped all his smiling and gave me a hard stare. "Why would there be word from the fleet? They ran out on us a week ago. What have you heard, McGill? Did you pull a move of some kind? Something illicit?"

I rubbed my neck and sighed. "I guess it doesn't matter much if it didn't work out."

Graves nodded. "I guess not. Thanks for trying in any case. I'm sending out a lifter to pick up your men—all of them. I'll pass on the suggestion about putting gremlins into power-armor—Lord help us."

He signed off, and I ordered my troops to fall back to the LZ. We were all going to have to board the lifter and scramble out of here. It was just as well, as the bears were starting to mass-up nearby. I had the feeling someone in command had decided to wipe us out once and for all.

When the lifter came, we rushed aboard, and I managed to get all the gremlins aboard with us—those who hadn't been knocked out by this time.

After we lifted off, I dumped a bottle of water into my face and drank a second one. Then, I checked the notes on my tapper.

There were lots of red ones from various officers. I flicked most of them off to the side unread. I didn't have time for recriminations or demands that I put a real primus into command. What was done was done.

The gremlin commander came to talk to me during the short flight to the center of the city. We didn't dare fly high or fast, for fear of being shot down. The ship had to creep between the buildings, sneaking her way into friendly territory.

"Big-man," Jink said. "You took us with you, as you promised."

321

"That's right. I always keep my promises." This was a bald-faced lie, and we both knew it, but he seemed pleased anyway.

"We must continue the retreat. We must get off this world. Have you managed to arrange this yet?"

Frowning, I shook my head. "It's not that simple, little buddy. We're going to be redeployed to fight in the inner city. To make a last stand."

The gremlin peered at me for a moment. "That is regrettable."

His eyes slid to one side for a moment, then back to fix upon mine. That was all the warning I got, but it was all that I needed.

Whirling and reaching out with my ape-like arms, I grabbed the second little bastard, who sure-as-shit was sneaking up on my six. I didn't go easy on him. Not this time.

I know that any field commander in a true starfaring legion had to expect some shenanigans every once in a while. He had to roll with the punches—or in this case, accept a friendly, vengeful electrocution now and then.

But I wasn't in the mood, and the timing was bad. Lord only knew when I'd get my next revive if I let these pricks fry me now.

Accordingly, I grabbed the gremlin by the neck and wrapped my other big fist around his tiny hands. A hot wire was in there, I could feel it buzzing at my gauntlet. I touched it to his chest, and I fried him. I fried him until there was hair burning and the stink of it filled my nostrils.

Tossing the corpse aside, I turned back to Jink. The gremlin leader looked a mite upset.

"Did you see him dance?" I laughed. "My hand might have been covering that up—too bad."

The gremlin showed me his teeth. "Very funny, big-man. You always did like to play. But you promised, remember? We take such things seriously."

"You should, you should. Listen here, if I figure out a way to escape Segin, I'll let you know first. Until then, this game isn't over yet. We're both still in it together."

He nodded, and he left me with the stinking corpse of his comrade. I tossed the body away and sank back into my seat. After I was sure there weren't any more comedians stealthing near, I went back to paging through my messages.

One of them—only one of them—caught my attention. It was from none other than Galina Turov, and it had been stamped urgent six ways from Sunday. How had I missed that one? It must have gotten buried in the flood.

Opening it eagerly, I read it, and I felt a rush of surprise. Standing up, I charged down the aisle of the lifter. Several people jerked their feet out of the way—but some were too slow. Those last unfortunates got stomped, and they howled and cursed my name. I waved over my shoulder at them—what else could I do?

-53-

Lifters don't have Gray Decks like bigger ships do—but they do have small science labs. I rushed up to the command deck, then past the revival machines to the lab. Throwing open the door, I had a look around.

The place was dead empty. I found notes, I rustled through computer scrolls... the last entry in the log was dated three days back. Apparently, the tech running this place had died back then and never been revived.

"Shit..."

I dug into the lockers, busting them open one after another. I wasn't too careful with this process, and I made an awful racket.

A hulking figure appeared at the entrance. "I should have known," Raash said. "What other piece of primate excrement could be found making such a mess?"

"Hey, Raash! You must have heard me all the way down at the revival chambers, huh?"

"Yes, madman. Explain yourself before I'm forced to take disciplinary action."

That's when I looked down and saw what he had in his crusty, bluish paws. There was a dripping syringe in one of them—the classic weapon of bio people all across the galaxy. At least he'd given me a warning. That was more than most of them would have done.

"I need your help. Our salvation is in here—at least, I think it is."

"Why do I feel compelled to aid your insanity? It is a curse. I'm warped by my biology."

"Yes, I'm sure you are. Get over here and open the lockers on the other side."

Grumbling, Raash walked in and began rattling the lockers. Unlike me, he was able to open the locks when they scanned his scales—something like that. I found this vaguely offensive.

"So the computers trust you, but they don't trust me?" I demanded.

"Naturally so. AI systems are excellent judges of character. What are we looking for, mad-thing?"

"You'll know it when you see it."

He opened more lockers, and I did the same. He didn't complain about me busting open the ones on my side of the room. That right there showed he wasn't your typical prissy type of specialist. Any human in a lab would have had a conniption over all the damage I was doing.

"Human? Is this…? I'm surprised."

I turned toward him, and I gazed over his shoulder. A big smile crept up and grew into a grin on my face.

Raash turned to me in wonder. "How did you know there were gateway posts here? How did you know—and why did you keep this secret for so long?"

I shook my head. "They weren't here an hour ago. That transmission I made with your spy rig—I called for help. They teleported the gear to this spot using a casting device."

"A what?"

"Never mind. Casting devices are just more monkey-magic to you. Forget I mentioned it."

"I would summon authorities and demand your arrest, but I can't deny the fortuitous nature of these results. I will reserve judgment. If these devices are operational, I'll upgrade my estimation of your capacities."

"That's mighty fine of you, Raash." I reached past him and grabbed the posts. Carrying them out of the place, I had to dash to a jump-seat and strap in while the ship lurched down to land abruptly.

"Uh…" I said, when I was loosening the smart straps again. "If I just take these into headquarters, the brass will be sure to seize them. Sateekas will probably confiscate them personally."

"They might do just about anything to avoid more of your primate antics," Raash agreed.

I ignored the grumpy blue reptile. My mind whirled as I considered the possibilities. The Mogwa, and the human brass… I wouldn't put it past any of them to arrange a quick one-way ticket for themselves right off this doomed planet.

Turning around, I went back inside the small, abandoned science lab. "Raash, I need your help again. Do you trust me?"

"Not at all. I trust only in your duplicity, your violent nature, your—"

"Yeah, yeah, okay. I get that. But I need you anyway. We all do. Everyone on this planet is going to die when the bears sweep through to these headquarters. You, me—everyone."

"These statements are obvious and therefore pointless."

"I can stop all that bad stuff from happening. But I need your skills."

Raash threw his hands wide and spread his claws. I tried not to flinch. It was kind of creepy, watching him simulate human gestures. "What can one elite nonhuman do in this sea of incompetence?"

"You can help me hook these posts up to the lifter's engines. Just the way you did with that little secret decoder radio-thing."

"You need to stop using such terms for my device. It is a hobby of mine to transmit random messages to the stars. There is nothing secretive or nefarious about my actions."

"Of course not. Can you do it? Can you hook me up?"

Raash looked troubled for a moment, but at last, he agreed. The second he left to get one of his dick-thick cables, I contacted Natasha. She was almost as reluctant as Raash to listen to me, but at last, she came into the lab and squawked about all the torn-up lockers.

"Settle down, girl. This isn't even your lab. Looky over here! Check out what I've got!"

I showed her the gateway posts, and she marveled.

"Where do they go?" she asked.

"I don't know. I would assume they'll connect to some ship in the fleet—or to Central."

"That's great! All you have to do is walk through and talk to the command staff. Surely, they can send a fresh legion or two."

I gritted my teeth and shook my head. "No. It won't work. The help won't come fast enough. First, they'll have to have about six meetings. Then, they'll send in some prissy high-level officers, and they'll realize this planet is doomed. My guess is they'll evac the important people and leave the rest of us behind to die."

"You really think so?"

I nodded.

She sighed and flopped onto a creaking office chair. "It's over, then. I'd hoped we could do better than this. We just came too late, with too little force. If only—"

I reached down a gentle hand and touched her shoulder. "Natasha? I'm not using these posts to go back to Earth. I'm not going to waste my time stepping through and begging for help they won't give us."

She turned around slowly, and her eyes were big. "That's why you contacted me, isn't it? To get me to change the connection point? Where are you thinking of going, James—and don't say the Core Worlds."

Laughing, I shook my head. Not even I was that crazy. "No way. The Mogwa on Trantor are even less likely to help us out than Central would be."

"Where, then?"

"Blood World."

She blinked, and she stared. Her mouth even dropped open a little bit. "Seriously? You want more near-humans? What makes you think—?"

"Can you do it? Can you fix these up?"

Raash had returned, and he was laying out cable and grunting. He had a big spool of the black stuff, and he had run it right down the passageways of the ship all the way to engineering. I had to give him props for speed and innovation, if not for subtlety.

"Can you do it or not?" I demanded.

At last, Natasha nodded. She went to work, and I watched like a nervous father in the maternity ward. Playing lookout, I loitered out in the passageway and handed out bullshit to anyone who asked what the hell was going on.

It was a temporary fix, but then, we didn't have much time anyways. This was going to work, or it wasn't. Either way, it was all going to be over with pretty quickly.

-54-

Less than an hour after I'd found the gateway posts in the locker—right where Galina had said they would be—I stepped through them to Blood World.

It was a dry, dusty planet with a lurid red sky and fine sand that got into everything. They had vegetation of a sort, but every plant I saw looked like it was on the verge of dying a horrid death.

Walking at my side was a certain miniature humanoid known as Jink. He'd provided us with the right coordinates, and we'd landed just outside the biggest colony of gremlins in the known universe. The town was, in fact, the *only* gremlin colony this side of Hell itself.

When I met up with a whole tribe of gremlins, my balls and the pads of my feet were crawling. Naturally enough, my balls were fearing a fatal shock, while my feet were itching to do some stomping and kicking. Gremlins always made me feel that way.

But I contained myself, and I grinned, and I introduced myself to them as the Champion of Blood World. I was quickly informed that my title didn't hold much weight here these days.

"Yes, yes!" screeched a gremlin female, one of the few I'd met. She bounced around the landscape like a gibbon with an itch. "I know this one! He ran out on us! He left in fear, shirking his duties! Gytha was mortified!"

"...mortified...!" cried several others, echoing her. They liked to do that sometimes.

"...Gytha...!"

"Hey guys," I said, looking as friendly as possible. "I remember you as well. Today is a great day. Today, you're going to do Earth and the Empire a great service."

This was met with catcalls and howls of high-pitched laughter.

The female gremlin crept close, she felt the seams in my spacer suit, down around my ankles. I checked her for needles and wires, but I didn't see anything.

Glancing around behind me, I saw no one sneaking up— but I didn't see Jink, either. "Damn that sneaky little bastard..." I muttered. "He's gone and run off on me."

Turning back to the gremlins, I grinned again. "Listen up," I said, "I'll take volunteers, and I'll take as many as I can get. Just step right this way into these glowing posts here, see, and—"

"Human?"

I looked down. It was the female gremlin, and she was peering up at me seriously. "Can you truly be so demented and foolish?"

"Uh... probably. What are you talking about in particular, Miss?"

She waved a tiny hand toward the curious circle of a hundred gremlins. More were coming out from the town. More and more every minute.

"Your guide has led you to this spot as a gift to us. We have a taste for unusual flesh. Was that not explained?"

My mouth sagged low.

Jink... he'd taken off for a good reason. It occurred to me that I'd promised him I'd get him off City World, and the moment I'd done so, he'd made off like a bandit in the night. He was home and on friendly ground—but I wasn't.

Lifting my tapper to my face, I pretend to talk to someone. Fortunately, none of the gremlins were tall enough to see the blank screen. "Gytha? What's that? You want these gremlins punished and abused? That seems extreme, ma'am, if you don't mind me telling you your business."

330

A few hissed and stepped around me, circling me. They were upset, and even the one tugging on my pant leg backed off.

"You can't be speaking to Gytha!" squeaked a voice from the back of the crowd. "It can't be so—it is a trick!"

The voice belonged to none other than Jink, who'd chosen this moment to show his nose again.

"And why can't it be?" I asked him.

"Because Gytha *hates* you. You are the McGill. The abuser. The evil male who abandoned her on her wedding day. Still, to this very hour, she has yet to take a new husband."

"Uh... really?"

"You don't even know her," the female complained. She began kicking dirt onto my boots like a cat scratching angrily in her box. "You defile her with your words."

"I do so know her. I know her sister Floramel, too."

This elicited a general gasp from the group. As one, they began coming closer with slow, predatory steps.

"...Floramel...?"

"...it lies..."

"...I wonder how it tastes...?"

Now, I'm a moron on a good day, but I was beginning to get a creepy vibe from these little guys. Their doll-like eyes were as black and flat as glass. They didn't seem to have an iris, or much of a white circle around that. They just had one giant pupil, or so it seemed to me. The overall effect was freaky, and I was soon surrounded by tiny people with the eyes of hunting snakes.

"Hey," I said, clearing my throat and taking a step toward the glowing gateway posts. "I think I'm going to go visit Floramel now. She's a good friend of mine, and—"

Suddenly, they surged forward. About a zillion of them grabbed me, and I would have shaken them all off and killed a bunch, except for one thing...

Jink and the female gremlin, they had a wire and a needle out. They were going to jab it deep, and they were going to watch me dance.

"Freeze, ape-man," Jink said. "Today you have committed fresh crimes. We're not just going to make you dance, we'll cook you alive and eat your flesh after!"

Shrieks of excitement and laughter came from the crowd. There were so many now—a thousand of them, maybe.

"We had a deal, Jink!" I complained. "I brought you home, just like I said I would. I kept my bargain, and you're breaking your word!"

Plenty of hissing went on, and Jink dared to come near. He lifted a wagging finger in my direction. "Wrong! We agreed not to play each other falsely. You speak of Floramel, the most beloved of our creators. We are her lost children, and we won't have you speak of her with a lying tongue!"

That brought back memories. When I'd visited Blood World during the campaign here, I recalled that the gremlins had all loved Floramel. They loved her more than anyone or anything. They loved her almost as much as they loved themselves—and she'd called them her children.

Could Floramel have had a hand in creating this particularly nasty off-shoot of humanity? It seemed clear now that she had.

"I can prove it!" I shouted. "Let me touch my tapper!"

"He lies!"

"He'll signal Earth!"

"He'll blow himself up and take us all with him!"

Jink considered, and then cuffed a few crazed gremlins that clung to my suit and lusted for my blood. "Prove it, ape."

I reached a finger to my tapper, and it took a few long moments of digging through archives, but I found Floramel at her apartment. We were chatting, and we were all alone.

The gremlins watched, fascinated.

"You see?" I crowed. "That's her, at her place on Earth."

"You must take us there!"

"We must see her again!"

"Uh…"

The gremlins were going wild again. They weren't a civilized folk even on a good day—and today wasn't a good day. They were hopping around and shouting all at once.

In the meantime, I noticed the video was still playing. I saw myself take Floramel's hand, and I kissed her knuckles, then I kissed her wrist, then her sweet forearm.

With a grunt of effort, because a dozen tiny hands were working to restrain me, I reached over and stabbed at the cutoff button. The vid stopped playing.

"He was about to defile her!" one of them shouted.

Others, fortunately, beat him down for having spoken heresy. He was beaten until his tiny skull was crushed and his dead, staring eyes peered up at me out of a mash of broken teeth.

"She isn't on Earth any longer," I said.

"Then where is she?" Jink asked.

"Only I know. It's a secret. She's hiding from Earthmen on another world."

"You will take us to her. You will help us reunite with her. You will do this, or you will be cooked and eaten."

I shrugged, and a few gremlins bounced on my shoulders. "If you do that," I said, "you'll never find her."

They hissed and complained for a bit. I waited patiently.

"What do you want?" Jink asked me at last.

"Thousands of your people must follow me back to City World. We'll train an army how to walk in the Mogwa walking-machines. You, Jink, will command them, and you'll listen to my commands in turn."

He looked thoughtful. "And if we do this? If we save those heartless walking spiders you love so much, you'll reunite us with Floramel?"

"I swear it."

"No!" shouted a few voices.

"Don't listen to him!"

"He's a false prophet!"

"He's a defiler!"

Jink looked around thoughtfully. He was taking it all in, and I knew he was my only hope.

"I brought you home, Jink," I said, talking to him directly. "You know I keep my word. Besides, you know your people will have a lot of fun tearing things up in power-armor. I'll even let you guys keep some of them and bring them back here to play with… if you want."

His nasty dark eyes lit up as I spoke these fateful words. Soon, he began to smile. I had no idea what his little brain was thinking—but I knew it was something wicked.

"We'll do it," he said at last.

-55-

When we returned in force to City World, it was quite a sight. There was shock and dismay written on the face of every human, Mogwa and Cephalopod alike who we marched past. Soon, their general surprise turned into disbelief as the stream of gremlins only increased in number and bouncing speed. A seemingly endless column of gremlins were flooding down the lifter's lowered ramp. Little did these witnesses know that the stream wound back through the entire ship to the tiny science lab and a pair of humming gateway posts.

"McGill?" Graves asked. He'd come up from the nerve center of the headquarters building to the roof, where this act of prestidigitation was taking place. "What the fuck is going on? Where did you find all these gremlins?"

"It's a funny thing, Primus. These gremlins are mighty small, see, and they can fit into the damnedest places."

He wasn't really listening to my bullshit. His head was too busy swiveling and trying to take it all in. "There must be thousands of them."

"Yessir, I do believe so."

He reached out a glove and grabbed up a handful of my spacer suit. "You fool! If you found a pair of gateway posts, why would you waste that golden opportunity on these weasels? I can't even think of a more useless and unreliable source of help. Even those frigging salamanders you dragooned into helping us back on Storm World could at least fight!"

"You mean the scuppers, sir? Well, that's where you're wrong. These boys might be small, but I don't plan to give them rifles and send them to the front."

"What then?"

He was still holding onto my front zipper, but I didn't take offense. Old Graves had special privileges in situations like this. Almost any other man might have found himself doing a facer after demonstrating such a lack of respect—but I liked Graves too much for that.

"Sir, I'm going to put them into Mogwa fighting machines. They fit in real good, and they're naturals on the field of battle."

I tried to show him a few highlights of the action we'd fought during the Rigellian advance, but he slapped my tapper away.

"All right... that worked before... Whatever. Do your worst, it hardly matters. The whole city is on fire. We're reeling back on every front. I'm surprised it hasn't all fallen apart yet."

I frowned. "Why would that be, exactly, sir?" I asked. "Why are these bears slowing down?"

"Two reasons. For one thing, this city goes deeper underground than it does on the surface. The bears are invading the lower levels as well, and that takes time. The other reason... it's too grim to talk about."

"Uh... can you give me a hint, sir?"

He looked up, and he looked troubled. The gremlins kept streaming by, led by Jink into the vaults to mount-up and undergo an extremely short training session. Graves was no longer able to see this spectacle, however. His mind was on other horrors.

"You know these bears are predators, right?"

"Of course. We are as well."

He shook his head. "Not like these little monsters. They're eating the Mogwa as they go. They seem to have a real taste for them. Dead, alive, young or old."

I stared at him for a second, and it was my turn for my jaw to sag to my chest. "Seriously? They're cannibals? They never seemed to be into that sort of thing when they were fighting on human worlds."

"No… I suspect the Mogwa taste better. At least they do to these bastards. No wonder the Galactics call us all barbarians."

He walked off, and I found myself being tapped on the back of my knee. Looking down, I saw Jink. He was grinning, and he waved with a flourish.

"Big man, it's time to fight! You promised us blood, and my people very much want to indulge themselves."

"Right. Let's go."

We didn't waste any time. After a few hours of organizing them into groups and giving every living one of the gremlins a very basic training course, we were ready to move out. I commandeered a fleet of skimmers from the Mogwa, who were dead and slumped over in their pilot seats.

Graves gave me more pilots, and together we glided slowly over the streets. Looking at the tacticals, I discovered Graves was right. A lot of the heaviest fighting was going on underground now.

We found a dark tunnel entrance, and it reminded me of those big tubes that crisscross the bottom of the oceans back on Earth. We entered the first one we found, and it didn't take long to find the enemy.

A few cohorts of humans came with us to offer support. It was a strange army, mixed with all kinds of humans and near humans. The only reason it worked was because Jink and I worked together.

When we met up with the bears, we had about a thousand humans and another thousand gremlins in Mogwa tanks. At first, we crushed everyone we met up with. Taken by surprise, the bears were destroyed in small groups.

Our tactics were simple. We used humans to recon and skirmish—then deployed the gremlins to do the serious killing.

The bears seemed to be sluggish and shocked whenever we appeared. I suspected they'd figured they already won this battle, and they'd lost some of their discipline. I'd seen this before, and I'd capitalized on it back on Ice World. The bears weren't really very well organized. They didn't march in ranks, they didn't fight like a pack under tight control.

They were really warriors, rather than soldiers. Back in Roman times, that simple reality had often won the day for the original legions. Thousands of skilled tribesmen would assault the legions, often with superior numbers. Even their gear and skill was excellent.

But the Gauls, the Celts, Germanic tribesmen and others weren't versed in the use of formations and tight control of their troops. They would usually just charge in a mad rush, attempting to break their enemy with sheer ferocity and numbers. If that initial charge didn't work, their armies fell apart.

Legion Varus troops combined with gremlins in their power-armor weren't perfect, either. We earthmen were well trained and disciplined. The gremlins were neither, but when we unleashed them, they did their grim work with glee.

Self-control was the main element we humans brought to the table. We'd fought and died for more years than any of these others had even been alive. With our help, the gremlins had at least a dash of discipline and organization.

Sometimes, they lost their minds and charged in when they shouldn't. Like old fashioned knights, they were hard to control, but Jink helped me maintain our lines. He backed me up in every disagreement. Now and then, he even had a gremlin pulled from his power-armor and torn apart by his fellows.

"That's a lesson for the others," he said.

I didn't argue with him. It was his show to run, and as long as he took my tactical advice I figured we'd do well.

We took the first level directly under the city streets within a day. Then things became too big for me to handle alone. There was too much territory, too many gremlins—I had to call for help.

Getting Graves on the line proved to be impossible, so I contacted Sateekas instead.

"Sir? Grand Admiral, sir?"

"What is it, McGill? I'm very busy losing this desperate war. There are signs of hope from below, with reports of Mogwa marines pushing the enemy back. But I'm not fooled by rumors of victory. They always come when defeat is inevitable."

"Uh..." I said, giving the situation a hard think. I finally decided to show him the battlefield I was standing upon, but I angled my tapper so the camera only saw the rear of the marching machines.

"The rumors are true, sir! I'm fighting alongside a brave company of your combatants right now. We're kicking ass!"

Sateekas boggled at the dead bears and the advancing forces as they streamed by me. They whirred and the turrets swiveled ceaselessly, searching for fresh game. Humans walked between the marching gremlin-drive machines on both sides.

"What miracle is this, McGill? How is this possible?"

"It's real simple, sir. When humans fight alongside your marines, they both do better."

Sateekas marveled. "Indeed, I see these reports from the lower levels in a new light... it's amazing. If only this could be repeated."

"It can be, sir," I insisted. "Give me access to every armory you have. Order Graves to send several units of human troops to every one of these locations. I'll send volunteers to man the power-armor. Together, we've got a chance."

Sateekas narrowed a half-dozen eyes in my direction. "Where are you getting these volunteers? How are they being trained so quickly? My own marine commanders—"

"Sateekas," I said seriously. "Listen to me for one moment please, sir. Do you really want to know how the sausage is made?"

"What? Is that some kind of idiom?"

"Yessir. It sure is. What it means is that if things are going your way, don't ask too many questions."

Again, he gave me that strange look. He knew something was up. He knew his people, and he knew they'd never step up like this. Not even when they were being overrun and slaughtered. Heroism just wasn't in their DNA. They needed to be conditioned or forced to fight bravely.

Despite all this, he also knew his situation was dire. He came to a quick decision.

339

"I will order Graves to release all his reserves as you suggest. May the countless suns at the Core bless us this day."

With that cryptic comment, he signed off. I turned to Jink, and I had a little argument with him.

"We've fought hard and long. I'm tired of the killing," he complained.

"That's as may be," I said. "But we're not done yet. This world can be saved, and you'll get your rewards only then."

"Floramel? A thousand fresh machines with ammo, fuel and spare parts?"

"Uh..." I said, blinking. I'd never really mentioned anything about ammo and spare parts. I'd kind of envisioned the gremlins would take a few banged-up machines back to Blood World and have fun jousting with them or something until they broke down.

Apparently, Jink had much bigger ideas.

I thought about laughing off his wild plans, but I knew I couldn't do it. Without the gremlins, we would lose in the end.

Sure, the bears were sated on Mogwa-meat and victory, but they were going to figure out pretty damned quick that someone was kicking their butts. The war had a long way to go yet, and we needed to press our advantage while we could.

Chewing on my lower lip for just a second, I nodded my head. "You've got it. The whole kit-and-caboodle. Floramel, a thousand machines—take some bear ears too, for trophies."

Jink gave me that freaky grin of his, and it was bigger than ever. I recalled countless admonishments about being careful when you dealt with the devil, and I knew I was ignoring that ancient wisdom today.

"You have a bargain, big-man. Let's win back this planet as quickly as we can."

We worked like thieves in the night after that. Jink sent back to Blood World for even more Gremlins, and we unlocked more Mogwa bunkers. Sateekas had indicated these spots, and they were full of power-armor suits that stood empty and waiting in vaults.

Graves did his part too, dispatching handfuls of weary Victrix soldiers from the revival chambers to march with us.

They seemed confused and disgusted by the gremlins, but they were disciplined to the last. They followed their orders.

There was trouble in paradise when the Victrix folk reported in, however. Crazy stories about hordes of gremlins eagerly piloting Mogwa equipment got back to headquarters.

Graves called me up, and he was in a foul mood.

"Have you gone mad, McGill?"

"Probably," I admitted.

"Do you know that more gremlins keep bubbling out of our cohort's lifter? The pilots are panicked, and they're telling me the gremlins won't let them anywhere near the science lab on their own ship. They plan to disengage the fusion core on their ship to cut the power."

"Really? Hmm…" I gave myself a scratch. "Uh… do you have a count on the total number of gremlins that have come through, sir?"

"You mean you don't know that number yourself? You've lost control, McGill. These creatures aren't trustworthy."

I laughed weakly. "That's a hoot, sir. They're helping us. They're pushing the bears back all over."

"Even if they do beat the bears, they'll end up taking over the planet or something. That won't go over well with the Mogwa back on Trantor. They'll blame Earth in the end."

"Yeah… maybe…"

He gave me a hard look, and his ire came through my tapper like my own angry dad's temper used to do. "You have to get a handle on these gremlins. Tell them anything. Stop this new invasion."

I signed off, and I turned toward Jink. He had been watching me closely. I suspected he'd heard every word.

"Hey Jink," I said in a cheery tone. "My boss wants you to know how thrilled he is about your enthusiastic support. Did you know that among all the brands of near-humans that were cooked up out on Blood World, your kind was held in the lowest regard? That's right, that's the sad history of it. But today, you've changed all that. Earth is forever in your debt."

Jink had been looking bored, but now he perked up. "In our debt? Forever?"

"That's a figure of speech. It's high praise."

341

He flapped a hand at me and went back to looking bored.

"Hmm…" I said, not knowing how to breach the next topic on my list. "What are your plans, exactly, after this is all over and done with?"

"Assuming we win?"

"Naturally."

Jink eyed me thoughtfully. "McGill, you are fast becoming my favorite man-puppet."

"Uh… what?"

"Just as I said. You are a thing that entertains and yet is useful. Best of all, you never think too hard about the fingers manipulating your innards."

"Huh… well, that's a mighty nice thing to say… I suppose."

"In your case, it is," he went on. "I want to make you an offer. This is a strange moment for one of my kind. I now see the magical spark buried in your servitude. The thing that possibly Gytha and Floramel once saw as well."

"Um…"

"Yes. I do not exaggerate. You're a servant of excellent quality. Knowledgeable, effective, but still an imbecile. Perfect, in a way. I will therefore make you an unprecedented offer."

"How's that?" I asked.

My hand had already crept down to my belt, and my fingers touched the butt of my service pistol. I hadn't drawn it yet, mind you, but I was quick with a gun. I knew I could draw and put a bolt through Jink's brainpan before he could spring off and run.

The trouble was I didn't trust my gremlin comrade. Never yet, in all my years of dealing with them, had I found them to be worthy of trust. As a convenience, sure, they could be levered into helping a man out, but they were like a wild animal sleeping in a cradle. There was always a worry in the back of any thinking man's mind.

Jink seemed oblivious to my thoughts. He prattled on in a high-falutin way. "Here's my offer. I will take you back to Blood World with me, after we own this planet. You may service Gytha as an added incentive—something she still wants, I believe. You will become a uniting figurehead on my homeworld. With your help, I think I might manage to do the unthinkable."

"Huh... really?" I said, having no idea what he was talking about, but the idea of "servicing" Gytha did sound tempting. The girl was quite a looker. "Uh... what's unthinkable about all this?"

"You may be able to unite my world and all its peoples. Remember, when Earth conquered my homeworld, you were the one we swore to follow. The more idiotic members of my brethren still recall and respect that distant day. Now they serve Earth, but with you in our midst, we'll bite that hand. We'll finally achieve the great awakening we've always been denied!"

I could tell he meant whatever he was talking about. There was a real light of excitement, madness and wild greed in his eyes.

"That all sounds nine kinds of fantastic, Jink," I said, touching my right hand to my chest. "I mean that from the bottom of my heart. But... isn't all this premature? We still have a battle to win. Can we have this talk later, when the fight here on City World is finished up and victory is in our hands?"

Jink thought it over. I could see the mad glee of success had gone to his head. But he managed to fight his sinister urges, to choke it all down. He nodded at last.

"Yes, yes. You're right. You are wise, if very stupid. We must finish one deal before contemplating the next. Let us march."

Our roles changed after that day. Instead of fighting in the broad tunnels and vast, lit-up caverns, we gave orders and coordinated troops from the rear lines. Jink was good at the work, but it kind of bored me.

The bears finally woke up to what was happening after the second full day of fighting. By then, however, we were coming on hard. There was so much territory, they couldn't defend it all. When they tried, it just meant we were locating small garrisons and destroying them with our superior force.

Like any army that's taken too much land all in a rush, the bears found themselves unable to defend it all. Sometimes, a

343

small army can win a war too quickly. That was the problem the bears had. They were unable to support or supply their scattered troops on the countless battlefields of the multi-level city.

Realizing the danger, the bears tried to retreat and regroup, but we trapped them underground, destroying them in small formations. The bears had no organized front, and our troops moved faster and hit harder than theirs did. This scenario had destroyed countless armies and conquerors in the past, and today it was happening to Rigel.

On the eleventh sub-level of the great City, we found six companies of bears abusing Mogwa in a massive underground living complex. Rather than rushing in, we encircled them and waited until they'd gorged themselves on helpless Mogwa citizens. That part of the plan was Jink's idea, and although I didn't like it, I had to admit it was effective.

When the false sun on the ceiling panels began to fade, we drove in from every angle, slaughtering the enemy without mercy. The living complexes were set ablaze, and choking smoke filled the passages—but not a single bear escaped us.

After that sickening battle, we found there weren't any more bears below us—so we turned upward, back toward the surface. We became unstoppable.

We took two more levels, driving the bears before us, when I noticed a change. When we arrived, the bears stared at us in what could only be called fear. Rather than face us, they tried to retreat—but we didn't let them. In the increasingly capable hands of the gremlins, the Mogwa machines ran faster than infantry could on foot and were more deadly. We ran the bears down and killed all we could catch.

When we returned to the surface, the other Blood Worlder troops joined our ranks and helped out as well. Heavy troopers, slavers—every variety of man yet created marched together. We fought with the gremlins in the lead, and together we threw the bears out of the center of the city.

The struggle continued as we pressed into the outer neighborhoods. The bears mounted counterattacks, and they had some wins, destroying three lifters owned by Victrix. But in the end, the story was the same. They were overwhelmed by our core army. They couldn't stand up to it.

Nearly a week after I'd gotten Jink to join me, the enemy seemed to vanish. They'd decided to rush aboard their invasion ships and retreat back up into space.

How had this happened? I think it was partly due to our more stubborn nature. We, the various kinds of men who made up Earth's legions, we were more determined than the bears. We were accustomed to dying down to a handful of troops—but after reprinting these lost souls by the thousands, we could come back. The revival machines provided a limitless trickle of reinforcements that often won tight battles.

The bears didn't fight that way. They generally let their dead warriors stay dead. They didn't believe in reviving their fallen, seeing them as failures. Eventually, this tradition led to a loss of morale and an urge to flee.

Whatever the cause, we pushed and pushed, we killed, and we killed. It took days, but at last, the bears got back into their ships. They left half their troops dead on the ground behind them, and they took off flying back to the stars.

Word had it they took a whole lot of Mogwa-meat home with them, but I couldn't swear to that part.

-56-

When it was all over and done with, you might have thought that someone would pin a medal on old McGill—but you'd have thought wrong. Like I've always said, there are heroic deeds in war—and then there are those who take the credit for them.

In this case the line was long and illustrious. People like Graves, Primus Collins, Jink and me—we were at the very rear of that long, long line.

As it turned out, Tribune Kraus had crowded to the front of the pack. Now, it was the God's-honest truth that old Kraus had been dead or at least missing in action throughout much of the dramatic finish, but the brass assumed that everything that went right had been his idea.

In fact, shocker of shockers, it was discovered that orders predating my trip to Blood World had been written by Tribune Kraus. These documents outlined the use of the gremlins in precisely the fashion I'd pioneered. The proof was irrefutable.

When all this came to light, there were naturally a lot of narrowed eyes and muttered conversations. Some discontents in my cohort and others dared to complain openly.

I wasn't among them. I laughed the whole thing off, suggesting that none of it mattered. We'd won the battle and saved the day. That was good enough. The newspeople back on Earth wanted heroes, and Legion Victrix looked like heroes. That was just how things tended to go.

346

As to what Earth decided to do about the gremlins, well, that part was sketchy.

"McGill?" Graves said, coming to my tent while I was taking a well-earned nap. "McGill!"

I rolled out of my bunk, scratching and groaning.

Graves looked me over. He nodded in approval. "You fought well out there."

"Thank you, Primus."

He hesitated, but I didn't ask him why he'd come. I knew he'd get around to it. The fact he wasn't talking right off indicated it was something bad—so I had a doubly good reason to keep quiet.

"McGill... there's an issue. With the gremlins."

"How's that, sir?"

"Did you promise them they could take the Mogwa power-armor home with them?"

So there it was. Jink had gone to the top officers and put in his claim. I'd kind of hoped all that would have gone away by now.

My jaw sagged, and my eyes flew wide. "What now? That's just crazy-talk, sir."

"Are you sure? The gremlins seem pretty adamant about it."

I laughed and stretched. "I know old Jink pretty well by now. We've killed a thousand bears if we've killed a single cub. You've got to know how the gremlin sense of humor works, see."

Graves squinted at me. I could tell he didn't know what to think. That meant my lies were working better than usual on him today.

He heaved a sigh. "We kind of thought it might be a power-play by the gremlins. Disappointing. We fought so well together."

"Uh... we sure did. What are you thinking about doing to resolve the issue, sir?"

Graves shook his head. "There's no way the brass will let them march machines back to Blood World. They'll start a revolution, or a coup, or something. Besides, the Mogwa want their machines back. If these little monsters would only see reason…"

My neck was feeling itchy, so I gave myself a good scratch. I shrugged and looked at Graves, who was clearly troubled. I didn't like to see that. He wasn't a man who was troubled by walking over a stack of his own dead corpses. Whatever was going on inside his brain—it had to be something real bad.

"Drusus wants you to do it," he said at last, looking back up at me.

"How's that, sir?"

He pointed a finger at me. "You heard me. Go to the gremlin camp. Talk to Jink—and kill him."

That floored me. I'd expected a dozen different things, but not that. My jaw set in a line, and I frowned back at him. We stared for a few long seconds. Finally, I shook my head.

"I pass."

"What?" Graves asked in disbelief.

"I'm not doing it. You can demote me, or shoot me… I don't care. I fought with those nasty little bastards for days. They're human, you know—sort of. They're kind of like primitives. Like some offshoot of our line that died out thousands of years ago—but they're still men. I'm not killing my comrade in arms as a final ending to this whole shitty campaign."

Graves sighed. He reached to his belt and drew his pistol. He aimed it at me.

"Aw now, seriously?" I complained.

"Let me get this straight, you're refusing to follow a direct order from your direct superior?"

"Yessir. In this rare instance, I'm doing exactly that."

Graves and I glared at each other for a few seconds. Neither one of us wanted to back down. We'd never seen eye-to-eye at moments like this. To Graves' way of thinking, an order was an order, and you either followed it, or your life wasn't worth spit.

But at last, to my surprise, Graves holstered his pistol again. He heaved a weary sigh. "All right, fine. I'll do it myself."

"What? Uh… sir?"

348

But I was talking to his back. He walked out and left me thinking hard. A part of me was regretting making big, bold promises to the gremlins. Promises that I couldn't keep. Maybe I should have bargained a bit more, or gotten the brass onboard with some of it.

Stretching out on my bunk, I decided that was all foolish thinking. I'd been in desperate straits. Arguing with the Blood Worlders or with headquarters would only have wasted valuable time. I'd taken the initiative, and I'd gotten the impossible done. After such success, there was no point in second-guessing the details.

At last, I fell asleep. Hours later, I was awakened again by a boot in my ribs.

I rolled up, snarling, and I found an angry-looking Primus Graves glaring at me. His hair was kind of... drippy.

"You tipped them off, didn't you?" he growled.

"Huh?"

"The gremlins, you moron. They were waiting for me. Jink talked as if it was all a big misunderstanding, he said it was all a mistake. While he spoke, one of his little frigging sidekicks snuck up on me."

"Ohhh... you didn't... like... do a little dance did you, sir?"

He glared at me. "I sure as hell did."

Looking down, I saw his pistol was there, in a white-knuckled grip. I shook my head.

"Sir, I fell asleep after you left. I didn't send any messages to any gremlins."

"I know. I checked. But I also know you're tricky."

"Come on, sir. I wouldn't set you up to be killed and laughed at—they did laugh, right?"

"They sure as fuck did!"

I nodded. "Right, right," I said, suppressing a grin. "That's kind of a tradition with them, see. They're a hard people to like."

"I don't see how you could stand working with them for days on end in close quarters. The McGill I know would have gone ape and killed them all within hours."

Raising my nose high, I sniffed. "Maybe I've matured a bit, sir. What with all my long years of life and experiences."

"Bullshit." Grumbling, he put his gun away, then he stalked out again.

I followed and caught him outside. "Uh… sir? What happened to the gremlins?"

"They took off. Almost all of them did, anyway. I guess they went back to Blood World. But they did leave me something. A note for you. That's why I figured maybe you tipped them off."

After a bit of wrangling, he gave it to me. I opened it up and read it.

You owe me, big-man.

That was all it said.

"Huh…" I said.

Graves was peering at me again. "What do you owe them? What deal did you make, McGill? They had to be fighting for something."

I thought it over, and I finally remembered with a jolt. I snapped my fingers. "Floramel…"

"What? Who…? Oh… that's right. That tall chick from Rogue World. You were sweet on her, right? But wasn't she permed years back?"

"That's right," I said. "She's dead and gone. But the Blood Worlders are sad about that. They want me to bring back her ashes to spread around in their deserts."

Graves was squinting at me. He was squinting real hard. "They're sad, huh? Those tiny psychopaths are feeling low about Floramel? This whole thing smells like Georgia horseshit, McGill."

"A fine earthy scent, sir. I know it well."

Snorting, Graves left me in peace at last. I had trouble falling asleep again, but I managed it after a few minutes.

-57-

The next day found me in high spirits. Sure, I hadn't gotten a medal, but the gremlins had cleared out without killing me for lying to them, and the whole legion was going home in a few days.

Our fleet rode the skies over City World, and it felt good to see those ships up there. The Mogwa citizens who'd survived the war—something like half of them—were out and about in spacer suits, cleaning things up. They weren't a very brave people, but they were industrious. I suspected they'd have their city patched up and spic-and-span inside of a year.

Now and then, I saw the Mogwa turn their gaze skyward. They marveled at Earth's fleet, and that was a fine thing to see.

Primus Collins came to talk to me at lunch, which was held outdoors on a scorched terrace. The spot had once been the Mogwa equivalent of a shopping mall, but we'd commandeered it for legion use.

"McGill?" Collins said. "Can I talk to you for a second?"

"Pull up a chair, sir!"

She did so, and she put down a tray of food opposite me. We blinked in the sunshine. I was smiling—but she wasn't. She seemed troubled.

"Uh… what's this all about, sir? Don't tell me one of my after-action reports is missing."

She snorted. "Hardly. I hear you rarely turn those in unless one of your adjuncts writes it for you."

"Hmm… yeah. That's pretty much how it goes."

We ate in silence for a bit. I could tell she had more to say, but I also knew that women would always get around to telling you what was on their minds eventually. You never had to push for that.

"McGill… I feel kind of guilty."

"How's that, sir?"

"Did you know I've been offered a post in Victrix?"

I looked up at her, blinking in surprise. I forced a smile. "That's great—assuming you want to go, that is."

She shrugged and poked at her food with a fork. She hadn't eaten much, and I was already scheming a way to get my hooks onto her tray.

"I *do* want the transfer," she said at last. "I'm taking it, in fact. Who wouldn't?"

I shrugged.

"I'm feeling guilty because… well, because I can't help but think you should have the position. Not me. You set up the winning tactic with the gremlins. I just helped organize things."

"Did you try to tell anyone that?"

Her face twitched. It was the fastest half-smile in history.

I laughed. "You sure as hell didn't, did you? You didn't want to blow it, right? Your ticket out of Varus? But now, you're feeling guilty. Who would have thought it?"

She sighed. "Look, I've come here to talk to you about it. To offer you my spot, if you want it. I'll tell them—I'll sell you to Kraus. I'll do that, if you want me to."

My jaw hit my chest. "Really? You'd do that for me? You hate me."

"Yeah, well… I don't like injustice."

"Hmm… well, fortunately for you, I don't want to leave Varus."

"You don't?" she asked in surprise.

"Nope. Just think about it. How would Victrix enjoy working with old McGill? I'd be drawn-and-quartered by Friday, then court-martialed on Sunday morning."

She burst out laughing. "It would only take a few weeks, I bet."

352

"That's right. Victrix and me—we're not a good fit. So you enjoy your transfer. I wish you well."

She smiled, and it was a real smile this time. "Thanks," she said, and her hand strayed across the table. She put it over mine, and she gave me a quick squeeze.

I ate quietly with her for another minute or so, finishing up my breakfast. "But we have something else to talk about," I said.

"What's that?"

"How you're going to repay this debt you've been talking about."

It was her turn to stare at me, open-mouthed. "What? Are you—?"

"Yes, I'm serious. You took credit for my ideas. You sold yourself hard to Victrix. You got what you wanted."

"Yeah, but you said you were cool with that."

I nodded. "Right, I'm not trying to stop you. But we're talking about some repayment, here. One favor deserves another—or maybe two, since this was a big one."

"Two? Two favors?" She blew her bangs up with a puff of air. "All right. Tell me, what do you have in mind?"

"You're agreeing?"

"Certainly not. Not until I hear these ideas of yours."

"Wise... wise. Okay, first off, you should insist on taking Adjunct Barton with you to Victrix."

She looked confused. Of all the things I could have asked for, I could tell this wasn't even on her list.

"Adjunct Barton...? That stern woman, your light platoon commander?"

"The very same. She's my best officer, and you know how good she is. You've seen her in action."

Collins thought it over and nodded. "All right. But why? I mean, if she's your best, why would you want to let her go?"

I shrugged. "Because she wants to go. Are you willing to do it?"

"If they'll let me."

I shook my head. "Not good enough. You have to insist. It's both of you, or nothing."

She rubbed at her neck, and she looked around. I knew she was probably thinking of ways she could get out of the deal if she had to—but I knew she'd at least try.

"All right. I agree. What else?"

"Huh?"

"You said there were two favors, James. I'm not leaving anything hanging over my head. When I leave Varus, I want a clean break."

"Oh yeah. The other thing."

I stopped talking, and I looked at her. I smiled. I smiled big.

It took a few seconds for her to catch on. After she did, she fussed a bit, but she also looked kind of flattered. In truth, I suspected that's what she'd wanted all along.

The rest of the day went pretty well, and after we were off-duty, I visited Primus Collins in her private quarters. We had a great night together. We had such a good time, in fact, I regretted she was planning to ditch old Legion Varus the minute we got back to Earth.

-58-

When I woke up the next morning, I was in a fine mood. The birds were singing in my head—but not in reality, as City World didn't seem to have any birds. They had some gigantic flying insects, but that really wasn't the same.

Breakfast came and went, and Primus Collins was called away by the end of it. I'd learned her first name was Cherish—a really sweet name for such a ball-buster of a woman—but I didn't call her that in public.

Still, despite our half-hearted efforts to keep our new found romance under wraps, people noticed.

Leeson was up and around again now that the fleet was in orbit, and we were running our revival machines at full capacity. He came to congratulate me the moment Primus Collins left.

"Bagging new game these days, McGill?"

"What?"

"That's what I heard."

He was grinning at me. I tried to play ignorant, but I soon gave up. I knew it wasn't going to work this time. I frowned at him instead. "Mind your own business, Leeson. You're just one step from being dead again."

"I'm kind of glad I didn't experience these last few days. I'm going to call it a forced vacation. There was some hard fighting involved, according to every report. I don't even like gremlins... or the Mogwa, for that matter."

"Yeah. It was rough." In my mind recent events were replayed. I saw fire, smoke, blood and thousands of permed Mogwa citizens.

"Say, how did Gary work out? As my replacement?"

"He did okay. At first, he was pissing his pants, but he got over that eventually."

"Harris was telling me about one death he saw—"

"Yeah, yeah, shut up about that. Harris likes seeing other people die too much."

Leeson laughed and walked away. I was glad to be left alone—but it didn't last for long. The next person to pester me was Gary himself. He'd changed somewhat, I could see it in his eyes. They were dark and a little bit haunted.

"Sir? Can I talk to you?"

"You sure can," I told him.

He took a chair and leaned forward. He glanced around, and when he saw no one else was listening, he started talking.

I was already bored, but I let him talk. He obviously had something he thought was important on his mind.

"Sir, there have been rumors going around that Adjunct Barton is leaving your unit."

"That's unofficial and unapproved. I'm surprised to hear you go in for gossip, Adjunct."

He shrugged. "I'm not interested for that reason, sir. I'm concerned because there's another rumor floating."

"What's that?"

"About me joining your outfit on a permanent basis."

We both stared at each other for a few moments. Gary didn't say anything. He just let his words sink in. I appreciated that approach, and I wished more people would operate that way.

"Holy shit..." I said. "Are you serious?"

"So it's true? Barton is bailing out?"

I shrugged. "She's applied to Victrix. That much I can tell you."

Gary looked more stressed and nervous than ever. "Look, Centurion, I don't want you to take this the wrong way, but—"

"But you don't want to serve in my unit forever? Are you sure about that? You'll get to see a new planet up close and

356

personal every year or two. Isn't that the adventure you're craving?"

I was quoting the recruitment vids, but Gary didn't seem to find that amusing. He looked like he was sweating.

"Sir, I don't want this to sound wrong, but I do not want to slog through any more alien planets with a rifle in my hands and a series of vicious deaths to look forward to."

"Harris was right. You are a big baby."

He bristled at that, and I was glad to see it. "Hey, look, I did my part. I served, I killed, I died. Isn't that good enough? Do I really have to turn pro to impress you bastards?"

I shrugged. "Nah, I guess not. You're no longer a full-fledged hog, Gary. You're a hog with an asterisk next to his name, now. That's a good thing."

"Great... well, can you help me out?"

"Uh... how's that?"

"Talk to Graves! Talk to Turov! Get me back to Earth in my nice, cushy office."

I considered it. "Hmm... you'll owe me one if I can pull that off."

"Done," he said, slapping a gauntlet on the table between us. The table was kind of flimsy, and it shook a little with the impact. "I'll owe you one even if you just try to help."

Nodding, I got up and left. I was done with breakfast, and there wasn't anyone else in the room who I wanted to talk to.

Being a man who believed in direct action when it was warranted, I went to find Graves at the headquarters building. He wasn't there, so I tried the lifters.

At last, I found him in the loading zone. He was already packing troops and gear.

"Uh..." I said, watching him shout and make windmill motions with his arms. "Sir? Can I have a word?"

Graves looked at me. He didn't look overly happy. The last time I'd seen him, the gremlins had just offed him and escaped to Blood World.

"What do you want, McGill?"

"I want to talk about transfers."

"Save it. I already talked to Primus Collins about it. Barton can go if she wants to, and Victrix agrees. We're not going to hold her to any fine print in the contract."

"That's good to hear, Primus. Now, about her replacement—"

Graves looked at me. "I heard about that, too. I guess it will work, if Turov is willing to give up Gary. I'm surprised you think he's as good as Barton, but... whatever."

I blinked a few times. I suddenly realized a lot of things had been going on under the waves around here. I'd gotten Collins to help with letting Barton go back home to Victrix, but I hadn't really expected her to move so fast. She was all over this. She'd even lined up Gary as Barton's replacement.

"Uh..." I said, taking a moment to think it all over until my brain hurt. "Primus Graves, sir? I don't think I want Gary on my team on a permanent basis."

Now I had his full attention. He turned on me and planted his fists on his hips. "What's this bullshit? Are you doing all this just to get some other woman into your unit? I'm not going for that, McGill. Everyone wants to play musical chairs and—"

"Wait, wait," I said. "I don't have anyone in particular in mind, sir. I'm just saying... not Gary."

"Who, then? I don't have another officer to give you."

I thought hard for a second or two. Eventually, I came up with an idea. "How about asking Victrix if they have anyone they want to get rid of?"

Graves snorted. "You want their trash?"

"Well, it worked out before with Barton."

He grunted. "This isn't a football team, McGill. We're not horse-trading."

"No, sir. We're gaining a good officer for another good officer. Or... maybe a questionable one for a good one. Anyways, what do you think of the idea?"

He shrugged. "I guess it doesn't matter. They're only adjuncts. Go tell Collins."

I did, and after I sealed the deal with a kiss, she agreed as well. Collins was a lot easier to deal with than Graves.

After all that rearranging, I was pretty pleased with myself. I'd gotten Barton what she wanted, and I'd gotten tacit approval from the brass to get Gary out of my face as well. That kind of maneuvering left a man thirsty, so I headed for the new victory bar the troops had already set up. It was on the sunny roof of a building that had miraculously withstood the war intact.

Sitting up there, I had to admit the big city was impressive, and I knew it went on much, much farther than I could see. Now that most of the smoke had cleared, the skyline was glorious.

As the afternoon wore on into the night, I held down my bench seat and slowly put away a lot of bad-tasting brews. The city lit up when darkness fell, and nearly half the buildings appeared to have power already. The Mogwa engineers were working hard, even if they were still wearing full environment suits.

Once night fell hard, the view was even more pleasant. They'd yet to turn on the dome above, so I could see the stars clearly. They were absolutely stunning. We were a lot closer to the galactic Core here in the Mid-Zone. That meant the Milky Way wasn't a faintly glimmering part of the sky. It was a full-on river of glowing gemstones. Even the rounded hump of the Core itself was visible.

Enjoying some boozing and relaxation, I drank and stargazed for hours. Around dinnertime, I began to think about leaving. I didn't want to ignore Cherish Collins for too long, as I had plans for some evening festivities.

Accordingly, I stood up, swayed a bit, and almost pitched over the side of the building.

"Whoa, Centurion! Careful, that's a hundred-and-forty-story fall."

Turning and leering, I made out the shape of a tall, skinny officer. I didn't know him.

"Who are you?" I demanded rudely.

He snapped to attention and threw a salute at me. "Adjunct Dickson, sir. Reporting for duty."

I squinted at him, taking in his whole look. He was in a clean uniform, but the wrong emblem patch was on his shoulder. Instead of the red wolf's head of Varus, he bore the crossed swords of Victrix.

"Adjunct who—?"

"Dickson, sir. Oh…" He took a second to remove his patch. "I'm afraid I don't have a Varus patch yet, sir."

Finally, the light began flickering to life inside my fridge. "You're from Victrix? You're transferring in?"

"Um… yes, sir. It's a prideful moment for me. I've always admired Varus from afar."

I shook my head and shook a finger in his face. "This unit already has an alpha-dog liar, Dickson. We don't need another."

"Right. Sorry, Centurion."

We stared at each other for a second or two. At last, another question hit my beer-fogged mind.

"Did you impregnate some officer's poodle or something? Over at Victrix?"

He looked evasive. His eyes studied the deck between us for a moment. "Something like that..."

I laughed. "Okay, I get it. I don't have to know anything else. I don't even want to know. You're here, and you're mine. That's all that matters."

It was the same speech I'd given Erin Barton about a decade or so back—but I was a little more boozy this time. Nevertheless, it had the same effect on Dickson as it'd had on Erin years ago.

"Thank you, sir," he said. He sounded both grateful and surprised.

I guess in his old legion any officer would have dragged the sordid truth out of him—but that wasn't the Varus way. If you wanted to serve in the worst legion humanity had yet to field, you got to serve.

No questions asked.

-59-

The next day Governess Nox and Sateekas came out on a tour. It was your classic meet-and-greet with the troops after victory had been declared.

Nox was really doing the kissy-stuff while Sateekas trailed after her, looking bored.

"I really don't see why this is necessary," he complained. "These are slave-troops. They aren't going to pass a referendum on your quality, or report back anything to the Core Worlds."

Nox turned on him in annoyance. "That kind of thinking is why you never got your fleet back. These animals are adored by the local populace. Those beaten-down citizens will be voting and sending notes home to any of their relatives who still recall their existence."

Hmm... Was there trouble in paradise? It seemed to me that there just might be. Or possibly, this was how a mated pair of Mogwa always treated one another. It was hard to know.

My job was to tag along with the two aliens, simultaneously providing security and a walking photo-op. I'd gained some fame among the population of surviving Mogwa. In their own way, they were grateful for my efforts. In particular, they'd been impressed to learn that I'd pioneered the idea of stuffing gremlins into Mogwa marine power-armor.

Marching after the two bickering VIPs, I tried not to make trouble. I was even a little flattered that they still trusted me over any of the other bodyguards they had to choose from.

After watching Nox glad-hand a few thousand Mogwa citizens and human troops, however, I was getting just as bored as Sateekas. It was time to make a suggestion.

"Uh… Lady Nox? Can I say something?"

She looked at me sternly. "It seems to me that you've already begun speaking without permission."

"Huh? Oh… yeah, I guess so…"

Sateekas made a calming gesture in her direction, so she relented. "All right, McGill," she said. "Let's hear your gem-like words of wisdom."

"Well sir, I'm afraid I'm fresh out of those. But I would like to know if you and Sateekas here are going to be flying back to Province 921 with us?"

"No," she said firmly.

This seemed to startle Sateekas. "What's this? You're not going back? What of your governing appointment?"

"What of it?" Nox asked him. "It's a thankless job that I loathe. Here, we have a beaten people and a chance to start over. The Imperial officials in the Core will be hateful toward us—but that's nothing new. They've already exiled us, and nothing is going to change that."

"This is… shocking…" Sateekas said. "What of our offspring?"

She stopped walking and slapping foot-hand things with the endless procession of Mogwa citizens. She turned on him. "I just stated my intention to stay. Are you still thinking of going back?"

He began to bristle. I winced as I watched this happen.

"You said it yourself," he pointed out, "how else will I ever gather a new fleet to my banner?"

"You don't even have a banner for them to gather around," she said, and I could tell she was getting angry as well.

She put a protective arm around her belly. Could she be pregnant again? Damnation, Sateekas was a randy old goat.

Sateekas got angry next. He puffed up like a cobra and looked at her sternly. I could just tell he was going to go off, being a man who'd done the same with women on countless occasions.

"Hey, hey…" I said. "How about this? What if you start building a new fleet right here, Grand Admiral, sir?"

He turned an angry eye in my direction. Most of his orbs were still staring at his mate. "What are you chattering about, primate?"

"Just this, sir. Right now, you've got a single battlecruiser. The pride of the fleet out here at Segin. That's something to start with, and it's better than nothing."

"He had to steal it," Nox said. She wasn't helping at all, so I made a calming gesture with my hand. This didn't work on her any better than it had ever worked on any female.

"It's time," she said, "to give up on childish fantasies of being a fleet officer again. You're my consort, and you did a good job with this campaign. I plan to run for the local governorship of Segin."

"City World is… a democracy?" I asked, surprised.

Nox threw a dismissive hand high in the air. "Of course. Why do you think they've been ostracized from the Core Worlds?"

Sateekas looked upset. "It's disgusting for personages such as ourselves to have to wheedle and beg for power."

"That part will only be for show," Nox said. "Their entire system is a sham to make the populace more docile. Look at the bright side: the absurd notions of the locals have created certain opportunities for us to exploit."

"I see that your mind is made up. You might well have informed me earlier."

"Would you have listened? Would you have cared? All you want to do is mate and talk about past glories."

Sateekas began to sputter. He was so pissed he couldn't even talk right.

"Hold on, hold on," I said, releasing a nervous laugh. "If you're going to run for office, Lady Nox, I think you might need a war hero at your side. All you have to do is put him in charge of the military. He's a natural."

The two looked at me, then each other. They seemed to calm down a bit. I could tell that there was friction just below the surface, just like there had to be with any power-couple like these two. They both had planet-sized egos and arrogance to spare.

"McGill makes a good point," Nox said at last. Being the politician, she seemed to be the one who was better at smoothing things over. She drew in a breath, and she lowered her hands to place all six on the ground again. "Ex-Admiral Sateekas, I would be happy to have you as my political appointee in charge of the military."

Sateekas scowled, and he shuffled around a bit like he had to pee or something. At last, he spoke up. "I will accept this offer—but I have conditions."

"What conditions?"

"You must run on a policy of rearmament. This planet was woefully unprepared for a barbarian invasion. I propose that one percent of the population be placed into a pool for conscription. I also need a vastly increased budget for the fleet."

Nox mulled that over. "Agreed. Your points should be easy to sell to the people. They've suffered greatly due to their lack of foresight."

They went on like that for a long time, but as they were no longer at each other's throats, I didn't much care. I soon grew bored and began to play around with my tapper. Seeing an urgent message or two, I was goaded into action.

"Uh... Lady Nox? Can I return to my unit? There seems to be a ruckus going on."

"Very well. We're done with the charade of campaigning for today."

I ditched them and trotted back to my unit, which was in the act of packing up all our gear. What I found wasn't what I expected.

Adjunct Dickson was standing tall over a recruit, one of Barton's light troops. Dickson had out a shock-rod, which he'd apparently used to discipline the man.

"What seems to be the problem, Dickson?" I asked.

"Ah, Centurion. Good to see you here. This man here," as he spoke, he toed the inert recruit with tip of his boot, "lacks any sense of decency or decorum. I have corrected him appropriately."

Frowning, I came forward and nudged the man on the ground. He didn't move, and after a quick glance at his tapper, I saw he'd red-lined. He'd been beaten to death, but Dickson didn't seem broken up over it at all.

Looking around my unit, I saw lots of angry glares. That wasn't good for Dickson. Maybe in Victrix you could get away with anything you wanted—but here in Varus, well sir, people had a way of getting even.

"Well, as I wasn't here to judge, I'll take your word for it," I said. "Everyone get back to work. Dickson, call in the revive."

As the new adjunct worked his tapper, someone shouted out from the back of the assembled troops. I knew that voice in an instant. It was Carlos.

"Hey, Adjunct," he called out. "I bet I know what they called you back at the academy."

Dickson eyed Carlos warily. "What's that, Specialist?"

"A sharp troop."

Dickson looked surprised and relieved. "Well yes, as a matter of fact—"

"I bet they said you had the stiffest spine on the training fields, sir. The hardest eyes, the longest—"

Moller didn't wait any longer. She cuffed him, and he shut up at last.

As we all settled down for the evening, I had to wonder if I'd gotten swindled in the horse trading that had rewarded me with Dickson.

-60-

The long journey home began the next day. We took off on our lifter, firing up into the strange skies of City World. Looking down through camera feeds wired to my tapper, I saw the entire massive blot of the city, which spanned countless square kilometers of natural land. All around the city, a fringe of green appeared as we went higher and higher, punching through the clouds. Those were the farms and supporting regions. Eventually, it transformed into a bulbous hump on the side of the planet.

Much of the city was wrecked, of course. The fires seemed to be out now, but the rebuilding and repopulating would take decades. Lowering my arm, I ignored my tapper. I was glad to see City World in my rearview mirror. I hadn't much liked the place.

When we docked with *Dominus*, I smiled. I was thinking of Primus Collins. We'd had a half-dozen fine nights together after the fighting had ended, and I wouldn't mind continuing that adventure.

To further that goal, I sent a note to Cherish the moment I stepped aboard *Dominus* and my tapper synched-up with the ship's grid. A frown came to my face a few moments later.

"No such person can be located in the…" I read aloud.

My boots stopped marching, and I stood stock-still in the middle of a crowded gangplank. Plenty of soldiers bumped into me and more than a few of them cursed, but I didn't care.

Where had she gone? Immediately, a single thought came to my mind. It was a dark thought, and it pissed me off.

Working my tapper with speed, I checked on the whereabouts of another woman. Since she was also in my direct chain of command, I quickly found that she was aboard *Dominus*.

"Galina…" I said, and the word came out like a curse.

She'd pulled this kind of shit in the past. I began walking again—faster than before. Now, rather than bumping into me, soldiers were being rudely rammed aside. They cursed and growled at me with even greater vehemence, but I cared even less than before.

My first stop was her office, up on Gold Deck. I found Gary there. He had a big smile on his face, and a pair of big boots on his desk. He seemed very happy to be back at his chicken-shit job.

On a different day, I might have found this amusing. I might have teased him about it, or threatened to tell Galina something—but I didn't do any of that today. I was too pissed off.

"Adjunct!" I shouted.

Gary ripped his boots off the desk and lurched up. "Centurion?"

I was glad to see he was still conditioned to jump at the sound of my voice. He'd gotten something from participating in a real campaign at least.

"Where is she?" I demanded.

Normally, Gary would have been surly and flippant in his answer. He might even have pretended not to know who I was talking about—but not today. I'd spent too many days with the power of life and death over him recently, and he'd forgotten none of that.

"She's in her quarters, sir."

"Alone?"

He blinked. "Um… as far as I know."

I turned to go, still storming, but Gary called after me. "Hey, McGill. I wanted to thank you for telling Graves to send me back to my office work. That was really cool of you."

I glanced at him, and I nodded. I took a moment then, since Gary wasn't to blame for anything I was suspecting Galina of right now. I instantly decided it was time to lie, and I went hard with it. "It's a shame, really. You did a good job out there. You were born to be a soldier, even if you didn't enjoy it. At least now you won't be wondering for the rest of your career how it might have gone in the combat arms."

Gary blinked in surprise, then he smiled. "Why... thank you, sir. It was good to serve under you."

There, I'd done my good deed for the day.

Marching out of the place, I headed for Galina's quarters. They weren't as sumptuous as they'd been in past years, but they didn't consist of a dusty bunk in a well-used module on the lower decks, either.

Hammering on the door until it shook, I waited a moment, then I hammered again.

The door clicked open, and it swung fractionally inward. I pushed my way inside without waiting for a formal invitation.

Inside, I found Galina Turov primping in front of a mirror. She was fancying up her uniform with meticulous care.

Normally, when any soldier arranges his dress uniform, it takes a bit of the old spit-and-polish, but Galina took such things to the extreme. She didn't just get her insignia straight and remove the smudges from her buttons. No sir. That was just the beginning. She liked to wear smart cloth, the kind that could be instructed on how to hug one's shape.

She had quite the shape to be hugging onto as well. Using her tapper, she touched a glowing spot on some kind of prissy fashion-app, and I watched as her pants cinched in, sucking in wrinkles and becoming form-fitting over her buttocks. It was like they were designed for this express purpose—which they were.

Despite my mood, I was distracted. Had she set up this scenario on purpose?

Dammit.

"Galina?" I asked.

"James? What's up?"

"Did you ship Primus Collins back to Earth?"

She stopped primping and turned slowly to look at me. Her head cocked, and what had been a smile faded into a red line of suspicion. Worse, her eyes were all slanty now. They'd been in a good mood before, as I recalled.

"What are you talking about?"

If there's one area of mental effort that my mind excels at, it's the glib excuse. I couldn't do much math, speak any foreign languages, remember promises, or even listen when people talked for more than a full minute straight—but I could switch directions on a dime when I had to.

This was one of those moments. Galina clearly had no idea what I was talking about. That meant that I was not only barking up the wrong tree when it came to thinking Galina had turfed Cherish to remove her from my reach, it also meant I was letting the cat out of the bag in real time.

"Uh..." I said, my mind doing a one-eighty. Less than a second later, my stern gaze turned into an affable smile. "I'm sorry, things were rough down there on City World."

"Yes, but what's this interest in Primus Collins?"

I shook my head. "If you don't know what I'm talking about, then I can see I've got the wrong idea. I'll just excuse myself and leave you to your meeting or whatever is coming up."

Her suspicions were flying high now. Higher than ever. Her fists planted themselves on her hips. "How do you know I'm going to a meeting?"

I gestured vaguely. "Uh... all the pant-tightening sort of gives it away, sir."

Her face soured, and she almost let me go—but not quite. "Hold on. Stand where you are, Centurion."

I froze and turned slowly back to face her.

"You came in here angry, didn't you? What did you think I'd done?"

Shrugging helplessly, I tried to look like a dumbass. That didn't take much work. "I don't know, sir. I just thought maybe you knew what had happened to my commander."

"Your commander? Primus Collins?"

"Yessir."

I proceeded then to explain that Collins and I had been thrown together on the battlefield. I described our heroic actions—but I left out all the salacious ones.

"That's very interesting. You two worked together on this nonsense of using Mogwa tanks with gremlin pilots?"

"Mogwa power-armor, sir. Yes."

She fluttered carefully painted nails in my direction. "Whatever. Why were you upset?"

There it was. Dodging had been my first line of defense, but now I knew I needed to move on into a straight-up lie to protect the guilty.

"Well sir, we were credited with a lot of the glory down there on City World. As you know, sometimes people like Winslade and Tribune Kraus... well sir, they aren't good at sharing the limelight."

She nodded slowly. "Okay. I get that. But why did you come here to accuse me of some vague crime?"

"Well... I thought maybe they'd come to you—seeing as you're the proper CO and all—and one of them might have gotten you to do their dirty work."

"Reassigning Primus Collins to some salt mine?"

"Yes."

Galina's eyes narrowed, and she slid them around. They weren't glaring at me. They were thinking hard. Evil thoughts were going on behind those eyes, I could tell.

"Those bastards..." she said at last.

"Huh?"

She pointed a finger at me. "You're right. I was lobbied to remove Primus Collins. She's been reassigned to Death World. She's running a garrison there now, policing those nasty women Helsa and Kelsa—whatever their names are."

"Uh... really?"

I was floored. My bullshit scenario had come true? I'd been winging it—but it did make sense. When a tribune has been shown up by an inferior officer, and that tribune is cagey, he might very well quietly shunt aside underlings capable of taking his job from him.

"So... I was right?" I asked, flummoxed. "Cherish really did get reassigned?"

370

"Yes, she… wait? What did you call her?"

"Primus Collins, sir. A meaner woman I've never met. She'll give those Shadowlanders a headache and then some."

Galina smiled vaguely. "Yes. I suspect she will."

Then she shrugged, and she smiled up at me. "James, from all reports you performed magnificently on City World. You even managed to unload those bumbling idiots Nox and Sateekas. I'm sure the poor Mogwa citizens who've inherited those two will come to regret their choices."

"Hehe…" I said, laughing hesitantly. "I'm sure you're right about that, sir. Did you say you were going to dinner?"

"I said I was going to a meeting."

"Oh yeah… will there be food served… by any chance?"

Galina eyed me, and she thought over my offer for a second or two. I let her do it. When the mouse sniffs the cheese, you don't snap the trap. You won't even catch a tail if you go off too early.

"All right. You may accompany me. Get your kit in order—you have… eighteen minutes to do so. Meet me down on Lavender Deck after that."

I smiled. "Yessir!"

Trotting out of the place, I had to wonder at my swiftly changing fortunes. I'd gone in there to chew Galina out for sending Cherish away, and I'd nearly blown everything.

Now, a less thoughtful person might say that I'd given up on my brief affair with Primus Collins too soon, but I was nothing if not a man who seized opportunities when they were offered. After all, she was gone and out of my reach. Galina was here and she was… looking pretty good.

The evening went well, and we ended up spending the night together. Along about midnight, I got a message—it was a deep-link transmission, which meant it cost real money.

The message was a serious text-wall. It was from Cherish, and it amounted to a lengthy apology. She'd gotten orders and been rushed away back to Earth, then to Death World. It was a great opportunity for her to run her own garrison command, and she hadn't been able to say good-bye properly.

I thought about tapping a message back to her, but I didn't dare. Galina was asleep beside me, but she was a notoriously light sleeper.

Instead, I swept away the message with a swipe of my finger, then I double-deleted it, even searching for the back-up on the cloud and nailing that, too.

You could never be too careful with such messages. They could bring all kinds of pain if the wrong people read them.

-61-

Months later, as fall began on Earth, *Dominus* finally parked in orbit. We disembarked and walked on solid ground again for the first time in a long while. Anxious to get home, I mustered out and demobilized. As quickly as I could, I headed home to Waycross.

Anyone who knows me might well suspect that I'd have forgotten my promises to a certain gremlin madman named Jink by the time I reached Earth. Such a hypothetical person would have been right on the money, too.

What with Galina distracting me, troops to demobilize, and a stuffed-shirt named Dickson to deal with, I plain forgot about Jink—but he didn't forget about me.

When I got back home to Earth, a package was waiting for me. I opened it, and I puzzled over the contents.

Inside, I found a waxy flower... it was clearly an alien growth, and it was both unfamiliar and familiar at the same time.

Finally, I remembered what it was. The strange-looking bloom came from Dust World. It looked kind of like a giant orchid the size of a cantaloupe.

I'd once plucked one of these things and given it to Natasha. That had been many long years ago... who might be sending me something like this now?

I thought over all the people I knew on Dust World. Etta was out there, fooling around with some kind of weird experiment with her grandfather again. Then there was the old man himself. He was a freak, but he wouldn't have sent me a sticky flower that grew in the marshlands around the lakes of his planet.

Who else lived out there these days...? Oh yes, of course. *Floramel.*

My eyes snapped wide. A thought had struck me, and it struck me hard. I'd forgotten about Jink. I'd forgotten about my promise to bring Floramel back to Blood World. Hell, I'd forgotten about everything I'd told just about everyone out on City World.

"Shit..." I whispered, climbing off my couch and slipping on boots in the dark. Fortunately, I was already wearing pants and such. I was sleeping alone, and it was the dead of the night in Georgia Sector.

It had to be Jink. There was no way Floramel or the Investigator would send me a flower out of the blue. Etta *might* have done it if it was my birthday or something—but it wasn't. It was a cold Tuesday in March, and not even close to Easter this year. Besides, Etta would have sent me a note or something.

Searching the box, I found there wasn't a damned thing in it besides some sticky residue from the flower. That was it.

Looking at the bloom again, I realized it had to be pretty fresh. Someone had brought it—probably by courier—through the gateway posts up at Central, and they'd secretly delivered it to me.

This was a chilling moment for old McGill. I had family here, and family out on Dust World. Someone knew about all of them, and where they were. In fact, a paranoid man might have concluded they knew about the flower I'd once given Natasha as well.

"Damnation... I've got to go out there."

I armed myself, packed a minimal ruck, and headed for the airport. I pretty much stole the family tram to do this, slapping her gently on the fender to send her back home. She knew the way.

After a long sky-train ride, during which the woman next to me sneered and made lots of remarks about people not

374

knowing how to wash these days, I found my way to Central. From there, I paid a fee and walked into a bug-zapper that sent my molecules all the way out to Zeta Herculis, better known as Dust World.

These days, just about anyone could buy a ticket and stand in line, zapping yourself to the world of your choice if humanity owned it. The weird thing about such travel to the stars was the prices. You would think that what with the power usage being the same and all, going anyplace would cost the same amount—but that wasn't how it worked.

Going to Dust World was dirt cheap. The only destination that was cheaper was Death World. Before anyone starts getting ideas about an exotic destination-vacation, however, you'd better check on the cost of returning to Earth. Coming back was expensive—especially from Dust World. I suspected the truth was that Hegemony Gov didn't really want people to come back from that place. They wanted people to migrate and stay put.

After walking down off a platform and touching my cap to some unsmiling hog guards, I was asked to state my business. That was easy to do for a man such as myself.

"I'm cruising for a hot date," I said. "I heard these local colonist girls are as easy as they are cute."

That elicited a gut-busting round of laughter from the guards. "You'd better think again, friend. The girls around here will cut your dick off as soon as look at you."

I pretended to be disappointed but headed to town anyway. After enquiring as to the whereabouts of the Investigator, I was eventually directed into the caverns that had been drilled into the stone walls of the valley.

Using my tapper, I searched for Etta. They'd apparently moved their secret lab deeper into the dank caves, but I found them on the third day of the search.

When I arrived, they were in the middle of an experiment. Floramel was there, with the Investigator at her side. He was observing, looking down into a lumpy tank of brown stuff that bubbled and smelled bad.

375

Etta was playing the part of the assistant. She made me smile, she was so intent on her work she didn't even know I'd arrived at first.

"Raise the amperage a milliamp," Floramel said.

"Done."

"Hmm… nothing. Let's try—James?" Floramel turned around and stared at me in surprise. "Where did you come from?"

"Floramel," the Investigator said sternly. "You're mixture is steaming…"

She whirled back to her nasty brown stew and ordered Etta to shut it down. After that, everyone greeted me enthusiastically—except for the Investigator. He was rarely happy to see anyone, especially when he was working some kind of disgusting magic in one of his tanks.

I pointed at the tank. "Don't tell me you guys are trying to revive someone in there."

"No," the Investigator said. "Let's adjourn to my office."

He walked away, and the two women followed him. The man had a natural authority about him which tended to make most people obey his every whim.

Naturally, I wasn't the most easily swayed of individuals. I lingered and put a finger into the soup in the tank. It was hot, and it kind of itched a little after I pulled it out.

"James!"

The three were standing at the exit, staring back at me.

"Coming!"

I trotted after them, wiping stinky stuff on my pants. I hoped it wouldn't eat my uniform—or my finger.

We found our way to a lantern-lit office of sorts. It had once been some kind of tech shop, I could tell that much from all the antiquated junk that lined the walls and shelves. There were jerry cans of fuel, sealed barrels of chemicals, and all sorts of dusty electronic gizmos.

"To what do we owe the honor of this visit?" the Investigator asked.

"Whoa!" I said, laughing. "Since when does a man need a special occasion to visit his genius daughter?"

This response pleased Etta and Floramel—but the Investigator didn't seem mollified.

"It's been my experience, over several decades, that you always want something specific when you come here, McGill."

"Well... that's true."

"It's Etta, isn't it?" he asked. "You're here to take her home, or arrest her, or something worse. Am I right?"

"Uh..." I said looking around at the three concerned faces. "None of those. Honest."

"Why then?" he insisted.

I sighed, and I pointed at Floramel.

"I'm here to see you, girl. Not Etta—not this time. But it is sure nice to lay eyes on you too, little lady."

I gave Etta a hug, and she returned it with one of her own. She was happier now, it seemed to me, and that made me happy as well. The last time I'd seen her she was still upset about her new, hybridized body. After all, any adult person can get kind of attached to having a certain height, weight and appearance.

With the new control over genetics that the Investigator had recently gained, it was possible to mix-and-match things like a person's heritage. That was freaky and kind of cool, but it was also a super-secret. Earth Gov didn't know about it, and neither did the Galactics. I would shudder to think that either might find out someday.

Hegemony would probably try to secretly use it to "fix" things the upper class Public Servants didn't like about themselves and others. The Galactics, on the other hand... well, they'd probably want to erase all Humanity for breaking their laws. Only one patent could be awarded in any province for any technology. To challenge that patent, you had to go through miles of red tape, Nairb butt-inspections, and all kinds of other bullshit.

As far as I knew, the Investigator had never even hinted to anyone he'd been working on this kind of thing for decades. Like a spider in the dark, he'd secretly and illegally recreated a homebrew revival system. This was dangerous and foolhardy, and sometimes it kept me awake an extra minute or two at night before I finally shrugged and passed out. I wasn't a man who worried much about things I couldn't control.

"Dad?" Etta said when she'd taken her arms from around my belly, "we've learned so much over the last year or so. I can't even tell you."

"Hehe... nope, you sure can't. Don't even *think* about telling me—I don't want to know."

Right then, a strange thing happened. I lifted my smiling face up toward Floramel and the Investigator—and I received the equivalent of a high voltage shock.

The Investigator had his hand resting lightly on Floramel's shoulder.

My jaw sagged low. I wasn't able to control it. Seeing this, Floramel cast her eyes down at the floor. Was she embarrassed? Maybe.

As for me, I was gob-smacked, floored, and kicked hard in the tail-pipe. It wasn't any kind of a jealousy thing, mind you. Sure, Floramel and I had shared some nice nights over the years. That was a well-known and well-documented fact. But I wasn't pining away for her, and she wasn't for me, either.

Mostly, I was shocked by the concept of the Investigator being interested in a woman of any kind. I'd known him for a long, long time, and he'd never shown the slightest inclination in that direction.

What's more, he was an old soul. He'd been older than me when I'd first met him, and even though he looked like a well-kept forty-something today, I knew that was the tip of the iceberg. He had to be pushing a hundred at this point—almost as old as the original colonists who'd come out here from Earth long, long ago.

Zeta Herculis was Earth's one and only true colony. The mission had been sent out before the Galactics had arrived, and by the time I was born, it had been assumed lost. That assumption had turned out to be horse-hockey, as the colony had reached Dust World, dug in, and begun their own civilization.

In all that time, I'd never heard of this old bastard having a girlfriend, a wife, or anything else. Sure, he'd once had a companion who'd given birth to Della, his only daughter and

Etta's mother—but as I understood it that woman had been enslaved by the Cephalopods and vanished forever.

The crazy old man had been wedded to his cryptic work ever since. Now, things seemed to have changed.

Etta was the one to break the spell, during which I stared in slack-jawed surprise.

"No need to swoon, Dad," she said. "Floramel and grandpa have been a thing for about a year now. They've got a lot in common, after all."

"Uh..." I said, and that was all I could get out of my lips.

My mind, of course, was doing loops and swirls. Not only was this a surprise from out of the blue, I was now thinking enough to understand there were unhappy consequences coming my way.

The number one problem was the simple fact that I'd promised one nasty little gnome named Jink that I'd deliver Floramel to him and his evil minions. That had been a tall order from the get-go, and now it was looking damn near impossible to accomplish.

The others were talking. They were telling me things, like how happy they were, and how I shouldn't feel weird about it—but I didn't listen. I didn't even hear them, really.

My head rotated, mouth still open, toward the caverns behind me. They were dark, dusty and quiet. They were full of secrets.

Jink had found these people. He'd found Dust World, and he'd delivered a flower to Georgia that could only have come from here.

Now, that could have been nine kinds of trickery. He might have bought a flower and had it transported out to my parents farm, for example. Improbable, sure—but possible.

Staring at the dark caverns though, I didn't think that was how things had gone. To my mind, the way this had happened had been much more sinister.

Jink and his people were natural spies and sleuths. They liked to slink in the dark. Why would such a bunch of nasty creepers resort to hiring others?

No, sir. They'd come out here and found Floramel. At least one of them had. And then they'd plucked that big, waxy bloom and sent it to my folks' house.

I knew it had gone that way. I knew it in my bones.

"James? James!" the Investigator boomed.

Snapping my fool head back around, I blinked and forced a smile.

"James?" the man said again, his intense gaze locking with mine. "Did you hear me?"

"Uh... I sure did. But what was that last part? I kind of spaced-out for a moment."

"Of course you did..."

Etta cleared her throat and took my hand in both of hers. "Daddy, Grandpa said that Floramel and he were engaged to be married. That makes you *really* happy for them, doesn't it?"

My jaw was low and hanging again. Dammit, I hated when it did that for a long time, or repeatedly. With an effort of will, I snapped my mouth shut.

My smile was back, and it was faker than ever. I sucked in a breath and thrust a hand out to the couple. "Congratulations!"

-62-

The Investigator shook my hand, and he gave me a cool smile of his own. That was nice to see, even if we both knew we didn't like each other much.

Floramel, for her part, had clearly been dreading this moment of revelation. Now that it was over, she lifted her eyes from the stone floor and met my gaze. We smiled at each other like we were both happy or something, and the uncomfortable moment passed.

Corralling my brain and getting myself under control, I suggested we break out some booze. They didn't have any, but there was a flask or two in my ruck, so we all managed.

After downing a blood-warm shot of bourbon each, everyone's mood improved. I talked big about attending the wedding with Della, and even promised a shocker of a wedding present.

The two girls seemed pleased and completely fooled. Only the old man knew better. Later, after we'd eaten dinner, he pulled me aside. The ladies assumed he would be wanting to speak to me in private, so they left us alone and went back to prodding whatever nightmare they'd been stewing up in the tank in the other room.

"James," he said, "I know this must come as a shock, and as an unwelcome change to your plans."

"Huh?"

"I'm talking about Floramel and her sudden, permanent removal from your list of feminine targets."

"What? Oh… no, no, no… that's not what I've been thinking about. That's not what I'm thinking about at all, sir."

"What then, pray tell, concerns you so much?"

For a long moment, I considered actually doing as he asked. I considered coming clean. I could tell him about my plans to spirit Floramel away from Dust World. My unpleasant mind had already come up with all sorts of nefarious schemes by which I could achieve this goal.

For instance, I'd considered telling her she was welcome back at Central. That they'd had a change of heart and decided to award her a medal of freedom, or some such nonsense. If that didn't work, there was always outright seduction—or even meaner things, like bringing Raash out here to tease her into leaving…

I'm not proud of it, but my brain had been working overtime on all kinds of smooth ways to get Floramel out to Blood World. Just for a visit, mind you—depending on what old Jink had in mind for us.

But all that skullduggery was out the window now. After reflecting on things, I realized I never could have gone through with any of it, anyways. Sure, I was still worried about Jink and whatever his evil band of midgets might do to me and mine, but there was no way I was going to shit all over Floramel's happiness. Hell, she was soon going to be Etta's newest family member.

The whole marriage idea wasn't a bad thing, anyways… It might even solve some of my problems. After all, Etta had murdered Floramel a time or two in the past, and that kind of nonsense would probably come to an end. This could mean peace in the family. Hell, Floramel might even give birth to some aunts and uncles for Etta. That had long been something she'd been denied in our too-thin family tree.

Heaving a sigh, I considered telling all this to the Investigator. He was a wise man, and he might even come up with some ideas as to how to deal with the predicament I found myself trapped within.

But old habits are hard to break. Just ask anybody. So... I lied instead.

"Sir, I have good news. Something I haven't dared speak to Floramel and Etta about yet."

He blinked at me. "What news is this?"

"The Blood Worlders—you know about those near-humans, right?"

"Of course. Unfortunate relatives of ours. Twisted things that should never have drawn breath."

"Uh... right. Anyways, they want to reach out to people like you—and Floramel. They want to have a dialog. After all, as you said, they're your distant cousins."

The Investigator stared at me. It was as if his mind was resetting itself. I knew that look well, and I waited for the reboot to be complete.

"This is quite a surprise, James. Almost as startling as our coming marriage must have been for you."

"Uh..."

We'd been sitting across from one another, both with our butts on stone ledges. The Investigator stood suddenly, and he began to pace around.

"I'm seeing all kinds of connections now," he said. "Surely, this can't come out of the ether. No. Hegemony sent you out here, didn't they? Who do you serve today? Galina Turov? Or perhaps someone placed even higher?"

"Huh?"

He didn't seem to have heard me. He was pacing around, thinking hard. Like a lot of smart people, he liked to jump to all sorts of conclusions.

"No. I'm seeing something worse than that. The hand of a Public Servant is behind this. One Alexander Turov, to be precise."

"Oh... wait a second..."

"You don't need to confirm or deny my suspicions. In fact, given your reputation for base mendacity, I'd rather you didn't bother. You should know, James, that I'm the closest thing this planet has to a sovereign. It is therefore my duty to know what happens in all connected affairs and relationships. In short, I know that you've had dealings with the Servant Turov."

It was my turn to be dumbfounded all over again. Sure, I'd been working as a shill for Old Alexander now and then. But I didn't think anyone outside Galina and her father knew about it.

"Now that we've laid our cards on the table, so to speak, I want to know exactly what you're proposing?"

"Well sir... I was kind of wondering if you and Floramel might want to step out to Blood World. There's this charming village full of gremlins, see, and they—"

"Gremlins?"

Here, the Investigator surprised me by spitting on the stones between us. That wasn't a good sign.

"Those beastly creatures are our greatest shame. Do you know one was sighted on this very world just a few weeks ago? I ordered that the beast be tracked down and slain, but somehow, it evaded us."

"You don't say..." I was feeling itchy now, and my finger began to probe my neck.

"In short," the old man told me, standing tall, "I have no intention of visiting a world full of abominations. The sentiments of my wife-to-be will only confirm this position."

"Hmm... okay! It was just a suggestion. No pressure, if you want more time to think about it... There would be no travel charges whatsoever, by the way. In fact—"

The Investigator took a step toward me. "McGill? Are you listening to me? Drop all your schemes and plans. Whatever they are, they're not going to happen. I say this as your eldest relative. Have some spine, man, and show some loyalty. You're a soldier of Earth, not a pawn for a politician."

That got through to me. I felt his words like a punch in the belly. I hadn't really thought of my family as extending beyond my folks, Etta, and maybe Della. But he was right. Even though Della wasn't my wife, we had a kid together. That was as close to a family as I might ever get.

"All right," I said, standing up and slapping my knees. "I'll convey your regrets. Let's go back to the ladies and celebrate some more."

He watched me warily, but I meant what I'd said. I got out my flask again, and together we ended up draining it dry.

384

A few days passed, during which I fished in the deep bubbling lake in the center of the valley, and caught up with Etta as best I could. We set up plans for the coming holidays with visits—the works.

Claiming that I was being summoned by Central, I left on the fourth day. I think only Etta was sad to see me go, but everyone was cordial enough. Compared to how my visits with relatives typically went, the trip was a success.

Returning to Earth, I only made one pit-stop inside Central. It took some wangling, but I managed to get a little help putting together a care-package. Kivi frowned at it, but she didn't ask any questions. She knew better by now.

With a brown box tied with a brown string under my arm, I put on a smile and stepped out through the gateway posts again. This time, I didn't head to Dust World.

I went to Blood World instead.

-63-

Blood World is an unpleasant planet. It's kind of like a hot version of Mars. Despite the climate, I wasn't given a terribly warm welcome when I initially arrived. Only after I did some name-dropping—especially when I invoked Gytha, who was their local ruler—did I get an enthusiastic response.

Almost immediately my tapper lit up. A pretty face, older and wiser but still lovely, peered up at me.

"James McGill?" Gytha asked. "Can it truly be my betrothed? Have you returned to complete your vows with me?"

"Huh?" I said. "Oh…"

She glanced down at the brown-box package I had under my arm. It was getting kind of drippy, but I didn't care. I kept it hugged up against me.

"A gift?" she exclaimed. "Is that a gift? You're going to ask for forgiveness, aren't you?"

"Well… that is…" I stopped, feeling at a rare loss for words.

I'd almost forgotten about Gytha. She was nice-looking and all that, and we'd had exactly one passionate encounter many years earlier. But that wasn't the important thing. The kicker was I'd been sworn to marry her, and she'd had really, really big plans in that regard.

On the day of our grand ceremony, a truly stupendous march had been held. Thousands upon thousands of Blood

386

Worlder soldiers had marched from her world to Earth. I recalled standing in near-desert conditions, watching them go by.

Being a simple man with simple needs and thoughts, I'd professed a powerful need to urinate. Then I'd slipped away to take a leak behind the gateway posts and—well, I'd accidentally stepped through them, returning to Earth.

Ever since then, I'd pretty much forgotten all about Gytha, Blood World, and all her big plans. Apparently, she hadn't been able to let go of the past quite as easily as I had.

"Stay right there," she said. "Guards! Contain the McGill! I will be there as soon as I'm able!"

My tapper went blank, and I was left dumbfounded and staring.

Two big paws the size of ham-hocks grabbed me by the biceps. I looked to one side, then the other. A big-ass heavy trooper, each a head and shoulders taller than I was, stood on either flank.

The brown box under my arm dropped on the ground, and I winced. A dark syrup leaked out at one corner, but no one seemed to notice or care.

"Hey, boys," I said. "It's good to be back."

They said nothing. They didn't even twitch their lips up in a grim smile the way a hog might have. It was disheartening.

Straining a bit, I worked my tapper with my longest finger. It was the only one that could reach. There was only one person who might be able to get me out of this, and I didn't hesitate to contact him.

About ten minutes later, a bouncy little guy with an evil cast to his face showed up. It was Jink.

"McGill?" he said. "Why are you alone?"

I glanced at my two huge partners and laughed. "I'm not quite alone, if you get my drift."

Jink slid his nasty eyes from one of the heavy troopers to the other. "I get it. Wait here."

"Heh…" I said, smiling at his joke. "Don't take too long!"

Several more minutes passed. I was getting sweaty, and it wasn't just due to the natural heat of Blood World. The big red sun beat down on the deserts outside, and every passing second felt like a grain of sand falling in an hourglass. How far away was Gytha? It was a big planet, but...

Suddenly, the trooper to my left stiffened and stood taller. At the same moment, I felt a stinging sensation in my arm. Fortunately, he was wearing non-conductive gauntlets and I didn't get a lethal dose.

After several seconds, the heavy trooper fell like a tree in the forest. He crashed down, and by the stink of it, I figured he'd shit himself.

The other guy on my right had finally figured out something was wrong. A dark look passed over his face. He drew a big pistol the size of a hog leg, and he aimed it at me.

Then he stiffened up, too. I ducked, and a huge boom sounded. The floor of the gateway terminal had a chunk taken out of it.

I scooped up my leaky box and looked around. A tiny figure waved, then disappeared. I charged after him.

Once out in the bright hot Blood World air, I recalled how much I disliked this planet. It was all deserts and evil-looking plants. Taking huge steps, I ran after Jink as fast as I could. We reached a flying vehicle of sorts—it was like an air-hauler, but smaller.

Jink climbed in and waved for me to climb up into the bed on the back. I got on, but I had trouble getting a good grip before he launched into the sky. I almost slid off, and when I did get a hold of the side rail, I could only do so with one hand. My other hand was gripping my package by the brown string. By some miracle, it didn't snap or untie itself.

Riding through the air for several minutes, we finally landed at the gremlin encampment. I climbed off the back of the mini-hauler. I was lightly bruised and impressed.

"Jink, that was pretty amazing. I can't even think how you managed to—hey!"

The hauler was surrounded by several of those walking-tank things. Gremlins piloted all of them, and their nozzle-like turrets were aimed directly at me.

"This is no way to greet an old comrade in arms," I complained.

"Where is Floramel, big-man?"

I looked at Jink. He wasn't in a charitable mood, I could tell.

Taking my package and setting it down between us, I pointed at it. "I brought you a gift. Check it out."

"What is this?" he asked suspiciously.

"A present, like I said. From one warrior to another."

He stared at it.

Now, you have to know something about gremlin psychology. It's kind of like that of monkeys, or lemurs. They're inquisitive beings. They're not trusting in any way—not by a longshot. But they are also easily intrigued by mysteries.

"You," Jink said, pointing to one of his gremlin sidekicks. "You open it."

Grumbling, the low-ranked gremlin crept forward. He poked at the package. When it shifted its weight, he sniffed and stared.

"Open it!" Jink demanded.

Others took up the cry.

"Open it! Open it!"

Finally, the sacrificial lamb of the group dared to touch the string—but then he bounded away, squalling and pointing. "It leaks! The package leaks blood!"

Jink's mouth dropped. He approached the box. Then he looked up at me.

"You would dare such an insult?"

"Uh… what insult?"

He pointed accusingly at the box. "You think I'm a fool? This is Floramel's head, isn't it? You weren't able to trick her into coming home to us, so you murdered her!"

The gremlins went wild at this. They hopped and screeched. Weapons and wired needles appeared everywhere. A bigger and bigger crowd had gathered to encircle us. The tanks with their turrets swiveled and pranced like horses.

"Such madness!" Jink wailed. "I knew of your barbarity, but I never would have believed—!"

"Hold on, hold on!" I shouted. "It's not what you think!"

They settled down a bit, and they stared at me and my box.

389

"What then, big-man? What would you dare to bring that could repay your debt?"

Stepping forward, I knelt over the box. I untied it, and they all churned and sidestepped all around me.

At last, I had it open. I lifted a giant bloom from the box. It was dripping sap like gore. It was a Dust World orchid, just like the one that Jink had sent to me.

"What's this?" he demanded, snarling and hissing. "Why would we want one of your stinking flowers?"

"It's a message, Jink," I said. "Just like the one you sent me."

Then, plucking at a tiny ring at the base of the flower, I set off a thermite reaction. This in turn lit off a much more powerful explosion—because the flower and the box were full of military-grade chemistry.

In less than a second, me, Jink, all his aunties and cousins, plus six stolen Mogwa power-armor were vaporized.

-64-

"What do we have?"

"He's a nine. That's rounding up, mind you."

"Good enough. Call the Servant."

Two bio people lingered over me. I'd been revived somewhere, somehow, and if the truth were to be told, I was kind of surprised.

Relaxing on the recovery plank, I wriggled my toes and fingers enough to realize I was locked down securely. The bio people left, and it was just me, some bright lights, and my cooling dick as the sticky liquids dried on my skin.

I almost shivered before anyone bothered to come talk to me. Why did they always keep operating rooms so damned cold?

Another figure arrived. It hovered near.

"Why is he unconscious?" asked a familiar old voice. It was the man from Belarus, the infamous Public Servant Alexander Turov.

"He's not," said one of the bio women. "He's faking."

"Of course he is... What else would an assassin do when he's in his enemy's power?"

I didn't like his turn of phrase. I opened an eye and pretended to wake up. Yawning, I tried to stretch. Bands of steel and chains jangled and rasped.

"Hey there, Mr. Servant. You're a sight for sore eyes."

"You, on the other hand, are not. I believe that you will have your cock out for display at your own funeral, McGill."

"That's probably true."

Alexander waved a skinny hand, and they released me. A few armed guards stared from the doorway.

Noting their distance and the fact they didn't have their weapons trained on me at the moment, I figured I could probably kill old Alex before they could stop me.

The old man watched me with interest. "I see the violence in your eyes. Do you always contemplate murder when you speak to your benefactors?"

"Uh... yeah. Pretty much." I shrugged. "It's an occupational hazard, I suspect."

Turov nodded, but the guards frowned harder. They brought up their rifles, just in case.

"Sir," I said, "I want you to know you have my heartfelt thanks."

"Why's that?"

"Because you revived me again, without any prior warning that I might need the service. I was kind of hoping I could get away clean, see... but it didn't work out that way."

Alexander nodded, and he studied the cold gray floor of his private revival chamber in Eastern Europe. "Why did you murder a large number of gremlins, McGill?"

"Well sir, that's kind of a private matter. Just something between their folks and mine."

Alexander squinted at me, like he was trying to figure me out. Countless authority figures had given me that precise look in the past, starting with my young mother.

"McGill, you are an enigma. Do you know that when I proposed using you for certain missions—I was warned not to?"

"By who, sir?"

He shrugged. "Pretty much everyone in your chain of command."

"Oh... well sir, they would know."

"Yes. I see now they were correct. What did that prissy fellow say?"

"Tribune Winslade?"

He snapped his skinny fingers and aimed one of them at me. "Yes! That's him. He said employing McGill was like using a blowtorch to trim the hedges—that the job would probably get done, but I might not be happy with the results in the end."

I laughed, but I was the only one who did. The bio people had melted away, and the guards were in a sour mood.

"Let us go over the specific cases that back up Winslade's claim," Alexander went on. "First, I suggested you should assassinate the Mogwa who came to commandeer our fleets and legions."

"Huh... is that what you were hinting about? I thought maybe—"

He put a hand up to stop me. "Do not embarrass yourself further."

"Okay..."

"Instead, you lost several of my ships and countless billions of credits worth of gear."

To my way of thinking, that right there was what was wrong with some of these Servants. They thought they owned all Earth's ships and soldiers. They were supposed to manage such things, not regard them as personal possessions.

These thoughts crossed my mind, but I was way too smart to say them out loud. I was still in the middle of old Alex's castle, and I owed him the courtesy of listening. After all, no one else had seen fit to revive me.

"The debacle at Segin was expensive, but the outcome was positive," he continued. "The Mogwa we helped there account us as friends now, and they shall treat us with greater respect in the future."

These words flat-out stunned me. I knew they were far from the truth. Most Mogwa didn't know which end of a thank-you was which. Someone—probably Winslade—had pumped this flowery sunshine into Turov's ear to make all our losses sound better.

Despite all these negative thoughts swirling around in my brain, I managed to smile and nod with enthusiastic agreement. "That's the plain truth, sir. We're practically allies now."

393

He nodded. "All right, then. Let us come to your most recent acts of heinous violence and destruction."

"Uh... which ones would those be, exactly?"

"I'm speaking of your actions on Blood World."

"Oh yeah, of course. Was that cool or not, sir? We couldn't let those gremlins have tanks and stuff."

"Right. You were sent out there as a cleaner. But what I want to know is *who* sent you?"

He stepped close and peered at me. He seemed full of suspicion and accusation. He clearly thought I was working for someone else, and he wanted to know who it was.

I looked stupid, which took no effort at all. I always looked like that when someone surprised me. The whole idea had been mine and mine alone—but I didn't want to fess-up to that. So, I just looked dumb and stared back at him.

"Not going to talk, heh?" Alexander asked. "I see... do you know that I have had every known revival machine monitored for the past several months?"

"You did? Is that why it's so bitterly cold in here?"

"Yes. It is now late November."

I whistled. "November? Holy shit. I hope Thanksgiving hasn't come and gone. I promised my folks—"

He gestured for me to shut up, so I did.

"I finally gave up on using that approach to flush out your handler. Whoever sent you on that mission was very cautious. Eventually, I grew impatient. That's why you're breathing again."

"And I want to thank you for that, sir—"

"Do not thank me. I'm considering torment to learn the truth."

"Oh..." I said.

"But I suspect that you will not tell me who sent you to Blood World. An agent that cracks easily is a poor one. You would also be less likely to do work for me in the future, should I resort to such extreme, but justified methods."

"Sound reasoning, sir."

Alexander tapped at his chin and muttered to himself for a bit. Finally, he sighed. "I have come to a fateful decision. I will allow you to live this life. Go now, and do not annoy me further."

I'm not a man who overstays his welcome. I pulled on some clothes they gave me, and I got the hell out of that creepy basement. It wasn't until I was up on the ground floor that I noticed I was wearing an honest-to-God tuxedo. I guess that's just what they had lying around in the Turov household.

Walking fast, I'd almost made it across the flagstones to the big arched doorway, when a woman's voice called out to me.

"McGill? Is that, you? James McGill?"

I pivoted on one heel. A woman came close. She was pretty. She also looked familiar—then I had it.

"Sophia? Galina's sister?"

She smiled. "That's me. I guess we've met, but I don't remember that day..."

A shadow crossed her face. The last time I'd been out here at her dad's place, it had been her wedding day. The Tau had raided the place, shooting her down. She'd caught a revival, but she'd forgotten years of events—including everything about her fiancé.

I reached out a big hand and put it on top of her two, which she held clasped in front of her. "If it makes you feel any better, Miss, I killed most of those Tau personally."

She glanced down at my hand, then up at my face. She lit up. "That's how I recognized you—from the vids of the battle. It does make me feel better, knowing those aliens are dead. Thank you for your service, Centurion."

We smiled at each other for a moment, and as the Almighty himself can tell you, I felt a tug of temptation. As I've admitted a thousand times over to anyone who'll listen, I'm a deeply flawed man.

Just then, however, a skinny old dude with crossed arms and a sour expression appeared in the hallway behind Sophia.

I glanced his way, then looked back down at his lovely daughter again. I took my hand off hers, but my big smile never faltered.

"Ma'am," I said, "I'm sorry, but I've got to be going. Official military business. I hope you understand."

"Of course..." she said, sounding just a touch disappointed.

Sophia glanced over her shoulder, but her father was long gone from the hallway. He was spry for an old fart.

After another smile and a wave, I quickly left the mansion and then the continent.

-65-

Less than a day later, I made it back home to the southern swamps of Georgia Sector. To my surprise, Etta was there. As it turned out tonight was Thanksgiving, and she'd come home for a visit.

Everyone was overjoyed to see me. They'd been worried, but they'd held the faith that I'd return eventually. They went on about how I'd disappeared and not come home, and how no one in the government would say squat about where I'd been all this time.

"It was another of those secret commando missions, wasn't it, boy?" my dad asked in the kitchen of the big house.

"Sure was," I said.

"Don't tell us a thing, James," Mamma said. "We don't want to know the harrowing details."

"Speak for yourself, woman."

"Dad?" Etta asked me. "Did you know we've got more guests coming tonight?"

"Huh? Really? Who?"

They all smiled. "It's a surprise."

Instantly, all kinds of worries popped into my mind. Chief among these was the idea that Floramel and the Investigator would come, possibly bringing Della. That thought had me a little freaked out. The Investigator was just about the oddest person I knew, and I couldn't imagine he'd be much fun at my family dinner table.

Steeling myself with a fake smile, I counted the empty chairs which I had just noticed at the far end of the table. There were exactly two.

"Huh..." I said, thinking that over. Who was coming to dinner?

Over the next several minutes, while we waited for the food to finish-up in the auto-cooker, I repeatedly suggested we should break out the wine. This idea wasn't greeted with enthusiasm.

Just before the dinner timer was up, there was a knock at the door. Etta jumped up to get it, and she came back into the dining room looking as pleased as punch.

"Welcome the Turovs!" she said.

I gaped, and everyone else stood up. Galina walked in first, but I looked right past her. I expected her father to appear out of the shadows, just as he'd disappeared into them the last time I'd seen him back in Belarus.

But that's not how it happened. Instead of a crusty oldster, a slim young woman with a charming appearance walked in Galina's wake.

It was Galina's sister, Sophia.

"There you are, James," Galina said. "I understand you've met my sister?"

"Huh? Oh, yeah. I remember her..."

Galina smiled. "She heard I was coming out to the states for this unique holiday, and she wanted to experience it."

Sophia offered me her hand in greeting, but it wasn't a handshake. It was one of those deals were she wrapped her fingers over my index finger. I figured I was supposed to kiss her knuckles or something, but since I was clueless, I gave her a brief up-down pumping instead.

She looked bemused and withdrew her hand.

"Hello, Lady Turov," I said. "Welcome to our humble home."

We offered the women chairs, and my dad and I pushed them in, seating them the old-fashioned way. This seemed to please everyone.

Along about then, the timer finally dinged, and I felt saved. My dad and I soon jostled outside the auto-cooker, plates in hand. We returned to the table with full loads.

The women were all talking a mile a minute, but they eventually got up and got plates as well. The whole party quieted down while we ate.

People asked me questions, I think, but I didn't answer with more than a grunt now and then until I'd cleared my third plate. After that, I was ready to hear what people had to say.

Dinner came and went, then we had wine and dessert. All too soon the good stuff was gone, and I had to listen to gossip, politics, complaints and other nonsense.

By the time our guests stood up to leave, I was ready for a beer and bed. After all, I'd been revived just this morning on the other side of the planet. It had been a long day.

At the door, Galina smiled at me and gave me a kiss. I slapped her rump as she turned away and walked toward her air car.

One more person lingered, however. It was Sophia. Her eyes had a certain light in them.

Uh-oh.

"Hey, thanks for coming," I said. "We don't get a lot of fancy people out here. I hope the food wasn't too crass."

Sophia reached a hand out and wrapped her fingers over mine again. "I enjoyed everything," she said. "Especially the company."

"Uh… that's great…"

She held onto my hand and stared at me for about two seconds too long, then she finally let go and walked off into the night. The two women got into their air car together and flew away.

I let out a big sigh and retired to my shack across the backyard.

* * *

Sometime after midnight, I heard a sound. I came awake with a machete in one hand and a pistol in the other.

399

It was a pinging sound, and it went off again. The proximity alarm was real quiet, because I'd set it that way. I wanted to have some warning just in case any tiny bastards from Jink's family decided to pay me a nighttime visit.

Stalking to the windows, I peeked out. None of the cameras showed anything on the tapper, but—wait. There it was. An air car parked out on the road.

Shit.

Opening my front door and turning on the porch light, I waited in the dark entryway.

A small figure approached. It was cold out, so she wore a big coat with the hood up. The hood was lined with fur.

What was I going to do? What if Sophia grabbed my hand again? What if she kissed me? Was I going to be able to keep my hands to myself?

I'm sad to say it, but I wasn't certain. I'm a deeply flawed man, and as many people have often informed me, I share many characteristics with goats, pigs and dogs. Apes, too.

So I waited. I waited in the dark.

At last, the girl's light step caused the boards of my porch to creak. She threw back her hood, and she smiled up at me. She smiled big.

It was Galina.

I grinned back at her. I was so relieved, my smile was completely honest in nature. She sensed how happy I was to see her—but not why—so she didn't hesitate. She jumped up and I caught her, lifting her butt up in the air. We made out right there in the doorway.

"I told my father to revive you," she whispered in my ear. "Did you know that?"

"I suspected as much," I whispered back, lying without a qualm. "I guess I owe you one."

"Yes. You certainly do."

The night went by nicely after that, even if it was a little cold. We didn't mind, as we made our own heat.

When I awakened in the morning, Galina was gone. There was only the lingering scent of her perfume on my pillow to prove she'd been there at all.

Yawning, I stretched and showered, then headed for the house. There were plenty of leftovers in the fridge after all, and I didn't want my dad to get more than his fair share.

THE END

Books by B. V. Larson:

UNDYING MERCENARIES
Steel World
Dust World
Tech World
Machine World
Death World
Home World
Rogue World
Blood World
Dark World
Storm World
Armor World
Clone World
Glass World
Edge World
Green World
Ice World

REBEL FLEET SERIES
Rebel Fleet
Orion Fleet
Alpha Fleet
Earth Fleet

Visit BVLarson.com for more information.

Printed in Great Britain
by Amazon

78727153R00234